THE
SUNDAY
MACARONI
CLUB

ALSO BY STEVE LOPEZ

Third and Indiana

Land of Giants:
Where No Good Deed Goes Unpunished

THE
SUNDAY
MACARONI
CLUB

Steve Lopez

Harcourt Brace & Company

New York   San Diego   London

Despite the presence in Pennsylvania of real people who
beg fiction, none of the characters in this book has a
living, breathing counterpart, or a dead one, for that
matter. They are entirely made up. Any resemblance to
actual incidents or persons is wholly coincidental. Some
actual institutions and events are featured in the book,
but the world they are presented in here is fictitious.

Library of Congress Cataloging-in-Publication Data
Lopez, Steve.
The Sunday Macaroni Club/Steve Lopez.
p.   cm.
ISBN 0-15-100264-9
I. Title.
PS3562.O673S8   1997
813'.54—dc21   96-44062

Designed by Lydia D'moch
Printed in the United States of America
First edition
A B C D E

For Alison, and no one else

Acknowledgments

My thanks to Michael Riverso and Joey "Mambo Joe" DelBuono, a pair nobody could have invented. And to George Parry, who used to chase bad guys for a living.

Also to Walter Bode, my editor at Harcourt Brace, who still does it the old-fashioned way. And to my friend and agent, David Black, whose faith and support, though no greater than for the Jets, keep me at it.

A special thanks to Robin Clark (1955–1995), a newspaperman, a poet, a soul. A friend.

THE
SUNDAY
MACARONI
CLUB

*I looked around at the little fishes present
and said, "I'm the Kingfish."*
—HUEY LONG

*I used to say that politics was the second lowest profession
and I have come to know that it bears a great
similarity to the first.*
—RONALD REAGAN

Ambition should be made of sterner stuff.
—WILLIAM SHAKESPEARE

CHAPTER 1

It was only since the slide down the East Coast, after the most private part of her life had become tabloid fodder in Boston, that Lisa Savitch found herself smoking before her morning run. It was a conscious development, not some nervous reflex. This was someone who did nothing by accident. She routinely jabbed cigarettes into her mouth one after another as if feeding a fire burning in the walls of her chest. A half-burned stick dangled now as she labored through her stretching routine on a steamy Saturday morning in Rittenhouse Square. A squirrel scampered past her and up a sycamore tree, its claws tip-tapping on the bark before it paused to look back at her. Groggy from a night as restless as all the others, Savitch was oblivious to the squirrel and to several gawkers who craned in her direction, fixed on this sketch of bad habits and good looks.

Savitch perched her foot on a bench and bent at the waist as she touched chin to knee. She wore a plain white T-shirt and blue nylon shorts, no hips to pooch them out, and it looked as though giving birth could kill her. A slim waist tapered down to the tight, evenly tanned muscles of her thighs and calves—the legs of a dancer, not an athlete. From a distance, one leg up like that, she looked like a ballerina on a cigarette break.

Savitch lived in one of the high-rises overlooking the square.

She'd been there a month and most of her boxes were still stacked around the apartment, making it look less like a home than a place where she had paused for an inventory. The coffee-maker was the only appliance she'd unpacked, and she wondered now if she'd remembered to turn it off.

The park, a city block of grass, trees, and benches in the middle of one of Philadelphia's oldest and priciest neighbor-hoods, held the usual summer mix of neighborhood residents—retired Jews with thick glasses and caved-in coat-hanger shoulders, gay men who sat tall and shiny and threw glances the way fishermen throw nets, floppy-haired young professionals in weekday dress shirts and weekend shorts, and resident manics and schizoids with plastic bags of secret goods. It was a crowd busy with newspapers, coffee, and bagels, but most of them watched as Lisa Savitch stood free of the bench and rubbed the sleep out. Feeling the park's eyes on her now, she locked her hand at her waist and stood there punctuating her irritation. You got a problem?

She was twenty-nine years old and had never understood that it was impossible for people not to look at her. It wasn't just the lithe body or the natural, low-maintenance looks, with fine blond hair that brushed her shoulders and was streaked by sun. What turned heads was the unmistakable fact—it was ap-parent even to strangers—that she didn't define herself by any of those things. In manner and looks, there was no pretense about Lisa Savitch, and the absence was like a nakedness. She didn't waste much of her day primping and posing, and had little or no patience for those who did. In high school, she had once plotted to spike the cheerleaders' lunches with Valium on pep day.

One captivating glance revealed that Lisa Savitch could be trouble. Look at her with the cigarettes—a runner who chain-smoked. A person had to notice. Savitch sucked hard one last time to feed the fire. The asshole in Boston had actually asked her not to smoke in his presence, and against every instinct, every microscopic scrap of her being, she had caved in. It wouldn't happen again. She expelled a cloud of smoke and flicked the butt into the bushes, scattering squirrels, and off she went. A deer shooting through the park, all attitude and legs.

The usual run took her to Fairmount Park and along Kelly Drive, named after the family of Grace, to whom Savitch bore a resemblance noted by a dozen men whose paths she'd crossed, each one thinking he was the first to bring it up. They were so much the same it had gotten to be a joke with her; how every guy thought he was the only man alive. Savitch liked Kelly Drive because it reminded her of jogs along Boston's Back Bay. Rowers were on the water to start each day, paddling in and out of the docks on Boathouse Row and up and down the Schuylkill River. But she wanted to clock another course, so she turned right on Market this time instead of left, passed City Hall, and headed east toward the Delaware River.

It was the first week of September, but the weather was midsummer. Only ten in the morning, and the pavement was already soft and tacky, the city beginning its daily meltdown. It was probably a lot cooler in Boston, Savitch thought, working up a sweat by the time she hit the Liberty Bell, her wet skin glistening in sunlight that fought through the trees of Independence Mall. Savitch wasn't a huge history buff, but her mother—who missed her daughter at least as much as Savitch missed home—had told her she ought to take advantage of her time in Philadelphia, regardless of how long she stayed. Savitch ran past the Liberty Bell Pavilion, swiping a glance through the glass housing, and circled around the back of Independence Hall, craning up at the clock tower that dominated the mall. She could now honestly tell her mother she'd taken in some history.

From there she ran north two blocks, then turned right at a cluster of tourists snapping photographs of Ben Franklin's grave. As she passed the crowd, Savitch wondered if Franklin had been the last honest politician in America, or if he just hadn't gotten caught at anything. She ran Arch to Second, Market across

Interstate 95 and down to Christopher Columbus Boulevard, the Delaware lapping at the foot of the city where William Penn had docked three centuries earlier and cut a deal with the Leni-Lenape Indians, or so claimed a historic marker. It was cooler along the river, but the breeze coming off the water carried a heavy metal odor, like the inside of an auto shop. Savitch pictured the clusters of refineries and other monstrosities that sat to the south, too far to see from here. The first time she flew in, she had watched them belch black clouds of exhaust like gigantic spewing Erector sets with big gray storage tanks and miles of spaghetti piping. Welcome to Philadelphia.

The thought took her back to the decision to leave Boston. New York had been an option as a place to start her life over, but Savitch wanted one major buffer city between herself and her ex-fiancé. She didn't want to make it any easier for him to schlepp down and beg forgiveness, which she knew he'd get around to at some point. As it happened, the district attorney in Boston knew the Philadelphia DA and made a call. Savitch, one of the rising stars in Boston, was hired on the spot and was told that a corruption case was waiting for her in the special investigations unit. A state representative and congressional candidate named William "Ham" Flaherty had gotten cozier with the Atlantic City gambling industry than the law allowed, and he was suspected of having set up his bimbo mistress, a casino cocktail waitress, with a no-show job on the state payroll. Stalking congressional wanna-bes was a change from Savitch's Boston dance card of burglars, rapists, and murderers, but it didn't appear to her, at first glance into the local petri dish, that Ham Flaherty was any higher on the food chain. After four years as a prosecutor, she had mixed feelings about leaving street crime. Politics and politicians were by nature corrupt, it seemed to her. Didn't that take some of the fun out of the chase?

Savitch began to hit her stride as she reached Penn's Landing, the river off her left shoulder. She had a smooth and effortless groove, no wasted motion, as if the wind were at her back and the ground made of air. It had been like that since she went out for cross-country in junior high, following in her brother's footsteps. Six-minute miles were nothing, and an hour of it was a routine workout. She was a natural, cigarettes and all. She had definitely had better runs than this one, though. She felt light-headed and slightly nauseated and realized that the metal odor had gotten stronger. A tanker was making its way upriver under the Walt Whitman Bridge, a thin finger of exhaust curling from the smokestack. Maybe that was what she smelled.

Her hair was dark at her neck, stringy and wet, and a ring of sweat starting at the top of her T-shirt seeped down to her breasts. She caught a deeper breath and wiped her brow, and she was shaking the sweat off her hands when she heard a car engine slowing behind her, followed by a male voice. "Not to be rude or nothin', Bambi. But those are the greatest fuckin' legs I ever seen."

"Unbelievable," Savitch muttered. It was the kind of line that apparently passed for courtship in this town, and it was the third time it had happened. She found it amazing that you could leave Boston and end up in a city with twice as many dickheads. Don't even acknowledge him, she told herself. Just keep running. But the car was alongside her and keeping pace, some greaser leaning out.

"Why don't you run up my leg, get something for all that sweat?"

Savitch thought about grabbing him by the neck and jerking him out of the car, but he wasn't worth the effort. For the time being, no man was worth it. She pulled off Columbus Boulevard and cut west, blazing past Mario Lanza Park and through narrow row-house streets that reminded her of Boston's North End. At Fourth Street she passed Ham Flaherty's legislative office, a converted row house with a storefront and a second-floor apartment, and the sight of it raised every doubt, every question, that had torn at her from the moment she left Boston. Why was she wasting her career on this womanizing creep of a politician? She'd left home to get away from that very thing. And shouldn't her fiancé have been the one who was run out of town and forced into a city of strangers?

Savitch picked up the pace. Maybe there were answers at a higher speed, or maybe you could just outrun the questions. The locals eyeballed her as she sprinted by, knowing she didn't belong in the same way dogs know when an interloping hound has crossed into their territory. Philadelphia was built for those who were born into it, and outsiders were instantly sniffed out and regarded with suspicion and disdain. Even the local accent, to Savitch's ear, was foreign, the vowels all stepped on and bent out of shape. One of the secretaries in the DA's office had asked Savitch if she had a mug, or if she wanted her coffee in a "star-fame cup there, hon." And people made fun of the Boston accent? Savitch had to sit in the ladies' room for ten minutes, mouthing the correct pronunciation over and over like a Gregorian chant—*Sty-ro-foam, Sty-ro-foam, Sty-ro-foam*—before she could get back to work.

The same scent she'd picked up down along the Delaware was sharper here, and although the sky directly above was blue, the light on the horizon was different, darkness creeping into it. As she turned left on Broad Street, the city's main north-south artery and a direct shot into South Philadelphia, Savitch heard sirens in the distance. She coughed and spit, a burning in her lungs. Was it the cigarettes? She knew it wasn't when two TV news vans streaked past, barreling south, and she ran in the same direction for more than a mile, behind them, all the way down toward the southern boundary of the city and a scene that looked like something out of a horror movie.

Cars were speeding through a park, some of them fishtailing and spinning out on the grass, and hundreds of people in berets and uniforms of red, white, and green were screaming and on the run; TV vans were circling and sirens wailing. Savitch's heart pounded in her ears. Only now, as it cleared the trees and moved overhead, did she see the billowing cloud rolling up from the vicinity of the refineries, filling the sky like a great yellow ghost. In the foreground, a banner stretched across the entrance to the park.

TUTTI BENVENUTI
MID-ATLANTIC STATES SENIOR OUTDOOR
BOWLING TOURNAMENT
HIGH ROLLERS BOCCE PAVILION

Savitch walked backward slowly, her eye on the cloud. It could be just a normal discharge from one of the refineries, she told herself, but it didn't look normal. It swelled across the sky as if it were alive and breathing, like a gigantic brain growing new chambers as it plotted over the city. Maybe there was a fire, or some kind of explosion, and she'd been inhaling toxic fumes for the last half hour. It could even be a killer chemical blast like the one in India. Her lungs would be heat-welded to her ribs, her nervous system would be shorted out, and they'd find her flopping around in the street like a landed fish, dying in the company of people who couldn't pronounce *Styrofoam*.

Savitch bent over and coughed hard, spitting up what tasted like cigarettes and sour coffee. She was at least as angry as she was scared, but she didn't know who to direct it at. Maybe the idiot in Boston who made her move to this industrial dump site of a city, or whoever the hell was responsible for this cloud. Some genius falling asleep on the job, contaminating half the city. Savitch was about to run for cover when she noticed that the TV crews didn't seem nearly as alarmed as everyone else. She heard one reporter tell a team called the Bocce Butanas that it was an accidental release of silica something or other, but it was nothing to worry about. It just stings the eyes and throat for a while. Another TV crew was interviewing a local man who had taken cover in his car; he and his wife were slumped down in the front seat, drawing their heads in like frightened turtles.

"It's like from a horror movie," the man said, his window

opened just a crack. "I'm ready to bowl and what should happen but it gets so dark I can't even see the pallino. I look up and here's this mustard gas falling down on me." He looked at his pale, slack-jawed wife before continuing. "Theresa, she's crying there, telling me this is it, we're going out in the Pontiac. This is the thing they're doing to us. They're killing us down here with all of this poison that comes out of the sky every day in this part of town."

The cloud was still traveling north, but it was thinning out now, raining a fine dust that looked like a light, sunlit shower after a thunderstorm. The talcumlike dust settled on Savitch as she ran back home, and sweat ran in yellow rivers across her body. When she got out of the shower, she sat on the bed and held herself, naked as the walls behind her. The room was cluttered with boxes that were still packed and sealed, and she followed the line of them past the closet, past the window, and all the way to the corner, where her suitcases were lying. It would be so easy.

CHAPTER 2

THE PHONE AND DOORBELL rang together, just as the water hit a boil. "Gesù Cristo," Senator Augie Sangiamino grumbled. He splashed extra-virgin olive oil into the water and sprinkled fresh basil into the marinara before running from the kitchen to get the door.

It was Joey Tartaglione, his loyal driver and bagman.

"Joey, do me a nice favor, will you? Get the phone. I got my gravy goin', the macaroni, the sozzich. What have I got, eight arms here?"

The senator, three months short of his seventy-fifth birthday, shuffled across the plastic runner in his living room and disappeared into a wall of steam in the kitchen. Joey, who tried to look after Augie without mothering him, wondered if the red splatter on his sleeveless undershirt was new or if he'd forgotten to send out the laundry again. Augie's gray slacks could use a pressing, too. Joey made a mental note of it as he picked up the phone in the living room.

"The senator can't talk right now, Mrs. Mangione. He's on the other line with the governor. What can I say? The governor needs a favor, he knows who to call like anybody else." Joey held the phone to his ear while he tossed his jacket onto a sofa sealed in clear vinyl and decorated with two lace doilies made by the senator's wife. "Guess what, Mrs. Mangione. How about you come by the office tomorrow, down Milly's Lunchbox? The senator'll be where he always is."

Joey set the phone in its cradle and turned toward the sound of sizzling sausage, pausing in front of side-by-side frames of Pope John Paul II and Mayor DeMarco. He made the sign of the cross before them, did a half genuflection, and went into the kitchen, where he filled his lungs with garlic-scented heat.

"Whadda we got?" Augie asked without looking up from his boiling pots. He had a wooden spoon in one hand, a long fork in the other, and he worked them like a maestro conducting an orchestra. The floor sagged from the weight of the refrigerator and the linoleum was worn to the wood in front of the sink and stove, where Augie stood now. His slippers, the backs crushed flat, fit the depressions like boats in their berths.

"It's Mrs. Mangione," Joey said, turning on the light. Natural light fell in through the window over the sink, but the senator's eyesight wasn't what it used to be. The overhead lamp lit the edge of the scalloped molding that ran along the top of the ceiling all the way around the room, dingy yellow on soft green walls. Pots dangled from hooks under cupboards, their bottoms burned black, and bouquets of wooden spoons sprouted from coffee mugs. A four-inch statue of Jesus watched over the entire operation from the back of the range, wearing a coat of grease. Augie was guided by the story of fishes and loaves being multiplied to serve loyal disciples. The greatest friggin' miracle in the book, the senator would tell people.

He was no longer a senator, but it was a mark of respect in South Philadelphia to refer to a person by the highest rank ever achieved, and nobody from downtown, with the possible exception of the late Mayor DeMarco, Mario Lanza, or Frankie Avalon, was ever more revered than Augie. As assembly speaker in the state house and later as a United States senator, the Prince of Pennsylvania, as he was known, had produced like no one else. Jobs, grants, fixes, broken noses, whatever the situation called for. At his height, Augie controlled labor, he owned more jobs than anyone in the state, and nobody in politics made a move before clearing it with him. He wasn't shy about his success, either, and used to brag that with one phone call, he could have the pope deliver a pizza.

These days, he let Joey make his calls, sparing himself the indignity of a thousand excuses about why someone couldn't come to the phone. It had all come unraveled twelve years ago when, halfway through his first term in Washington, an FBI bloodhound sniffed out a pack of no-show employees on Augie's payroll. Among those who did make it to the office, three ran a bookmaking operation that fed Augie's reelection kitty.

That was the Augie Sangiamino Joey was looking at now— a fallen man who had committed the second worst sin behind not using the power of office to steal for his people. He had gotten caught.

"Mrs. Mangione," Augie repeated, turning her name into a little song. Augie was six feet even and thin as a wing, and his voice climbed narrow pipes and squeezed through a beak he referred to as solid proof God put him on the planet to cook. The whole thing is in the allfactories, he would say, wagging his head as he talked, as if it wound up the machine that ran his mouth and hands. He licked marinara off the wooden spoon and closed his eyes in ecstasy. Opening them, he asked, "What now with our girlfriend Mrs. Mangione? She's got a problem with some parking tickets again?"

This was the kind of thing Augie had been doing since he got out of prison ten years ago and set up a consulting business. For a price, he could still put in a small fix, like making tickets disappear, and he occasionally gave advice to pols who knew Augie wrote the book on pulling money out of thin air and votes out of the ground. But his stable of candidates, once huge, was down to two glue horses, and he was on the edge of the track now, standing in a shadow.

"Nah," said Joey, who had posted Augie's bets while the

senator was in jail. Joey was the one who picked up Augie on the day of his release from prison, and on the ride home, Augie hired him as his right-hand man. "She's all worked up about this stuff flyin' out of the refinery there yesterday. She wants to know can she paint her house on Liberty Oil's dime."

A look of irritation floated across Augie's Mediterranean blue eyes. "I got everybody bustin' my chops with this thing," he said, drawing his shoulders up in a shrug. His hair was still dark and thick, lathered in pomade and stroked back, clean. With his pencil-line mustache—a pair of accent marks—Joey thought he looked like a Venetian gondolier. "How's this time so different from all the others, Joey? Can you tell me that?"

Joey walked over to the sink and leaned against the counter, his finger scraping over a chip in the olive green tile. He knew it wasn't just silica alumina that had fallen out of the sky. It was political opportunity. In his prime, Augie would have been all over it. But he had to have pictures painted now. Joey said, "Those two old ladies? They're still in serious condition, you know."

"The ones down William Penn Homes?"

"Yeah," Joey said. "There's still a couple of kids in the hospital, too, their lungs full of that stuff. Little colored kids that was outside. Usually the wind takes it the other way, but this time it comes right down on top of the project there, the other side of the park."

"Maybe we're lucky we left the tournament to go see my Angela," Augie said. "But what I heard, this irritates your eyes is all. So don't be surprised if the coloreds aren't scamming a payday here, Joey. Tell me if I'm wrong that a bus has a little fender bender in this town and inside of two minutes, you got four hundred coloreds in neck braces across the city. They're not as slow on the take as you think."

Joey decided to let it simmer, like Augie's marinara. Something would bubble up. He rinsed the wooden cutting board

Augie had used to chop tomatoes and put it in the drainer. Augie's wife had been in a nursing home three years, and housekeeping was never the old man's strength. Joey took a dish towel and squeezed his round body behind the kitchen table to wipe down the steamed windows of the china cabinet in the corner. All the cups and saucers were lined up in there just like Angela had left them before leukemia and Alzheimer's took her down. He stood on his toes to get high enough, and one clean swipe painted his picture on the glass. A head like a melon and a chin that doubled as a neck.

Joey went over and wiped the window on the back door, too, looking out at the patio. Vines climbed a wooden overhang, and in the center of the patio stood a three-foot-tall statue of the Virgin Mary. Resting on a wine barrel, she gazed reverently upward at the voting booth that sheltered her, the curtain pulled open. Augie knelt for a daily prayer in front of the statue, and on election day, he called in whatever candidates he was sponsoring and recited an entire rosary. Then they went out and stole every vote they could.

Augie sprinkled more basil into his gravy and asked over his shoulder, "What kind of registration we got down William Penn Homes?"

Joey smiled with relief. "About thirty percent," he said. "Somewheres around there. Why?"

Augie turned all the way around and licked a bit of basil off his finger. "Open your fuckin' eyes, Joey. The way the coloreds got nailed with this silicone? Let's get somebody down there, see if we can't get them registered."

Joey said it was a good idea, a damned good idea. He'd make the calls.

"Fuckin' A right. Maybe we can get something going here to put our boys out front before this campaign even gets going. What'd you tell Mrs. Mangione?"

"I told her come by the office tomorrow."

"Mrs. Mangione," Augie said, a reminiscence welling as he turned to Joey again. "You know what? She used to be a beautiful woman once."

Joey nodded and began setting the table. He wished he could set it up for the boss to get laid, but it wasn't his place to do that sort of thing. It wouldn't be professional.

Joey took the basket of fruit and the bowl of nuts off the table and put them on the hutch—the senator always sliced apples with his pocketknife and cracked almonds and walnuts after a meal. He set out plates for Augie, himself, State Representative William "Ham" Flaherty, Common Pleas Judge Isadore "Izzy" Weiner, and Democratic City Committee boss Lou Canuso.

Ham was running for Congress, Izzy for state supreme court. Neither was expected to win, and Izzy didn't even have a prayer. But that didn't stop Augie from dreaming, and there was no better day for believing your own lies than Sunday. On Sunday, the red gravy simmered same as ever and the boys came over like they always had, and Augie still ran things the way they were meant to be run, performing good and noble deeds for God-fearing people, even if it meant pulling off the occasional felony.

They'd done this every Sunday for ten years. Augie Sangiamino, last of the great ward heelers, and his loyal henchmen—dinosaurs conspiring against the future.

Augie called it the Sunday Macaroni Club.

"Joey, you wanna cut a piece of the sozzich, see if it's done?" the senator asked.

Joey was already moving in with knife and fork before Augie got the words out. He took a bite and lifted his eyes.

"Senator, that's a nice sozzich."

A knock at the door.

"Must be Ham," Augie said. "I told him get here early."

Joey knew Ham always rang the bell. So did Izzy. Lou Canuso, a former boxer and bricklayer, always rapped on the door as if his knuckles needed a fix.

Lou threw his coat on top of Joey's and paused in front of Mayor DeMarco and the pope for the ritual bow. "Fuckin' Iggles are down seventeen in the first quarter," he mumbled, a voice rattling up from the bottom of a pile of cracked ribs. Lou had five hundred riding on the Eagles. At the height of his boxing career, he once bet on himself to lose and accidentally knocked out his opponent. "They can still get into this thing," he said, turning on the TV.

"Yeah," Joey said. "And I can still pork Marilyn Monroe."

To Joey's eye, Lou had the look of bad sculpture, like God had too much clay and too little time that day. All of his features were too big for his face, and some were rearranged from his days in the ring. Toward the end of his boxing career, Lou lost seventeen straight fights. His nose was an inch closer to his left ear than his right.

Lou waited for a commercial before going into the kitchen, where Augie stood proud and erect, holding out a hunk of French bread. He said, "Here you go, cousin."

Lou, hairy as a coconut—he even had hair on his nose— leaned over the range and dipped the bread into Augie's cast-iron gravy tank. He pulled it up dripping red.

He sniffed, eyes closed, then tasted.

Silence.

Five hundred times they'd done this, as if the taste changed from week to week. And each time they all stood around tense, expectant, as if they were working on a cure for cancer.

"You son of a bitch," Lou said. "That's beautyful, Senator. Fuckin' beautyful." Augie always reacted with polite surprise and then a gracious laugh, as if there were a chance Lou Canuso, who owed everything to Augie, would find something wrong with his gravy. "Senator, how's Angela today?" he asked.

"I seen her yesterday," Augie said, waving the wooden spoon like a magic wand, as if it could make his wife appear. "She didn't know who I was, but she said she wanted to go to the track." The senator's eyes misted. "How do you like that, Lou?

My Angela still remembers some of the beautyful moments we had together."

The doorbell rang again.

"This must be Ham now," Augie said, though Joey knew it wasn't. Ham always held the ring an instant longer.

Izzy Weiner looked like his name. He was a little guy, wiry, horn-rim glasses. His opponent had picked up on a resemblance to Groucho Marx and was running a TV ad in which Izzy's name was superimposed on Groucho's desk in a snippet from *You Bet Your Life.* The secret word, dropped down from the ceiling in the clutches of a little bird, was *hack.*

Izzy's nomination was a fluke. Two other Democrats, infinitely more qualified for the supreme court, had negated each other in the primary. Izzy, meanwhile, went to the track two weeks before the election, hit an eighty-thousand-dollar trifecta, and dumped it into a TV blitz that gave him the win by a nose.

"Hello, Senator," Izzy said, extending his hand.

"Izzy, you're not gonna believe it. Tell him, Lou. Tell him."

"The gravy's out of this world," Lou said. "It's a beautyful thing."

"Tell me about it," said Izzy, a cross-cultural cousin who'd grown up in a Jewish pocket around Fifth and Ritner. "I hadda go up Mayfair yesterday, the Clover Club's puttin' on a little spaghetti feed. Go ahead, they're tellin' me. Eat, eat. I said get outta here with that *farckuckteh* macaroni, you crazy micks. You don't know from Italian. You spoil me, Senator. You spoil me."

They'd been together so long, Izzy could throw in a *farckuck-teh* or a *fishtunkenah* and the others could come back with a *mezza-mezz* or a *fongool,* and not only did they all understand each other, but it sounded like they were speaking the same language. At campaign time, Augie always made a point of telling Jews the beautiful thing about Yiddish is how the words sound like what they mean. "Take *farckuckteh,*" he once said during a rally for Judge Edith Schmeltzer at Famous Fourth Street

Delicatessen. "I don't care if you're Chinese, you know *farkuck-teh*'s a mess of some type."

Augie smiled at Izzy's story and then turned serious.

"Anyone know what happened to Ham?"

No answer.

"If he's with this new cupcake again, I'm gonna smack him," Augie said, throwing a backhand at the air. "He drops this election, we're out of the game, boys. And he can't keep it in his pants? Fifty-two years I'm with my Angela. Fifty-two years, and not once did I wet my whistle outside the domicile."

Joey and Izzy nodded gravely, as if Augie had just delivered the eleventh commandment: Thou shalt not wet the whistle outside the domicile. The silence was broken by Lou's voice, which roared in from the living room. "Get your head out of your ass, you son of a bitch! Fuckin' Iggles are down twenty-eight in the second quarter."

Joey made the salad and put it on the table while Augie poured the macaroni into the colander, disappearing in the steam that mushroomed up. The doorbell rang and Augie stepped out from behind the cloud. "There's our boy," he said, lighting up. For reasons Joey never understood, Ham was like a favorite son to Augie. The more he strayed, cutting deals behind Augie's back, the more protective Augie seemed to be.

After a thoroughly undistinguished career in the state legislature, Ham was running to fill out the term of Congressman Albert "Bitty" Reed, who had stiffed Augie for years, never so much as returning his phone calls. But as he usually did, Augie got even, and cleared a path for Ham in the process. Reed, who had a long history of heart trouble and hadn't been under three hundred pounds since high school, died in the Kubla Khan room at the Trump Taj Mahal, where Augie had set him up with a hotel belly dancer. Augie, still beaming over the genius of it, thought of it as his greatest work in a long career of public service. The perfect murder.

"What's for dinner?" Ham asked, filling the kitchen with enough cologne to peel the wallpaper. "Chop suey?"

It was Ham's standard setup for Augie.

"We fought three wars so we wouldn't have to eat that shit," Augie said, dumping Parmesan on the penne. "I got your chop suey right here. Listen, Ham, we got some business. Where the hell you been?"

"You gotta be kiddin' me," Ham said, his palms open to the heavens. "It's Sunday in the campaign season. What am I, stupid? I been to mass eight times today. I hit every goddamn church in the district."

"That's my boy," Augie said, patting Ham on the shoulder of his fifteen-hundred-dollar suit. Ham, who'd had a brief spin in Hollywood on a connection made by Augie, thought he was still there. He shopped only at Boyd's, where he bought top-of-the-line European suits, and he wore two or three pounds of gold at any given time. He also spent an hour a day in a tanning salon, and fair-skinned Irishman that he was, the lamp had melted his freckles into a face the color of mahogany wood putty. The lamp also appeared to have damaged his toupee, cinching it up slightly at the edges and giving it an orange tint.

Joey studied Ham suspiciously. Mentally, he bet the house that if Ham had been on his knees, it had nothing to do with Holy Communion.

Augie said, "You know, we're still strong in the church. Izzy, you oughta show up at a mass or two in the next couple of months. Alls you do, you say an Act of Contrition before you take Holy Communion, then it's not a sin that you had no confession. Of course, being that you're not even in the faith, you can probably skip the prayer."

Izzy gave it a nod.

"I gotta tell you somethin'," Ham said. "There's a lot of gripin' about this silicone dust, whatever the fuck they call it, that come out of the refinery there yesterday." He lit a cigarette and dropped the match on the floor. "That stuff'll fuck you up."

"Guess what," Augie said. "That's what we gotta do, is jam it up their ass a little bit, this Liberty Oil. The prick bastards. I was tellin' Joey here earlier."

Joey tossed the salad with oil and vinegar and thundered off to the living room to put an album on the phonograph. His weight sent a wave through the weakening floor and the refrigerator swayed slightly.

Ham said, "He's gonna bring down the house one day, this fuckin' bull."

Augie wasn't much for modern conveniences. No cassettes. No compact discs. He had a scratched-up Mario Lanza or two, a Jerry Vale, and every Sinatra song ever pressed onto vinyl. Joey settled on *Songs for Swingin' Lovers*. First cut, "You Make Me Feel So Young."

Augie, an occasional guest vocalist with the house band at the Triangle Tavern, a blue-collar pizza and macaroni house in South Philadelphia, sang along in the kitchen. " 'You make me feel so young. You make me feel like spring has sprung. And every time I see you grin, I'm such a hap-py in-di-vidual!' Come on, you crazy goombahs, *mangia, mangia.*"

Augie put the macaroni on a platter and set it in the middle of the table, then ladled his gravy over it. He breathed in the aroma that wafted up and smiled like a proud father. "How about that, boys?" The five men took their places, closed their eyes, and bowed their heads. Augie began to pray.

"We thank you, Lord, for this wonderful macaroni dinner. But we could use a little help, tell you the truth, in this campaign."

"Amen," Izzy said.

"I ain't fuckin' finished," Augie snapped. "All my life, only three things mattered to me. You, my family and friends, and the river wards. Constituent service is what this is. We work for Mrs. Mangione, who's got silicone all over the house, and even the coloreds that went down in the same mishap there. We work for the good Roman Catholic boy who needs maybe a starter job at the Parking Authority. Good causes, all. But we're light on the campaign funds here, which puts us behind the eight ball. So if we could catch a break with the lottery, or maybe Izzy hits another one at the track, there's a cut in it for the church. And please don't forget to keep an eye on my Angela. Amen."

A round of amens.

"Father, Son, and Holy Ghost," Izzy said. "Who eats the fastest gets the most."

Sinatra was singing "Too Marvelous for Words."

Everyone stood and lunged at the food while Augie poured Chianti all around. The glasses met in the center of the table.

"*Salud*," the senator said. "We're gonna show the bastards we're not done yet. *Salud* and *mangia*."

CHAPTER 3

MIKE MULDOON always parked near the art museum, no meters out there, and walked the several blocks along Benjamin Franklin Parkway and into the lap of Center City. He enjoyed the morning stroll even on a gray Monday like this, the city stepping out, one building at a time, from behind the fog.

He had to admit it: One week back from retirement, he was enjoying himself. Sure, he missed the golf. But he'd gotten a rush over the weekend, just like old times, when he hid a camera in the ceiling of congressional candidate Ham Flaherty's office. Muldoon was leaning against telling Lisa Savitch he did the job without waiting for court authorization, just so surveillance could begin the moment the papers came through. She was young, and the young ones always went by the book. Besides, Savitch, a thoroughbred all the way, was already enough of a handful. Muldoon shook his head, threw his trench coat over his shoulder, and clip-clopped along in his wing tips.

The parkway was modeled after the Champs Élysées in Paris, a broad tree-lined boulevard decorated with the flags of the world, the Rodin Museum at the midpoint. Just past the spray of Logan fountain was the Cathedral Basilica of Saints Peter and Paul, where Muldoon was married twenty-five years ago to a woman he met while investigating a bank robbery. Beyond that, rising up at the far end of the parkway like an overdressed circus elephant, was City Hall.

The hall was Second Empire style, a look that suggested a French brothel or burlesque house, and it sat at the very inter-section of the city's two main thoroughfares, stubbornly in the path of anyone who needed to get anywhere. The gargoyled main building was topped by a clock tower and a statue of William Penn, who had arrived from England in 1682 to begin what he called a holy experiment. An experiment that had led, three hun-dred years later, to Muldoon's substantial career in removing the sinners.

Muldoon stopped at Logan Circle and bowed his head before the Basilica. He said a short prayer for help in bringing charges against Ham Flaherty, Augie Sangiamino, and what was left of the crooked Democratic Party machine he'd spent so many years dismantling. To his left, Logan fountain gurgled and hissed. Straight ahead, City Hall seemed heavy enough to sink, all that money in the pockets of the thieves who worked there.

Muldoon had hidden in closets, taped bugs under desks, planted cameras in ceilings. All City Hall's whispers and all its secrets were his. That was what brought him back now, one year into early retirement. He had left because the building had got-ten to him; he was back for the same reason. Walking into City Hall through the northwest entrance, Muldoon recalled the DA's pleas for help. She had literally tracked him down on the golf course and begged him, telling Muldoon she'd assigned a young prosecutor to the case, someone who had just moved down from Boston and needed to be pointed in the right direction. Besides, she asked, would you rather be teeing off on golf balls or the troglodytes of this city? The question had answered itself.

Twelve years ago, this same DA, Kevinne McGinns, was in the U.S. attorney's office and drew the corruption case that be-gan her career in politics. She was the one who brought down U.S. Senator Augie Sangiamino. Not that it was a particularly brilliant prosecution. McGinns had been handed a case she couldn't lose, thanks to the work of the FBI agent who set her up. Thanks to Muldoon.

Two months, tops, Muldoon figured as he headed for the elevator. These were not the brightest crooks in the world. By election day, one of them had to slip up, and Muldoon would be back in heaven, knocking long ones down the fairway.

The district attorney's office was across the street, but Muldoon and Savitch worked in a small annex on the sixth floor of City Hall. Muldoon strained to see himself in the hazy reflection of the elevator door on the way up, adjusting his tie and patting his reddish hair. He was six feet tall, about two hundred pounds, with a mustache he groomed now with a comb. He liked making an entrance—the celebrated FBI agent coming in to inspire the yearlings with his mere bearing, like a major leaguer visiting the minors to give batting tips.

The elevator doors rolled open heavily and Muldoon's size thirteens kicked echoes through the block-long corridors of City Hall. The annex was behind the first door on the left, and one step inside, Muldoon was reminded why everyone called it the Hole.

The FBI it wasn't. The roof leaked, ceiling panels were missing, the walls had yellowed, and the lights flickered. A foul odor hung in the room, too, like nervous sweat, feeding the legend that a former judge, who was occasionally spotted roaming the halls in a growing state of disorientation, had been living on the sixth floor since his retirement seven years ago.

A half dozen prosecutors and two secretaries were stationed behind government desks the color of lead, all of them facing the door, when Muldoon walked in. The room was a firetrap, with boxes of files, some of them going back fifty years, scattered everywhere. Muldoon casually returned nods and hellos as he weaved through the cluttered aisles toward the back of the room. Savitch's office was in the far right corner, Muldoon's at the other end. He stopped at her door and when he was sure no one was looking, he smoothed over his mustache with his fingers. She didn't look up when he walked in. Head down, eyes on the newspaper, she asked, "Muldoon, you see this quote in the paper from Jim Carville, the political consultant?"

Muldoon, fifty-four, was almost twice her age. Every time he saw her, that blond shag, golden skin, sad brown eyes, she looked better. Not that she looked bad the first time. "No," he said. "What did Jim Carville the political consultant say?"

He hung his coat on the back of the door, which barely cleared the edge of her desk when it swung all the way open. This had been a storage room before Savitch arrived. There was nothing in it but the desk and two chairs, and the dartboard that was on the wall by the window when she moved in. Muldoon sat on a chair that had stuffing coming through the vinyl cover like wisps of cotton candy.

"Pennsylvania is Pittsburgh and Philadelphia, with Alabama in between."

She looked up to see how that played, and her eyes, wet from the sting of the smoke, found him staring at her. Muldoon had never seen a woman look this good without makeup, and he often studied her face in search of powder or eyeliner. She had to be wearing something.

"Does he say Alabama is the good part?" he asked. He walked over to the window, which looked onto the parkway. The fog was lifting and he could see the Basilica. George Washington was beyond that, near Muldoon's car, heading into town on his horse.

"Did somebody once tell you you were funny?" Savitch asked.

"No, Savage. It happens all the time."

She didn't seem to mind the name he'd given her, and she hadn't thrown one back at him. One of the DA detectives had been calling Muldoon "Irish Mike," which he thought was a little informal for a man of his stature, but Savitch hadn't repeated it. As long as she didn't call him "Duldoon," which he used to get from one of the smart-ass females in the U.S. attorney's office.

A secretary knocked on the door and slinked into the cramped office with two coffees. She wore high heels and a tight red dress, green eye shadow spreading to her temples like the wings of a butterfly.

"Here you go," she said, setting the cups on Savitch's gray desktop. "This one's for Lois Lane; this one's for Clark Kent. And if I was you two, I'd watch out for the boss. Everyone's saying she's a bear today. Something about what a bunch of boobs are on the state supreme court."

Muldoon watched Carla leave, a wiggle straight out of a fifties movie.

Savitch watched him watch.

"Let me guess," she said, coughing and then clearing her throat. "The look works for you."

Muldoon glared back at her.

"That woman haunts me," Savitch said in a confessional tone. "I keep having this dream where everybody in Philadelphia looks like her and they say *starfame* like she does."

"They all *do*," Muldoon said dryly. "What's your point?"

Not that he would tell Savitch, but yeah, he thought Carla Delmonico looked pretty good, as a matter of fact. She had it and she flaunted it. What was wrong with that? With Savitch, you couldn't tell. She wore a plain black skirt and loose-fitting gray cotton shirt, and Muldoon didn't know what was under there today or any other day, just like he didn't know what was behind those brown eyes of hers.

Muldoon pulled the darts out of the board. He puffed his chest and moved away from the window in his upright FBI manner, a man who couldn't have been anything else. Savitch had written "Nov. 5" on a yellow note and pinned it to the bull's-eye on the dartboard. Election day. Muldoon set his coffee on the corner of her desk and lined up his first throw. It hit the metal rim on the edge of the board and fell to the floor like a dead pigeon.

"You're showing improvement," she said without looking up, buried in the newspaper again.

"You know something, Savage? I've never seen you try this."

His voice, built to his size, left a bass hum in the room.

"You wouldn't be able to handle it," she said.

His second dart caught more metal and joined the first one on the floor. Muldoon examined the dart he still held as if there were something wrong with it.

Savitch said, "I thought you people were born with a dart in one hand and a mug of beer in the other."

Muldoon let the dart fall and it stuck in her desktop, piercing the newspaper. He said, "That would be the British, sweetheart."

She didn't appear to be listening, but looked up to say, "Excuse me. Beer in one hand and a potato in the other."

It had been like this since they met. A first-class ball-buster, she was. Muldoon didn't know if she'd been born this way or if it had something to do with the stories he'd heard around the office. Savitch had allegedly been two-timed by the star prosecutor in Boston, his affair becoming the subject of a scandal that chased Savitch out of town. Muldoon had a call in to an FBI buddy in the Boston office to see how much of it was true.

Muldoon tapped his foot deliberately. "What are you reading?" he asked. "I'd like to get this thing moving, if you don't mind. These guys are probably out digging up graves and robbing banks while I watch you read your horoscope, or whatever the hell you're doing."

"Listen to this," Savitch said, clearing her throat and then coughing. A hard, dry cough. "Whit Pritchard, owner and chief executive of Liberty Oil, said silica alumina can irritate the eyes, nose, and throat, but is not believed to present a serious health risk to reasonably healthy people."

She looked up for his response. This was how she really got to him, the way she could look nineteen sometimes. Fresh-faced. The center of her top lip turned up and her small round mouth so perfect. Muldoon asked what her point was.

"What the hell does it mean?" she asked, the edge there already, this early in the day. " 'Not believed to present a serious health risk to reasonably healthy people.' What does that mean?"

"Just what it says, is my guess."

"Well how comforting is it that they're not sure? If they're that incompetent, they shouldn't be in the business. Did you see this thing on the news?"

"The yellow cloud thing?"

"I was in it, Muldoon."

"What do you mean, in it?"

"Running. I was doing a run down there Saturday when this thing happened."

"You told me you always run on Kelly Drive, along the river."

"I didn't this time. I wanted to find a different route and I ended up in the middle of this disaster. I've probably got cancer."

Muldoon threw his head back and laughed. "You don't have cancer," he said.

"How do you know? This boob from the refinery doesn't even know."

"This happens all the time down there, Savage."

"Oh, that's reassuring."

"Does it say what went wrong this time?"

She looked at the article. "A valve, they're saying."

"On a catalytic converter?"

That got her attention.

"How'd you know?"

"That's where they break down crude oil to make gasoline."

"What are you, George Bush's son?"

Muldoon crossed his legs. "It's pretty basic stuff," he said. "A faulty valve is not an uncommon thing. But I still don't see why you're so interested."

"Let's just say that I am, all right? Just on general principle, I take notice of negligence and greed. Two women went to the hospital in serious condition, Muldoon. It's no different than being hit in the head with a brick, and this businessman is saying, Hey, it's no big deal. Don't worry."

Her eyes were riveted on him, but she seemed to be somewhere else. Muldoon watched her look away and out the window to that place, wherever it was.

"I'm just saying it's not toxic," Muldoon said. "Silica alumina? Let me tell you something. It's the air you can't see that you should be scared of."

She looked at him like he'd finally said something she agreed with.

"You're supposed to go indoors," he went on. "Did you go inside?"

"No."

"Well then you're right. You probably have cancer."

"Muldoon, how am I supposed to just go indoors if I'm out in the middle of this park?"

"I'd see a doctor if I were you."

"I've been coughing ever since."

"There you go. Cancer, emphysema. Maybe if you have another cigarette."

Muldoon fanned the smoke and then tried opening her window, something he'd done every day for a week. She insisted on keeping the door closed, probably to discourage guys from coming in and hanging around, trying to get to know her. A half dozen of them had already pulled that. The window, which probably hadn't been opened since World War I, wouldn't budge. Muldoon grunted and tried again. Nothing. He cursed and sat back down hard.

"Jesus, Muldoon. I run five or six miles a day and you give

me shit for smoking a cigarette or two. You try to open a window for two seconds and you're about to keel over."

Muldoon mashed his tongue against the side of his mouth. You couldn't win with her.

Savitch opened a drawer and pulled out a sheaf of paper, waving it with a smile. "A little present for you," she said. "Your court authorization to wire Ham Flaherty's office. How long will it take to set up?"

"Not long."

He definitely wasn't going to tell her. Novice that she was, she had no idea how long it could take in this town to get the courts off their ass and push some simple paperwork so they could get the investigation going. The DA's Hack Hotline had begun picking up anonymous tips on Ham Flaherty in the summer. Nosy neighbors, suspicious of payola and upset that they weren't getting a piece of it, reported daily shipments of furniture, electronics, and various other perks to Ham's South Philadelphia house, including installation of a rooftop hot tub and deck. The usual graft, Muldoon called it, and he frankly had bored of chasing after two-bit cases like that. But there was another element to this one.

One tip said Flaherty's campaign for Congress was going to be secretly bankrolled by Atlantic City casinos in return for consideration of gambling interests. The casinos, located just an hour from Philadelphia, drew thousands of suckers out of their row houses every day. If the tip were true, Muldoon had told Savitch, Augie Sangiamino was the likely go-between, so they had to keep an eye on him as well as Ham. Nailing it down could be tricky, but if a second tip were true, they might catch a break. One of the first payments from a casino was the service of a cocktail waitress who moonlighted as the house hooker. Ham was said to like her work so much, he gave her a no-show job on the state payroll to supplement her income. All Muldoon and Savitch had to do was get to the woman, twist her arm, and maybe she'd give up the whole scam.

"You set up the surveillance on the bimbo yet?" Savitch asked.

"It starts tomorrow morning."

"Maybe we'll get lucky and close this thing early," she said.

"What. You're tired of working with me already?"

"I just can't believe the amount of small-time sleaze around here," she said. "It's a city of bottom feeders. With no bottom."

Muldoon had grown up in Scranton, three hours north, where his father was a cop and his mother a schoolteacher. The combination of organized crime, the state's mutant politics, and his father's silent influence got Muldoon into the business. But he could be defensive about his home state, especially with Savitch treating him as if he were personally responsible for whatever problems existed.

"It's not like this in Boston?" he asked.

"No, for your information," she said, kicking off her shoes. "It isn't."

"No machine politics left at all?" Muldoon asked, an eye on her feet as she walked around the desk to get another pack of cigarettes out of her pocketbook. Somehow her shoeless feet seemed to reveal more of her body than the amount of skin exposed. She had slender ankles and tight, shapely calves. A thin run in her stocking started in the middle of her left calf and continued past her knee.

She went back behind the desk and fixed a stare in his direction. Her left eye wandered slightly, and Muldoon wasn't always sure exactly what she was looking at. It was an imperfection that added to the allure, like the way she bent her cigarette hand back between puffs, almost as if she were mocking a Hollywood look.

"There might be some similarities," she said, her Lauren Bacall voice roughed up by the smoke. "But there's one major difference between Boston and Philadelphia."

"And what would that be?"

"When the pols get out of prison in Boston, they don't start work the next day as political consultants."

"That's an exaggeration," Muldoon protested.

"Is it? I did a little research on Augie Sangiamino. The week he got out of jail, he got a consulting contract to help design the new prison."

"Who could be better informed?" Muldoon shot back. Not much else he could do with that. "At least in Pennsylvania the hacks usually have the good sense to limit themselves to local and state politics."

Savitch tapped a finger on the desk, looking at him like he was an amusement. "Who, exactly, are you talking about?" she asked.

"Where should I start? Ted Kennedy? Mike Dukakis?"

"My God," Savitch said, dunking a cigarette in the half-full coffee cup. She smoked only half of every cigarette and drank half of every coffee, a habit that had suddenly begun to annoy Muldoon. "I forget. How many years ago was Mike Dukakis?"

"Not that long ago," Muldoon said, his voice a little stronger now. "Remember when he climbed into that tank and put on the Army helmet? That was a good look. I had a bobbing-head Phillie in the back of my dad's car when I was a kid. Same thing."

Muldoon stood up and jingled the change in his pocket like he had something to celebrate. She wasn't half as smart as she thought she was, but that's why he was here. The DA knew Savitch needed a guide to take her through the sewers of the city, and McGinns wanted to blow Ham Flaherty out of the water in the worst way. She wanted to nab him in the middle of his congressional campaign and take Augie Sangiamino down a second time because she had her sights on bigger and better things for herself. Senator, governor, vice president. Whatever, it wouldn't hurt her cause to add these meatballs to her trophy case.

McGinns had told Muldoon that they raved about Savitch in Boston, saying her instincts were uncanny for someone her age and that she had destroyed a half dozen veteran defense attorneys her first year in felonies. McGinns also wanted a fresh eye on this one. Someone who'd been in town a short enough time so that her mouth still dropped open when they pulled the net up off the street at the end of every day.

"Speaking of incompetent men," Savitch said, "you happen to see that TV ad this weekend? It's a Groucho Marx clip with Izzy Weiner's name on it, and the secret word is *hack*."

Whatever she said, something unsaid always went with it. Muldoon found himself in the awkward position of defending the very hacks he'd spent his whole career putting away.

"Look," he said, "it's not that bad in this state anymore."

"Then what the hell did it used to be like?" she asked. "Aren't you the one who told me you could still buy a judge in this town for coffee and a doughnut?"

He sat down, crossed his legs, and pulled out his handkerchief to buff a spot on his wing tip. His neck felt hot against his collar. What could he say? One member of the state supreme court had just called the only black justice a descendant of King Kong, another had accused a colleague of trying to spike his coffee with drain cleaner, and another was being accused by his secretary of forcing her to take dictation while he sat in the nude and played with his gavel. Eight state judges were in jail for assorted types of graft, six were under indictment, and the state attorney general had just gone down for killing an investigation into the activities of a porn distributor who'd bankrolled his campaign.

Muldoon was better off just keeping his mouth shut.

"Face it," Savitch said. "Pennsylvania's not a state. It's a lounge act."

For this, he came out of retirement? Muldoon loosened his tie. "Well if that's how you feel, then why don't you just go back to Boston, Savage?" His face got rosy with any amount of exercise or agitation, and it was flaming now. He folded his handkerchief carefully, square corners, and tucked it away. She might have a fancy Yale diploma and he'd gone to lowly St. Joe's, but he didn't need a civics lesson from an Ivy League brat. A New Englander, no less. Philadelphia might not be perfect, but it had a lot going for it. More golf courses, probably, and the weather was better so you could get more rounds in. And sports fans in Boston were all lunatics. Savitch was right. She probably was better off in that overrated icebox of a town.

The irony, it occurred to Muldoon, was that he was the envy of every guy in the office. Traditionally, most of the deputy DAs shunned the Hole. But since Savitch's arrival, it wasn't uncommon to find a dozen guys hanging around, waiting to catch a glimpse of her or strike up a conversation. They were particularly intrigued by her complete lack of interest in any of them, which they referred to in hushed conversation as a kind of sexiness they couldn't quite articulate.

Muldoon himself, for all the grief she gave him, couldn't help but think of slipping his hands under that little black skirt. She walked past him now to take a look out the window and he caught a whiff of her as she went by. Lemon-scented smoke. She puffed at the window, her back to him, and he followed the line of her calf up the back of her leg and under that skirt. He was telling himself to forget it, she wasn't his type and he was happily married, anyway, when Carla Delmonico appeared in the doorway.

"I got Judy Garland on the Hack Hotline," she said. Judy Garland was the code name they'd given to their chief tipster.

"Put her through," Savitch said, coughing again as she went back to her desk. "And Carla, could you get me a printout? All the newspaper stories, this year and last, that mention Liberty Oil."

"What do you say, Muldoon? You think we're ready to tell

her we know who she is?" Savitch looked at him and then at the phone.

"Too soon," he said. "Way too soon."

"All right," she said, picking up line six and saying hello to Judy Garland, who was married to William "Ham" Flaherty.

CHAPTER 4

Augie Sangiamino, trim and natty in a new three-piece suit of pastel green, threw the door open and stepped into Milly's Lunchbox with his arms outstretched, as if everyone in the place had been waiting for him. The dozen customers turned at once, as if he were right.

"How we doing today, Milly? Everything all right? Atta boy. How about the rest of you dingdongs? Beautiful." Joey rode Augie's tail as the boss patted everyone on the back and handed out campaign buttons. Four men sat on fountain stools and eight others at tables in a narrow space the size of a shuffleboard court. "You guys hear Milly hit a number last night? Everything's on the house today or we take our business elsewhere, boys."

Augie had a table all the way in the back with his own phone and a nameplate that said, simply, THE SENATOR. The owner, Emiliano Falcone, had insisted for forty-two years that no one sit there without Augie's blessing, and the table was vacant the two years Augie was in prison.

"Smells good," Augie said to Falcone, who pushed a sizzle of eggs, potatoes, and scrapple over the grill. "You're finally getting the hang of it, Milly."

Once, while Augie was in the Senate, the president called the luncheonette, hustling votes for his budget plan. Augie was in the men's room, so Falcone picked up and asked, "President of what?" When he realized who was on the line, Falcone told the president there was a lot he could learn from Augie Sangiamino about how to take care of the little guy. Before hanging up, he promised to send a shipment of pepper-and-egg sandwiches, Italian hoagies, and veal grinders down to the White House, no charge.

Augie's daily routine was to make morning mass at St. Mary Magdalen, stroll the Italian Market, then come by Milly's, where dusty trophies lined the shelves, the Christmas garland never came down, and the radio played standards all day long unless the TV was on. Some of the regulars came in early and stayed until Falcone shooed them out for napping, or until their wives came in after them. Augie gradually made his way across the chessboard tile floor to his table, where the morning paper and two cups of coffee waited. Tina, the waitress, always set him up the second he came in. Augie sat facing the front door, and the wall behind him was plastered with photos of Augie hosting one visitor after another at this corner table, going back to when he was a young man. The angles of his face had hardened and his shoulders had softened, but the look in his eyes was the same as in the photos. It said, Work with me or I'll bury you.

From this modest corner, in this blue-collar neighborhood hangout at Eighth and Christian Streets, Augie Sangiamino once ruled the world. A ceiling fan moved slow as the years above a red-checked table that was confession box, altar, bank, courtroom, and woodshed. Augie carried himself as if it were still all those things; as if he still commanded respect and fear. He still had some respect.

"They make the pickup yet?" Augie called to Milly.

"Not yet."

Augie took a twenty out of his wallet and handed it to Joey. A retired cop ran a numbers game every day in the neighborhood. Augie hadn't hit one in six months. "Take care of that for me, will you, Joey?"

Augie grabbed the phone. His first call every morning was to Lou, who grabbed odd jobs for him at Democratic Party headquarters in Center City. The offerings weren't as fat as they once were. In fact, Augie and his gang were like buzzards who always got to the carcass ten minutes late. Maybe a political candidate was looking for dirt on an opponent, for example. For a job like that, Augie might charge two hundred dollars, payable in cash only. He'd call one of a dozen cops he still had, the cop runs a check and feeds Augie the dope. A few days later, maybe the cop comes by Milly's for lunch and Joey hands him a brown bag with a twenty inside.

Lou said he had nothing yet, so Augie hung up and opened the morning paper to the racing page. Joey, who checked for bugs first thing each morning, was on hands and knees under the table. He'd once seen a quote in the paper, DA Kevinne McGinns saying that anytime Augie Sangiamino was involved in a campaign, a special prosecutor ought to be appointed automatically.

"Joey, we're in the seventh today," Augie said, slurping black coffee and holding a finger on the racing grid. "How do we look?"

"She'll show," Joey said, popping back up. "That's all." Augie had owned two racehorses that were handled by a disbarred attorney who had been his cell mate for a period. One of the horses, I Didn't See Nothin', was in the seventh race at Garden State. A second filly, My Angela, had bowed a tendon two months ago and had to be put down.

Tina, a northern girl, fair-skinned like Augie, came by to see if they needed more coffee. Augie used to have her sit on his lap, but either he was getting too old or she was getting too heavy. "Again with the horses," she said. "You boys got a gambling problem or something?"

Augie threw his hands up, and his gleaming eyes were two small blue lakes at the base of a mountain. "We gamble," he said. "That ain't a problem. It's like breathing."

Augie had done more exhaling than inhaling in his life. The

track, the numbers, the weather—he'd bet on anything. As a boy, he used to ride his bike down to Roosevelt Park with a pal, throw bread into the middle of the lake, and bet on which duck would get to it first. That was one thing he loved about politics. It was just another horse race was all.

"The campaign posters come in, Joey?"

"I got some in the trunk, Senator."

"Good. Let's get them out on the street already. And this place, fix it up for me so it looks like fuckin' campaign head-quarters."

Tina brought Joey his regular breakfast. Bacon, egg and cheese on a roll, and two soft pretzels with mustard. Augie, who didn't eat breakfast, noticed that Joey's eye followed Tina away from the table.

"This girl's really porked up, Joey. You take a shot yet?"

"She's a nice girl, Senator. Nice girl like that don't go with a crazy nut like me."

"The hell you talking about, Joey? Healthy young man like yourself? I was in your shoes, I'd be all over that. She's your type, besides, the way you go for those pie-eating champions."

Joey finished breakfast and went out to the car. He plastered the front window of Milly's with Ham and Izzy posters, and when he went back to Augie's corner with a cigar box full of campaign buttons, Augie was looking up from the paper and slamming an open hand on the table. The results of the first poll were in, and the news wasn't good. Izzy Weiner was a twelve-point underdog to Debra Sharperson, his opponent for supreme court. Ham Flaherty was four back of Ron Rice.

Joey pulled a wrinkled scratch of paper out of his pocket. He'd written his predictions on it a month ago. Eleven and four. He was only one point off, but Augie reacted as if it was a surprise.

"Sharperson I could understand, the backing she's got,"

Augie said in a sharp, whining tone. "But this *schvartze* don't know night from day, Joey. Colored guy like that, never held no office. What the hell are people thinking?"

"It's the football," Joey said. "I told you that thing would bite us in the ass, Senator."

Ron "Minute" Rice owned a piece of a waterfront restaurant and had no political experience, but he had been a flashy wide receiver for the Philadelphia Eagles fifteen years ago and for Notre Dame before that. His nickname grew out of his reputation as an instant scoring machine. The black vote in the district was less than 40 percent, but in some white neighborhoods, his having gone on to the pros from Notre Dame was the equivalent of having won the Nobel Prize.

Augie couldn't handle the idea of a political novice coming out of nowhere like this when guys like Augie, professional pols, had paid a lifetime of dues. He'd been running into this kind of bullshit for ten years, ever since the Young Turks took over, and it wasn't just because he was an ex-con. To some people, that was a badge of honor. The problem was that big-city bosses like Augie couldn't muscle people the way they used to, when anyone who stepped out of line got smacked, or, in extreme cases, was removed forever from the warmth and goodness of the public teat. Organized labor had lost its punch, the proud traditions of patronage and nepotism were being held up to public ridicule by asshole media types, and political parties were splintered. "It's getting so you can't even buy off a fuckin' judge," Augie had complained at Sunday's macaroni dinner.

It wasn't that Augie was too old a dog to learn new tricks; he just preferred the old ones.

"This Ron Rice had to knock somebody up at that gigolo club he runs. I'd bet my left nut," Augie told Joey, head wagging. "Either that or he's laying on his bills. Check with one of our boys at the 'lectric and gas companies, Joey. We gotta get something on Sharperson, too. Get Lou on the phone and tell him I want somebody knocking on the door of every putz this broad ever knew for five minutes." With *ex-con* in front of his name, Augie had to lay back, calling the shots from behind the curtain. Even in Pennsylvania, running for Congress or a seat on the highest appellate bench with a former crook as your campaign manager could cost you a few votes. Joey had no official title, either, but handled the money for both campaigns.

"She wants to play hardball, let's show her who invented the game," Augie said. He slapped the table for punctuation and the old fire flickered momentarily—the same look that was in all the photos over his shoulder. "She puts out the trash, I wanna know what's in it. Somebody's gotta have something on her."

Joey knew it was over for them unless they came up with a miracle. Augie did, too, but for Augie, knowing and believing were two different things, and that was something Joey admired. Augie Sangiamino would go in the ground trying to get over on the fucking gravedigger.

Sharperson, as the undisputed favorite, had attorneys waving money at her from every corner of the state so they could cash in when she won the election. Ten thousand dollars here, five thousand there. Izzy's first fund-raiser, meanwhile, was a central Pennsylvania bull roast that brought in $348.00 from the Association of Retired Steamfitters. He was so bad off, he couldn't even buy airtime to respond to her Groucho Marx ad. Ham, meanwhile, was waiting on a promised stream of cash from Atlantic City, but so far, all they'd come through with was a few toys for him to play with. Augie had lost his clout in A.C., too.

"Joey, you wanna find Ham for me? We need to get him in here and go over some things."

Joey was about to dial when Augie yelled past him. "Mrs. Mangione—how's my girlfriend?" Augie stood up and put a hand on her fanny as they hugged, winking over her shoulder at Milly Falcone. Her head came barely to his chin.

Joey always gave up his seat to the visitor and stood at

Augie's right side like a sergeant at arms, hands clasped in front of him. They might be going down, but they were professionals, and they were going down with style and pride. Augie always wore his hat for these consultations, so if he wanted to cut a conversation short, he could say they were on their way out.

"Listen, how's your boy doing?" Augie asked. Mrs. Mangione had come to him when her son was suspected of torching the bar where he worked in an insurance scam. He'd done a pretty good job, in fact, and Augie thought he had potential. He set him up as a court crier at City Hall.

"Everything's fine," Mrs. Mangione said. "He sends his best."

She was Augie's age, wide and sturdy. She'd worn black, including a veil, every day since her husband died of liver failure ten years ago. He had worked at Liberty Oil for forty years and got sick six months after retiring.

"They should right now paint my house," Mrs. Mangione declared. She leaned over the table and whispered in a grave tone, "Those rich 'merigan bastards." She took a napkin and swept off her side of the table. Joey could see wrinkles and folds through the veil, her eyes like black dots.

"Joey, you wanna make a call down Liberty Oil there later on, see what they can do for our girlfriend Mrs. Mangione?"

"No problem, boss."

"I want a rug shampoo," Mrs. Mangione added. "I had open the windows."

"She wants to wash the rugs," Augie said. "Sit on those guys for me, Joey. See what we can get out of them for Mrs. Mangione's inconvenience." Mrs. Mangione nodded her appreciation.

"Listen, help yourself to a couple of buttons here," Augie said, pushing the cigar box at her. Mrs. Mangione took two, polished them with her sleeve, and pinned them over her breast. GET BUSY VOTE IZZY, and HAM CAN.

"Beautyful," Augie said. He took her hand and kissed it. "We'll let you know. And remember—vote early and often."

For the rest of the morning, anybody with a cracked sidewalk, a parking ticket, or any one of a million bureaucratic hassles or jams dropped by Milly's Lunchbox to see if Augie could make it go away. "No problem, cousin," Augie would say over and over as Joey quietly recorded names and phone numbers and pushed the box of buttons toward them. They'd all be called on election day. "You can bet Augie Sangiamino drives his foot up somebody's ass on this thing."

Joey took another call and covered the mouthpiece, whispering something to Augie. Augie took his hat off as he took the phone. "Jesus, I'm sorry to hear that, Cheech. He takes the good ones, you know. The ones too good for this rotten world we got. No. It's no problem. Listen, it'd be my honor to be a part of that. And whatever else I can do, you'll let me know?"

Frankie "Cheech" Napolitano had come to Augie for help seven months ago. He'd lost his job at the naval shipyard, and without health insurance, St. Bartholomew Hospital had refused to admit his Joey, who was in the final stages of leukemia. One call from Augie and the boy was set up in a private room by the end of the day. Napolitano was calling now to thank Augie again and to let him know his son had died. The boy was twelve. He told Augie he'd be honored if he came by the funeral, and Joey was making a note of the day and time when Augie hung up the phone.

"Gesù Cristo, Joey. You hate to see a thing like this, kid that young. He'll never be with a woman. Never vote." Augie checked his watch and stood up to leave. They made a trip to the home every day at this hour so Augie could visit his wife. They were on their way out when Augie heard a TV talk-show host introduce his next guest—Ron Rice. "Fuck me," Augie said, stopping at the counter and turning toward the television, which sat on a shelf over the grill. The Notre Dame fight song played as Ron "Minute" Rice walked onto the stage, juking two or three imaginary tacklers.

"I'm runnin' Ham fuckin' Flaherty for office and they're playing the Fighting Irish for this smoke," Augie whined.

"He ain't so bad a guy," Joey said quietly, but Augie didn't hear him.

The host droned on about his memories of Rice's acrobatics, and said he looked in good enough shape to go out there right now, show some of these kids how it's done.

"What a fuckin' blow job," Augie bellowed.

After several minutes of fawning blather, the host turned serious and asked if it wasn't true that Rice had an important announcement.

"That is correct," the candidate said, opening a briefcase. He said he'd spent time in the hospital with the old women who were laid up after inhaling the silica alumina from the refinery, and he'd also met with members of Not in Our Backyard. "The time for sitting back and doing nothing, as those in public office have done for years, is behind us," Rice said. Augie snorted and took off his hat, figuring he'd better hear the end of this. Rice brandished a bill he'd drafted and promised to introduce it ten seconds after they told him which chair was his in Congress.

"In lay terms," the host asked, "what does this mean for the health and safety of those of us who are exposed to risks every time we take a breath?"

"What it means," Rice said, "is that the free ride has ended. This bill will require all petrochemical industries located in areas with above-normal cancer rates to do weekly self-reporting of their emissions to a regional field office, and it also provides for monthly unscheduled surprise visits by the Environmental Protection Agency for additional testing."

Augie was slowly crushing his hat in his hand. Ham hadn't

even checked in with him since the Sunday macaroni dinner, when Augie told him to jump on the refinery with both feet.

"Joey!" Augie screamed, startling a Milly's regular who had dozed off. "Get Ham on the phone and get him now! I don't care if you have to call every fucking woman in the city."

CHAPTER 5

DISTRICT ATTORNEY Kevinne McGinns kept two cats and six yellow finches in her ninth-floor office, which had wall-to-wall carpeting, a fireplace, and furniture more suited to a living room than to the city's crime-fighting control room. "Look at those two," she said from her rocking chair. The cats, one gray with white paws and the other black, sat on opposite arms of a sofa, their gaze fixed on the birdcage that hung in the center of the room. Lisa Savitch sat between the cats, wondering why she'd been dragged up to the boss's little zoo. McGinns had called her at home, saying she wanted to see her in thirty minutes. No clue what it was about.

McGinns did a mechanical back and forth in the rocking chair, grim and dour, a practiced countenance. On each forward motion, a holstered gun peeked from behind the edge of a cardigan that framed a schoolmarmish gray suit. McGinns had used the gun twice, once plugging a mugger in the leg and another time killing a drug dealer who had stalked her and drawn on her after his release from prison. McGinns had been known to suggest that she would ride those two bullets into the governor's mansion one day.

Savitch coughed and covered her mouth.

"You allergic?" McGinns asked.

Savitch shook her head until the coughing stopped. "No. I was running on Saturday when that cloud came up from the refinery, and I can't get rid of this cough."

"They'll have us all dead soon enough," McGinns said.

"I was actually thinking of talking to you about looking into it," Savitch said timidly. In Boston, she could throw out ideas to the DA as she pleased, but she didn't know if McGinns was open to that sort of thing. "I had a similar situation where I grew up, actually, sort of similar, anyhow, and you know, this boy who just died of leukemia lived less than a half mile from the refinery. I did some checking, and the cancer rates in that part of town are incredible. There's got to be a correlation."

McGinns tapped stubby fingers, the nails chewed down, on the arm of the rocking chair, like she was measuring out the cadence of her response. "*A*, number one," she said, her mouth a small slit and her lips barely moving, "Liberty Oil is not in the city, it's in the next county, my dear. *B*, number two, the area from Boston to Norfolk happens to be an industrial corridor, so your information about cancer rates is neither new nor surprising. And *C*, number three, you have not been assigned to figure out why anyone died of leukemia. To summarize, it is not your concern."

Savitch put her hands up, half apology, half surrender.

"Your job," McGinns yammered on, "is to bring me the heads of these dinosaurs so we can stuff them, mount them, and put them on display at the Academy of Natural Science. And I don't want you getting distracted by anything in the process, or anyone, for that matter. Do we understand each other?"

McGinns raised an eyebrow on "anyone," which Savitch took as a cheap reference to Boston. She'd traveled three hundred miles, and she still couldn't get away from it. "Fine," she said politely, snuffing an urge to stand up and walk out the door. They barely had probable cause, let alone any solid evidence. But she didn't want a fight now. "I understand."

"Excellent."

McGinns kept the rocker going in a steady, maniacal rhythm. She was in her fifties, hair the color of morning frost, and she wore it short, just over the ears. Savitch wondered if she'd always looked this severe, or if it came from having prosecutorial responsibility in a city that averaged more than a murder a day, seven or eight on busy weekends. Eleven murders were being tried right now along with assorted rapes, robberies, and drug cases, and dozens more were waiting where they came from. The DA's situation was pretty much the same in every major American city—it was a job in which you never made the slightest bit of progress—and Savitch was willing to concede that it could put you in a rocking chair ahead of your time.

"Five years we've been together in this office," McGinns said, staring at the cats and birds again. "Five years, and there they are." Savitch wore a fixed smile. Was she supposed to tell the boss stories about pets she'd grown up with? She'd had a professor at Yale who was like this, always speaking in metaphors and parables, hoping the class wouldn't be able to figure out the profound insight he held. Savitch, who liked things straight and direct, found him pretentious and boring, and he punished her with her only college C.

"Can you see a way the cats might get to the birds?" McGinns asked.

Jesus, Savitch thought. It's like an episode of Mr. Rogers.

She glanced around the room, looking for the answer to McGinns's little pop quiz. The desk wouldn't help the cats get to them. It was off against a wall. The bookshelves were too far away, too. Photos were everywhere, McGinns with smiling mayors and governors, McGinns with a smiling President Bush and a smiling President Reagan and a smiling Charlton Heston. Savitch noticed that as the years marched on, McGinns's smile became more like the smile of the people she posed with. "No," she said, answering the bird question. "Not unless they've got a little trampoline."

McGinns didn't react, and Savitch wondered if she'd been

too flip. She also wondered if this crazy lady just liked torturing the cats.

"You've missed the point entirely," McGinns said coldly. Savitch wanted to look away, but McGinns froze her in place with a witchy stare. "Those cats could be here twenty-five years," she said, "and they'd still sleep with one eye open and wake up thinking this is the day they're going to get the birds. That's all they care about."

McGinns walked over to her desk and the finches fluttered as she passed under them, throwing birdseed out in nervous spasms. She picked up the calendar and flipped ahead two months, counting as she went. "My dear, you don't have twenty-five years," she said. "I count seven weeks until the election."

If she'd been here longer, Savitch would throw a line back at her, tell her they weren't in the business of politics, or at least they shouldn't be. The case was the case, and it should be decided on its merits and in its own time, not on the political agenda of an addled, sexually repressed bull dyke. That would probably go over well. Savitch, wearing a black suit—she'd be in court later on—crossed her legs tight, tying her attitude in a knot. She picked at the skin around her nails, tearing back little flaps until it hurt. "I think we're moving along just fine," she said, pushing the words past lips as wooden as McGinns's. "We're set to brief the grand jury this afternoon."

McGinns had insisted on seating a grand jury because it was the only way to get anything out of Augie Sangiamino and his outlaw band of apes. As she had put it to Savitch, the doctors pulled them out of the womb, slapped them, and they all squawked, "I don't know nothing." The advantage of a grand jury was that if they refused to talk, they could be thrown in jail for contempt.

"The beautiful thing about a grand jury is that those people walk in there not just as jurors, but as grand jurors, a job so important it's performed in complete secrecy," McGinns said, walking back from her desk and sitting in the rocking chair again.

Savitch nodded appreciatively, as if McGinns were telling her something she didn't know.

"They can almost be made to think they're doing God's work. And I can give you a valuable tip about Mr. Muldoon," McGinns said, pausing there. "So does he."

McGinns waited for the weight of her wisdom to be fully appreciated, then she went on. "I've never known a more righteous man, and I mean that in a flattering way. He still thinks people are supposed to be naturally good and he's personally offended when they're not. Put him on the stand as often as you can, especially early on, since you don't have a lot to go with yet. Let Muldoon and the jury get to know each other—everybody loves an altar boy, my dear—and you and I are going to be happy girls come November."

Savitch gave her a nod she hoped wasn't too obviously patronizing. She frankly couldn't see Muldoon putting up with someone this overbearing.

"I wish you luck," McGinns said, smiling. "Not that I expect it to come down to that. My friends in Boston can't say enough good things about you. And they all ask how you're doing, by the way."

Savitch and Muldoon went to a French bakery across the street from City Hall to go over their strategy, but all Savitch wanted to talk about was McGinns. "This is just what I need," she lamented. "I've got Annie Oakley for a boss, and she's constipated to boot."

They were at a table in the window, and when she fell into silence, Muldoon wondered if she'd been hypnotized by the traffic that moved in slow circles around City Hall. Her sandwich lay untouched on a plate, and Muldoon had his eye on it as she went for more coffee. She lit a cigarette when she got back and returned to staring out at the street.

"I don't think you need to worry about it," Muldoon said. "She likes to play the hard-ass with everybody. She give you the jungle book lesson?"

That got a halfhearted smile out of her.

"Everybody gets it," he went on. Savitch looked like she might cry, which he wouldn't know how to handle. Maybe he could prevent it if he just kept talking. "You really start to wonder when she pulls it on you in consecutive days. But don't worry about her. She's just a little bomb-rattled, and that office has become her foxhole. But she's a strong DA and she'll always back you up. You should have seen her at trial back in her day. Trust me, you would not have wanted to be a defense attorney and draw Kevinne McGinns. It's like she was angry at the world—still is—and I could never figure out why. All I know is she takes it out on crooks and sleazeball attorneys. The woman lives for that. I don't think she ever even married."

Savitch lifted the sandwich but put it back down without taking a bite.

"Look," she said, "I'm just going to tell you this so you'll know, all right?"

He nodded.

"I was seeing this prick, the chief of the homicide unit. Against my better judgment, of course. He kept asking me out for a drink after work, and I was telling my mother about it, to see what she thought."

"Your mother?"

"She's more like a big sister. I guess because I had the two brothers, no sisters. Also, my mother quit law school to raise us and ended up helping out at my father's business. He's an oral surgeon. Anyhow, the last thing I wanted to do was let an office relationship get in the way of my career."

She made a point of looking at him when she said it, forcing a reaction, and Muldoon gave an exaggerated nod, like that was good thinking. What dummy didn't know office romances were a bad idea? "So what did your mother say?"

"You're not a little girl anymore," Savitch began, reciting it like something she'd been back over a thousand times. "You're an intelligent woman, and I can't decide things for you. I trust you to know the risks, and I trust that if he ever once treats you without proper appreciation or respect, you'll nail his prick to the floor, set the DA's office on fire, and hand him a rusty razor."

Muldoon spit coffee on himself.

"My mother had a saying," he said, dabbing at his lap with a napkin. "The acorn doesn't fall far from the tree."

"I am my mother," she said, as if she'd just realized it. "I told you, we're like sisters. Anyway, six months into it, we got engaged. Three months later, he's on page one of the morning paper. A mistrial was declared in a double homicide he was prosecuting after the defense attorney backed out of the case, the slut, giving as her reason the fact that she was sleeping with the prosecutor. That was how I found out—from the papers."

Muldoon, dabbing his lap with napkins, imagined Savitch with a hammer, nailing her fiancé's pecker to the floor. He found it hard to believe that anyone would two-time Lisa Savitch. What the hell must the other woman look like?

"I was stalked by these squirrelly reporters trying to turn it into some sort of celebrity scandal," Savitch said. "A courthouse tryst in the middle of a murder trial. Big fucking deal. They followed me everywhere and shouted out the same stupid questions. Every time I turned around I had eight microphones in my face. It was worse than getting mugged, and you feel so helpless."

She paused, and then spoke as if this had been the worst part: "I had them camped outside my apartment. Then one morning, I go out on the back balcony to water the garden, figuring I'm safe back there, and a tabloid photographer is hiding in the bushes across the way. It was a full-page photo on the front cover of the fucking paper. Me in my bathrobe, flipping him off."

Muldoon knew all about it—and what the headline said, too:

JILTED DA SAYS EX IS NO. 1!

Muldoon could feel the blood rushing to his face, part lust and part anger. He didn't know who he wanted to smack first—the parasitic reporters who stalked Savitch or the gigolo prosecutor who shamed her. One thing he did know—he wanted to gather Lisa Savitch in his arms, carry her to the nearest hotel, and fuck the demons out of her.

Every muscle in Savitch's body had tensed and then relaxed with the telling of the story. She looked exhausted now, but softer. She brushed her blond hair back with her hand and let it fall, a look of contentedness crossing her face. A look that said, It could be worse. "The problem in this business," she said, and Muldoon wondered if he saw tears forming in her dark brown eyes, "is you work day and night, and the only guys you meet are attorneys, drug dealers, and killers. I should have had the sense to make attorneys a last resort."

Muldoon was so fixed on her he didn't catch the joke. He grunted an unintelligible response and asked, "So, did you get into the business because of your mother quitting law school?"

Savitch ran her tongue over her lips as she considered the question. She looked in his direction when she answered, but she wasn't focused on him. It didn't look like she was focused on anything.

"When I was thirteen, I got home from school one day and there were a dozen cars parked in front of my house. All the relatives. My mother met me at the front door and took me over to this little bench we had in the yard. My brother Noah was on a break from Yale to earn some money for a trip to London. He was studying acting and wanted to get into a theater program over there. Anyway, he was working at a logging mill up near the Canadian border and my mother said, 'Lisa, they had an accident where Noah works, and your brother was in the wrong place at the wrong time.'

"They never talked about the details of what happened, but

I started to pick up on it. My father sort of disappeared to his den and he hasn't really come through it even now, all these years later. But I'd hear him on the phone in there, talking to lawyers, or I'd see a letter on the counter in the kitchen. The company that owned the logging mill had four or five other mills and they all had a history of accidents. But they also had the best law firm in New England defending them against every lawsuit and every attempt to force them to clean up their act."

"I'm sorry," Muldoon said.

Savitch did focus on him now. "To answer your question, I don't know exactly why I went to law school. You know how it is when you're young. I mean, when you got into the FBI, didn't you think you were going to save the world?"

Muldoon didn't answer. "And what's the story with your other brother?" he asked.

She dropped a cigarette into her coffee and watched it float on the surface. "I'll save that one for another time," she said, looking at her watch.

She was smiling when she said, "Let's go nail Ham Flaherty's prick to the floor."

CHAPTER 6

COURTROOM 598 IN CITY HALL had served as the grand jury assembly room for roughly a year, ever since the common pleas judge who normally presided in it went to jail for fixing cases on behalf of the law firm that had sponsored his campaign fundraisers. It had been Mike Muldoon's last roundup before he retired to the golf course.

The hundred-year-old courtroom was designed in the English style, with oak furnishings including a waist-high wooden railing that surrounded the defendant's table like a minijail and a witness stand that was like a small fort. It had everything but attorneys in powdered wigs.

Portraits of two dozen former judges, six of whom had been indicted at one time or another, looked down from gilt frames at the twenty-three citizens who had just been officially seated as members of the grand jury. The fourteen women and nine men, most of them middle-aged or older, sat behind a railing in a steeply terraced gallery, which was divided into five rows that looked like church pews. Ten yards in front of them on a platform, the judge's bench loomed with the seal of the state on its facing. The stenographer sat in front of it, and behind it, dressed in black, was Lisa Savitch.

"My guess is that we'll be meeting at this same time and

place once a week, and I can't emphasize enough the importance of absolute secrecy surrounding these proceedings," Savitch said, pausing as a subway train passed underneath City Hall. The rumble sent vibrations and a low-frequency groan up five stories of concrete and steel, and she felt it in the floor. "Discussing what you hear in this room with anyone on the outside, and that includes a wife or husband, not only has the potential to jeopardize our investigation, but constitutes a crime in itself. Believe me when I say that violators will be prosecuted."

Savitch swept a piece of lint off the sleeve of her suit. Wearing black was a trick she learned from her ex-fiancé. Dress like a judge and sit at the judge's bench at least occasionally during the proceedings, he had said. Makes the grand jury think you've got more authority than you actually do. Savitch, who had assisted on one grand jury investigation in Boston, explained to the jury that no judge would be in the courtroom at any point. If jurors or witnesses raised questions she couldn't answer, or if legal rulings were required, she, the witness, and the witness's attorney would go before a judge in another courtroom to get a ruling. Then they'd return and pick up where they left off.

"The idea here is to gradually build a case, and if we reach a point where you believe you have heard sufficient evidence for charges to be brought, you will be given the opportunity to sign what we call a presentment. If that document is signed by you and by the presiding grand jury judge, those charges will be filed against the targets of this investigation, and you'll all be dismissed."

Savitch watched them shift in their seats and glance at each other. She could see a rush of excitement and nervousness sweep through the group. They were ordinary people who walked in off the street and suddenly had more power than they'd ever had in their lives. She thanked them in advance, drawing them in, putting them on her side.

"All right, then. Does anyone have any questions?" She looked around. So far, so good. "Fine. Now that you understand the general process, I'd like to call the first witness." Savitch went to the door and asked a sheriff's deputy to retrieve the witness, who marched in like a soldier reporting for duty. Dark blue suit, fresh haircut. A trench coat was folded over his arm, and he handed it to the deputy in a way that suggested it better not come back wrinkled.

"Please state your name and occupation for the record," Savitch said.

"Michael Patrick Muldoon. Special agent, Federal Bureau of Investigation, United States Department of Justice."

Savitch suppressed a smile and reminded Muldoon he no longer worked for the FBI, a fact that almost seemed to bewilder him. In the two hundred or so times he'd testified in court, he'd never been anything else.

"And you've been hired by the district attorney for the city and county of Philadelphia, am I correct?, because of your expertise in the area of political corruption, and your extensive involvement in how many cases would you say?"

Muldoon grinned and said, "It would be literally in the high dozens."

Savitch, with McGinns's voice in her ear, asked Muldoon if he had ever conducted an investigation in City Hall.

"You could almost say I had an office in the ceiling," he said.

Savitch let the jurors chuckle and elbow each other. When they settled down, Savitch asked Muldoon what he meant.

"I spent quite a few hours running surveillance equipment in the ceiling here. Video and audio."

"In other words, you planted cameras and microphones?"

"We also wired a number of people who'd flipped."

"Could you explain what you mean by that? *Wiring* and *flipping*?"

"Wiring is just that. Secreting a microphone on someone's person for the purpose of recording conversation. Let's say someone admitted to a crime and decided to cooperate with us, secretly, in an ongoing criminal investigation, meaning that he had flipped from their side to our side. We might conceal a wire under his jacket and have him engage in a conversation with a suspect, and the recording could be used to make the case against that suspect."

"Mr. Muldoon, would you say this sort of thing happened only occasionally, or was it a regular occurrence?"

Muldoon sort of peeked up at her to field the questions, then turned his shoulders square to the jury. He was so damned upright and earnest, she thought. And the G-man outfit was perfect. You could leave the FBI, but the wardrobe was forever.

"My entire career in the Philadelphia field office, twenty-five years, I don't remember a time when there wasn't an active investigation of crime in this building. Sometimes that involved wiring someone and sometimes it involved, among other things, setting up cameras. This particular courtroom, in fact, was the focus of a surveillance operation that took place in the ceiling."

Savitch picked at dead skin, index finger to thumb. No cigarettes to hold on to. She looked up at the ceiling, waiting for the jury to look up there, too. "Right here?" she asked, pointing up.

"Not the courtroom itself. That door behind you? It goes into the judge's chambers."

"And you were in the ceiling there?"

"Yes."

"Would you mind telling us about it?"

"It was actually on two different occasions. The first one— that was about thirteen or fourteen years ago—I was in the process of placing a camera in the drop ceiling on a Saturday afternoon when the judge and attorney I was investigating at the time surprised me by coming into chambers."

He stopped there, and she pushed him along. "What happened next?"

Muldoon looked at the jury and then faced her this time to answer. "I arrested them."

"But you were in the ceiling, am I right? And they were down below you?"

"At the time, that was the case."

"Would you mind explaining how you resolved that problem?"

"Well, there's a weak spot between the beams, and I was stuck in that precise location because if I moved, they'd hear me."

"So you didn't move."

"No. I tried not to."

"And what happened?"

Savitch was violating one of the basics. Never ask a question you don't know the answer to. But she couldn't help it.

Muldoon said, "The ceiling gave way."

If they were anywhere else, she would have burst out laughing. He hadn't told her this story. Savitch looked at the jurors and saw the question on their lips, so she asked it of Muldoon. "And then?"

"I crashed through the ceiling and fell on top of the judge."

He said it with more self-deprecation than Savitch thought he was capable of, and she chuckled along with the jury. "So you've crashed through the ceiling and you're on top of the judge," she said, drumming her fingers on the bench. "What exactly do you say in a situation like that?"

Muldoon had a sheepish grin on his face. "I said, 'Freeze.' "

McGinns was right, Savitch thought as she looked out at the jury. They were already in love with him.

"You said, 'Freeze'?"

"Well, the attorney had started to run, is why I said that. The judge didn't move. I don't think he could have if he wanted to, because I weigh over two hundred pounds. Two-twelve, actually. But this other guy was making a break."

"What came of this little episode, Mr. Muldoon, if you don't mind wrapping up the story for us?"

"I arrested both men and they ended up confessing to a fee system used by the judge. This attorney, and the other attorneys in his firm, would represent a man accused of burglary, say, and for a set fee, say two hundred dollars for burglary, maybe five hundred dollars for robbery, the judge would find a way to let the defendant off. The judge had a drug appetite, cocaine, and this was how he fed it."

Savitch climbed down off the bench and walked around the front of it, toward the jury. She had authority in this room, yes. But she was one of them, really—an ordinary, taxpaying citizen. She tapped a pen on the railing in front of the jurors and asked, "Mr. Muldoon, was there anything particularly memorable about that case?"

"Yes, there was. That judge flipped and we wired him up for contact with the participants in an illegal gambling operation— it was sports and numbers, basically. Roughly two hundred City Hall employees were gambling on a daily basis, often using money paid in cash by the taxpayers of this city. Water bills, license fees, that sort of thing."

"Mr. Muldoon, can you tell the members of the grand jury who ran that gambling operation?"

"Yes, I can. It was run out of the office of United States Senator Augie Sangiamino."

"And he was indicted for that crime, am I right?"

Muldoon's pride showed now. "Indicted, prosecuted, convicted, and sentenced," he said. "He and eight others, most of whom have since died, if I'm not mistaken. They also had a nice little system using Teamsters who worked for the *Philadelphia Journal*. The drivers would drop off papers at newsstands each day and pick up bets from the news hawks. It was about a twenty-thousand-dollar-a-day book at its height. But people tend to forget that that wasn't the only thing we got Mr. Sangiamino on."

"What else was there?"

"Ghost employees. Six of them."

"Can you explain that for any of our jurors who might not be familiar with the term?"

"Employees who get paid, with your tax dollars, I might add, for jobs they don't have to show up at. Basically, a job like that is a payoff for somebody you owe a favor to."

Savitch went back up to the bench and pretended to be going over her notes. She wanted the jury to pause over Augie Sangiamino's criminal résumé for a moment. When she looked up, she asked Muldoon what brought him back to the ceiling of this courtroom the second time.

"That one involved the judge who was in here until about a year ago. We got him on bribery, two counts; mail fraud, sixteen counts; and obstruction of justice, three counts."

"What exactly did you catch him at, if I might ask?"

"I secreted a camera and microphone in the ceiling and got him working a deal with two attorneys involved in his campaign. He was going to do what he could for them when their law firm had clients up before him. He actually used the words 'You scratch my back, I scratch yours.' And he said he had a big itch."

"And the man with the itch, Mr. Muldoon, can you tell us if this person has had a free moment to scratch it?"

"He's in the Loretto Federal Correctional Institute, which is a low-security facility in the central part of the state."

"You didn't crash through the ceiling and fall on him, too?"

He seemed a little defensive. "No, I did not."

"Mr. Muldoon, over the course of your career, do you have any idea how many convictions came of your investigative work? And for the moment I'm just talking about convictions of people in public office, and not the work you did in the area of bank robberies, armored car robberies, kidnapping, and terrorism." Muldoon wet his lips and Savitch thought to herself, He's like an overgrown Boy Scout. She had a classmate in a grade school class who always stood a little more erect than everyone else for the Pledge of Allegiance. Muldoon was that kid.

"Eleven judges, six state legislators, five city councilmen, a councilwoman, a United States senator, the state treasurer, the state labor secretary, the state attorney general, the boxing commissioner, the lottery commissioner, two members of the liquor control board, half the board of the port authority, and fourteen members of the turnpike commission."

One of the jurors started clapping and several others joined in, one of them whistling. Savitch let them have their fun.

"That's quite a trophy case you've got," she said.

Muldoon leaned back, stretched, and then snapped back to upright. It was sort of like cracking his knuckles, Savitch thought. "There were fifty-four others who were public employees but would not be classified as being in public office. If you want their names and departments, I could provide that. Then there are quite a few nonpublic subjects I was involved with, as you mentioned."

"Thank you, I don't think that will be necessary. Now, Mr. Muldoon, are you familiar with a man by the name of William Flaherty?"

"Yes, I am."

"And how is that you happen to be familiar with him?"

Muldoon told the grand jury that Flaherty had first come to the attention of the FBI more than twelve years ago, during its investigation of Augie Sangiamino's gambling operation. Flaherty had been indicted as a recipient of the proceeds, but the charges were dropped when the one person who could have made the case against him refused to cooperate.

"And who might that have been?"

"Augie Sangiamino."

Savitch didn't look at Muldoon when he gave his answers. She looked at the jurors to read their reaction. At this point, Muldoon could have told them Augie Sangiamino and Ham

Flaherty were in on the disappearance of Jimmy Hoffa, and they'd sign the presentment. She brought Muldoon back to the present and he told the grand jury about the tips on the Atlantic City casinos.

"Mr. Muldoon, in your investigation, did you happen to examine Mr. Flaherty's voting record as a member of the state legislature?"

"Yes, I did."

"And did you find anything of interest?"

Muldoon told the grand jury that in the spring, a Chamber of Commerce proposal to establish riverboat gambling in Philadelphia came up for a vote in the legislature. "Most of the casinos lobbied against the proposal because they didn't want the competition. The vote ended up in a tie, but one legislator was ill and missed the vote, so they brought it up again for another vote when he came back."

"And do we know who that legislator was, Mr. Muldoon? The one who had been ill and then came back to cast the deciding vote?"

"Yes," Muldoon said. "It was William Flaherty."

"And which way did the vote go?"

"The riverboat gambling proposal was defeated," Muldoon said. "William Flaherty cast the vote that killed it."

The second witness surprised Savitch, who'd only spoken to her over the phone. Judy Garland, whose real first name actually turned out to be Judy, wore a simple brown dress and her hair was pulled back and tied rather than teased, tinted, and piled high in the local custom. Savitch didn't expect someone this understated to be married to a man like Ham Flaherty.

Yes, Judy Flaherty said, she had called and and written to the DA's office anonymously to report the shipments to their house. "This sort of thing has happened through his whole career," she said.

"Mrs. Flaherty, what made you decide to do something about it now?"

Judy Flaherty wept while she told of her husband's constant philandering, but it didn't appear to Savitch that she cried for her husband. She cried for being such a fool. "I suspected but didn't know for sure. Other people knew, though. Somebody—I don't know who it was—even wrote to me about it. They wrote poems." Savitch thought about her own situation and wondered if other people knew she was being cheated on while it was happening. She said, "You say someone wrote poems to you about your husband having affairs?"

"Yes. But you don't want to see it, as the wife, and so you become defensive and you get very good at telling yourself lies. I guess I finally got wise enough to stop believing them." Mrs. Flaherty said she had filed for divorce and was preparing to move out of the South Philadelphia house she shared with Ham. Savitch wanted to ask what she was doing with him in the first place, but this wasn't the place. And besides, who was she to judge?

Savitch thanked Judy Flaherty for coming and then she dismissed the grand jury for the day. She and Muldoon still had a long way to go, but this wasn't a bad start.

CHAPTER 7

AUGIE'S HOUSE was a two-story red brick row on Latona, a half mile from Joey's and about the same distance from the house he was born and raised in. He and Angela had moved in the day they were married fifty-two years ago and never considered living anywhere else.

Augie could walk to the bakery or the butcher shop. He could buy fresh gnocchi and ravioli two corners away. If he needed anything else—olive oil, cheese, wine, fresh produce—it was a short drive to the Italian Market with Joey, or he could even walk there. He was a simple man, in most ways. That was the life he'd chosen.

The green-and-white aluminum awnings over the windows were Angela's touch. Same with the flower boxes under the first-floor windows, dark green to match the awnings and the front door. Augie had struggled with the flowers in the three years his wife had been gone. He had no knack for it, but thought he'd be letting her down if he didn't at least try, so the boxes had a scraggly mix of dying plants.

The morning sun came to Latona from the Warnock side, same as Joey, who turned the corner in a '56 Oldsmobile. It was two-tone burgundy and cream, like an oxford shoe, and it was washed and buffed twice a week so people knew these weren't a couple of meatballs coming down the street. This was Senator Augie Sangiamino and his personal driver Joey "Numbers" Tartaglione doing business in style. You heard about your Meals on Wheels, Augie would say. This here is Deals on Wheels.

Joey, who sat on Yellow Pages to see over the hood, always pulled up to Augie's at 6:45 sharp. Augie had been telling him for years to just blow the horn, but Joey never did. Augie deserved full respect at all times. Joey rang the doorbell, and Augie's voice came up from the back of the house.

"All right, all right. I'm comin', Joey. Hold your pants on." Augie always looked natty in the morning, his white shirt starched at the cleaners up the street, his suit like it just came off the steam press. He wore a suit every workday, this one the color of tree bark, with a maroon paisley tie and an Izzy button on his right lapel, a Ham on the left.

"Joey Tartaglione, son of Enrique, how are you today?"

"Good, good. How you doin', Senator?" Augie had a dab of toilet paper on a shaving cut at the corner of his mouth, and some hair grease was clumped on his forehead.

"Couldn't be better, Joey." Augie held onto the iron railing coming down the three steps of the porch. He was still in pretty good shape for a man his age. But Joey had noticed a more careful step in the last few months. "Here we go," he said when he hit the sidewalk.

Joey got the car door for him. Augie slid in, made a little bow to the plastic St. Christopher glued to the dash, and crossed himself for safe travel. "OK, Joey. *Andiamo.*"

The Oldsmobile was a gift from the local mob and the weekly detailing was done in one of their body shops on Passyunk Avenue. Augie had struck a deal years ago, when the local don passed on with a bullet behind the ear and the undisciplined sons and nephews took over, going after headlines instead of profits. Augie went to the kids with a warning. You stay out of my business, I stay out of yours. *Capeesh?* He didn't like violence. A smack in the nose, a broken arm or leg, OK. But this bullet in the head thing showed no human consideration.

Joey drove the Oldsmobile like it was a float in a Sunday parade (he had actually loaned it to the PuertoAmeRican Club for that purpose on several occasions, in return for consideration at the polls) and the senator waved to everybody—pedestrians, motorists, people on benches and stoops. He even waved if he saw someone in the window of a house, just in case they recognized him by the sight of the car. And then he'd ask, "Joey, who the hell was that?" He often talked under his breath, a series of hmmms and yep-yep-yeps for the pleasant thoughts and *fongools* and *bastas* for the unpleasant. He looked out the window as they traveled, his thoughts as predictable as the next rowhouse block of brick and awnings. People dressed up their houses in South Philadelphia because the house was who they were. They put ceramic knickknacks on the front sill along with religious figurines and framed photos of grandchildren, and they went nuts at Christmas with garlands and ornaments.

On some streets, double-parking was standard procedure. Everybody knew everybody else, so they knew what door to knock on if they got jammed in. Nobody ever got ticketed, either, unless a new cop was on the beat and hadn't yet been indoctrinated as to the rules of South Philadelphia, most of which had been written by Augie. The median of South Broad, for instance, had been cleared for free public parking going back thirty years, to a time when Augie went to a funeral and couldn't find a legal spot, so he parked in the middle of the street and got ticketed. Augie had the mayor, the police commissioner, and the parking authority chief in his office in ten minutes and warned every one of them that if he or anyone else ever got a ticket for parking in the middle of South Broad again, those three palookas would be hawking pretzels on street corners. Nobody had challenged the arrangement in all these years because there was history in it, unwritten agreements that might as well have been added to the Bill of Rights: free speech, free assembly, and free parking in the middle of South Broad. Keep your hands off the fuckin' car.

South Philadelphia was the kind of neighborhood where, on warm nights, people gathered on their front steps to talk about the days when your taxes got you something in return and you knew everybody on the block, and certain types of people had the sense to stay in their own neighborhood. They also talked about the ponies and the numbers, everybody working an angle, looking for an edge on the next guy. It wasn't a question of need or greed. It was a hard-boiled, old-country belief that whatever someone else might take, you were entitled to grab for yourself. From this petri dish came the mutant strain of politics that, at its best and worst, produced an Augie Sangiamino. If you wanted a visionary for health-care reform or a balanced budget, call somebody else. But if you wanted help with common daily struggles—say you needed a job application speeded up or a tax audit killed, a dead tree hauled away or a competing restaurant harassed by inspectors—Augie was the grand pooh-bah and high priest of all time.

The black-and-white posters were plastered everywhere. On telephone poles, storefronts, steak and hoagie shops, automobiles, row-house windows. The face of a smiling boy—it looked like his school yearbook picture—under the words: HOW MANY MORE?

"Who the hell is this kid?" Augie asked Joey as they drove to morning mass. "He's got more campaign posters than Ham and Izzy combined, the little prick."

"It's the kid died of leukemia," Joey said. "The one's funeral we got today after mass."

"Oh. All right. What was his name?"

"Joey. Joey Napolitano."

"That's it," Augie said. "I'm putting Ham in with the boy's old man, Cheech. You call the TV people, Joey?"

"I got your buddy Louis Bonguisto over Channel Nine. He says he'll be there."

"Beautyful," Augie said. He'd known Bonguisto for years and threw the reporter a bone now and then, diming out a crooked pol or blowing the whistle on somebody who was stealing more than he was. In return, Bonguisto did an occasional puff piece for Augie. "Now we're talking."

Augie looked out the window for a while and when he spoke again, his voice was thinner. "Geez, this kid went fast," he said as Joey turned onto Seventh Street and sunlight filled the car. Augie always sneezed when the sun first hit him like that.

"God bless."

"Yep yep yep."

Joey said, "There's two more kids that got diagnosed with leukemia. It's in the paper today."

"*Madonna*, what the hell's happening?"

Joey shook his head. "Fuck if I know, Senator. But everybody's worked up about it, I'll tell you that. You know how they are historically about all this crap we got down here with the factories and all. Ever since that shit come flying out of Liberty Oil, that's half our phone calls. And now with these kids falling, everybody thinks they're dying."

Joey could tell Augie was warming up for a lecture. His head started moving to wind it up. "It's something I learned years ago," he began. "A crime wave, a natural disaster like flooding from a storm, a case of pollution like this here—I don't care what the fuck it is—there's votes in it, Joey. Ron Rice got out of the gate first, but watch and see if Ham doesn't lap the bastard. Now all we gotta do is figure a way to get Izzy involved."

Augie was uncharacteristically quiet after his lecture. Joey glanced over and caught the boss's profile sharp against the sun. Like a hatchet was sitting there wearing a hat. Joey wondered if all this news about leukemia had him more worried than usual about his wife. He said, "You know, Senator, they got different types of leukemia. Some of it spreads faster than others. Some of it, you'll see people beat it altogether."

"That's right," Augie agreed. He'd forgotten most of what he learned about the disease from Angela's doctors, but that part of it rang true. "They got all different types. She's got what they call the genius type, I think it is. Milo genius, or some such. We'll see her after this kid's funeral, huh, Joey?"

Joey wheeled the Olds into the parking space that was permanently reserved for Augie in front of St. Mary Magdalen. Pastor Frank D'Anunzio put two orange cones out there to mark it off. Joey came around and opened the door for Augie and the two of them walked up the steps and under columns of polished granite and blue marble.

Just inside, pamphlets on the first Italian church in the USA sat on a table. Augie wasn't exactly a history buff, but he respected his heritage. Joey remembered a line from Augie's keynote address at a national Knights of Columbus convention in Scranton: "I don't know if you're aware of it, but it was us people that started most of these things like opera and all the paintings that stood up over the years, not to mention the food."

Augie took off his hat and placed it over his heart, dipped his hand in holy water, and made the sign of the cross. "OK, Joey. Let's go."

Joey, in a Christmas sweater and overcoat, walked two steps ahead of Augie up the center aisle, leading him to the front row. The thirty or forty regulars knew to leave those seats empty at every weekday mass. On the wall behind the altar, Mary Magdalen genuflected, arms extended, surrounded by angels. On the ceiling was the Assumption, Mary ascending into a pastel heaven the color of Augie's eyes. That was the thing you had to love about the Catholic Church, Augie liked to say: Hooker, virgin, or crook, they took you in.

Joey and Augie knelt, sat, stood; knelt, sat, stood. They said all the prayers aloud, but didn't hear themselves. Neither paid attention. Joey stared up at Mary Magdalen and wondered if she had really been a hooker, and if so, if Jesus had nailed her. Then his thoughts wandered. He thought back on the last woman he was with and wondered if she preferred the man she was with now. Augie went over the list of people who owed him favors, he counted the jobs he still controlled, and he tried to think up new ways to steal votes and raise the dead. It was something to pass the time.

Father D'Anunzio's sermon, which Augie and Joey missed in its entirety, was about the eternity of good deeds. The pastor always made sure to drop Augie's name, especially during an election, knowing there was no better investment the church could make. This particular day, he remarked on the overnight storm and happily noted that the church was dry as a bone. "Senator Sangiamino, through our good friends at Pennies from Heaven, arranged a generous donation for much-needed roof repairs, and his timing couldn't have been better. Good hearts, good deeds, and God's reward awaits."

Augie missed the plug. He was thinking they had to figure out a way to raise some money or they were dead in the water. With a few bucks, they could start going negative on TV. Bang the shit out of Debra Sharperson and Ron Rice, show them what happens to amateurs who try to play ball with old pros.

The Italian Market was a block and a half from the church, and for Augie, it was no less a place of worship. He had grown up on Kimball, off Ninth, the son of a produce man who was up at four every morning, and of a woman who cooked three meals a day for her family, every day, the last fifty years of her life. That was where she went out, too—a heart attack right there at the stove, her last pot of red gravy simmering away as she collapsed on the floor. Augie's hands were calloused by the time he was ten, all those boxes of Idaho potatoes and Jersey tomatoes. Do something else with your life, his father told him—words Augie could still hear. Do something noble. And don't fuck up your back.

The market had changed over the years, losing some of its charm as the neighborhood turned. Some vendors sold cheap clothes and tacky toys instead of tomatoes and melons, and there were nearly as many Asian vendors now as Italian. But it was still the Italian Market. Presidential candidates didn't stop by the ACME or Super Fresh, but they never missed these several blocks of slat crates, striped canvas awnings, wooden baskets of live Maryland blue crabs, and rolling slopes of fruits and vegetables. Great hunks of waxed cheese, nestled in twine slings, hung from rafters, and skinned, muscled carcasses dangled from hooks in butcher-shop windows. A touch of the old world, ten blocks below the city's shimmering new skyline.

Augie paused to cinch up his tie and seat his hat squarely on his head when they got to Ninth Street. He turned to the north, like this was the starting line in a race, and a light grew in his eyes as he opened himself to the city. "OK, Joey," he said. "Here we go." Six days a week he'd been making this pass like a runway model, going on fifty years, and each time, no matter the weather and no matter the mood that came with him to this street, Augie floated. This was his stage, and when Joseph Augustine Sangiamino walked this walk, he owned the city. Any problem could be disappeared and any election was winnable, even if the polls had you dead and buried.

Augie, who was called the "splendid splinter" by his high-school basketball coach, moved north on Ninth with a slightly bowed walk, head before feet, arms swinging, ageless and elegant. He had a smile and a wave for everyone—the shoppers, the people who lived in the flats above the shops, the merchants. They were Augie's age or older, the merchants, their old-country faces beaten by the weather. They wore gray stubble and hats pulled low over dark eyes, and they got shorter each year from the weight of the crates they carried, their bodies evolving to the task, turning into small forklifts.

"How you doin', Senator?" asked a produce man building a pyramid of cabbage on the very spot Augie's father had owned for half a century.

"They got a space for me at church, Billy, but they're not sure about heaven," Augie answered, never breaking stride, throwing a nod or a wave to six other people in the time it took to answer the cabbage man.

As a boy, Augie awoke each morning to the sounds and smells of the market, and by the time he was five, he knew everything he needed to know about politics. His father paid bribes to the faceless black-suited men from the health department and from licenses and inspections, and he paid the First District councilman protection from even bigger fees. But these weren't thought of as bribes. That word was never used. It was the process of survival, a part of doing business in the city: You kick something my way; I kick something back. The morality of the streets. When Augie was on city council, it was generally accepted that nobody was ever better at it. At his height, one call from him could get L & I off your back ten minutes ago, or it could have them coming out of the woodwork at your place of business to bust your balls for this or that. Jobs were power, and Augie owned more than anyone.

"Yo, Augie," a produce man named Jimmy called from in front of DiBruno Brothers' House of Cheese. He was ancient and elfin, bent up with back pain. "Look at this," he said, waving disgustedly at piles of trash. "They ain't picked it up again. See what you can do for us, Senator."

"Joey," Augie called, looking over his left shoulder. Joey was on his right. He could anticipate Augie's next words and even his thoughts, but he always messed up this part. "Jesus Christ, Joey, where the hell are you?" Augie whined, wheeling back the other way. "Take this down, will you?"

Joey had already pulled a notebook out of an inside pocket of his overcoat and was writing "Trash Pickup, Nine Hundred Block Ninth Street."

"Jimmy, let me explain something, here," Augie said, his face twelve inches from Jimmy's, his right hand chopping his left palm. "You know what we got today in City Hall? Do you know what we got?" Jimmy didn't know whether he was supposed to answer. "I'll tell you what we got, Jimmy. We got these fuckin' Ivy League pinheads sittin' in there pullin' their puds. They got their law degrees on the wall, they got their feet on the desk, and they got a stack of papers on how they're gonna reinvent government."

Augie brought his shoulders up to his ears and turned to Joey, palms to the sky. "Am I kidding here, Joey?" Joey had taken a half step back. Augie tended to gurgle and spit when he was worked up. His voice, forced through those narrow pipes, could get nasal and shrill, and he looked like he might cry over the sheer stupidity and incompetence of the people in power. Joey shook his head.

"You see what I'm saying, Jimmy?" Augie sounded like a cat in distress. "It's not like the old days, when you had us eagle-beavers workin' up the Hall. Tell you what, Jimmy. You let me take care of this. I'll go up City Hall, stick my foot up somebody's ass, and get a truck down here yesterday. You can count on it."

Jimmy said he appreciated it. Appreciated the sentiment, anyway. Augie had been making empty promises since he left prison.

"Joey?" Augie called, turning the wrong way again. "Joey, give my friend Jimmy here some buttons, will you?" Joey handed a half dozen buttons to Jimmy, who pinned an Izzy to a potato and a Ham to an onion. "There you go," Augie said. "Take a few more of these cocksuckers. And don't forget, cousin"—he grabbed Jimmy's arm and gave him a wink—"vote early and often."

The Anthony Faggioli Funeral Home was on the first floor of a brick fourplex on South Broad Street, the same building that had been Congressman Bitty Reed's office before his coronary in the Kubla Khan room at the Taj. Members of Not in Our Backyard had set up a table on the sidewalk in front of the funeral parlor, with the blessing of the Napolitano family, and were handing out buttons with the same image of Joey Napolitano that was on all the posters. Augie took one and pinned it next to the Ham button on his lapel. A stack of afternoon papers was on the table next to the buttons. Augie hadn't noticed them at first, but now the bold black headline jumped off the page at him:

LEUKEMIA OUTBREAK FEARED BY DOCTORS; ONE CHILD, 12, DEAD, TWO MORE DIAGNOSED

Augie felt a rapid flutter in his chest and had trouble catching his breath. "Joey, I'll run in, see if Ham's here," he said faintly. "You wait for the TV guys. Maybe we can set something up right here, this newspaper in the background, the family coming out of the funeral home. You see what I mean?"

Augie was hit by the scent of flowers and burning candles the moment he opened the door. It was the smell of death and it had always made him queasy, ever since his mother was laid out right here in this very home. Anthony Faggioli was in the foyer, extending a hand. They all looked alike to Augie, these gravediggers. Like they'd soaked up some of the embalming fluid over the years.

"Senator, it's always an honor."

"I'm fine," Augie said, shaking hands and then wiping his hand on his pants. These guys had their hands on corpses all day. "Listen, Ant'ny, you seen Ham in here?"

"No, but he could have come in when I was in the office."

"How about this Napolitano boy, where you got him laid out?"

"Chapel B."

"Thanks."

Augie hurried down the hall and pushed open the door

slowly, not wanting to draw attention. He took one step inside and was scanning the room for Ham when his eyes fell on the boy. From a distance, it looked like Joey Napolitano was sleeping on a cloud. The pillow all puffed up and lacy under his head. The casket, charcoal gray, glowed with the reflection of candles.

Napolitano's family was in a receiving area to the left of the body, the mother sobbing and supported by her husband on one side and another man on the other. The seventh-grade class from St. Thomas Aquinas was moving in a line past the casket, and the sight of her son's classmates was too much for Joey Napolitano's mother. Her cries came from a deeper and deeper place until she hit bottom and threw herself on the floor at the children's feet. Several of them jumped back, terrified. As Mrs. Napolitano was helped into her chair, some of the children burst into tears.

Besides the students, there were maybe twelve or fifteen people in the chapel. Augie checked again. No Ham. He was about to leave when he realized the father had spotted him. Son of a bitch. Now he'd have to make a pass by the casket.

Augie's legs turned to rubber at funerals. He didn't fear death as much as dying, but he thought the open-casket ritual was barbaric. He took a deep breath, walked slowly to the casket, and knelt to make a prayer. There was no avoiding it now. The boy was right in front of him, and he'd have to at least glance at the body. Show proper respect.

Joey Napolitano was small, frail, and gray. He wore a blue suit and had one hand over the other. Augie was surprised by how easy it was to look at him. The face was sweet, no pain on it, and he didn't seem as dead as other dead people Augie had seen. Maybe that was why such a horrible thought was coming to him now, a thought he tried to fight back—having someone cast a vote in the boy's name. Augie said an Our Father and apologized to God, telling him he just couldn't help it sometimes. Then he went over and hugged the boy's parents.

"I'll never forget what you did for us," Frankie Napolitano

said. Augie told the mother it would be OK, her son was in a place with no suffering. Through her sobs, she thanked him for coming, inhaling the words.

The fresh, cool air outside was a relief. So was the sight of the news van. A crew was setting up just where Augie thought they would. Augie figured Ham must have shown up, but he hadn't spotted him yet. He saw Bonguisto, the reporter. And then Joey.

And then Ron Rice.

Bonguisto was getting a cue from his cameraman and now they were rolling. Rice, wearing one of the Joey Napolitano buttons, promised to get to the bottom of this horrible plague before there were hundreds of Joey Napolitanos.

Augie made eye contact with Joey and held his hands up. Joey shrugged. No sign of Ham. Augie stormed back to the car, his fists clenched and the veins in his face pushing up at the skin.

"Do me a favor," he said when Joey was behind the wheel. "Keep driving until we find the cocksucker. I'm going to cut his balls off."

CHAPTER 8

ONE MILE UP Broad Street from the Faggioli Funeral Home and nearly in the shadow of City Hall, a black limousine pulled up to Republic, one of the city's most prestigious old-money clubs. The chauffeur, who wore driving gloves and a cap, came around to get the door, and out stepped A. Whitney Pritchard III, the only grandson of the founder of Liberty Oil.

A red-walled Victorian with oxford gray trim, Republic had sat in this spot since 1880 and was considered one of the city's architectural treasures. Brass handrails, polished daily to a fine gloss, framed a wide, elegant stairway that splashed onto the sidewalk in the heart of the city's commercial center. Philadelphia had long been a region of two cities that rarely met: a city of society and wealth, most of it spreading west to the wooded colonial estates of the Main Line lords and philanthropists, and a city of brick-row-house dwellers who, in the best of times, worked for them. This building was the first and largest gathering center of the former.

Pritchard looked up and down Broad Street, as if checking to see if his arrival had been noted. He wore a tailored charcoal gray suit with braces and a rep tie, smokestack tie clip, and a monogrammed shirt with cuff links. Pritchard, in his fifties, wore an American flag button on his lapel.

Following him out of the car was Richard Abbington, Pritchard's legal adviser and political consultant. The only time Abbington had ever been past the front door of Republic was with Pritchard, whose grandfather was one of the founding members. Abbington opened the door for his boss and followed him into the dark foyer, blinking as his eyes adjusted to the light. The entrance was decorated with chalices, coats of arms, and other Anglican playthings, but like the rest of Republic, it had lost some of its luster in recent years.

"Good afternoon, Mr. Pritchard," a short, jacketed deskman said, making a half bow.

Pritchard nodded and moved past him. Abbington, who wasn't a member—you had to be sponsored, and Pritchard had never offered—followed the boss into the oak-paneled Stratford Room, which resembled an Old English dining hall. Pritchard's regular table was in the far corner on the left, and he ate lunch here three or four times a week in the company of gray hair and good breeding. A hand reached up from one of the tables and stopped Pritchard as he made his way to the back.

"Whit, how are you?"

"Hello, Judge. Not too good, actually. I still haven't recovered from the beating you gave me last weekend. What was it, seven strokes?"

"Nine."

"I stand corrected. Judge, have you met Dick Abbington?"

This was one of Pritchard's games, acting like he was the only one who knew anybody important. Abbington, who was used to it, took the judge's hand and said, "It's good to see you again, Justice Ricks."

"Come on out and play with us next time," Ricks said. "I'll gladly take your money, too."

Pritchard exchanged several more handshakes and hellos on the way to his table, where a tuxedoed waiter pulled his chair out for him. Pritchard asked for a bottle of his regular merlot, and when the waiter left, he leaned over the table and said in a low voice, "The place is going to hell. Did you catch who was at Ricks's table?"

Abbington shook his head. He'd actually had his eye on a woman at the same table. Abbington, who was single, often ended his days in the Library Lounge at the top of the nearby Bellevue Hotel, entertaining expensive women and later billing Liberty Oil for what he said were business meetings.

"It's Tom Myers. A shill for the trade unions. They're letting riffraff like that in now."

Abbington had to listen to this every time they came in. The club wasn't exclusive enough for Pritchard, who probably wouldn't be comfortable unless it were all robber barons and captains of manufacturing, like it had been in the beginning. The club had been forced in recent years to admit women, Democrats, blacks, and Jews. Pritchard had welcomed them and then, with several other local alums of Dartmouth College, planned the establishment of a new private club, which they intended to call the Green Room.

"He's one of ours," Abbington said. "I don't care who he sits with, as long as he doesn't forget who got him elected."

"I'll give you that," said Pritchard, who was handsome in what Abbington considered a mannered way, with a grass-court tan and fifty-dollar haircut. His hair had gone nearly all gray since he took over the reins of the company from his father five years ago, and Abbington, noticing that Pritchard suddenly looked old and tired in the low light, ran a hand over his own hair, which was dark and thick and combed straight back. "Ricks has been good to us for years. Very trustworthy," Pritchard went on, his tone signaling the disappointment he was about to express. "It's more than I can say for Debra Sharperson."

Pritchard was in a swoon that began the moment Abbington stepped into the office this morning, but that was becoming routine. Profits at the nation's fifth largest refinery had been slipping ever since Pritchard took control, and each quarterly report was another blow to the ego of a man obsessed with proving he could run the company as well as his father and grandfather had. To further frazzle him, they had a public relations nightmare on their hands with fallout from the silica alumina incident, which had carried over into citywide hysteria about leukemia. And now, mercilessly, Sharperson was piling on. Liberty Oil had pumped thousands of dollars into her campaign, counting on her as someone who would watch out for their interests on the state supreme court. But in a televised interview on the morning news, she said she had problems with the state's emissions monitoring system, as well as with "the spirit" of a Liberty Oil lawsuit the high court was scheduled to hear in the coming calendar year.

"What exactly did Sharperson say when you called?" Abbington asked. He knew Pritchard was single-mindedly committed to winning that case, because it would mean his vindication. In his first major exercise of authority after taking over from his father, he had blundered into the purchase of a storage field from another refinery, only to discover that oil had been seeping through the tanks and into the soil for decades. In the words of one environmentalist, it was as if a dozen *Exxon Valdez*es had collided under the city. Parts of South Philadelphia essentially were floating on an oil slick. The extent of the damage to groundwater, the health risk, and the cost of the cleanup were the subjects of a lawsuit that had already cost millions. The next stop for the case was the state supreme court.

"Nothing very satisfying," Pritchard said. His hair had moved to a higher starting point in recent years, making his long, triangular face even longer. From a broad forehead, his face sloped down to a chiseled jaw, which he stroked now as he recalled the conversation. "I told her we were frankly shocked that she'd have her hand out in the primary and then turn around and slap us like this now, just because of all of this irrational hysteria among the great unwashed."

"And?"

"And the insolent bitch says, 'Whitney, I didn't ask for a campaign contribution. You came to me.' "

"That's it? 'I didn't ask for a campaign contribution'?"

"She also said, 'Politics and law are two different things.' "

Abbington had a look of resignation. He'd been in politics long enough that no amount of hypocrisy could surprise him. "The cock and the hand are two different things, too, but one serves the other," he said. "At this point, I doubt she'll be there for us with the heating oil permit."

Pritchard stared across the room, plotting something behind those small, pale blue eyes, Abbington was sure. Probably something spectacularly stupid or ruthless. He'd become verbally abusive lately with bankers who were holding down Liberty's credit line and with loyal congressmen who showed signs of bending under pressure from the environmental protection lobby. He had confided in Abbington that he suspected his father's contemporaries, and his own, judged him to be in over his head, and he constantly schemed to prove them wrong. Part of his plan to save Liberty, which shipped three hundred thousand barrels daily of gasoline and diesel up and down the East Coast, was to expand into the heating oil market. He was convinced, despite the advice of a consultant, that it was the only way to stay competitive. There was just one problem. The state had denied Liberty's application for a building permit, arguing that pollution in the area had to decrease before any new construction would be approved. Liberty sued, challenging the state's authority, and lost. That case, like the groundwater contamination case, was headed for the state supreme court.

The waiter poured wine while Pritchard examined the cork and pronounced it acceptable on that test alone. He ordered veal medallions; Abbington got the crab cakes. "I don't know what else can possibly go wrong," Pritchard said, swaying back in his chair, his eyes heavy on the shelf of his aristocratic face. "Silica dust is probably the least harmful thing blowing out of our stacks, and it's got the whole city worked into a lather."

"You're overreacting," Abbington said. "You just need to relax."

Pritchard accidentally clinked his glass on his plate and spilled some wine. He looked around the room to make sure nobody noticed his state of anguish, then leaned closer to Abbington and spoke softly. "Dick, we've practically been accused of killing children, and you want me to relax?"

"We haven't been accused of anything. And it'll all blow over, so to speak."

Pritchard licked drops of wine off his fingers, his eyes glued on Abbington. "Temporary minor respiratory problems blow over, Dick. Leukemia doesn't. Not that we're responsible for it, by any stretch of the imagination. But the public and the press are too stupid to know that, and it's attention we certainly don't need at this point. Pilgrim Petroleum is squeezing us out of New England, we're down six percent in the last quarter, and the timing of the silica event couldn't have been worse. It puts Ron Rice up my ass like a June bug—a bloody football player, for God's sake—and now Sharperson, of all people, endorsed by every business lobby in the state, betrays us."

The waiter set their salads in front of them and Abbington refilled Pritchard's wineglass. "Eat your greens," he said. "It's good for digestion."

"I honestly don't understand why you're so smug about this," Pritchard said, picking up his fork.

Of course he couldn't understand. He was born with a CEO job waiting for him and he grew up on his family's Main Line estate, a pampered prep. He'd never had to fight for a thing. That was why he hated and envied Abbington, who was always one step ahead of him. Abbington, who didn't carry the burden of family history, was born to working-class parents who divorced when he was young. He had worked his way through law school, inspired by an attorney from Delaware County's Republican machine who had brilliantly inflated the settlement when Abbington suffered a soft-tissue back injury in a car accident.

"It's because I have a plan," said Abbington, who had been troubleshooting for Liberty Oil since Pritchard's father had hired him as a lobbyist. Shortly after A. Whitney III took over and came to grips with his own shortcomings, he began relying more on Abbington.

"And this would be the plan you mentioned at the office?"

"Yes."

"Well let me have it, and I hope it's better than the last plan you had. Wasn't that when we bought the fifty storage tanks that turned out to be gigantic colanders?"

Pritchard had been doing this routinely. Saying things that weren't true. Abbington wondered if he was aware of it, or if he'd begun inventing his own reality. He said, "That was before I was this involved, if you'll recall. Your father had just retired to the fairway."

Pritchard said, "Speak of the devil, he hasn't even spoken to me in two months. Not that I should take it personally, I suppose. He didn't speak to me when we worked in the same office and lived in the same house."

The problem, as Abbington saw it, was that Pritchard had neither the smarts nor the guts his father and grandfather had. He did, however, have a greater desire to succeed, and Abbington had nearly perfected the art of using that to his advantage. "Your father's probably not as worried as you are," he said. "He had his valleys, too, you'll remember. It goes in cycles. One way your father got out of the bad ones was to take risks. Not stupid ones, but bold, calculated chances. Like when he went after Asco Oil's market in Virginia. Like when he took a two-year loss on the construction that eventually doubled production. It's the same kind of chance you and I took when we broke the union and when we lobbied like hell to strip the Clean Air and Clean Water acts. You know it as well as I do, Whit. You sit on your ass in business today and you're dead."

The waiter took Pritchard's unfinished salad and set his entrée in front of him. Pritchard put a fork in a medallion, but didn't lift it off the plate. "So let's have it," he said. "Tell me how you're going to rescue me from myself this time."

Abbington clucked crabmeat from the back of his teeth and swallowed. There was no other way to do this but to just put it out there. He took a sip of wine and said, "We back Isadore Weiner and William Flaherty."

Pritchard's expression didn't change. He looked around to see if anyone might have heard those names, then he put the forkful of veal into his mouth. He chewed deliberately, staring at Abbington the whole time without giving his thoughts away. Then he swallowed, cleared his throat, and said, "That isn't funny."

Abbington knew he'd have a fight on his hands. "You're the one who runs the books, Whitney, so you know what's at stake here. Why shouldn't we give it a shot?"

Pritchard snickered condescendingly. "Because we've never backed candidates with nicknames, Dick. That's why. You really aren't kidding, are you? I knew you had no morals. Now I'm wondering about your intelligence, as well."

"Is it just because they're Democrats?" Abbington asked.

"Democrats? No, it starts with a *D*, but it's not 'Democrats,' Dick. They're dinosaurs. You've seen them on television. They're throwbacks. This is what the Democratic Party was before it discovered secondary education."

Pritchard turned his gaze across the dining room, but didn't focus on anything in particular. He brought his hand up to the silver smokestack tie clip he wore every day and fidgeted with it absentmindedly. Abbington couldn't read exactly where he was going, but his instinct was to lay back. "Look," Pritchard finally said, "I don't mind having a few congressmen down to the property in Barbados, though God knows it's getting more crowded there all the time. And I never bickered when you insisted we hire enough lobbyists to escort every frapping senator in D.C. out to dinner on the same night. We've supported pro-business Democrats and you know it as well as I. But William 'Ham' Flaherty and Isadore 'Izzy' Weiner? That's an entirely different element. Do you realize their role model is Augie Sangiamino? The man's been to prison, Dick. Federal prison."

The plates were cleared, Pritchard's meal virtually untouched, and the waiter brought his regular dessert, lemon meringue pie. Pritchard stuck a fork through the meringue topping and said, "There's a public relations problem with it, anyway. If we start writing checks for them, don't you think the intent will be obvious to the public? The sad thing is, it might be as much an image concern for them as it is for us. What candidate wants money from a baby killer?"

Abbington dropped three sugar cubes into his coffee and stirred like he was ringing a bell, licking the spoon when he was done. "First of all," he said, "you're way out of control with this baby-killer thing. Nobody is saying that. And as for us helping these guys out, it doesn't have to be public. Trust me, I know guys like these. I've worked with them for years and I know how to handle them."

Pritchard put his elbows on the table and leaned in, lowering his voice. "It doesn't have to be public? What are you telling me?"

"Would you let me handle this, Whit? We get them some money through the PAC, maybe through the party. The state and national committees could help with that. There are dozens of ways to do this."

Abbington could tell Pritchard was only half listening now. He was probably going through one of his mental balance sheets, like he did with everything, weighing benefits versus risks. "Look," Abbington said, "we've got half the state supreme court right now. Izzy Weiner gives us a majority, which we absolutely have to have with these two cases coming up. And if we can get Flaherty in, we don't have to worry about Ron Rice going down to Washington and beating a drum for regulation. You're the one who's been saying one more bad break and we could be in trouble, Whit. I'm telling you, as unnatural as it might seem, these are our guys."

Pritchard shook his head in agreement, but Abbington knew it wasn't an endorsement. He was still chasing down his thoughts, trying to fit them to an answer, and a look of recognition was forming in his eyes.

"They're killing off business in this country," Pritchard said in a low, even voice, as if he'd visited a truth so powerful it put him in a trance. "Emissions regulations don't need to be ratcheted up, they need to be relaxed. They're burying us with regulation and accusation. Leukemia. Lung cancer. Emphysema. We're greedy. We're bad guys. Now we're killers. Here we are, paying good salaries to four hundred uneducated people, manufacturing a product thousands of people rely on every damn day of their lives, and with a few people getting sick they want to shut us down."

Abbington pounded the table hard, rattling the coffee cups in their saucers. "That's exactly what I'm talking about," he said.

When the vibration stopped, the unanswered question was back on the table. Should they back Izzy Weiner and Ham Flaherty?

"There's a problem with it," Pritchard said. "A fundamental problem."

"What's that?"

"Neither one of them can win. Weiner's getting crushed and Flaherty is so miserable a candidate he's trailing a football player. Have you seen the polls, Dick? These guys are already out of it."

Abbington all but yawned at Pritchard's assessment. "This is why it's best that you leave politics to me," he said. "There's two months left in the campaign. In this state, anything can happen in two months. And I know people who've worked with Augie Sangiamino. You put money in his hands, they say, and the man is a miracle worker. That's their only problem right now—that they've been out of the loop for a while and they don't have anything to work with. We could give them a start— a start that could bring them back."

Abbington knew he had a chance when Pritchard asked, "Does either one of them even have a pro-business rating? I mean, how do we know if they'd even be willing to work with us?"

"Whitney," Abbington said, as if addressing a child, "they're politicians. Do you understand what that means? They may be old school and somewhat unrefined, with the gravelly voices and the hairy fingers and all, but in a fundamental way, they're like every other politician we work with. If there were money and votes in it, they'd be in favor of train wrecks."

Pritchard asked the waiter to put lunch on his tab. On the way out, he told Abbington he wanted to think about it.

"Fine," Abbington said. "But don't take too long. If we're going to move on this, we've got to move soon."

Back outside, the chauffeur stood at the curb, opening the door of the limo. Pritchard paused at the top of the stairs, squinting into the midday light as a long funeral procession slowly made its way up Broad Street.

CHAPTER 9

PLAYERS IN THE Half-Century Basketball League had to be at least fifty, but the teams occasionally tried to sneak in a younger man who looked older because of advanced hair loss or some other degeneration. Ham Flaherty, due to longtime exposure to tanning salons, tobacco, and booze, had joined the league at forty-three. Games were played on Eighth Street, a block from the Italian Market, in a warehouse that had been converted into a community recreation center by Robert Magnifico's House of Beef and Pork. It was a gesture of gratitude to Augie, who had kept the health department out of Magnifico's butcher shop for years. The gym floor was bare concrete, large flakes of asbestos insulation floated down from the ceiling like absentee ballots, and a smiling cow and pig were painted on the wall at one end of it.

Triangle Tavern and Inzerello's Vestments & Religious Articles were finishing up their game, with Augie Sangiamino's team waiting to play Johnny's Roast Beef in the second half of the weekly doubleheader. The Triangle players wore tank tops with a cocktail glass logo, and Inzerello's had T-shirts designed as holy cards, only instead of saints, they had their own likenesses. But the class of the league, sartorially speaking, was Augie's team—the Fifth Amendments.

Augie had come up with the name after years of being advised by lawyers that no matter what kind of jam he or his cronies were in, they would never have to incriminate themselves. The name of the law firm that sponsored the team—Roe, Barry, and Murray—was burned across the backs of snappy white satin uniforms with red trim. Under the sponsor was a number and each player's name or nickname: NUMBERS, HAM, IZZY, LOU, SENATOR. Augie also wore No. 6565347 on his back—his prison number.

"Where the hell is Bonguisto?" Augie asked Joey as he paced the south side of the gym, keeping an eye on the door. "That son of a bitch promised me, and now he's gonna stiff us?" Augie, desperate to get some exposure for Ham and Izzy, had called the Channel Nine reporter and talked him into doing a story about how two candidates took time off from the rigors of a tough campaign. Before Joey could answer, Augie had climbed into the bleachers. He was handing out PUT IZZY ON THE BENCH T-shirts to the old men from the neighborhood who showed up every week to watch the ball games. Maybe Bonguisto could have his crew point the camera up there. If not, maybe the bumper stickers would get some airtime. Joey held them in his hand as he watched Augie step carefully down off the bleachers and hustle back toward him. Augie was always in a hurry, knifing into the next thought, the next event. Especially at election time. "Come on boys, get in here," Augie called out to the Fifth Amendments as he took the stickers from Joey. "Slap these cocksuckers on the back of your jerseys. Come on, you yo-yos. We ain't got all night." One said HAM CAN, the other said GET BUSY, VOTE IZZY.

Izzy said it would look tacky, and Ham griped, too, but they followed Augie's instructions. When they were done, Ham said, "I gotta go take a piss. I'll be right back."

Izzy winked at Joey. Ham, who was already carrying a load, was going out to his car for a quick pop.

"Hurry up," Augie said. "This game's almost over."

Joey was just glad Ham had finally shown up for a scheduled

event. Not that he cared personally if he ever saw him again, because Ham had never shown proper respect for Augie, as far as Joey was concerned. But this was probably Augie's last election, and Joey wanted no trouble for the boss. Augie had met privately with Ham earlier in the day and he came away saying Ham had promised to shape up. We'll see, Joey thought to himself. That day Ham blew off Joey Napolitano's funeral, it turned out he was in Atlantic City, boffing the cocktail waitress and sleeping through lunch. He had no discipline. No fucking respect. Here he came now, sloshing back into the gym and drawing hard on a cigarette. The way he walked, half bagged, it looked like he was taking steps in a rowboat. The bad toupee, the belly, the toothpick legs—he was a mess, Joey thought. But in a freak of science, still handsome somehow, in a Vegas kind of way.

Izzy waited for Ham to get right up on them, then he asked, "The hell you got on your feet?"

Ham looked down as if he wasn't sure what he'd find. "Hush Puppies," he said. "You got a problem?"

"Yeah. Where's your sneakers?"

"I couldn't fucking find them," Ham said.

Izzy tapped Ham's arm and said, "Couldn't remember what bed to look under?"

"How 'bout I stick one of these dogs so far up your ass you start barking? How'd that be, Schlomo?"

Joey stepped away and looked up at the smiling cow and pig. Sometimes it was a little too scary for him, the level of intelligence he was working with.

Augie, who never played unless they were short, went with the usual lineup of Joey and Izzy at guard, Ham and Lou's cousin Dominic at forward, and Lou at center. Lou was shorter than Ham and Dominic, but his reach gave him a half-foot advantage over both of them. "Joey, don't be afraid to put the ball up tonight," Augie said, looking across the gym at the Roast Beef center, who stood six-four. "I don't know if Lou's gonna be able to work on this fuckin' giraffe they got." Lou was the Fifth Amendments' leading scorer at twelve points a game. Joey had a good two-handed set shot, and Dominic could always be counted on for a few buckets. Izzy, who quarterbacked the team, had been a gym rat as a kid and had some ballhandling skills. His hero was Bob Cousy, the Boston Celtic Hall of Famer.

"Ham, listen to me," Augie said, putting his hand on his protégé's shoulder. "I got a little beef going with one of the assholes on Johnny's, all right? All I'm asking, you gotta bust your ass tonight, up and down the court. Your best effort. *Capeesh?*" They got little scoring and no defense out of Ham, and were happy if he made it through the game without coughing up a lung or having the toupee fly off his head, which happened once on a charging violation. Ham preferred to sit and watch, but Augie had been playing him the entire game as election day drew closer. He wanted him so tired it would cut into his whoring.

Ham sucked hard on his cigarette, hacked out a dry cough, and waved OK.

"How you feel?" Augie asked.

"What do you mean?"

"The campaign. You all right?"

Ham had a here-we-go-again look on his puffy red-brown face. "I'll take him," he said. "I don't care what the fucking polls say. A colored can't beat me in this district. Besides, what I went to Atlantic City for, it was to straighten out this financial thing."

"I can help with that," Augie said. "I go way back with some of these people."

Ham nodded yes, but it meant Yeah, thanks, but no thanks. "It's all right. I got a relationship with them that if I don't handle it, maybe it gets fucked up. If you could dig up something on Rice from this end, is all, we'll be in good shape."

Joey had inched in close enough to eavesdrop, and he had a brief urge to smack Ham. Augie never would have stood for that kind of bullshit in the past, Ham telling him to lay off. Augie must be thinking he stood to lose Ham if he crowded him now. "I'm working on it," Augie said. "Son of a bitch has paid his taxes, his gas bill, everything. He even pays his fuckin' parking tickets, this bastard."

Augie had told Joey about an idea he had for a TV spot in which Ham would wear a gas mask and say something about air pollution, but he was having trouble raising the money for it. That was probably half of Ham's problem, that Augie couldn't bring it in like he used to. Even Joey had to admit this was pathetic, praying that some fuckwad reporter showed up at an old-timers' game so they'd get what, maybe ten seconds of free airtime?

The buzzer sounded, ending the game between Inzerello's Vestments & Religious Articles and Triangle Tavern. Augie looked around once more for Channel Nine. "He'll be here," Joey said. "He owes you."

It was true. Augie had cemented Bonguisto's career in Philadelphia twelve years ago when the reporter, new in town, was doing a story about why South Philadelphians call spaghetti sauce gravy. Bonguisto, informed that there was no higher authority than a certain congressman and gourmet chef, sped down to Washington with a crew and interviewed Augie on the steps of the Lincoln Memorial. "Well then, Senator, explain this," Bonguisto said to Augie in one of the senator's defining moments. "If it's gravy, how come when you go to a store to buy a jar of Ragu, it says sauce on it?" Part of Augie's answer got bleeped, but it was unmistakable. "Guess what, Mr. Bonguisto," he said, looking away from the reporter and directly into the camera, Abe Lincoln over his shoulder. "We don't buy fuckin' Ragu."

"All right, boys, get in here," Augie called.

The Fifth Amendments gathered around, each one putting a hand into the ring. "Jesus," Augie said, sniffing. "What the hell is that?"

"What's what?" Lou asked.

Augie said, "Smells like a balsamic vinaigrette."

They all looked at Ham. It was the combination of booze and cologne.

"Fuck you, guys," he said.

"All right, listen up," Augie said. "This is important. Lou, I need you to set up a meeting of ward leaders next Friday night, downstairs at the South Broad Diner. Ham and Izzy, bring all your lit'rature, whatever you got, and be prepared to make a little speech. And I don't want you getting fancy on me, understand? It's law and order, clean streets, and the good strong family values we all grew up with. *Capeesh!*" They nodded. "Now, Joey, you gotta get our 'lectrical guy, what's his name?"

"I already called," Joey said. "Nicolosi Electric."

"Yeah. You had him do Ham's office? Because we can't trust this fuckin' DA for a minute."

"Tonight, he does Ham."

"You tell Nicolectric we need a sweep of the diner, too. We'll see him down there a half hour early. And you know what?"

"I told him we need to check Milly's, too."

"There you go," Augie said. "The ceiling, too. Have him check the ceiling, the floor, everything. You blink, and these pricks'll stick a wire up your ass."

The buzzer sounded for the start of the game.

"All right," Augie said. "Let's show these Mamelukes a thing or two."

Augie wore a PUT IZZY ON THE BENCH T-shirt and planned to walk up and down the court all night, advertising his supreme court candidate while he coached. This was the kind of thing he excelled at in a campaign. Handshakes, hustles, old-fashioned neighborhood stuff. It had been his strength and now it was his weakness. When he got out of prison, he was the hottest political consultant in the eastern half of the state, but the business had been taken over by marketing majors and multimedia whiz kids. Electronic parasites, Augie called them. They might have been to school and opened a book or two, but they hadn't been on the street. What the fuck could they know?

When the teams met at center court, the Johnny's Roast Beef center said something to Lou about the hair on his back. Lou gave a push, and the referee called a foul.

"What're you, kidding me?" Augie called out. "You can't call a foul before the game starts. Get your head out of your ass."

The ref whistled again. Technical foul on Augie.

It was a league record. Two fouls on the Fifth Amendments before the game had started. Augie turned and played the crowd, leading a cheer when the Johnny's shooter missed the free throw. "All right," he called, pacing the sidelines and clapping. "Now we're ready. Now we're ready."

Lou won the opening tap, guiding the ball over to Izzy, who was too wound up and dribbled it off his foot and out of bounds. "Son of a bitch," Augie muttered, reminded of Debra Sharperson's attack ad. The way Izzy bent over when he dribbled, glasses strapped to his head with a black elastic band, he did look like Groucho Marx.

Izzy was more patient bringing the ball up court the next time, and he whipped a no-look pass to Joey at the top of the key. Joey, whose shorts came to his knees, spotted Ham on the baseline and almost fed him the ball, but realized at the last instant that Ham had a cigarette in one hand. Nobody else was open, so Joey put up a fifteen footer. It thudded like a medicine ball off the fiberglass backboard—not what Joey intended—but banked in.

"Beautyful," Augie crooned. "Now everybody hustle back on defense."

On the next possession, Izzy threw his defender off balance with a stutter step that got a reaction from the old men in the bleachers. He slid into the lane and dished back out to Joey, whose twenty footer flew over the entire backboard and rattled around behind it.

"I'm standin' wide the fuck open in the lane," Ham moaned

as they trotted back to the other end of the gym, "and you're shootin' the ball out of the freakin' gym."

Augie, still waiting on the TV reporter, called time-out to stall. "Where is that fucking guinea?" he was barking as his sweaty players came his way. "We got Izzy playing like Julius fucking Irving, the crowd's into the ball game, and that dago cocksucker don't show."

Bonguisto hadn't shown up by halftime, either, when Augie led his players to the middle of the court, out of earshot, and had them kneel down around him. From a distance, it looked as if he were diagramming plays on the floor and pumping up his team. He was.

"We gotta start hitting the absentee ballots hard," he was telling Lou. "You tell the committeemen we're goin' a buck a ballot this year. That's all you gotta do. It stirs a certain creativity." Augie always got absentee ballots to people who didn't ordinarily go to the polls, or didn't even know there was an election—the sick, the elderly, the ignorant. The non-English speaking were the easiest. You show up with some appearance of authority and those people signed anything. They'd sign their own death warrant, Augie said. He didn't think of it as deceit; he thought of it as public service. They were better off with his politics. He made things happen. He got potholes filled and trees trimmed and tickets fixed.

"Senator," Joey said, "the problem I see, we got so many of these Portarickens and Vietnamese in the district now, we could have trouble finding enough runners who understand what we're talking about."

"A problem? Joey, it's a gift from God," Augie said, crossing himself. "We hire a couple of these nice 'ricken boys, a couple of Viet Cons, whatever the fuck they call themselves. These chinks especially are so happy just to be in this country they'll work their asses off. I seen some of them, Joey. They're eagle-beavers."

"That's how my father come off the boat," Lou said. "He

didn't have ten cents in his pocket and he worked his way up from nothing. You gotta respect some of these Orientals who are the same way. It ain't like the coloreds, with their hand out from the day they got here."

"Lou, guess what," Izzy interrupted. "They were brought here as slaves."

Augie had had enough of this. "Would you guys shut up for five minutes, for cry seven-up? My point is for a buck a ballot, half of San Juan and Hanoi are gonna vote in this election. We'll get Vin Ho to work this block, Ying Yang to work that block. When the first Viet Con votes from his grave, we'll know these people have achieved full citizenship."

The lead seesawed back and forth the rest of the way, neither team able to take control. Lou kept getting whistled for traveling, fouls, and lane violations, and the referee had threatened to eject him if he didn't stop complaining about the calls. Augie called all the time-outs available to him, trying to drag it out until the TV crew arrived. He used the time to review ways to rig the tally sheets when the polls closed on election night. "Eight minutes left," he said during one break, "and Bonguisto's got us standin' here with our dicks in our hands." Joey asked Augie if he wanted to get into the game, maybe it would calm him down.

"Anybody need a breather?" Augie asked. Ham raised his hand. "Jesus, Ham, I need you in there right now, buddy. The game's on the line, I gotta have my best five on the floor. Can you make it?" Ham—who actually thought he was one of the more valuable players—said he was OK.

Izzy pushed the ball up court, looking for Lou inside. Lou was backing into the big center, rear-ending him for position, and Izzy snapped a pass to him on a drive down the lane. Lou put up a smooth hook that hung the net, giving the Fifth Amendments a one-point lead, but the whistle blew. "Three seconds in the lane," the referee shouted, waving off the points and leaving Johnny's up by one.

Lou came apart. He had the same look he used to have in the ring when he decided he wasn't going to take another shot between the eyes. Joey was the first who tried to hold him back.

"Keep that son of a bitch away from me," the ref said, back-pedaling.

"You're bustin' our chops," Izzy said to the referee. "That call is *for-schimmel.*"

"Excuse me?" the referee said.

"For-schimmel," Izzy repeated. "That call is *for-schimmel.*"

"For shit," Ham explained.

The ref whistled another technical.

"On who?" Ham asked. "Izzy, for saying you're shit, or me, for translating?"

Augie missed the exchange. He was trying to help Joey calm Lou down. The Johnny's Roast Beef center had moved in closer and said, "Put this moose back in his cage before he hurts somebody." Everyone threw hands for the next five minutes, but with the exception of Lou, who broke two noses, no one's punches were any more accurate than their basketball shots. The referee blew his whistle the entire time before calling off the game, awarding the victory to Johnny's Roast Beef, and stalking off the floor with one eye over his shoulder, making sure Lou didn't follow.

That was when Augie noticed the glare of a TV light and saw Bonguisto with a smile from ear to ear. He'd shown up just in time to catch the fight.

CHAPTER 10

A SECRETARY PEEKED into Lisa Savitch's office and said there was some nut on the phone. Somebody saying she was Judy Garland.

"Put it through," Savitch said. Muldoon watched the secretary leave—it was somebody new—and asked what happened to Carla Delmonico.

"She called in sick the last couple days. Why, you miss her?"

"Just wondering," Muldoon said.

Ham's wife, who'd moved out on him, was calling to say she went home to pick up some things and overheard Ham on the phone, telling someone he had to cancel an appointment. He said he had a ten-thirty strategy meeting in his office and it couldn't be rescheduled.

Muldoon looked at his watch. Ten o'clock. "You wanna go watch it?"

"Anything to get out of the office," she said, putting the Ham Flaherty file back in her drawer, "so I don't have McGinns calling every half hour to see if I've done my homework."

Besides, maybe they'd catch a break. It had been two weeks since the grand jury met, and Savitch had nothing new to give them. The shipments to Ham's house had stopped cold. Muldoon was sitting on three Atlantic City contacts, but if anybody knew anything about a payoff to Ham, they weren't talking.

Muldoon had one detective tailing Ham and another dividing his time between Augie Sangiamino and a couple of Sangiamino's A.C. connections. Nothing but blanks.

On top of that, Ham's girlfriend, the cocktail waitress, was coming out of her house in Voorhees, New Jersey, at eight every morning and driving to the Turnpike Commission office in Plymouth Meeting. She was putting in eight hours there, then driving to Atlantic City for the swing shift at a casino. So much for the no-show state job.

"You sure you wanna drive?" Muldoon asked as they walked through the parking lot. He hadn't said anything the first couple times she was behind the wheel, but she drove the car like it was a delivery truck, quick stops and starts on every corner.

"I'm fine," she said, jingling the keys.

"Because I can drive if you want."

"No thanks."

The DA's office had a fleet of sedans. This one was maroon. Savitch got in and lit a cigarette before she turned the key. "Could you at least crack your window?" Muldoon asked. "So I don't get emphysema?"

Savitch gave him a look and started the car, opening the window as she pulled onto Fifteenth and made the half circle around City Hall and onto South Broad. "Emphysema's high around the refineries, too," she said. "Lung cancer, breast cancer, emphysema."

She was still on this kick, Muldoon thought. "What is the deal here?" he asked. "Could I just name any disease, and you're carrying statistics around in your head?"

She looked at him with that left eye wandering out there again, swinging free just slightly. She was wearing a baggy sweater and snug-fitting blue jeans, getting more casual as she got comfortable with the job. The jeans showed more of her than Muldoon had seen before today, and he was biting his lip. She looked tight everywhere.

She asked, "Do you read anything besides the sports page, Muldoon?"

He didn't even look at her.

"The papers have been full of it," she said. "You see it's up to four kids now with leukemia, plus the one that died? It's starting to look like another Love Canal, and they still don't have a clue what's causing it. I'd be all over this thing if I were McGinns, but she doesn't give two shits."

"She has no jurisdiction," Muldoon said, no attempt to hide his feelings about Savitch's preoccupation with a case other than the one they were supposed to be working. McGinns had come to him, asking what Savitch's problem was. Muldoon wanted to tell her she was busy chasing her brother's ghost, but he hadn't.

"Jurisdiction? Fuck jurisdiction. You realize that in ten years, Liberty Oil has been cited for emissions twice as often as the next refinery down there?"

Muldoon watched her as she ranted. Her top lip, with that upturn in the center, revealed the bottom of a front tooth. Muldoon had seen something on one of those entertainment news shows about actresses doing that to their lips. Shooting something in there to puff them up. He could see why. It made you want to touch it. Put your mouth there. Muldoon would have bet a week's salary Savitch wasn't the type who'd let somebody shoot something into her lip. That had to be the real thing.

The light changed and she hit the gas hard, jerking Muldoon's head back, even though traffic was stopped a half block in front of them.

"I talked to McGinns," he said. "She told me you said something about a situation like this in Boston. Pollution case of some type."

"What, is she griping about me to you? Telling you to baby-sit the bitchy new girl?"

"Do you have to overreact to everything? She brought it up in casual conversation that you knew about a similar problem up there. That's all it was. Besides, she couldn't pay me enough to baby-sit you."

If she was insulted, it didn't show. "You see where the state fined Liberty ten thousand dollars for that little blowup?" she asked. "What a joke. They're publicly traded, worth about two hundred million, and the state fines them ten thousand dollars."

"So what was this pollution case in Boston? When McGinns first told me, I thought she'd misunderstood you. I thought it was the industrial accident—your brother getting killed in the logging mill."

She said nothing and Muldoon wondered if she'd heard him. The ash on her cigarette was long and curled, like it usually was, a habit that didn't fit Muldoon's first take on Savitch. She was so revved up all the time, so twitchy, you'd think she'd be tapping it off every ten seconds. But maybe this did make sense. This long, slow, distracted burn.

"When I was twelve or so I got this baby-sitting job," she said. "A boy in my neighborhood. It was about two years altogether, and then later, I'd see him around town wearing a knit cap no matter what the weather was. He'd lost his hair. I didn't know what to say because it scared me, so I just sort of pretended I didn't recognize him."

She stopped there as if it were the place in the story where she always stopped.

"What happened to him?" Muldoon asked.

"It was his liver. His liver or his blood or both, I don't remember for sure. He used to play in this field near an abandoned railroad yard in our development, and they found PCBs in the dirt. He died when he was eleven."

"The family sue?" Muldoon asked.

"It's still kicking around, millions of dollars in legal fees later. The company's trying to wear them down and the family can't give it up." She looked at him and said, "It's the same thing here—little kids dying. Aren't you the least bit curious as a human being, if not as a career cop, as to what's killing them?"

Muldoon pointed a finger at her. "The FBI doesn't hire cops," he said in a grave tone. "If that's who you think you're working with, some fucking patrolman, maybe you should find another partner."

If nothing else, it took the edge off. She looked like she was trying to hold back a laugh.

"Excuse me," she said. "I keep forgetting I'm working with Eliot Ness. Maybe it's because we're three weeks into this investigation and we're worse off than we were the day we started."

Another dart aimed at his heart. Muldoon let it go, but he wasn't particularly proud of the way things were going. The usual channels were dry, for some reason. Nobody talking in the drop-a-dime capital of the United States. Something wasn't right and he hadn't figured out what it was, but he would. In time, he would.

"You do actually look more like a cop than an FBI agent," Savitch said more gently. "Especially with that big mustache and the red in your hair. An Irish beat cop, like the ones I saw in the courthouse all the time in Boston."

He didn't take it as a compliment, but he felt like the schoolboy who finally gets noticed by the girl he's been daydreaming about. "All I'm saying," he said, "is that kids get leukemia all the time. One kid dying and four kids getting sick, in a region of five million people, doesn't strike me as an epidemic."

Savitch said he could be right, but she had to do this, whether McGinns sanctioned it or not. She had to. She was meeting with a professor at Temple University later in the day. The guy who'd been quoted in a lot of the stories, speculating as to the causes of the leukemia.

"Why don't you just go to work for the EPA?"

"Because they're part of the problem, Muldoon. They had their teeth yanked out by the kinds of people you probably voted for."

It wasn't worth it, he told himself. Just leave it alone. It was easier to see now, after three weeks at her side, why the guy in Boston dumped her.

They were stopped at a red light and Muldoon grabbed a bag off the floor and took out a pair of sunglasses and a motorman's cap. He slid down in his seat, his knees touching the glove box, and put them on. Savitch watched closely and Muldoon could tell she was working on some smart-ass little comment. Here it came. "Now I see the edge you've got on cops," she said. "What does the FBI have, a special undercover class? He's a chauffeur. No, he's a paperboy. Couldn't be an FBI man. Irish eyes, blue suit, Efrem Zimbalist sedan."

She hit the gas hard and Muldoon grabbed the door handle to steady himself. "Look," he said. "I didn't just get to town, all right? There's a few people know me down here. Now could you please watch the road?"

"If you really want to blend in," she said, "why not just fatten up on hoagies and Tastykakes and get a bad toupee?"

Muldoon was sloped back, like he was riding a sled, flailing for a brake pedal on his side of the car. "Tell me something, Savage. Is this how everybody drives in Boston?"

"There's nothing wrong with my driving. I've never even been in an accident."

"You don't drive safely enough to be in an accident. You're gone by the time they happen. I think I'm nauseous."

"Nauseated," she said.

"I'm going to puke, how's that? Look, if you can see from a block away that it's a red light, why do we have to speed up and then slam on the brakes?"

"I'm trying to eject you through the windshield," she said. Muldoon buckled his seatbelt. "Have a cigarette," she said. "It'll relax you."

"I don't smoke."

"Does your wife smoke?"

Why would she be asking about his wife? Muldoon looked out the window. "No," he said. "She doesn't smoke. Why?"

"That's a gorgeous building," Savitch said. "What is it?"

"Republic. It's a private club for people with money. Big money. And this here's the Academy of Music." Muldoon had seen on TV that Ricardo Muti, the former maestro, was back in town from Milan as guest conductor of the Philadelphia Orchestra. It wasn't his thing, but Muldoon had gone there once with his wife, tickets from an FBI pal who couldn't make it. It wasn't a bad show, but he thought it would have been better if they had a singer or something. Maybe Barbra Streisand.

"I thought I smelled tobacco on you before, in the office, so I wondered if she smoked," Savitch said.

"You probably smelled it on yourself."

"How come you never talk about her?"

"What would you like to know?"

"How come you never had kids?"

He shot her a look.

"If it's too personal, don't answer," she said.

"I didn't."

"Fine. I'm not trying to be nosy; I'm just making conversation."

"It was because of my line of work."

"You mean the long hours, the nights, the weekends?"

"No. The danger involved. And then the kids would have no father."

She couldn't hold back the laugh this time. "Muldoon, you're an FBI agent, not a Green Beret."

Muldoon looked out the window at nothing. He needed this?

"You didn't answer me," she said. "How come you never talk about her?"

There was no point. It didn't matter what he said, she had some comeback.

"Look," she said. "Let me tell you something about my parents."

Wonderful. She put him in the same age bracket. Actually, he probably was.

"It took them a while, but they finally realized something about twenty years into their marriage. They had two choices. Either fix it or end it. But they couldn't let it drag them both to their graves."

Muldoon pretended not to be interested. She turned left on South, cutting off a car coming up Broad Street. Muldoon, sounding as bored as he could, asked, "So what did they do?"

"I'm not telling," she said.

Muldoon took off the shades and looked at her. "What are you, sixteen? What do you mean, you're not telling?"

"The point isn't what they did," she said. "It's what you're going to do."

"What makes you think I need to do anything?"

"Guess what, Muldoon. You think there's a man alive who can hide anything from a woman?"

He cocked his head and tapped his knee. Finally, she'd left him an opening. "Yeah," he said. "I can think of at least one. Lives in Boston?"

"Touché," she said.

"Damn right."

Ham's office was a corner storefront on Fourth Street in Queen Village, a mixed-race row-house neighborhood just north of South Philadelphia. Muldoon had wired it and run cable over the back roof and into a vacant house on Fifth Street. He preferred using a direct line to running the signal through a microwave repeater, because he'd once had the signal fade out moments before an attorney handed a wad of cash and a pair of Sinatra tickets to a judge. The DA's office had rented the house on Fifth Street under the name Allenwood Real Estate and hung a sign in the window saying they'd be open for business the first week of November.

"Nobody's on to this?" Savitch asked, parking across the street.

"Why would they be?"

"I don't know, I mean, what do people think when they see you going in and out of here?"

"We usually put our guns away and take off our FBI jackets before we tiptoe in," Muldoon said.

A county detective, one of four who'd been assigned to Muldoon, answered the front door wearing a blazer that had Allenwood Real Estate embroidered on it. Muldoon told him to take a break, come back in an hour. The TV monitor was tucked into what had been a closet or a pantry, no windows in the room. Muldoon pulled a second chair in and closed the door behind them. Sitting that close to her, he got another whiff of Savitch's lemon-scented smoke and the question hit him again. Why had she asked about his wife?

Ten twenty-five. Muldoon futzed with the focus on the TV and brought in an overhead shot of Ham's desk. The equipment was junk compared to what he used at the FBI. Muldoon popped the tape out of the VCR to make sure it was fresh. He started the reel-to-reel and then hit the pause button. Savitch smoked and chewed on a fingernail. "All right," he said. "We're set."

He left the room to go to the bathroom, and when he returned, the door to Ham's office was opening. "Here we go," Muldoon said. He couldn't remember how many times he'd done this, but it never got old. You were like a ghost when you ran surveillance. You were right there in the room with the crook and he had no clue. It was a feeling he got nowhere else, and he realized now, putting his hand in his pocket to free up some room for his excitement, how much he missed it.

From this angle, they saw Ham's head, shoulders, and sloped belly. "Jesus," Savitch said, "you can see a seam in the top of his toupee." Ham got on the phone to his secretary.

"No calls when she comes in," he said. "Nothing."

"She?" Muldoon said. "Maybe it's the cocktail waitress from Atlantic City. This could be just what we're looking for."

Ham opened a drawer, two liquor bottles and some cologne in there. He sprinkled cologne on his hands, patted his face and neck, then reloaded.

"Maybe just a little bit more," Savitch said.

Ham undid the middle buttons of his shirt and wedged a deodorant stick under his arms, then pulled a rubber band out of the drawer and cleaned his teeth. "Lovely," Savitch said. He squeezed off two shots of breath spray and straightened his tie, and his secretary called to tell him his appointment was in. State Representative William "Ham" Flaherty, a four-term fixture in the legislature and a candidate for Congress, threw his feet up on the desk to strike a casual pose.

The woman shimmied into the office. From this angle, all they could see was hair and cleavage.

"Hmmm," Muldoon said.

"What, you seen those before, Muldoon?"

"I guess it's the casino girl, but I don't know," he said. "Can't make out the face."

"Like you looked at the face."

"Something about the walk, though," he said. She slinked around the desk, pivoting on a finger.

Ham hadn't moved. "Hello, doll," he said. The sound was broken up, like the speaker was cracked. Muldoon banged the side of the television. "I don't fucking believe this," he said. "These voices sound like they're coming from underwater."

The woman was standing over Ham, whose head half disappeared in the crack of her breasts. His voice was muffled, but it sounded like, "How are my girls doin' in here?"

"They're good," the woman cooed. Savitch groaned and Muldoon turned red. The woman pulled back and sat on the edge of Ham's desk, her skirt riding up her thigh. Ham put a hand on her knee and walked his fingers up. Muldoon's cheeks were flaming. Savitch said, "I'd rather have a tarantula crawl up my leg."

"You need anything?" Ham asked.

"Maybe," the woman answered, working the top button of his shirt.

Ham was under her skirt now, his arm going in there like an eel. "You know what, doll? I don't know if I mentioned it, but you are one beautiful lady."

"Intelligent, too," Savitch said.

"And you know Ham loves you, am I right?"

She was undulating on the desktop, cantaloupe-sized breasts heaving.

"But we got a little problem now, don't we?"

"I guess so."

"What did I tell you when we got this whole thing started, me and you?"

"You said you loved me."

"I'm not talking about that," Ham said. "What else did I say?"

"That you're involved with someone else. Aside from your wife."

"That's right. Now what the fuck? I bump into you at the track, you gotta respect that. You understand what I'm saying?"

"I understand." She spoke in baby talk. A remorseful toddler.

Ham stood up and worked his hand into the crack of her breasts, a shark diving. "I got a reputation here," he said. "I'm in the midst of a 'lection campaign and I got you flashin' these tits in front of me at a fuckin' horse race."

"I'm sorry."

Ham shook his head, both hands cupping her breasts like he was weighing them. "What am I gonna do with you?"

"Spank me?"

Savitch choked. Muldoon, his head on fire, said, "You know, we don't have to watch this. It's not what we were looking for, exactly." He had to offer, at least. It was the decent thing to do.

But there was no way he was leaving this room. One of the things he had liked best about chasing these apes for the FBI was the occasional free peep show. All of the women were good-looking, too. It was amazing. He made sure the VCR was running, so he'd have the tape for future reference.

"There's something familiar about her," Savitch said. "Can't you get their voices to come in any better?" Muldoon played with the feed lines, but it didn't help.

Ham asked the woman if she was ready to play their little game.

"Ready," she said, perking up, her breasts about to pop out of her dress. Muldoon swallowed hard.

"OK, who am I?"

"State Representative William Flaherty," she said. "Soon-to-be congressman."

"And who got your job for you?"

"You and Augie."

"Who?"

"Just you?"

Muldoon cranked the volume all the way up.

"You play this little game with Augie, too, or just Ham?"

"Just Ham," she said. "Augie says he don't play around."

"That's what you tell people when the plumbing goes," Ham said. "How about Ham lays some pipe right now?"

The woman cooed again. Savitch stuck her finger down her throat.

"Who takes care of you?"

"You do."

"You need anything?"

"No."

"Tickets for any shows down 'lantic City?"

"No."

"You like boxing? I could put you ringside."

"I don't like bloodshed."

"How's your family?"

"We're fine."

"You gonna bring me some more paperwork?"

"Yes."

"All the latest?"

"There hasn't been none lately."

Muldoon said, "Paperwork?" Savitch begged the woman to lean back, show her face.

Ham was saying, "Now what do you call me when we're alone together? It's not William, is it?"

"No. It's Ham."

"And what are you?"

"I'm a Ham slammer."

Savitch put her hand to her mouth. "You all right?" Muldoon asked. Savitch said, "I'd ask a jury to come back with chemical castration for him. For her, I'm thinking death penalty. Who the hell is this bimbo? I've seen porno flicks that aren't this degrading."

She turned Muldoon around with that. "You've seen pornographic movies?"

She didn't answer. "What is this woman thinking? I mean, what the hell does she see in him?"

"You heard it. He's her sugar daddy. Anything she wants. Jobs, whatever. That's how the local economy works. All she has to do is put out."

The woman moved to the edge of the desk. Ham, standing between her legs, appeared to be working his zipper.

"Tell me again," he said.

Her hands came off the desk and disappeared under Ham's belly. "I'm a Ham slammer."

"Oh my God," Savitch said, and it sounded to Muldoon like she was in pain now.

Ham, his neck going rubbery, said, "Slap that prick. There you go, there you go."

"Thank God for the angle," Savitch said. "If I had to actually see this . . ."

Muldoon, his breath quickening, turned to Savitch just as she was turning to him. They broke up together. "I feel like I need a vaccination," she said.

Ham was still asking, "What are you?"

"She's a Ham slammer!" Savitch and Muldoon shouted together.

"OK, doll," Ham said, pushing her back onto his desk and climbing up. From a kneeling position, he dropped his pants.

"Yes," the woman groaned, pulling him in. "Yes, yes, yes."

The baby voice was gone, the regular voice more familiar. As her face came into view for the first time, Muldoon and Savitch leaned into the screen together and almost bumped heads.

Savitch shrieked.

Flat on her back, Ham Flaherty riding her like a horse, was the lovely and talented Carla Delmonico.

CHAPTER 11

Joey Tartaglione, who lived in the Pennies from Heaven bingo parlor and clubhouse on Tenth near Carpenter, was an incurable insomniac. On a good night, he got three or four hours. With all the spare time, he watched old movies and wrote.

No one knew this about him. He was Joey Numbers, not Joey Letters. But he'd been scribbling out little rhymes ever since his fourth-grade teacher, Sister Mary Thomas Roberta, complimented him for a poem he'd written about Jesus hitting the lottery and giving all the money to the Italian Market merchants. Some people showed you everything they had. Joey, like his father before him, held most of himself back, even from his closest friends. Maybe it was the Sicilian blood, or the fact that if you hung out with the Augie Sangiaminos of the world, it was difficult to work literature into the conversation.

Joey slept on a sofa. Underneath it, he'd cut a neat hole in the floorboards and built a compartment, sort of a safe-deposit box. Part of his life savings was down there, and his journal, too, which he pulled out when the dead of night put words in his head. Lately, he'd been writing a lot about Augie and Angela.

It was six in the morning. *On the Waterfront* had ended at four, and Joey had one verse to show for two hours of work. That was about average. There was no rush. No publisher waiting at his door.

His one verse:

That she loves him
is no longer in her eyes
but lies at the edge of her thoughts
a small pale forgiveness of lies

Joey read it over and over, rethinking it each time and deciding it was fine. He'd fallen in love with Angela, in a manner of speaking. Joey liked the idea of having a partner, but it had never worked out for him. They wanted you to do this; they wanted you to do that—every coming and going was a fucking drama. This way, say you ate a big meal and wanted to sit on the can for forty-five minutes, blow your brains out in there, it was no problem. You didn't have to answer to anybody. Someone locked up in a home, where you could see her now and then, that was the perfect woman.

Another poem he'd been working on, not about Angela, was more typical of Joey's work.

Once was a man
cooked the books in autumn
raped the boys
spanked the girls
clawed his way to the bottom

Joey put his journal back under the sofa and checked the clock. He and Augie had a seven-thirty meeting out at the lake. A meeting Joey hoped would change things for them. The rate they were going, they could bring in more money if Ham and Izzy set up lemonade stands.

The shower was in the back, off the kitchen. Joey used the

pantry as a closet, and opening it now, he stood before an end-to-end rack of sweaters on coat hangers. Three dozen of them, at least, representing every color in a crayon box. Augie bought him another one every year for Christmas, and so did relatives, and he never threw one out until it disintegrated and fell off the hanger. It was all he ever knew to say when anyone asked what he wanted for Christmas or a birthday, and he wore them year-round, except on the hottest days of summer. Joey picked a blue-and-gold one and set it on one of the plastic milk crates stacked on the floor of the pantry. The crates were turned sideways to make little cubbyholes, and Joey kept his gray slacks and underwear in them.

Augie had suggested Joey stay in the Pennies from Heaven clubhouse temporarily, after he was thrown out of a house he shared two blocks away with an Italian Market fishmonger. That was eight years ago. The fishmonger told Joey she loved him, but complained that she came third in his life, after Augie and bookmaking. For Joey, it only affirmed his sense of priorities. The first two, he knew, would never leave him. Besides, she stank so bad of fish all the time it was like fucking a walrus.

The clubhouse was fine with him, even though it wasn't a house. It had been a hardware store, and when the business folded, Augie was in the legislature and managed to finagle a state grant to buy the property, saying a charity would operate out of the building and serve various community needs. It was called Pennies from Heaven because one of the more urgent needs, as deemed by Augie, was transportation to Atlantic City for Frank Sinatra concerts. It was nothing fancy. Aside from the kitchen, there was one room, forty feet square, with linoleum flooring and long, cafeteria-style tables. Pennies from Heaven hosted bingo games and an occasional dance, and neighborhood men dropped by in the evenings to play cards or watch a ball game on the big-screen TV. This also served as campaign head-quarters for Ham and Izzy, whose posters covered the walls.

When the neighborhood theaters had shut down years ago,

Augie turned Pennies from Heaven into a movie house for kids the first Saturday of every month. He stood at the door and charged twenty-five cents, which got them a can of soda and a bag of popcorn. Although he constantly promised to get some new movies, he showed *Cinema Paradiso* so often some kids had seen it ten or twelve times. Augie always made a little speech before Joey popped the movie into the VCR. He told the kids the whole idea—the movie, the neighborhood hangout, the company of friends—was to teach them what the world used to be like and what it could be again. Then he watched the movie with the kids—he said they were the kids he and Angela never had—and tears filled his eyes every time the old man died.

Joey finished up in the shower and walked naked from the bathroom to the pantry closet, tracking wet footprints across the rust-colored linoleum in the kitchen. He put on a pair of boxers, an undershirt, and black socks, carrying the rest of his clothes, and his Colt nine millimeter and shoulder harness, out to the sofa.

The gun went back to a mob war for control of bookmaking, when both factions were hitting up Joey and other bookies for the weekly street tax. Joey, who had no fear of death, had no fear of the punks who roamed the streets like wanna-be gangsters, either. He had, in fact, written a short story about a man who is pushed too far and begins instantly shooting anyone who gets on his nerves. The kid in the street, car stereo blasting, who tells him to fuck off if he doesn't like it? Boom. The wise-ass who cuts him off and then flips him the bird when Joey blows the horn? Boom. On and on it went, Joey touching on every frustration and every afront to decent people. He sent the story, which he titled "The Loss of Civility in America," to four magazines, two of which didn't respond and one of which sent a note suggesting Joey see somebody about his hostility. The fourth, a drugstore detective magazine, said his story was under consideration for publication.

Joey got the Colt from one of his clients as collateral for a gambling debt. When a beef about the mob's street tax led to a fistfight in front of Pennies from Heaven one night, and the collector reached for his piece, Joey plugged him once in each leg and grazed his ear with a third shot. "You show your ass back here, the next one is between the eyes," Joey had said, standing over his whimpering victim with the gun aimed at his head. A call from Augie took Joey off a hit list, and he had been respected, ever since, as someone not to be fucked with. But he kept the gun anyway, because there were jerkoffs out there who might not know who you were.

Joey, who was right-handed, strapped on the Colt and cinched it under his left breast, the nose pointing into his arm-pit. He pulled the blue-and-gold sweater over it and sat on the sofa to tie his shoes. On the wall behind him was a framed cam-paign poster. Augie in his thirties, handsome, and fully aware, by the look in his eye, of how easy it all would be.

Joey's earliest memory of Augie went back to when he was twelve or so, sitting through a dinner table argument between his mother and father, a French-bread-truck driver who'd just been laid off. It was the first and last time Joey was afraid. His mother, in tears, was pleading with his father, a quiet, proud, and stubborn man, to go see Councilman Augie Sangiamino be-fore the family starved to death. Finally, the old man agreed, and like it was yesterday, Joey remembered his father coming home and calling everyone into the kitchen. He pulled a dark blazer out of a garment bag, put it on, and told them they were looking at the newest employee of the court of common pleas.

Augie had sized up Joey's father as a decent and dependable man, asked him who he had voted for, and made a call to a judge who owed him a favor. Just like that, Joey Tartaglione's father was a court crier. He'd have vacations, health benefits, and four-teen paid holidays including Flag Day and election day. From that day through his early adulthood, Joey froze when he heard Augie's name or saw him on television. Augie had turned misery to joy in this one little house, which was Joey's world. His parents talked about taking a vacation down the shore in Wildwood, like other families in the neighborhood, and it became their annual retreat. And not once did Joey walk along that boardwalk on a summer night, drunk on the warm salt air, without silently thanking Augie Sangiamino for the privilege. Years later, when he announced he was going to work for Augie as soon as the senator got out of prison, his mother cried and his father hugged him. To celebrate, they went to the Melrose Diner and then to the racetrack.

When Augie got the call from Liberty Oil, it sounded important enough—curious enough, anyway—to cancel the morning routine of mass, market, and Milly's. Augie suggested they meet at the bocce courts next to the lake in Roosevelt Park. He said he liked feeding the ducks, and told Richard Abbington to bring some bread. Joey picked Augie up at 7:15 and Augie said his good morning, but he took a longer time than usual coming down the stairs and his face was flat, his eyes empty. They got out to Broad Street and turned south before Augie said anything.

"You see it, Joey?"

"Yeah. I seen it."

"How bad was it, do you think?"

"It wasn't too bad."

"It was bad, Joey. Am I right?"

"Nah. It didn't look too bad." What could Joey say? Debra Sharperson and Ron Rice both had new ads on TV last night featuring clips from the basketball game. The Fifth Amendments looked like morons.

"Fuckin' Bonguisto," Augie said. "I offered him a few bucks to bury that thing, too. The prick."

Izzy was on the edge of things, sort of shadowboxing, FIFTH AMENDMENTS stamped across his chest. A male voice-over said: "Meet Izzy Weiner, candidate for state supreme court. Here, Izzy gets together with an ex-convict and various other friends, colleagues, and advisers for an evening of policy making, leadership training, and general goodwill. And you thought things couldn't get any worse on the state supreme court? On November fifth, do your part to put the Democratic Party machine where it belongs. In the hall of shame. Paid for by Citizens for Reform and Friends of Debra Sharperson."

Rice's ad was slicker, in Joey's opinion. The former ball-player in a sharp suit out at the Vet, the bronze sculpture of the football players behind him. Joey caught the ad four times, and by the last time, he was reciting along with Rice. "This year in the South Philadelphia district I call home, there's a clear difference for voters," Rice said, strolling past the statue. "It's as clear as the difference between amateurs and pros."

The next image on the screen was Ham, in an alcoholic daze, in his Fifth Amendments basketball uniform. The skinny legs, paunch, gold jewelry. The Hush Puppies. Ham then dissolved, replaced by a considerably brighter image. An Eagles highlight clip showed quarterback Ron Jaworski dropping back to pass, looking, looking, and throwing over the middle to Rice, who ran like a gazelle. The clip faded, giving way to what looked like a bad night at the Russian circus. The Fifth Amendments' brawl again, Ham in a headlock, toupee akimbo. Then back to Rice once more, hauling in a touchdown pass to the roar of the crowd. "For a whole new game," Rice said in a voice-over, "vote for me on November fifth. Working together, I know we can score for Philadelphia."

Broad Street was clear at this hour except for delivery trucks, and Joey sailed through the commercial heart of South Philadelphia. Augie waved as they passed a line of people in front of a doughnut shop waiting to catch a bus to Atlantic City for the day, but it was a halfhearted gesture and no one returned it.

Joey peeked over at him as they passed Oregon, Veterans Stadium coming up on the left and the park on the right, and Augie looked like he was still replaying the ads in his mind. Then, suddenly, he dropped his head back and closed his eyes. "I'm fuckin' drownin' here, Joey. Thank God for this beak, 'cause that's all I got above water." When he opened his eyes, he said, "Izzy, he was a long shot any way you sliced it. But I got Ham, won't get off his ass, losing to this black Sambo on my own fuckin' turf. My turf, Joey. You understand what I'm saying?"

There wasn't much Joey could say. Their prospects looked grimmer every day. But with Liberty Oil calling, who could say what might happen? "You know it better than anyone, Senator," Joey said. "These polls don't mean a thing. You show me one person ever got called for one of those things, I'll buy him dinner."

Augie brightened up a bit with that. "They did call me once, years ago," he said.

"What'd you tell them?"

"I told them they better call me back a hundred times, because that's how many votes I was good for. Put that in your fuckin' poll."

Joey turned right on Pattison, just beyond the shuttered Naval Hospital, and cut left into Roosevelt Park, a three-hundred-acre plot with a golf course and lake. The park was designed by the same man who planned New York's Central Park, and Roosevelt clearly was not the gentleman's best work. Swedish fur traders had settled in the area in the 1600s, after the Dutch and before the English and Irish Quakers, each European group pushing the Leni-Lenape Indians farther from their homes along the banks of the Delaware and Schuylkill. The American Swedish Historical Museum was in the park, and Augie had tried unsuccessfully while in the legislature to have the property turned over to the High Rollers Bocce Federation, arguing that he seldom saw Swedes in the park, or anywhere in South Philadelphia for that matter, but Italian Americans were everywhere.

"That's gotta be him," Augie said as Joey circled the lake. Clouds of white exhaust curled up from a black Lexus parked in the picnic area by the bocce courts. Joey drove through the clouds and pulled in next to the Lexus, and the driver was out of the car and standing at Joey's window before the Oldsmobile came to a stop.

"Richard Abbington," he said, sticking his hand in when Joey opened the window. Abbington leaned down and looked past Joey. "And there's Mr. Sangiamino," he said. "Nice car you boys've got here. I had a fifty-three Chevy when I was in high school."

Joey got out and buttoned his overcoat, and Augie was blowing on his hands when he came around the car. The sky was low and gray and this was the first good chill of the season, a month or so ahead of schedule. Abbington, wearing a camel hair overcoat, was asking Augie if he remembered him from Harrisburg or Washington. He did some lobbying for the oil industry and a few other people.

"I meet a lot of people," Augie said.

Abbington, who was about the same height as Augie and had a small, boyish face—peach fuzz and all—didn't look like any lobbyist Joey had ever seen. Those guys were under your feet and over your shoulder and gone, coming through doors that didn't exist and disappearing the same way. Abbington had a little bit of show in him—the snazzy coat, Italian loafers, his hair slicked back. He looked like he didn't know how to go invisible.

Abbington looked at the bocce courts, sixteen of them corralled by a waist-high chain-link fence, with picnic tables off to one side. The sign on the concession stand said HIGH ROLLERS BOCCE FEDERATION, and under it, in smaller letters, SEN. AUGIE SANGIAMINO, FOUNDER. "I was having a look at the facility before you got here," he said. "I've never played, but I hear it's a good time."

"You oughta come out, give it a shot," Augie said. "Maybe win a few bucks."

Abbington smiled and said, "What have you got, bowling for dollars here?"

"We've been known to lay a wager," Augie said. "That's one hundred percent crushed imported seashells on those courts, by the way. From Sicily, by boat."

"That's got to cost."

"That's the thing," Augie said. "We could always use a little help down here. Matter of fact, we lost a few bucks three weeks ago when you had that little sneeze at your place and sprayed silicone all over us down here. That thing put the kibosh on a tournament we had going, teams in here from five states up and down the coast." They were standing between the two cars and Augie put his hands on the hood of the Oldsmobile to warm them. Joey watched as the boss then looked in the direction of Mercer, the small town just south of the city. Joey had never noticed, but Liberty's smokestacks were visible from here, dark spikes stabbing the clouds.

"That's one of the things I wanted to discuss with you," Abbington said. "You know what? One of our guys fucked up. There's no way around it. You try to hire the best people, but every once in a while, some loafer slips through. You know what I mean?" Augie nodded. "Anyhow, we'd like to cover any losses. But beyond that, because we consider ourselves a member of the community, we wondered if there was anything else we could do for you here."

Augie looked at the courts and at the shack that served as an equipment room and concession stand. Joey's eye stayed on Abbington, who had his hands in his pockets. It struck Joey that the camel hair coat was bulky and heavy. The perfect place to hang a wire.

"What did you have in mind?" Augie asked, turning back to Abbington. Joey wanted to go over and nudge the senator, remind him they couldn't trust this guy yet.

"I don't know," Abbington said, taking in the layout again. "A set of bleachers, some landscaping, more courts. Whatever you think serves your people. We've built ball fields and parks on both sides of the company's property, and it's inappropriate that we've neglected this area until now."

If Joey was reading it right, there was caution in Augie's eyes. "Constituent service," Augie said. "All my life, that's what I been doing."

"In some ways, Mr. Sangiamino, I think we have some of the same interests. I've followed your career from the time I was starting out in Delaware County, so I know your whole thing is to be there for the little man."

Augie nodded and took a step toward the lake, asking Abbington if he'd brought any duck food. No, he said. He forgot. Joey grabbed the loaf out of the Oldsmobile and the three of them walked over to the asphalt path that circled the lake. Two joggers were doing laps, but there was nobody else in sight except a few golfers in the distance. A half dozen ducks had spotted them from across the lake and were paddling over. Augie stepped down to the water's edge—this was where he used to lay bets on the ducks—and threw in one piece after another to a symphony of quacking and flapping. He went through the entire loaf in less than a minute, tearing and throwing.

"It looks like you really enjoy watching them eat," Abbington said.

"No," Augie said. "I enjoy watching them fight."

Abbington started to laugh and then cut it short when he realized Augie wasn't joking. They made small talk as they moved around the lake, Joey trailing close enough to hear everything. Augie talked about growing up in South Philadelphia, the kind of place it was before the coloreds and Orientals came in. Abbington said a few things about the pressures of running a big business in the global market. Mr. Pritchard's goal was to keep it strong, he said, because that meant job security for hundreds of employees, a lot of whom lived in South Philadelphia.

Joey took in Abbington's greased hair and studied the way he carried himself. He hadn't met any executives from oil companies, but he never would have guessed they'd walk with a swagger like this. One thing he was sure of, though. Abbington was no cop. He was too much of a fag.

They were almost back to the car when Abbington said, "Mr. Sangiamino, can I be perfectly frank with you?"

Here we go, Joey thought. Now they'd see what this was all about. He was more relaxed now because Augie was as smooth as ever. He hadn't put too much of himself out there, and he wasn't going to commit to anything until they knew more about Abbington. This meeting smelled a little too much like Mike Muldoon, frankly. Put a wire on this butt-fuck and send him out here to set them up.

"Can you be frank?" Augie asked, chuckling at the question. "Mr. Abbington, I didn't come here to have you lie to me."

They kept walking, but slower now. Abbington said, "We've been looking to back up our commitment to the community by getting behind the right candidates in this election." Joey, trembling, blew on his hands and accidentally whistled. "People who share our views, frankly, about promoting business instead of putting our balls in a vise every chance they get. We're thinking more and more that Izzy Weiner and Ham Flaherty might be just the men we're talking about, depending on their views, of course, about some of these things."

Their views? Joey thought. They had one view. That they needed a shitload of money in a hurry or they were through.

"But if this is something that works out," Abbington went on, "we would get involved behind them in a way that everybody's happy with. Not raise a problem for you or for us."

If Augie wanted to jump out of his shoes, he gave no hint of it. He was all business, head down in careful contemplation. A pro. He asked, "How involved you intend to get?"

Abbington looked down and pointed at the ground. "Right here, where we stand, we're on top of oil," he said. "Five years ago we come in and buy these storage tanks from another refinery, and six months later we find out they leak like sieves. The oil is sloshing around down there day and night, Mr.

Sangiamino. South Philadelphia floats on an oil slick. And the courts tell us the cleanup is our responsibility."

Joey stared down, wondering if it was possible that the ground could open up and they'd all get sucked down there, drown in a pool of grease. What a horrible way to go.

"All we're looking for is somebody with a sense of fair play when these things come up, whether it's an underground situation or something in the air," Abbington said. "Somebody who understands the kind of regulatory harassment we deal with every day, which makes it difficult to stay in business and keep people in jobs. That's somebody we'd put a lot of weight behind."

Joey had to admit that Abbington had some polish. Knowing how to say things without saying them was essential in this business, and he wasn't bad at it. Augie said, "I like the sound of it," and then he paused. "But I don't know."

Perfect, Joey thought. Perfect.

"You want to give it some consideration?" Abbington asked.

Augie looked out on the lake, where one duck was chasing after another. "What I'm thinking," he said, "we got a ways to go to catch up, and not that much time left. What is it, five, six weeks now? This is a situation where Debra Sharperson spends maybe a million dollars, Ron Rice goes a couple hundred thousand."

Joey could tell he was trying to nail down whether Abbington realized how expensive, and risky, this could get. There wasn't enough time left in the election for Liberty Oil to legally pump that much cash into the campaigns. Some of it would have to be laundered. And if Abbington wasn't talking about a sizable chunk of dough, what was the point of the risk?

Abbington grabbed Augie's arm and they both stopped. Abbington said, "We've got a few dollars to play with, Mr. Sangiamino."

It was all in the look. Opportunity was in there, and risk, too. Augie Sangiamino, in his bones and in his soul, was a junkie for both. Ten years out of the loop, Joey was thinking, and now this. Liberty Oil wasn't some nickel-and-dime outfit. It was huge.

They walked back to the car, and Augie, still handling it as if so many corporate executives threw money at him he was bored by it, told Abbington he'd sleep on it. Joey opened the door for him and Augie was almost in when he thought of something and popped back out. "I don't know how closely you've followed the campaign," he said to Abbington, who walked over toward him. "But neither one of my guys has been out there like the others, busting your chops for this little mix-up three weeks ago. You won't see Izzy Weiner or Ham Flaherty doing a grave dance with this cancer scare that's got everybody hopped up."

It was true, too, though not by design. Ham had never gotten off his ass like Augie had been telling him to, and Izzy had been campaigning out in the western part of the state—Pittsburgh, Johnstown, Erie. Abbington, a half smile on him that wasn't a smile at all, said yes, they'd noticed.

"Some of these fuckin' politicians today, they'd exploit their own mother for a vote," Augie said, shaking his head. "A difference in style is what we offer here."

"Well I'll tell you what, Mr. Sangiamino. I know you're a very busy man. Why don't you have someone on your staff get in touch with me and we can work out the details without pulling you away from your schedule."

Abbington handed Augie a card and Augie gave it to Joey. "This is my staff," he said.

Joey's hands were trembling again. From where he stood, as the man who'd have to figure out how to wash the money, he saw more risk than opportunity, and he wasn't the gambler Augie was. But this might be the only shot they had.

Augie watched Abbington's Lexus pull out and he followed it north toward the Center City skyline. It caught a flash of sunlight that had broken through the haze, and before it disappeared, Augie said, "Look at that thing move, Joey. Smooth, ain't it?" When he turned to Joey his eyes were lit from inside and he wasn't an old man anymore. Augie had talked about the past so much, it had come and taken him back. "Run a check on this fuckin' weasel," he said, gazing at the spot where Abbington's car had disappeared. "You never can be too careful, Joey. But if this putz is for real, we just hit a gusher."

CHAPTER 12

MULDOON'S FIRST JOB as an FBI agent was a bank heist at a small branch in Maple Shade, New Jersey, on Halloween. The doer came in early in the day wearing a rabbit suit, gun drawn, no customers in the place. He ordered the manager and three tellers to strip naked, then handcuffed two tellers to the manager and had the third teller clean out the tills. Before leaving, he threw their clothes into a pile, poured lighter fluid on them, and set them ablaze. One teller, a petite, fragile, and attractive young woman from Cherry Hill, New Jersey, broke down while going back over it, and Muldoon promised that if it was the last thing he did as a soldier of the United States government, he'd bring the perpetrator to justice.

Muldoon worked day and night, sometimes cloistered in the office long after the other agents had gone home. When he made the arrest a month later, after another bank job in which the robber came in eating a carrot, Muldoon drove back to the bank in Maple Shade and took the teller out to lunch at Olga's Diner. Six months later, they were married.

Looking back over a quarter of a century, it was hard to say when things might have changed in the marriage, because there weren't really any highs or lows. Maybe it hadn't changed at all. Maybe this was the way it always had been and Muldoon had never noticed how flat it was. Flat like that little line on a heart monitor when a patient goes.

Lisa Savitch had made him notice. She wasn't just beautiful; she was difficult. Muldoon always thought he liked easy, but that was until difficult came along with her little turned-up lip and her little thin waist, those legs, the sad brown eyes, and a comment for everything.

Muldoon was coming out of the shower when his wife called from the kitchen. "You don't want pancakes?"

"Not today," he yelled back. "I have an early meeting."

"You getting any closer on this one?" she asked, the tone of someone who didn't expect an answer.

She did this all the time, talking to him from other parts of the house, and he had never given it much thought. It was one of those patterns you get into and maybe you don't like it, but there it is. You end up living with things you don't like. Accepting them as part of a contract you never really read. Then one day you wake up and read the fine print. Right now, going to the den to get his jacket, it was annoying the hell out of him. "I can't hear you," he whined back.

"I said are you getting close with this case?" She was probably watching one of the morning talk shows Muldoon hated. He couldn't even be in the same room with her when she watched those idiots. Especially the two who yammered on about nothing every day, the guy thinking he was in vaudeville or something. Yadda yadda yadda.

"It's going to be a while," he called back.

His jacket was in a closet off the den, near the door to the garage. This was the room where Muldoon spent most of his time when he wasn't playing golf. Plaid sofa, matching easy chair, paneling, a deep pile carpet, sports magazines in a rack next to the easy chair. Muldoon's slippers next to the rack. A man's room except that everything was neat and organized. The magazines arranged by the month.

The walls were decorated with sports trinkets—a pennant

and framed Phillies ticket from a 1980 World Series game—and FBI commendations. On the mantel was a silver cup the other agents gave him as a going-away present. The name of every public official he'd ever arrested was engraved on it, and when Muldoon decided to go to work for Kevinne McGinns, he turned the cup so Augie Sangiamino's name was facing out.

"Be careful," he called to his wife. He always told her that, as if her job at a department store in the Cherry Hill Mall exposed her to some great risk. He'd talked her out of the bank job when they were first married.

"All right," she said. "I'll put something together for dinner."

Muldoon backed his Ford Bronco out of the two-car garage and sped through the Squirrel Run development, not realizing he was going faster than he normally did. He took Route 38 past the mall and onto the Ben Franklin Bridge, the Philadelphia skyline opening up ahead. He thought about Lisa Savitch the entire way.

Muldoon read people, that was part of his training, and Savitch wasn't as tough as she pretended to be. There was something softer under that, something that showed itself now and then, like when she told him about the guy in Boston or about her brother and the boy she used to baby-sit. This was somebody who was reaching out, alone in a new city. A hundred guys in Philadelphia wished they knew her, and he was the only one who did. He knew her better than the others, anyway.

She'd left a message for him last night while he was out with his wife for her birthday, taking her to Red Lobster and giving her a gift certificate from the store she worked at. Come by her place Saturday morning, Savitch said. They had to talk. About what, she didn't say. She just asked him to pick up something for breakfast if he didn't mind. Muldoon had fallen asleep with the message playing over and over in his head, his back to his wife.

One time he almost did it. One time maybe six, seven years

ago. A secretary in the office had been flirting with him and he started flirting back. Innocent stuff. Like asking if she wouldn't rather go to the movies with him than with her boyfriend, if she had one, which she had to have had because she was young and single and nice looking. Not a movie star or anything—actually kind of plain, to be honest—but pleasant looking enough, and interested in him, Mike Muldoon. Wouldn't she rather go down the shore with him? Wouldn't she rather go to lunch with him? One day Muldoon's worst fear materialized. She said yes.

There they were, Muldoon sitting across from her in the Olde City Tavern, scared to death someone would see him. He was turning red and then he spilled a soft drink in his lap, making the red redder, but it only made her come on stronger. She thought it was cute that he was nervous around her. She asked if he wanted to go dancing with her one night after work and Muldoon said yeah, sure. Maybe. But he didn't dance. He hated to dance, as a matter of fact, and he suddenly realized this wasn't going to work. So that was where his one affair ended. With Muldoon hurrying through lunch and letting her pay half when the bill came, so she didn't get the wrong idea.

Muldoon found a meter with some time on it at Twentieth and Locust. Breakfast, Savitch had said. Get something for breakfast. Outside of chain-smoking and guzzling coffee, Savitch must have a fairly healthy diet, looking the way she looked. That left out the only three things Muldoon ever ate for breakfast: bacon and eggs, pancakes slathered with butter and syrup, and jelly doughnuts.

He was headed to a bakery he knew of on Nineteenth when he saw a sign across the street: FBI. He walked up to the door.

Fairmount Bagel Institute.

"Son of a bitch," he muttered. Certain symbols and institutions were sacred, as far as Muldoon was concerned, and shouldn't be commercialized or trivialized. But bagels were supposed to be good for you. The smell of fresh bread and coffee was trapped inside the small diner, tables squeezed in close to each other. Most of the customers appeared to be Savitch's age or younger. They sat reading books and newspapers and Muldoon imagined her in the corner with a cup of coffee, a cigarette, and a pile of news clippings on factory emissions, blind to the men ogling her. It struck him that only six or seven years ago, when he was pushing fifty, Savitch was in college.

Muldoon ordered a half dozen bagels. Two plain, two raisin cinnamon, two onion. Then he pondered the cream cheese selection through the glass display case. "Can you get a little bit of several?" he asked.

"No," said a ponytailed male clerk with three rings in one ear and a fourth in his nose. "It's against the law."

Muldoon looked up from the case and locked onto the clerk. He'd like to remove the kid's earrings with pliers, but he restrained himself. He took one plain, one strawberry, one rum raisin, and walked through Rittenhouse Square thinking there had to be a combination in there Lisa Savitch would like. She had him frazzled, he had to admit. Here he was rethinking his marriage and wondering if this case—Augie Sangiamino and his gang—was no good or if Savitch was just too much of a distraction for him to really concentrate. Savitch had been spending more and more time looking into the leukemia stuff, and Muldoon wanted to cover for her by getting a break on the hacks. Prove himself to her. But every day was another strikeout.

Rittenhouse Square was an upscale part of Center City West. A lot of chichi shops and restaurants built around an elegant little park, European in scale and design, high-rise apartments surrounding it. Savitch's building was on Eighteenth, the east side of the square, and Muldoon was cutting in that direction when he heard a rustling in the bushes and moved toward the sound. This was a good neighborhood, statistically safe. But it was still the middle of the city, and the park attracted various psychos, sociopaths, and derelicts. Muldoon peered over a row of shrubs and his blood boiled into his face and head. A park resident was relieving himself.

What had always set Muldoon apart from other FBI agents
was emotion. FBI work was science, and you weren't supposed
to let emotion enter into it. But Muldoon couldn't help it. Sometimes that had worked against him, but usually not. There were
times when he didn't think, he just acted. Like now. Muldoon
rushed the bewildered man, a raggedy urban camper, and grabbed
him by the collar. Muldoon had chased gangsters, bank robbers,
and crooked politicians, but nothing steamed him more than
disregard for public property and basic decency. If people were
allowed to use parks as their own personal toilets, you might as
well give up the whole war for civility, because it was lost right
there.

"Get off me," the bum protested, trying to spin away.
"What're you, some kind of pervert?"

Muldoon held on, but his bag went flying, bagels rolling under the bushes and cream-cheese containers sliding after them
like hockey pucks. "You son of a bitch," Muldoon growled as
teams of squirrels raced for the bagels. "Look at this." He identified himself as a special agent and the man, who had religious
stories from magazines and newspapers pinned on his clothing,
asked what he had done wrong.

"Public urination," Muldoon said flatly.

"I'm being arrested by the FBI for pissing on a bush? Why
not tack on the Kennedy assassination and we'll both feel better
about ourselves?"

"Pick up the trash and keep your mouth shut," Muldoon
ordered. He led the man to the police gazebo in the middle of
the park, identified himself, and told the officer to call for a unit.

"What's the crime?" the officer asked.

"Public urination," Muldoon said. "I want him locked up."

The police officer seemed as bewildered as the park resident.
Muldoon pulled his notepad out of his breast pocket and wrote
down both their names before leaving. "The Garden of Eden had
no toilets," the man called after him. "Was public urination the
original sin?"

"Fucking nutcase," Muldoon mumbled as he headed back to the FBI, where the same clerk greeted him. "You've come to turn yourself in for ordering more than one cream cheese?"

This was why he'd never live in the city. Between the bums and the freaks, nobody had any respect for anything. Muldoon spoke through his teeth. "I want the same thing I just got."

"What happened?"

"I had to arrest someone and I lost my bagels."

"Arrest someone for what?"

"For asking too many questions. Can you hurry it up, pony boy?"

Lisa Savitch lived on the seventh floor of the Rittenhouse Regency, a stately high-rise made of brick the color of autumn. Muldoon flashed a badge at the doorman and took the elevator up, ringing Savitch's bell three times before he heard a sound inside. She answered the door in a white terry-cloth bathrobe, hair mussed, eyes half open.

"I don't believe it," she said, rubbing her eyes. "I overslept."

"That's nice," Muldoon said. "How about if I just stand here in the hall while you wake up?"

"I'm sorry. Come on in."

She led him to the kitchen, a small space with brand-new appliances, everything white and shiny. It almost looked unlived in. Nothing in the room said anything about her except the ashtray filled with half-smoked butts and the Chinese take-out cartons on the counter. Past the kitchen, Muldoon saw unpacked boxes in what would be the dining room if it had any furniture in it. If someone walked in here who didn't know, they wouldn't be able to tell if she was moving in or moving out, and Muldoon wondered if Savitch knew herself.

Muldoon walked into the living room, where she at least had a sofa and chair. A picture window looked out on Rittenhouse Square and to the high-rises across the way. "My God," he said.

"This is a great view." Savitch popped around through the dining room. "Yeah, I love it. That's what sold me on this place." Muldoon looked down to see if the police had sent a unit to pick up the guy he just collared, but the guard shack was obscured by the trees. They went back into the kitchen, where Savitch put on some coffee and apologized some more.

"Don't worry about it," Muldoon said, watching her reach up into the cupboard, the curve of her calf muscles flexing. The flap of the robe fell open slightly, revealing one leg just above the knee. Her tan was even, all the way up there, and dark against the soft white of the robe. Maybe it wasn't a tan. Maybe that was how she was. She'd said her grandparents moved to Boston from a village on the Adriatic Sea.

"I was up half the night with the case," Savitch said, setting a cup in front of him on the small butcher-block table. "Mc-Ginns is in a state. Let me take a quick shower and I'll tell you about it."

She peeked inside the bag first.

"Strawberry. You got my favorite, Muldoon. Don't you love that place?"

Muldoon nodded as if he were a regular. "The name's a little too cute," he said.

"Well try to get over it. I'll be out in a minute."

As he watched her disappear around the corner, the detective in Muldoon went to work. Did she really oversleep? She calls him over to her place, rather mysteriously. She opens the door in a robe, probably nothing on underneath. And now she goes into the bedroom. Was he slow on the uptake?

All Muldoon's friends—most of them agents or former agents—had more women than he did before they were married, and they had affairs while they were married. At least that's what they said. Muldoon never thought he was capable of an affair because it was dishonest. This was where the Catholic training twisted you around. Hell, it was against one of the Ten Commandments. But did he want to be one of those people who lie on their deathbed and think back on all the shots they never had the courage to take?

Muldoon got up, took one step after Savitch, then stopped and listened. Was she waiting for him? He felt like a teenager. The problem was he was thinking too much. In half a century, he'd never let thinking get in the way of anything and he'd done all right for himself. Muldoon took another step and then another, off the kitchen tile and onto the carpet in the hall that led to Savitch's bedroom. Not thinking, just doing. It felt good, too, but at the very moment when he knew he'd broken free of something, he stopped dead. Muldoon held his breath for a few seconds before tiptoeing back to the kitchen. He sat down like he'd been hit, his brain numb, his heart beating in his ears.

Savitch lit a cigarette and squinted through the smoke as she spread the strawberry cream cheese thick on her bagel. Drops of water fell off the ends of her hair onto a white T-shirt. "You get anything in Atlantic City?" she asked.

He shook his head no. She had a look like, What else is new?

"So McGinns calls me in yesterday after you left," she said. "It's the second time I've had to cancel an appointment with the professor from Temple, and she's doing this thing again, watching the cats and the birds like it's National Geographic. So I'm thinking all right, what is it this time? I'm assuming she's decided what she wants to do with Carla Delmonico, but then she asks if I'm devoting any time at all to this case. I said, 'Excuse me?' She says she hears I spend all my time looking into Liberty Oil and the leukemia."

Muldoon was shaking his head. "I didn't say a word. Honest."

"Whatever. Somebody did. Then she asks if I've been following the election."

Muldoon had spread cream cheese on both sides of the bagel and put it back together like a sandwich. He was having trouble getting the whole thing into his mouth.

"I asked what she meant and she tells me Ham Flaherty is suddenly all over TV, he's got posters everywhere, and people are standing on corners in Center City passing out buttons. He's cut Ron Rice's lead in half."

Muldoon wiped cream cheese off the corner of his mouth. "We know all this. What's her point?"

"That he's struck it rich somehow, and she wants to know what we have on it and what we're planning to do. Same with Izzy Weiner. The money has to be dirty, she says. Follow the stink, and it'll take you to Augie Sangiamino. That's why I called you over. She wants us both in her office first thing Monday morning, telling her exactly how we plan to proceed and when we plan to call the grand jury back in."

"What did you tell her?"

"You know what I wanted to tell her?"

Muldoon chewed and swallowed. "I could make a pretty good guess."

"That I want off the case."

He put down the bagel. "You don't want to do that," he said, maybe a little too emphatically.

"Of course I do. I'd like nothing more. Why would you say that?"

Muldoon took another bite so he'd have time to think up an answer. "What I meant was I think she'd hold it against you. She could bury you, too. Put you in domestic relations or something. Arraignments. So what did you tell her?"

"That we're still looking for an Atlantic City connection, but it's coming up dry, probably because of the reports that walked out of here with Carla. And she has this look on her face, like she couldn't care less about my problems. She shows me the calendar again and points to the date, as if I don't know the election is less than a month away. Bitch."

Muldoon watched Savitch sag back on the chair and cross her arms. Her face looked smaller with her hair wet, and she didn't look as pretty, but she looked sexier. He could smell her hair from across the table. Smell the wetness of it.

"I almost told her, Look, we've already got Ham for this stunt with Carla Delmonico. We've got the damn thing on tape. Conspiracy. Theft. Obstruction of justice. We could charge now, ruin his campaign, and then I'm out of this nightmare."

Muldoon shook his head. "You know she wants more than that. She wants a roundup. Big headlines. Besides, if you indict Ham for infiltrating the DA's office, stealing everything we have on him, it's not the most flattering look at her administration."

Savitch took a bagel out of the bag, stood up, and flung it against the wall. Muldoon got sprayed with water that flew off her hair. "This is exactly what I'm talking about," she said, falling back down and sucking so hard on a cigarette it creased her cheeks. "I'm not interested in Kevinne McGinns's image or her political career. I'm begging you, Muldoon. Get me off this case and I'll be indebted forever. There's got to be someone else you can lean on to find out where these guys are getting all this money. Who in their right mind would give them a nickel when they're not even expected to win? It doesn't make sense."

Muldoon couldn't take his eyes off her. How was he supposed to concentrate? "I did have an idea with Carla," he said, trying to organize his thoughts. "What's the deal, is she still out sick?"

"Supposed to come back tomorrow. She still doesn't know that we're on to her."

"I had two ideas, actually. First, we could fake a memo saying the investigation is off and make sure it falls into her hands. She feeds it to Ham and the boys, and maybe they get sloppy because they think we've gone away. The other one is we call her in, tell her about the tape and explain how much trouble she's in if she doesn't cooperate, and have her wear a wire."

"This I like," Savitch said.

"The first or the second?"

"The second. It'll be quicker."

"We could have her go see Ham and Augie Sangiamino, too. Try to bring them out a little."

"The only problem is hiding the wire," Savitch said. "The cleavage is out for sure. Come to think of it, you'd have to surgically implant it somewhere."

"Let's see what McGinns says. In the meantime, I'll go to work on Pennies from Heaven. That's a front they use to launder money through bingo. They also have a bocce club that handles some money, and then there's this bank in South Philadelphia where some of Sangiamino's meatball pals are on the board. That's where the campaign accounts are. I could try a couple guys, see what they know, but I don't think we want to go in there waving search warrants yet."

"You said Pennies from Heaven?"

"Yeah. I could never nail it down, but they had a scam going with a few of the labor unions. Let's say the iron workers offer life insurance to their guys through Pennies from Heaven, telling the rank and file it runs fifty dollars a month when it's really only thirty-five. Sangiamino and the union boss split the difference, which gets multiplied by thousands of union members. They had another stunt with two or three nursing homes, where they had the estates paying membership dues even after the patient was dead. Like pennies from heaven. Get it?"

"What happened to the case?"

"Nobody sees nothing, nobody hears nothing, nobody knows nothing. Back when they were younger, they had a boxer who went around breaking noses, and they put the fear of God in people. So nobody talks even to this day. The other problem is they're not geniuses, but they aren't stupid enough to put money in checking accounts or make cash deposits of more than twenty-five hundred dollars, because they know the bank has to report them. Here you are, trying to follow a paper trail with these guys, and they've got cash in mattresses and coffee cans. They're also very good with the campaign disclosure forms.

Every time they fill one out, it's a creative writing assignment. These guys could all be writing novels if they wanted to."

Savitch snuffed her cigarette and immediately started another, but Muldoon could see the edge was gone now. He went back to his bagel, wondering if she had any more faith in him now that he'd at least thrown out a few ideas. He had to get over the fact that he was working with someone he wanted to jump and start concentrating on the case. Maybe he'd get going on some of this stuff over the weekend. Show her what he was capable of.

"Even if none of this checks out," he said, "it buys us some time with McGinns, and something will break later on. There's always a weak link with these guys. Somebody who's on probation and gets nervous, or some moron of a bagman. You find out who that is, bring him in and muscle him, and the whole thing comes down like a house of cards. Trust me."

He was fixing another bagel when the doorbell rang. Savitch asked, "Who the hell could that be?" as she went for the door. Muldoon heard a man's hello, but nothing from Savitch. He couldn't see them from where he sat. The man said something else, Muldoon couldn't make it out, and then Savitch said, "What the fuck do you want?" in a tone he hadn't heard out of her. He got up and moved to where he could see a loafer in the door. He took another step and knew instantly that it was the asshole from Boston.

He was about six feet tall, athletic. Very good-looking, like out of a fashion magazine or something. Muldoon didn't like the expression on his face. He was someone who knew he looked pretty good and figured that made it OK for him to be a jerk. Look at this. No consideration for whatever situation he might have walked in on. But it wasn't Muldoon's business and he retreated to the kitchen, rattled because of what this guy had done, but also because he'd had Lisa Savitch.

The ex said, "I didn't figure you for this fast a recovery. This guy's a little old for you, though, don't you think?"

Muldoon bolted up and went back to the door.

"Mike," Savitch said, "would you mind stepping into the living room for a second? I'll be right with you." Muldoon didn't move. He kept his eyes on the ex a few seconds longer, then did what she asked. He tried listening from the living room, but he couldn't make anything out. Not until Savitch's volume picked up as she was warning the ex that if he didn't leave, she'd call security. Muldoon could tell that the guy had wormed his way into the kitchen. "Everything all right?" he called out. When she didn't answer, he went in to check on her.

"Look, pal," the ex said, "this is between us, so if you could just go back in there and smoke a pipe or take a nap or something."

Muldoon smiled at him. A cool, pitying smile. The stupid prick.

"Alan, listen to me," Savitch said. "I didn't ask you here and I'd prefer to never see you again. So I don't care that you drove all night. Now you can drive all day and go the fuck home."

The ex sat down at the table and took a bite out of the bagel with Savitch's teeth marks in it. "I just want to talk about it," he said.

For someone as combustible as she was, Savitch was strangely composed, Muldoon thought. He remembered feeling her humiliation when she told him the story, and he hoped she wasn't going to fall for anything. This big sleaze had some nerve coming down here like it was no big deal, assuming she'd jump into his arms at the sight of him.

Savitch said, "There's nothing left to talk about," and now Muldoon saw her composure for what it was. This guy had nothing on her anymore. She didn't give a shit about him, and the lug was too dumb to see it.

The ex said, "How about if I meet you later, after your boyfriend here leaves? I'll take you to lunch or something."

Muldoon was beginning to enjoy this. This guy actually thought he was Savitch's boyfriend.

"You have two seconds to leave," Savitch said. "After that, I'm not calling security. I'm calling the police."

When Alan took another bite of the bagel, Muldoon walked over and put a hand on his shoulder. "Is it Alan?" he asked, his voice deep and strong. "I think you better leave, Alan."

"Well I really appreciate your advice, dad, but I'm not leaving until she gives me a chance to explain everything."

In one smooth move, Muldoon had Alan up and off his chair, his face squished against the kitchen wall, and his arm bent halfway up his back. "I'm not asking you," Muldoon said. "I'm going to turn you loose, and when I do, you're going to walk out of here and leave her alone."

The ex turned around, fixing his collar and brushing his hair back into place with his hand. When he thought Muldoon had relaxed, he pulled his arm back, but that was where it stopped. Muldoon's first shot, to the gut, doubled him over. The second caught him under his eye. Then Muldoon grabbed him by the collar and flung him out the door as if he were tossing a dummy. Alan bounced off the wall across the hall and Muldoon watched as he crumpled to the floor.

Savitch was on the phone to the management, telling them if they saw this guy near the building again to call the police. Muldoon made sure the ex got on the elevator and then he went back into the kitchen. "You all right?"

Savitch was leaning against the refrigerator, lighting a cigarette. "Yeah," she said, but her hands were shaking and her brown eyes looked like they were filling up. "I'm fine."

Muldoon watched her blow smoke. Watched the way she held her lips. He wondered if he was right. That she'd let him hold her now if he offered.

CHAPTER 13

JOEY WENT TO THE window and peeked out. No sign of anyone. He pulled the cord tighter on the vertical blinds, squeezing out shafts of light that fell like daggers on the Pennies from Heaven floor. Augie was in the back, by the big-screen TV, tidying up the money in neat stacks on a long and narrow bingo table. "Take a whiff of that," he said as Joey came toward him. "Sweet, ain't it? I fuckin' love that smell."

Augie had made sixty identical stacks of twenty-dollar bills, four hundred dollars in each. He squared up each pile, and when he was done, he said, "Joey, take my hand." Joey didn't particularly want to hold hands with the boss. It wasn't in their daily routine. But things were a little different now with all this money coming in. Augie saw it as a care package from God, and he'd been more spiritual, occasionally even listening to the sermon at morning mass.

Joey wiped sweat off his hand before taking Augie's hand. Augie, in a brand-new cappuccino-colored suit he'd picked up earlier in the day, skimming a little off the top, held his brown fedora over his heart, bowed his head, and began to pray. "Our Father, who art in heaven, halo be thy name. To kingdom come, thy will be done, on earth and also in heaven as well. Give us today our daily bread, and forgive us for trespassing, as we forgive those who trespassed over us. Lead us not in temptation, but deliver us from evil, now and again at the time of our death. And please watch over my Angela. Amen."

It was so much money that when Augie opened his eyes, he felt his chest tighten up and he grabbed the edge of the table for balance.

"Senator, you all right?"

"Jesus, I almost took a heart attack there, Joey. Just a little dizzy is all."

"Sit down, Senator. Let me get you a glass of water."

"I'm fine, Joey. Just a little excited is all. It's a sight, ain't it?"

Joey looked at the money and nodded. "One time I had a neighborhood girl in here, Senator, right there where that money is. A virgin, believe it or not, even though she was seventeen, eighteen. Nobody would go with her because of a little weight problem. And guess what, she's lying there naked, and she didn't look this good."

Augie seemed a bit confused as to the point of the story, but he nodded anyway. "Joey, you know what I need?"

Joey grabbed a box of envelopes off a shelf over by the wall poster of Augie in his thirties. The one with the eyes that saw all of this unfolding.

"There you go," Augie said, dropping the first stack of cash in and licking the envelope. "Help me stuff these cocksuckers, will you? Make a nice little gift pack for our boys." The money would be passed out like candy to ward leaders in the basement of the South Broad Diner. It was flowing now. Flowing like it hadn't since before Augie went away. In the week since the meeting with Richard Abbington, Liberty Oil had pushed all the money it could through legal channels. The political action committee. The city Democratic Party. The state Democratic Party. Now it was coming in under the table with Richard Abbington making daily deliveries to Joey. Liberty Oil, one of the richest companies in the state, was trying to buy its own survival through a regular neighborhood guy who worked from the back of a diner, fielding calls about cracked sidewalks. There was poetry in that, Joey knew. Not that he had the opportunity to use it. Even though he was only catching two or three hours of sleep a night, there was no time for his journal or for old movies. He was burning up his nights working the campaign books. He was the one who had to make it all square up on paper. If you spent twenty thousand dollars on a TV ad, the election commission wanted to know where that money came from. You had to fill out forms, and the task drew on all of Joey's writing skills.

Not that Joey "Numbers" Tartaglione didn't know a few tricks, most of which he'd learned from the master himself. He'd already started passing money through relatives and good friends of the Fifth Amendments. Lou had a big family. Eight brothers and four sisters. And Izzy must have forty cousins, half of them up in the Northeast and the other half down the shore in Ventnor, Margate, and Longport. Emiliano Falcone and the regulars at Milly's were on board, too, and everyone knew the drill. If Muldoon or one of his dobermen came around asking how they happened to come up with a couple thousand dollars to give to Ham Flaherty or Izzy Weiner, they had a big day at the track or they hit one at bingo. It wasn't like you had to get out a blackboard and draw diagrams with these people. But you did have to be careful. The broader the conspiracy, the greater the risks. And you didn't want to cut your own throat, because Mike Muldoon would be there to suck the blood.

Augie looked at his watch. "Joey, I almost forgot. It's six o'clock. We gotta look at TV."

Izzy's first ad was supposed to run during the news.

"What channel?" Joey asked, turning on the big-screen.

"We got it on all three shows at six and eleven."

Joey turned to Channel Nine, where the first story was the last thing Augie wanted to hear. Another kid dead of leukemia. Augie slumped down like he'd been hit in the gut. This one was a seven-year-old. A boy from the town of Mercer, home of the Liberty Oil refinery.

"Jesus, will you look at this?" A photo of the smiling boy filled the screen, taking Augie back to the funeral home, Joey Napolitano's tiny body laid out in the casket, his mother throwing herself at the feet of the schoolchildren.

Joey sat across from Augie and put his head in his hands. Did Liberty Oil have something to do with this? And if so, how long would it be before the FBI, the EPA—somebody—started watching every move Liberty Oil made? Richard Abbington kept saying the whole thing was bullshit. Nobody knows how a person gets leukemia and nobody could ever know. Especially in an area with dozens of factories. You didn't even know it was the factories, first of all. And even if it was, how could you single out one of them?

Joey didn't know what to make of that, but there was one thing he did know. As the speculation grew, Liberty seemed more desperate to buy protection, and they had a hell of a slush fund over there. It was like a drug habit now. The bigger the story got, the more Liberty wanted to give. And the more they did, the more Augie wanted. Joey felt like the designated driver in a car with no brakes.

Augie pushed the front of his hat up higher on his head and watched as the TV anchor said Not in Our Backyard was doubling in size every day. They showed demonstrators blocking entrances to Center City offices of companies listed in the newspaper as the top polluters in the region. Cops were dragging some of the demonstrators away, throwing them into a wagon and carting them off to jail. "It's like the sixties," Augie said. "Back when you had all those hippies runnin' around chaining themselves to trees and whatnot." The report ended with the news that the American Cancer Society and the Leukemia Society of America were sponsoring a conference to address "the causes and implications of the region's disproportionately high disease rates."

When they went to a break, Augie looked across at Joey. "You think they can nail down a thing like that, Joey? It ain't like taking a bullet or getting hit by a truck, as far as how somebody dies." Joey didn't know what to say. Fortunately, Izzy's ad came on before he had to answer.

"Here we go," Augie said. "Here we go." Izzy was standing in front of the Liberty Bell in his black robe, Independence Hall over his shoulder. Augie said, "Izzy looks good, don't he? He looks like a freakin' scholar and a patriot, the way they got him set up there."

Neither word had come to Joey's mind.

"Hello, I'm Common Pleas Judge Isadore Weiner, and I'm here to tell you that I like the idea of the Eagles and the Steelers trying out a few untested rookies this season."

"The hell's he talkin' about?" Augie muttered, pulling his brim down. He'd had nothing to do with the ad other than to say he wanted to turn Debra Sharperson's academic background into a negative. The marketing outfit from Harrisburg had put the thing together.

"And when I got my house painted recently, I didn't mind hiring the College Pros and giving a break to a few young students."

Augie could see where it was going now. "That's right," he said. "Tell me about it, Isadore Weiner."

"And at the racetrack, I might take a two-dollar gamble now and then on a young horse that hasn't been tested under pressure."

Augie got up out of his chair. "I fuckin' love this thing," he said. "And right in front of the Liberty Bell and all that other historic stuff. Now we're talkin'."

Izzy, shaking his head, brought his voice down an octave. "But there's one place where I'd never trust someone who's untested and inexperienced."

"Forget about it!" Augie shouted.

"The one place where all citizens, whether they live in a high-rise condo in the city or on a pig farm in the country, should expect the highest level of experience, expertise, and leadership. I'm talking about protecting your interests and upholding your rights at the highest appellate level in the state judiciary, the state supreme court, for which I, Isadore Weiner, am a candidate."

Joey said, "You're right. He don't look this good in person." Augie shushed him.

"I have twenty-five years of solid experience in the courtroom," Izzy said. "Five as a tough-minded prosecutor, five in private practice, fifteen as a judge. And as a judge, I've sent hardened criminals to prison for the maximum allowable terms, and brought quick resolve to complex civil disputes that directly affect you and yours. By contrast, my opponent works in a classroom setting. There, she teaches law. Beginning law."

Izzy picked up the cadence during the next part, just a hint of sarcasm in his voice as he counted on his fingers the problems with Debra Sharperson's candidacy. "She has not been a practicing attorney for over ten years. She has not prosecuted criminals. She has never spent a single day on the bench at any level. Not even traffic court."

Izzy chuckled at the thought of it. Then he said, "Ever hear the saying, Those who can, do. And those who can't, teach?" Izzy shook his head, then looked reflectively at Independence Hall. When he turned back to the camera, he wore a serious, almost sad expression.

"My friends, the Pennsylvania Supreme Court is not a ball game. It is not a home-improvement job. Alas, it is not a horse race. On November fifth, don't gamble on justice. Vote for dependability and the wisdom of experience." Izzy gave a gracious hello to a group of tourists entering the Liberty Bell Pavilion, then looked back at the camera.

"Vote for me, Judge Isadore Weiner, and become a voice for honesty, hard work, and integrity. Thank you."

"Fuckin' A!" Augie bellowed. He took off his hat and flipped it across the Pennies from Heaven clubhouse like a flying saucer, his eyes lit with the glow of the TV.

"You got a bag, Joey, something you can throw that money into?" Joey dropped the envelopes into a St. John Neumann gym bag he'd had since high school.

"I can feel it, Joey. All right, so we got a little problem with Ham, but nothing we can't straighten out. And Izzy's strong with this thing. I want him comin' out of TV sets from York to Erie, Philadelphia to Pittsburgh, I don't care what it costs. One of these pig farmers out in the sticks turns on his TV, I want Izzy climbin' his freakin' rabbit ears. We got a shot now, Joey. We got a shot."

The '56 Oldsmobile was plastered with campaign paraphernalia, grille to trunk, and Joey, propped up on Yellow Pages, did the slow drive through the streets of South Philadelphia, Augie waving all the way. Joey had run two flags up the antenna. One U.S., one Italian.

"I'll tell you what this is, Joey. We're like Robin Hood, is what's going on here. You take my father, your father, God bless them, those guys broke their backs their whole lives to make a buck. Am I right or am I right?" The head was bobbing, the finger jabbing. "Now you take some asshole who grows up in money, the cocksucker is born on third base and thinks he hit a triple. You see what I'm saying?"

"You got it," Joey said.

"Liberty Oil is full of these people, Joey. What is the company worth, eighty gazillion dollars?" He patted the gym bag.

"Twenty, twenty-five thousand dollars is chicken feed to these people, but it means a lot to the working stiff who gets a cut. You show me something more noble in all of politics than a redistribution of the wealth, and I'm a fuckin' Chinaman."

It was the old Augie—scheming, bragging, philosophizing. It was like he'd come out of a coma, and it was so good to see, Joey told himself it was worth all the risks. He had pleaded with Augie not to say a word about Liberty Oil to anyone. Not even

Ham or Izzy. Joey would handle the whole thing. It was the closest he'd ever come to giving the boss an order, but Augie didn't seem to have a problem with it.

Joey turned right on Broad Street, City Hall straight ahead a mile or so. The sun was setting in a hazy sky and the tops of skyscrapers were turning pink and purple in waves. The tallest one, sixty stories high with a needle on top, was corporate headquarters for Liberty Oil. To the right, William Penn was in knickers atop the City Hall tower, briefcase in hand. Augie, who claimed to know enough to put away half the politicians in Pennsylvania, liked to say that he kept his secrets hidden up there, in Billy Penn's briefcase.

Joey hadn't even told Izzy about the deal with Liberty Oil, although he had assured Richard Abbington that Izzy was on board. Izzy, who had good instincts, didn't ask questions. He was enough of a pro at this to just take whatever money came his way and keep his mouth shut. Anything happened, he could plead ignorance. Ham, on the other hand, wanted every fucking detail. He had even pitched an idea that they blackmail Liberty Oil into coughing up more. Threaten to blow the whistle unless they double or triple the ante.

Joey, who had moments when he would find his hand sneaking across the front of his chest on its own, making a move for the holstered Colt, hadn't told Augie any of this. He wanted to keep some distance there. In case they got jammed up. It was safer like this anyway, because Augie had a habit of talking too much, emboldened by a logic and morality he considered superior to what could be found in the penal code. It didn't make sense to him that a businessman could pass money to a candidate through a PAC, a lobbyist, or a political party, and that was legal. But put that same money in a bag and hand it directly to the candidate, which seemed more honest to Augie, and that was illegal. What kind of bullshit was that? Joey had to admit, the boss had a point.

"Senator," he said, "you sure we're OK with Carla Delmonico?"

Augie was waving to a family coming out of a fried chicken joint. The kids were pointing to the car. A moving billboard, flags and all. "Her uncle worked alongside my father for forty years down the market, Joey. I know that whole family. Carla we don't gotta worry about, I don't think. Ham's handling that thing."

They looked at each other the moment the words were out of Augie's mouth. Ham couldn't be trusted with anything. They'd put Carla in a tough spot, Joey thought. Having her boost reports right out of the DA's office. "You can't forget who's working this thing, Senator. Muldoon's no moron."

A shadow moved across Augie's face and took the color out of his eyes. "Joey, you gotta throw that at me now?" Augie respected Muldoon, who had nailed him fair and square, the way he respected anybody who did the job they were hired to do. He didn't like being reminded that Kevinne McGinns had dragged Muldoon out of retirement to chase after them. "That fuckin' mick could shine a light up your ass without you knowing it, Joey. But what could he have on us? We got two candidates trying to steal an election fair and square, and with Carla in there, we got them beat at their own game. Relax, Joey. This ain't no group of amateurs you're working with."

Augie had his hand on the bag of money like he was guarding the key to the next world. When they reached Center City, Augie saw a sign for the Vine Street Expressway exit to Jersey.

"Tempting, Joey, ain't it?"

"What's that, Senator?"

"We run to the track, maybe Atlantic City. This much to work with, we could double our money. Triple it."

"Don't get carried away on me, Senator."

"You play my Lotto numbers today, Joey?"

"Every day."

"Attaboy, Joey. I think our luck's changing. Not that I believe in luck."

Augie liked to hit the popular restaurants in South Philadelphia as often as possible in a campaign season, especially Friday nights, when people came from New Jersey, Delaware, and Southeastern Pennsylvania to eat in some of the finest Italian dining establishments in the United States. The rooms were always full, most of them loose and informal, and Augie would make a goodwill pass, shaking hands and flirting with the ladies.

Joey made the ritual lap around City Hall first and Augie gazed up at the Philadelphia Electric Company message board on Market Street. Electronic messages flashed left to right, wrapping around the top of the twenty-nine story building, and could be seen for miles at night. Festivals, commemorations, parades. It was all up there.

"Joey, we still got Dominic at PECO?"

"Dominic from the Fifth Amendments? Yeah."

"What did we get for him? He's a night security guard, am I right?" Joey could hear the gears spinning.

"Give him a call tomorrow, will you?"

"Senator, I'll call him tonight from the diner."

"Yeah, Joey. Ask him is it possible we sneak one or two messages up there. Jeez, that'd be beautyful, huh?"

Their first stop was Felicia's, then the Saloon, and then Ralph's on Ninth. The walls of Ralph's were lined with photos of luminaries, and Augie had a prominent spot between Dom DeLuise and Bobby Rydell. South Philadelphia restaurants loved to fuss over celebrities, and Augie was greeted like a war hero in most of them.

At Michael's Ristorante, around the corner from Ralph's, Augie gave the owner a bear hug, kissed him on both cheeks, and asked to be introduced to a table of four women. They were just inside the main dining room, highlighted against a white wall. The restaurant had a clean look—a lot of white, good light-ing, simple furnishings—and the feel of a comfortable living room. The women were out-of-towners and they'd never heard of Augie Sangiamino, but they said they didn't mind him pulling up a chair. "Youse're all dolled up," he told them, his hat in his lap. "The gowns, the diamonds, the whole nine yards. Beautyful. Where you girls taking me tonight?" They said they had tickets for Vic Damone, the late show down the shore.

"Vic Damone? Ladies, I do a little crooning myself. You come by the Triangle Tavern tonight, Augie Sangiamino'll show you some pipes." Augie called the owner over and whispered something in his ear. Michael nodded and Augie peeled fifties and hundreds like play money from a clip he kept in his front pocket.

Joey was back by the bar with an Italian beer, studying every detail in the picture. This was the way he wanted to remember Augie. Exactly like this. Out on the town in the campaign sea-son, money to throw around. Augie was half vaudevillian and half politician, a natural showman. People loved to watch him because he was an original, but they also realized they were looking at the end of a time that wasn't so bad, after all. Today's politician might look clean and sophisticated by comparison, but all he really had was a more lawyerly way of getting away with things. And he had none of the character. Augie was kissing one of the women on the cheek now and the others were giggling, saying they wanted theirs. Joey honestly didn't know if he could pull out the election for Augie. Even with Liberty's bottomless pockets, it was going to be tough. But he wanted nothing more.

Michael clinked a spoon on a wineglass and Augie did a shuffle step to the center of the room, looking like he might do a tap dance in that new suit. Michael poured a glass of wine and Augie held it up, his other hand playing with the gold chain at his vest pocket.

"Ladies and gentlemen, on behalf of Ham Flaherty and Izzy Weiner, both of whom would appreciate your consideration on election day, I'd like to announce that the wine of your choice will be delivered to your table. Compliments of Ham and Izzy." Augie got a standing ovation. He wagged his head and raised his hand to quiet the crowd. "And I'd like to thank these four lovely ladies for the pleasure of their company, and for letting me nibble on their ears the past twenty minutes. Put their dinner on my tab, Michael."

Augie bowed for the ladies. *"Salud* and *mangia,"* he said, downing his wine in one throw, turning to the door, and knifing into the night with his forward lean and Joey trailing him into the street.

He sang three numbers at the Triangle, ending with "Nice Work If You Can Get It," and had a pizza sent to every table.

"All right," he said when they were back in the car. "Take me to work, Joey. I'll rest when I'm dead."

Richard Abbington grabbed his briefcase and turned off the light in his office on the top floor of Liberty Oil's corporate head-quarters in Center City. He planned to go home, shower, and change before meeting his date. He was almost past the reception desk and into the elevator lobby when he heard voices. He followed the sound down the hall to the conference room, where Whitney Pritchard sat alone, watching television.

"Whit, what are you doing? It's Friday night. Go home to your wife."

Pritchard turned slowly, his triangular face blue-gray with television light. He poured two fingers of bourbon from a de-canter, plopped in an ice cube, and took a long sip, then set the glass back down on the massive oak conference table. He looked back and forth between the television and the lights of his refin-ery on the horizon. The city wrapped around them on three sides, the foreground of a spectacular view that took in parts of three states. Pritchard had once confided to Abbington that he felt almost supernatural up here in the sky over the city, a perch his father built, but that the power tested his faith in himself.

He loosened his tie now and cleared his throat. "One of the girls told me a commercial was on earlier," he said. "Isadore Weiner's ad. I called the television station, anonymously, and they said I'd be able to see it at seven minutes after the hour. Why don't you have a seat, and we'll see what we're getting for our money."

Pritchard looked at his watch and started to say he had an appointment. He'd seen the ad, and he didn't want to be here when Pritchard watched it.

"No, really. Sit down," Pritchard said. It didn't have the tone of an order, but that was what it was. Pritchard had been snarling at staff all day, the pressure playing on all his insecurities. Abbington had spent most of the day down at the refinery, where he and Pritchard both kept offices, just to stay out of his way.

"It's closing in on us," Pritchard said, gazing out the window.

Abbington sat down and could smell the bourbon from across the table. "What is?"

Pritchard's arm swept left to right, taking in the city. "The row-house people, the small-minded politicians, the idiot media. A century of work has been put into this business, and with a few deaths, they want to bring it all down."

"You've seen the polls, Whit. These guys are coming up fast. It's working, and everything's going to be fine. You just have to have a little patience now."

Pritchard took another drink and stared at the glass. He was starting at lunch every day now and didn't stop when he got back to the office. He put the glass down and grinned, and the grin grew into a deep, husky chuckle. "It better be working," he said, running his hand through his perfect haircut.

Abbington knew what this was. It was Pritchard covering his ass again. If the gamble didn't pay off, he'd put it all on Abbington. This was your idea, he'd say. I was against it from the moment you mentioned their names. And if it worked, Pritchard would probably strut into Republic like he used to, and maybe even run out to the Main Line and tell his father about all the slick moves he'd made to save Liberty Oil.

Abbington said, "I went to the refinery today, reminded them to direct all press calls to me, or to you if I'm not around. I also talked to them about the possibility of shutting down the number two cracking unit temporarily. What it would mean to production."

Pritchard bristled. "Production? What do you think it would mean to public perception? It's bound to get out, and then it's like an admission of guilt."

Abbington looked away. He couldn't stand the condescension in Pritchard's tone.

"What are you saying, Dick? Are you saying you think it's possible the benzene or something else is what's killing these kids?"

"No. As a matter of fact, I think it's virtually impossible."

"Well then why would you suggest such a thing?"

"It was just a thought. But you're right. We're going to be fine."

The commercial came on as Pritchard was refilling his glass, and Abbington reached for the remote control and turned up the volume.

"Hello, I'm Common Pleas Judge Isadore Weiner, and I'm here to tell you that I like the idea of the Eagles and the Steelers trying out a few untested rookies this season."

Abbington looked at Pritchard, who appeared to have fallen into a coma, mouth open and eyes wide. Abbington wasn't sure he was breathing until Weiner talked about taking a two-dollar gamble at the racetrack.

"What in God's name is this?" he demanded. "This is an ad for my supreme court candidate? It looks like a used-car commercial."

Abbington knew he'd flip. And he had to admit the damn thing started out slow. Joey Tartaglione, the little thug, had told him not to worry. They had professionals involved. "It's picking up steam now," Abbington said. "Look—he's talking about experience and leadership. This isn't bad."

"Experience and leadership? He's a candidate for supreme court, and he's talking about pig farms and horse racing. How many hundreds of thousands of dollars am I paying to these thieves? Listen, I want this done right or I might as well be blowing the money right up the smokestack. Are you watching this, Dick? It's like something from the amateur hour."

Abbington reached for a glass and poured himself a drink. "Look at this now. Here you go. He's talking about sending people to prison. That's all anybody wants to hear, Whit. Look, now he's going after Sharperson. Did you realize this? She hasn't been out of the classroom in ten years."

"Yes, but now he's saying the supreme court is not a ball game or a horse race again. Who the hell thought it was? And Lord, I had no idea he was such an unattractive guy from his pictures. It almost looks like he's wearing those fake glasses and nose."

"You're missing this, Whit. Did you hear the tag? He just said a vote for him is a vote for honesty, hard work, and integrity."

"Listen, I've got my neck out there for these guys. We're handing them money in brown paper sacks, for crying out loud. I can't even believe it myself. Do I want to go to prison for these clowns? You get them on the phone, Dick. No, forget that. You go tell them in person that I want more say in how they handle this money, or I'm out."

"They said they didn't—"

"I don't care what they said. It's my money, and I am not going to get fucked up the ass with my own money. You tell them they're going to do this our way, or else."

Abbington felt intimidated by Joey Tartaglione as it was.

Now he had to go back to him and bitch about how they were handling the money? "Or else what?" he asked.

Pritchard went to pour another shot and the decanter slipped out of his hand. It shattered his glass, spraying bourbon and shards of glass over the table. "I don't know," he said. "Let's just hope we don't have to find out."

CHAPTER 14

THE SOUTH BROAD DINER was a classic stainless steel model, designed like a railcar and set on the southeast point of an intersection that had a church, a check-cashing outlet, and a wig shop. Joey parked the Olds between the yellow lines in the middle of Broad Street and handed a twenty to a pretzel vendor working the median strip, four pretzels for a buck. "Keep an eye on the car for me, will you pal?" Joey asked. He took a sandwich board out of the backseat and propped it on top of the car. Southbound it plugged Izzy; northbound Ham. Lou was waiting for them at a booth inside the diner.

"How's it look?" Augie asked. He was still wound up from his performances at Michael's Ristorante and the Triangle Tavern. He flashed a smile, the accent marks of his mustache forming a steeple, and patted Lou on the back.

"My best guess, you're lookin' at ninety percent, Senator. The word's out that there's some street money in it now. Guys we haven't seen in ten years say they'll be here."

The city was broken into wards, sixty-nine in all, each one with a Democratic and a Republican boss. In the old days, residents of a street dimpled with potholes would call their committeeman, who would call the ward leader, who would call the councilman, who would call the streets department, and when everyone in the process had managed to extract something from someone else, the potholes would be filled. These days, the city ran from the top down instead of the bottom up. The mayor's complaint office handled pothole calls, and a work order would be sent down to the streets department, bypassing the tentacles of the ward heelers. The mayor and other politicians, who had passed themselves off as reformers, had their hands out in places where the return was better—in four-star Center City restaurants, where they dined with corporate bigshots. It was graft of a much higher order, while down at the bottom, Tammany Hall relics like Augie were left to fight over the scraps.

Augie had been voted ward leader in his neighborhood two weeks after getting out of prison. Being the senior member of the group carried no particular clout, but now Augie had the one thing that did—money.

"Ninety percent ain't bad. Not bad at all," he said.

Lou said, "I would've went and seen all of them, I had the time. But I got to about fifty wards and called the rest."

Lou, who wore a blue Philadelphia police windbreaker over a TropWorld sweater, had gone into the collection business right out of the ring, then worked as a bouncer in Atlantic City. That was where he met Augie. The senator was helping a cement contractor who needed someone on city council to carry legislation to pave over the entire Boardwalk. Lou was Augie's muscle, and although the deal fell through, Augie took a liking to him. Loyalty carried ten times the weight of intelligence with Augie, and Lou was like a puppy brought home from the pound. Before going to prison, Augie had him installed as chairman of the Democratic City Committee, a job in which he baby-sat all the ward leaders and leaned on anyone who tried to steal more than his share. Through Lou, Augie kept a hand in it from behind bars.

"What'll you have, boys?" a waitress asked. Only Lou was

eating. Probably his fifth or sixth meal of the day, Joey figured. He watched him study the illuminated photos of dinner platters that hung on the walls.

"I'll have the chopped sirloin. Peppers, onions, and gravy, the whole nine yards."

"You get two vegetables with that, hon."

"What are they?" Lou asked.

Joey had his eye on the waitress, a heavyweight, as she put her hand on her hip and looked at the ceiling, like she was reading a list up there. "Baked mashed fried string beans red beets onions zucchini cucumber salad buttered carrots lima beans applesauce."

Lou took French fries and applesauce. "That come with dessert?"

Joey could tell Augie was getting impatient with this.

"Coconut cream pie. Chocolate ice cream on the side. The ice cream's extra," the waitress said, and Lou couldn't decide whether to spring for it. Augie watched him think it over for maybe ten seconds before jumping in.

"Lou, you throw five hundred dollars on a freakin' donkey baseball game and you don't wanna spring for a piece of pie? We got the meeting of our lives in twenty minutes. Honey, bring him a half dozen vegetables, the pie, the ice cream, whatever he wants. He's a growing boy."

"And a glass of milk," Lou said.

Augie said, "Just walk a cow over to the table, if you've got one back there."

Joey looked at his watch and then out the window. It still wasn't right between Ham and Augie. Ham was still trying to break free without admitting as much, and Augie was getting tired of it but denied there was a problem. Augie scooted up in his seat to watch a car pull in out front. "It's Izzy," Joey said.

Augie jumped up when Izzy came in, gave him a hug, and patted him on the back. Feeling for wires was as involuntary as a sneeze. In the middle of an election, you trusted no one. Not even the guys on your own side. "I'm proud of you, Izzy. From the bottom of my heart, I'm proud. That's the best political ad I seen in years. Huh, boys?"

"Beautyful," said Lou, who was carving up his chopped sirloin. He had to cut the whole thing before he took the first bite.

"Supreme Court Justice Izzy Weiner. Get used to the sound of that," Augie said, loud enough for the entire diner.

"Lou, what kind of goulash you got there?" Izzy asked.

"It's a freakin' hamburger steak," Lou said, fisting his fork. "What're you, stupid?" Izzy took Lou's spoon and helped himself to a piece.

"Get the fuck outta here," Lou said.

"Not bad," Izzy said. "Not bad."

Augie looked out the window and then pulled a gold pocket watch from his vest pocket. He carried it for good luck. "Where the hell's Ham, Joey? I told the son of a bitch we needed him early to go over some of this stuff."

"He promised me, Senator. That's all I know. He said he'd be here."

Augie put the watch away and pulled out his pocketknife. He opened the blade and felt the sharpness of it with his finger, not watching what he was doing. Joey thought he saw a drop of blood forming when Augie closed the knife and put his hand under the table.

Ward leaders straggled in and stopped by the table to say hello and shake Augie's hand before heading downstairs to the Roman Forum, the basement banquet room. All of them promised to deliver their wards, but Joey could pick out the ones who were just talking. The way Augie looked people in the eye, connecting with something inside, threw the liars off guard. If they looked away, they'd give themselves up, so they moved something other than their eyes. The hands, usually. A tug of an ear, a scratch—the liar's itch.

By Joey's count, Augie had about half of them with him. But most had shown up only because of the money—they were like the ducks at the lake who didn't give a fuck about you if you didn't have something to throw them—and would remain loyal only as long as it kept coming.

"We better get started," Augie said, his disappointment unhidden. "I'll run outside, see if Ham's here yet. We'll meet you downstairs."

Augie paced the parking lot, hands in pockets. A train pulled in on the Broad Street line and a half dozen people came up from the subway station and walked like robots to the newsstand, a shabby blue shack on the sidewalk. They bought lottery tickets and turned away from the stand, one by one, to walk home with their hopes in their pockets. Cars were pulling into the lot, and with each one, Augie's heart rose and fell. Here they were, something to work with, finally. All Ham had to do was show up. A squad car went by on Broad Street and the officer, someone Augie had gotten into the academy, waved. Ham's father had been a street cop, then a sergeant, and then president of the Fraternal Order of Police. He delivered the police at election time, and Augie got them the richest employee benefits package in the United States, public or private. He also hired Ham as his legislative aide in the statehouse, and when Ham's father got jammed up on a kickback deal, Augie steered the case to a judge who stalled it long enough for Ham's father to die with a dirty liver but a clean record.

Joey knew Ham resented the perception on the street that he'd be nowhere without Augie. Joey checked every car that came in, too, just like Augie, and he even prayed. He prayed that Ham didn't show up.

"And so without further ado, I give you the one, the only, the Prince of Pennsylvania, Senator Joseph Augustine Sangiamino."

"Thank you, Lou. Thank you very much. Boys, welcome to the lovely and elegant Roman Forum, a fitting place for a group that, if we play our cards right, could take back the empire."

The room had faux crystal chandeliers, exotic artificial

flower arrangements, and molded white tables with red velvet high-back chairs. Two-foot-tall Roman figures stood atop half columns evenly spaced around the perimeter of the room, and a fresco of the Forum was on the back wall. Every seat was filled, so some ward leaders were leaning against the back wall. Augie, stalling for time on the chance Ham might still show up, acknowledged individual ward leaders and related stories about how far back he went with them. "Nicky, I knew your father at Allenwood. A fine judge and a quality human being. If you could see the tireless work that man put in, preparing briefs on behalf of his fellow inmates, you would have been proud." Augie looked toward the door after tearing each vignette from the book of his life.

"Boys, I don't think I need to remind any of youse that in this room, in the person of yourselves, we have the most influential group of people in the entire Commonwealth. This being the largest city, and primarily Democratic, the outcome of many an election, up to and including president of the United States, has been swung by this very group of goombahs."

An Irishman called up from the back. "Yo, Augie, I ain't no dago."

"That don't matter," Augie said. "You're in South Philadelphia tonight, you're an honorary goombah. Even our good friends Nat and Lucien over here, and the others." Augie pointed to a dozen black ward leaders sitting together. He planned to toss them a few extra bucks, hoping they'd pull some of the colored vote away from Ron Rice.

"The windup, boys, is that if you deliver your wards, get your people to pull a lever for Ham and Izzy, we've got this state by the balls again. With our good friend Ham Flaherty moving up to Congress, a couple of our boys still strong in the statehouse, and Izzy Weiner calling shots on the supreme court, that means jobs and programs for all of you and yours. Anybody wants anything, they come to us, I don't care who they are.

"It goes without saying, of course, that Ham and Izzy happen to be head and shoulders above their opponents. If you seen the new TV ad for Izzy, which is a beautyful piece of work, by the way, that makes me proud to know him, you know this Debra Sharperson hasn't been in a fuckin' courtroom since Eisenhower. It's an outrage, boys. This Ron Rice is another story, and I'm sure Nat and Lucien will agree with me when I say he has a real good future ahead of him down the road. But he's gotta pay his dues first, like all of you did, like your fathers did, like my father did, who landed here off a boat with nothing in his pockets and made a life through hard work and honest living, God bless him." Augie made the sign of the cross.

"I'm reminded at this time, boys, of another great It'lo-American, the late Mayor DeMarco. It was DeMarco who said, 'We need real stand-up men like Columbus today.' Stand-up men like Izzy Weiner and Ham Flaherty, I might add. People we know will go to bat for us if we got a problem of any type. But guess what, boys. Don't take my word for it that they're worthy of your support and hard work. Joey, can you..."

Joey held up the St. John Neumann gym bag to cheers.

"Boys. Quiet down now. Quiet, please. Boys, some of the finest individuals in the city believe in Ham and Izzy, and they have spoken with their wallets. I can assure you that it's only the start."

When the cheering stopped, Augie turned to Lou and asked if he'd announced the buck-a-ballot program for absentee ballots. Lou nodded. "Any questions about that?" Augie asked.

"How much muscle you want us using?" one ward leader asked.

Augie said, "All I ask, that you be as honest as you possibly can at all times." Everyone nodded.

"Anything else? All right, then at this time, I'm going to turn it over to the next justice of the state supreme court, the Honorable Isadore Weiner. Among his many accomplishments, Izzy is the one ruled in a vote fraud case that as long as you've got a suit of clothes in a given division, you can legally vote there, and I know we all thank him for that and hope to capitalize on it in a few weeks." Augie gave one more look toward the back entrance, then glanced at Joey, who shook his head, feigning regret.

"Let me say that Ham Flaherty is hoping to stop by, but he happens to be at a very important fund-raising event this evening, collecting money that will, of course, be passed on to you as soon as possible so you can put it out on the streets to turn out the vote.

"Gentlemen, with the kind of support we're getting, and with your continued cooperation, I believe we could give our opponents the voting machines the night before the election and still beat the cocksuckers. I thank you, and as always, I ask that you and yours remember to vote early and often."

Most of them stood and clapped and some whistled as Augie stepped away from the podium. He smiled and waved, but Joey knew the support was lost on him.

"I shouldn't have had that glass of wine at Michael's," he whispered to Joey in a corner alcove. "It's burning a hole in my stomach. Jesus, the *aciata* Ham is giving me, that fuckin' potatohead." Joey gave Augie some antacid tablets—he'd been keeping a supply on hand the last couple of weeks.

Izzy was halfway through his speech when Ham appeared, tripping on the last step and stumbling into the back of the room.

"Look at this," Augie said. "He's fuckin' lit again." Augie motioned Ham to another alcove, and they met there, out of view of the ward leaders. But Joey could see them. He could see Augie jawing, Ham shrugging his shoulders defensively and holding his hands up.

When Izzy was done with his speech, in which he promised to be available on the state supreme court to anyone in the room who needed help with anything, Augie took the bag and told Joey to start sending ward leaders upstairs one at a time to meet with him. After Augie went upstairs, Ham fielded questions on what type of programs qualified for a discretionary state fund he claimed to have tapped into.

"Yes, I believe that is a definite type of situation that goes to the heart of what this program is about," Ham said when asked if the Pollock Town String Band could get a state grant for new banjos and plumed costumes to wear in the Mummers Parade on New Year's Day.

Joey stood sideways against the back wall, feeling his Colt nine millimeter press against his ribs. He imagined Ham catching the bullet and collapsing on the floor, the blood sucked out of his head by the Roman Forum carpet. Joey could see his eyes. That stunned look people get, like their ghost already climbed out of their skin.

Augie sat at a booth in the diner upstairs, saying something personal to each ward leader who slid in across from him. He put the envelope on the table and tapped it as he recalled something they had done together, or told a story about a time when he worked with their parents. Then he'd push the money across the table, holding a finger on it while he asked if everything was OK with their family. "This is just a little somethin' to tide you over," he'd say. "And whatever I can do to help with anything, you know I'm at the Lunchbox every day." The money was supposed to put people on the street, knocking on doors with campaign literature. But Augie knew half of it would end up at the track. Operating losses, he called it. You had to figure it into the equation.

When Augie was done, Ham was waiting in the parking lot, one hand in his pocket. His tan showed up even in the dark, as unnatural looking as it was by day, and his gold chains were picking up neon from the check-cashing shop across the street. He looks like a cheap whore, Joey muttered to himself. Ham dropped a cigarette and twisted it out with the toe of his shoe as Augie approached. He said, "Augie, listen..."

"Listen to what? Another cockamamy story about why you're late? To another bullshit apology?"

Maybe this was it, Joey thought, silently cheering as Augie turned without another word and headed for the car. But something stopped the senator and he walked back slowly, looking at the ground until he was face-to-face with Ham, his slender frame loose, his eyes cool. Not giving himself away. "I'm an old man," he said, "and maybe I'm not what I used to be." He reached up and tucked Ham's shirt collar back under his overcoat, then waved at the stale smell of alcohol and cologne that came out of Ham's pores. Augie was smiling now. A smile with something sharp behind it. He said, "You wanna try this on your own, feel free. But maybe I'm not as old as you think, cousin. You take from that what you want."

Augie tipped his hat as he turned away, and was almost to the car when he realized Joey wasn't with him.

Ham's car was a half block down a poorly lit side street. He was almost there, fumbling for his keys in his pockets, when he realized Joey was following him.

"The fuck you want?"

Joey was sweating and the neck of his sweater felt like steel wool on his skin. He wanted to cap him so badly, he ached. He thought about the mob flunkie he'd shot, remembering the look on his face. He remembered the faces of two gangsters who died on the street, bullets behind their ears.

"This is the man that made you," he said. Ham, opening his car door, ignored him. Joey grabbed him by the arm and spun him around. "This is the man that put up with your shit when nobody else would. You show proper respect, you ingrate piece of shit, or I gotta get involved here in a way you don't like."

Ham took out a cigarette and lit it, looking at Joey out of the corner of his eye. He said, "Listen to me, Spanky. I don't fuckin' need to hear from you what I gotta do, all right? You keep puttin' the money in the box, and you remind your boss I'm his juice. It ain't the other way around no more, except in his dreams." Joey found the fingers of his right hand crawling across his chest. Ham wasn't done.

"You know what his problem is? I'll tell you what his problem is. He's been telling the same stories so long he forgot it was all bullshit from the beginning."

Joey's first punch was to the gut. When Ham doubled over, the second one caught him flush on the mouth. Short blows, but good leverage, all of Joey's weight behind them. Ham was flat on his back in the gutter before he knew what happened, and Joey put a knee on his chest, yanking at the toupee. It made a ripping sound when it came unglued, and the top of Ham's head was white as a baby's ass. Joey balled up the toupee and began stuffing it into Ham's mouth. "Eat it, you bald-headed prick."

Ham gagged and tried to fight him off, but Joey popped him once more in the mouth. "Eat the motherfucker," he yelled at him.

It was a tight squeeze, but Joey managed to stuff the entire toupee into Ham's mouth. He left him gagging and choking in the gutter, one edge of the toupee visible, Ham looking like he'd been attacked by a raccoon. Walking back to Augie, Joey said a prayer to Mary Magdalen, hoping Ham would choke to death. What a headline that would make.

CHAPTER 15

THROW OUT THE ENGAGEMENT in Boston and Lisa Savitch was a success at everything she'd ever tried. In sixth grade and ninth, she won the Framingham city spelling bees. In high school, she was in the state cross-country championships, as her brother Noah had been. She dated the guys she wanted to date, attended Yale on scholarship, went on to the law school and graduated with honors, and turned down offers from the most prestigious law firms in Boston to join the district attorney's office at a third the salary.

It had something to do with her older brother, Noah, and the justice he never got. She never really knew him because of the eight years between them, but his death, in a strange way, had allowed her to form a closer relationship with him. He had struck her as being rebellious to a fault, challenging authority at a time when she was subservient to it; arguing with their parents at a time when she thought they were the wisest two people in the world. But the older she got, the better she knew him, even though he was gone. He came home from Yale for Thanksgiving one year wearing a plain silver ring she fell in love with. When he came back home for Christmas, he brought her one just like it. As her hand grew, she moved it from her index finger to her ring finger. She wore it now on her small finger.

It had something to do with her younger brother, David, too. When Savitch was in her second year of law school and David was seventeen, he was carjacked on Commonwealth Avenue in Boston after a Red Sox game. He had no memory of the man who crushed his skull with a brick. The seizures began a month later. Five years had passed since then, and David, who'd become a drifter, would disappear for long stretches. When Savitch moved from Boston to Philadelphia, they hadn't heard from him in six months. At the time of the crime, David was planning to study at Berklee. He played piano and wanted a career in music, and Savitch, who had been more than a sister to him, was the one who encouraged him to keep at it when doubts clouded his dreams. Savitch often wondered if the brick had damaged David's psyche rather than his brain. She hoped so, because in time, the soul could heal. The one good thing about leaving Boston, she had thought, was that now, every time a defendant stood in front of her, she wouldn't have to wonder if he was the one with the brick.

With one brother lost to greed, the other to violence, Lisa Savitch could have been paralyzed by anger and cynicism. But she had no time for either. She was too busy trying to get her father back by honoring her brothers in the work she did and in the way she did it. Her father was lost to her now—he had been for years—his heart hardened by his own helplessness to save his family. He loved her through Savitch's mother, the only person he could share his feelings with. Savitch had decided she would never let it happen to her; she would never feel helpless.

Savitch drove through North Philadelphia on her way to Temple University. It was a part of town she hadn't been to, and it was the place from which most of the DA's business came, hundreds of thousands of people living in dead neighborhoods around the shut-down factories that had been the lifeblood of the city. The new economy was drugs, everybody carrying a gun, and kids worked the corners before they were in their teens. Once-grand churches were falling apart and so were the old theaters and turn-of-the-century houses of red brick. The Amtrak station looked like it had been hit by mortar fire, the hulking London Fog and Botany 500 buildings stared across the street at each other with broken windows that were like empty eyes, and flower boxes were painted on walls to make abandoned houses look occupied. Savitch thought of it as a newsreel—What Went Wrong with America—and her windshield was the screen.

Temple University was a break in the gloom. The hospital, a modern brick building, was on the right side of Broad Street and most of the medical schools were on the left. Dr. Jack Singer had told Savitch that the School of Public Health was in the one farthest north. She parked in a lot next to the sports medicine office and walked across the street. Twice she'd canceled, and now she was trying to squeeze this in on a lunch break while Muldoon went down to South Philadelphia to see about wiring Pennies from Heaven. Savitch carried a briefcase containing her file of all the stories she'd clipped, along with the rest of her research into Liberty Oil and industrial pollution and related diseases. She'd gone to the Leukemia Society of America office on Fairmount Avenue and grabbed up all their literature. She felt like a student now, on her way to a meeting with her teacher. Given the black jeans and blue denim shirt she was wearing, no one would know she wasn't.

A security guard directed her to the basement. Savitch took the stairs and then walked down a long hall that looked like it was part of a utility or storage area. She was thinking this couldn't be right when she came to an open door and peeked in.

"Dr. Singer?"

"Jack," he said from behind his desk, waving her in. He pointed to a chair, but books were piled on it. Somebody had a worse office than she did.

"Just throw those anywhere," he said, closing the text he was reading. The office was about the same size as her own, but it looked smaller because it was crammed with books and other materials. There wasn't much room on the desk, and every inch of wall and shelf space was taken. The office wasn't cluttered, just overstuffed. It looked like Dr. Jack Singer needed three times as much room.

Savitch sat down thinking that nothing about him was what she expected, including this little cinder-block cave of an office. He was maybe forty, whereas she'd imagined a man twenty years older. He wore a faded sweatshirt; she had expected a white lab coat or something. He was too normal looking—too good-looking—to be an academic.

Singer wore reading glasses that he took off as he pushed brown hair back off his forehead, showing a slightly receding hairline. Savitch was thinking about her college professors and the way many of them had a condescending air toward the entire nonacademic world. Jack Singer didn't give that impression at all. His face was open and there was a gentleness in his eyes.

She said to him, "You don't look like your quotes."

He said, "You don't look like your voice."

Meaning what, she didn't know, but she blushed. Savitch noticed a gym bag in the corner, next to a tennis racket, and wondered if she was holding up a game.

"Now tell me again," he said. "This is or it isn't part of an official investigation of something?"

"No," she said. "Not yet. I've been following the story in the papers and I know you're the person everyone's running to to make sense of it all."

"My fifteen minutes of fame," he said.

She asked if he was a medical doctor.

"By training. But I've been in research, epidemiology, since I got to Philadelphia about five years ago." He said he grew up in Connecticut.

Savitch reached into her pocketbook absentmindedly. Her hand went for her cigarettes, but stopped. If he knew so much about pollution, he probably didn't smoke, and she didn't want to make a bad impression. "I'm from Boston," she said, pulling out a notebook and pen instead of a cigarette. "I just moved here about a month ago."

"So what do you think?"

She smiled. "I miss New England."

Jack Singer said, "This place grows on you." Savitch asked if he had family in the area.

"No, they're all back home."

"Mine, too."

He was playing with a ruler, slapping his hand with it. It suddenly occurred to Savitch that it might be his way of counting the seconds. She began by telling him about her run the day of the yellow cloud incident. "You live down there?" he asked. "South Philly?"

"Rittenhouse Square."

"Oh. I live right by Graduate."

Savitch nodded, but didn't know where that was. She tried to continue, but she'd lost her train of thought. She said something about silica alumina and Singer stopped her.

"If you want to know whether you can get seriously ill from that, the answer is no." He didn't sound annoyed. He just sounded like he'd been asked the question a million times. "It's just a coincidence that it happened right before these cases started coming up," he said. "Something more would have to be coming out of those smokestacks, or someone else's, to cause leukemia. And it wouldn't happen overnight. It takes years."

Savitch said she knew enough to understand that. She tried picking up with her story, but then just jumped ahead and told him about her older brother.

"Corporate negligence," Jack Singer said, putting it together for her.

"Yes. There's another piece of it, though."

She told him about the boy she used to baby-sit, and when she said he had played in an old railroad yard, Singer said, "PCBs."

"You know the story?"

"It's not an uncommon thing. An abandoned railroad yard or industrial storage area. Polychlorinated biphenyls were used in electric transformers before they were banned."

Savitch nodded. "Well the kids played near this yard, and the boy ended up dying."

Jack Singer had been sitting forward, elbows on the desk. Now he leaned back, hands behind his head. Savitch saw a twinkle in his blue-green eyes when he said, "So you want to know where the railroad yard is."

Savitch smiled. "I can't help it," she said, opening her file on the desk and fanning the news clippings. "I lie awake with unsolved mysteries."

Jack Singer walked around the desk with the ruler and pointed to the wall behind her. A map of the city. Savitch noticed it had clusters of pins in the area around South Philadelphia and Mercer. "The red pins?" he said, looking at her. "Every one is a child with leukemia." He wore nice-fitting jeans and tennis shoes and he was tall and lanky.

Savitch got up and stood alongside him. He was nearly as tall as Muldoon, her eyes at the level of his shoulders. She asked, "It's up to seven now?"

"As of this morning. And the black pins? Each one of those is an industrial site—a chemical plant, a sewage treatment plant, an oil refinery, a petrochemical storage facility, an incinerator, a landfill. Things of that nature."

She didn't count, but there were at least four dozen. "That's unbelievable," she said, looking at the red pins in the middle. "They're surrounded."

Jack Singer talked while looking at the pins, reading a story off the map. "This is something I've been testifying about before the legislature and Congress. There's a concentration of these kinds of places in a lot of cities around the country, obviously, basically in your blue-collar and poor areas. A factory may shut down, but it's replaced by a landfill that takes shipments from places that wouldn't dream of dumping the stuff in their own communities. The town loses its tax base when the factory closes, so it's willing to take the risk, and to keep whatever jobs it can. The sites keep multiplying and the health problems keep getting worse, but I might as well be testifying to the trees." He backed up and sat on the edge of his desk, looking at the map for a while and then turning to her. He said nothing.

Savitch checked her watch and said, "I can go, if I'm keeping you from something."

"No," he said. "I was just wondering if maybe you wanted to get lunch. We can talk about it some more."

Savitch thought about Muldoon, and about Kevinne McGinns, who wanted to see her again after lunch. "I'd love to. But with this case I'm working, I only have a few more minutes."

"Fine," he said, curving back around his desk. "I'll get to the point. All the black pins, that's what makes it so difficult to pinpoint a specific culprit. There's too many railroad yards, so to speak. And the further complication is that we don't know all the causes of leukemia, or any kind of cancer for that matter. Then you get into the whole argument where one expert tells you there's no safe level of exposure to a carcinogen, and the other tells you we're exposed to low levels all the time, and most people don't get cancer."

Savitch hadn't sat down. She looked at the map and then at him.

"Well if someone's exceeding emission standards," she said, "isn't there some record of it?"

Jack Singer pointed at her. "There it is," he said. "You've hit on it."

She sat down now and crossed her legs. Her hair hung in her eyes—she hadn't had it trimmed since the move—and she swept it back.

"The beauty of the situation for these guys is that they do their own testing. For the most part, it's self-testing and self-reporting. Don't forget that the owners of these companies tend to be powerful people with a lot of money for the right political candidates and a huge lobby. Then you've got the regulatory agencies, which have to beg every year for enough funding to do their jobs. In this state, they've been stripped away to almost nothing."

Savitch pointed over her shoulder with her thumb. "So it could be that one or a combination of these black pins is the source of whatever's causing the epidemic," she said.

"I wouldn't use the word *epidemic*, from a medical standpoint. *Cluster* might be a better word for this many blood disease cases in such a short span. The boy today? I just talked to his doctor. The diagnosis is aplastic anemia."

"Depressed marrow," Savitch said.

He smiled and said, "You have some background?"

"Just what I've been reading lately," she said, pointing to her file on his desk.

"Well, the marrow is depressed and stops making blood cells, red blood cells especially. It's often what happens before the bone marrow turns malignant. Anyway, *epidemic* is too strong a word, but I think it's understandable that the community would be frantic. The mystery itself—where it's coming from— is frightening. I've been asked to work with this group that's looking into it, actually. The cancer society and the leukemia organization are putting together a summit of some type."

Savitch had semiconsciously written "political candidates," "regulatory agencies," and "summit" in her notebook. She asked why it was kids getting sick and not adults.

"Adults may be getting exposed, too. But with children, there's some evidence that sensitivity is higher and the gestation period is shorter, although it could be as simple as higher exposure. Kids playing outdoors, for example, where they're closer to the source."

Singer pivoted to his computer and tapped a key, lighting the screen. He started typing and asked Savitch to come around and have a look over his shoulder. "These are the names of all the companies represented by black pins," he said. "It's fifty-three total. Now, what I've done on this other file is x-ed out all the ones that seem least likely to produce any known or suspected carcinogens. And this here, this is the list of the most likely. There's seventeen of them."

He leaned to his left so Savitch could bend in over him and read the names. Toward the bottom of the list was Liberty Oil.

Savitch walked back around the desk with her eye on the black pins, trying to locate Liberty Oil. When she sat down, she looked at the notes she'd scribbled and then lifted her eyes to him. "Dr. Singer."

"You can call me Jack."

"Taking Liberty Oil, just for the sake of discussion, what kind of health risk might a place like that present?"

Jack Singer looked at his watch and then back at her. He asked, "How much time did you say you had?"

CHAPTER 16

AUGIE HAD BALKED at first, intimidated in his old age by the idea of being on television across the state in a live debate about election reform, but Izzy had talked him into it, saying he might be an ex-con, but at least he didn't look like Groucho Marx.

Joey cleaned up the knot on Augie's crimson tie, pulling it snug against a shirt as white as a Communion wafer. Augie wore a silver sharkskin three-button that hung like silk on his skeletal frame. His hair was cut, his mustache trimmed, and his nails, freshly manicured, looked like wet glass.

"How do I look?" he asked.

"Like you just robbed a bank."

"Thanks, Joey."

They were at Channel Nine, and Augie was about to go up against Debra Sharperson's top aide, Modesta Quatermaine, one-on-one. The subject was one of the more important, but least discussed, campaign issues: the question of whether the state should try to clean up its unprecedented judicial malfeasance by appointing judges on the basis of qualifications or continue to elect them on the basis of who could grease the right palms, make the biggest promises, and grovel before the most contributors and party hacks.

Augie, patting his forehead with his handkerchief, was for keeping elections. The senator measured off the studio, the heels of his loafers sounding like hammers on the plank flooring as he stepped over cables. Joey was on his shoulder at every turn, trying to keep him calm. The set, the place where Channel Nine did the nightly news, was nothing more than a low mauve desk with a mural of the city skyline behind it. The mural was being wheeled out by a work crew, replaced by a backdrop of white-tailed deer in a field of mountain laurel. The state motto was superimposed over the scene. Virtue, liberty, and independence. Augie buttoned his coat and unbuttoned it and buttoned it again. He'd told Joey on the way over that he was a ward heeler, and he'd always been more comfortable on the street than in a TV studio. Sure, he'd done some television and could come up with a few good lines in a short interview, but this was a thirty-minute debate. And with Izzy gaining on Sharperson every day, there was pressure to keep the rally going.

"Joey, what do we know about this Asbestos broad?"

"Modesta. She's an attorney's all I know, with that outfit takes people can't afford no lawyer."

Augie looked across the studio at Modesta Quatermaine, who calmly studied material that had just been handed to her by an aide. "What the hell's she lookin' at, Joey?"

Joey shrugged.

"Jesus, I got nothin'," Augie said. "She's over there lookin' up information and whatnot, probably statistics of some type, and I'm standin' here with my finger up my ass."

Joey wondered what Augie expected him to do. It's not like they ever prepared for any of his public appearances. They'd just show up somewhere and Augie would wing it. "You want I should stroll by, peek over her shoulder?" Joey asked.

They both took a few steps toward her. Augie said, "Modesta what?"

"Quatermaine. Modesta Quatermaine."

"Jesus, will you look at her, Joey? If that's a lady, I'm an astronaut. My twenty to your five, that's a carpet muncher." Joey took a closer look. Augie might be right.

"I could be in over my head with this thing," Augie said. "Jesus, she looks like my nephew Frankie, the one who got jammed up with the video poker machines."

Joey reached up and flicked lint off Augie's shoulder and caught their reflection in the window of the control room. He was half a foot shorter than Augie, but his head had twice the mass of Augie's. It was hard to distinguish between head, neck, and chin, the whole unsculpted block sitting on his chest in one piece. "Senator, let me ask you something," he said, still trying to take the edge off. "All these people sitting home right now, waiting to look at TV, you think most of them's like her or like you?"

Augie squinted as he imagined his way into living rooms across the state. "You're right, Joey. You get ten minutes outside the city, you're in the sticks. Very conservative. That's my edge, I guess. That I'm the one's normal."

"Guess what," Joey said. "Sometimes people are too smart for their own good. This Modesta Quatermaine, maybe she could talk your ear off about anthropology or Zen macrobiotics, some such subject as that. But she don't have the common sense of the street."

Augie seemed to be contemplating the wisdom of Joey's observation. He tugged at his lapels and sharpened the corner of the handkerchief that poked up from his breast pocket, his fingernails giving off pink light. He was nodding when he said, "I do know the street. That's for sure."

"This thing's simple," Joey said. "Two hundred years ago in this very town, what should happen but great men got together and guaranteed the right of self-determination to all of those people sitting home right now. It's called democracy, Senator. That woman over there, Modesta Quatermaine, who don't know which side of the plate to eat off of, is trying to take that away."

Augie brightened up. "There you go," he said. "That's all you need is a theme, Joey, and everything else works off of it." Joey nodded, the student again. He patted his boss on the back as Augie was called to take his place on the set. The moderator introduced his guests, laid out the issue, and asked if the combatants cared to make an opening statement.

"Two hundred years ago in this city ...," Augie began, head wagging, finger punctuating. There was a time when he didn't need the kind of prompting Joey had just given him. But if his mind wasn't as sharp as it once was, the spirit was as strong as ever. Joey stood back, admiring his mentor, and thinking that their only problem, still, was Ham. If the tune-up Joey had given him outside the diner knocked any humility or sense through his thick skull, there was no sign of it. Ham was insisting that the money gushing in from Liberty was further proof that he could sever ties with Augie. He even threatened to cut Joey out as middleman and deal directly with Richard Abbington.

Joey had managed to talk Ham down, convincing him it was foolish to risk laundering so much money on his own. But as for a long-term solution to the problem, Joey remained stumped. Shooting him in the head was still a consideration, but Joey thought it lacked creativity, given the level of betrayal. There was justice, but no poetry, in a bullet behind the ear.

Lost in conspiracy, Joey hadn't noticed the woman next to him, let alone heard her. "I'm sorry?" he said. "Oh, Joey. Joey Tartaglione."

"Maggie," she said.

"Maggie. That's a beautiful name." She was short, cute, curly dark hair. She ate well. The way Joey sized up a woman, he imagined what she'd like, and then he put himself there. This one wanted to be sweet-talked, that one wanted roughhouse. Maggie he figured for a party girl. Kitchen floor, back door. His type of woman. "Maggie," he repeated, inching away and sniffing discreetly at his underarm. "I like that."

"It's short for Magdalena."

"The saint," Joey said, brightening. "I take Communion every day there at St. Mary Magdalen downtown." He asked her if she worked for the TV station.

"No. For Debra Sharperson."

Now it came to him. The woman handing papers to Modesta Quatermaine.

"I'm with the senator," he said, pulling out a handkerchief and wiping his brow.

"I know. I saw you talking to him."

"A good man," Joey said defensively. "I known him since I was a kid. This is a stand-up guy, Augie Sangiamino." Joey took a half step back and nearly fell, his foot snagging on a camera cable. He wasn't used to someone from an enemy camp getting this close, unless it was to plunge a knife. They stood quietly a few minutes, watching the debate and moving to their right when one of the robot cameras wheeled in front of them. Joey strained for a better look at Maggie without making it obvious. She had a nice round face. Chubby cheeks. "Jeez, it's hot in here, ain't it?" Joey asked, stretching the neck of his sweater.

"I'm freezing," Maggie said.

Joey looked back at the set as Augie made a point he was obviously pleased with. Augie, it turned out, had underestimated himself. Modesta Quatermaine was getting crushed by the weight of her own argument, which was precise and substantive, but dry as a bone. Augie, meanwhile, was spinning yarns and speaking in parables. He chased every question with a story—dancing, juking, jabbing—and though he never actually answered a single query, he came across as the more engaging of the two. He'd actually been ahead of his time, Joey thought, getting by on personality and simple slogans long before TV was a factor in politics. He was a natural, the camera in love with him.

"How long you been with Sharperson?" Joey asked Maggie, his eye still on Augie.

She answered in his ear, whispering close enough that he felt her warm breath. "Since before I was born."

Joey nodded, and then it sank in. She was Debra Sharperson's daughter.

Modesta Quatermaine was just starting in on how Sharperson was going to clean up politics and government when Maggie was back in Joey's ear. She was a head shorter than he was and put a hand on his shoulder for balance, standing on tiptoe. Joey felt hot and cold at the same time. "You didn't get it from me," she said softly, "but Miss Reform owes about twenty-five thousand in back taxes on an apartment house in North Philadelphia."

Joey scratched the back of his neck. He looked at Maggie and back up at Augie. What the fuck was this? The little porker was diming her own mother?

"Check it out," Maggie said, whispering in his ear again. "You'll find people there with no heat. A couple of them with no plumbing. Dear old Mom's a deadbeat slumlord."

Joey felt a drop of sweat roll behind his ear. Maybe he had missed something. "This is your mother you're telling me about?"

"It's a long story," Maggie said. "Let's just say I found out recently she's not the person I thought she was." Joey nodded. "I can tell you more," she said. "Buttonwood Apartments, eighth floor. Come by at noon today."

Modesta Quatermaine made a strong closing argument for the appointment of judges. How can any lay person step into a voting booth, look at dozens of names on the ballot, and make an intelligent choice, one judge over another? Get rid of elections, she said, and you get rid of the corrupting influence of money, special interests, and televised mudslinging. She added that you'd also get rid of the muscle and sleaze from "political gargoyles the likes of Augie Sangiamino."

Augie ignored the insult. He thanked his worthy opponent

for a good clean debate, spoke of his love for his constitutents
and his Angela—Father, Son, and Holy Ghost—and finished up
paying tribute to the wisdom of the forefathers in guaranteeing
the right of "intelligent people like all of youse out there to
make decisions for yourself rather than trust the government to
make them for you."

Outside, Augie was waving to invisible supporters before
Joey had steered the '56 out of the parking lot. He jabbered all
the way home about how "these young kids getting into politics,
they could learn a trick or two from a few of us old-timers." Joey
congratulated him on his performance and dropped him off
home so Augie could get the macaroni dinner started. It was
Sunday, and they had good reason to raise the glasses.

"I'll see you in a few hours," Joey said. "You sure you don't
need nothing?"

"I'm fine, Joey. Couldn't be better."

Joey had sweat through the pits of his sweater. He went home
and showered, gargled, and shaved. He put on a pair of fresh
boxers, pressed slacks, and his best Christmas sweater. The last
one his mother had given him. It was dark gray, with a diamond
pattern on the chest in red and green.

The Buttonwood Apartments sat just north of the Ben Franklin Parkway near the Rodin Museum. He had to be twice her
age, Joey was thinking as he parked. The last eight years, he'd
probably been with a dozen women, none of them as young or
as good-looking as Maggie Sharperson. They were weekend deals
down the shore, some of them drunk, most of them hookers, all
of them big. In his mind, it went back to high-school football,
those summer practice sessions where you had to line up and
throw yourself into the blocking sled. The sled itself was heavy
enough, but some fat fuck of a coach would stand on it and you
had to plow him around, too. Ever since then.

Joey ran from the car to the building, but it looked more like
rolling than running, little penguin feet wheeling him along.

He told himself to keep his priorities in order. He was here for Augie, and the first piece of business was to allow Maggie Sharperson all the time she needed to rat out her mother. If he got laid, that was gravy. He called her on the house phone, combed his hair on the way up in the elevator, and threw out his plan when she answered the door naked.

Joey took her down right there on the hardwood. She was giggling and he saw that she was three-quarters of the way through a bottle of red. She wasn't in the same weight class as some of the others, but she was no fucking ballerina, either. Joey had his sweater halfway up and his pants halfway down and she was cackling like a schoolgirl as he ran his tongue up her leg, around the knee, over the thigh. Joey thought this was a good way to get a relationship started, because the girl figured he was the kind of guy who might always put her first. Maggie's body tensed, and Joey took that as a cue to draw his tongue down. It always made their brains explode. Maggie convulsed, went limp, and seemed to have passed out. When she came to, she took Joey's hand and tugged him over to the sofa. One whole wall was windows looking out on the Ben Franklin Parkway and the city skyline. A nice apartment, great view. She killed the bottle of wine while Joey stripped off the rest of his clothes, his gun thudding to the floor. "What's that for?" she asked, reaching for it.

Joey kicked the gun away. "You don't wanna play with that," he said.

"Maybe I do," she said, turning onto her stomach, her giggle back.

Joey climbed up, and through the window he saw George Washington on the parkway, riding into town on his horse. He knew Maggie wasn't doing him so much as she was doing her mother, but he figured this was no time to take it personally. With his fat fingers dimpling her fleshy white back, his stubby body pounding and his jowls flapping, he worked up the sweat of a lifetime, bumping an end table by the sofa and sending a vase crashing to the floor. He'd been blocked lately with the writing, but now he was blasting through the wall, words and images gushing. He'd write like a motherfucker tonight.

Joey went into the kitchen when they were done and came back with a towel to wipe up the mess of the broken vase. "Don't worry about it," Maggie said from the bedroom. She'd gone to get a robe.

While Joey put his pants back on, Maggie told Joey she had found out her mother was sleeping with Maggie's boyfriend.

"You gotta be fuckin' kiddin' me," Joey said.

"I decided to do it this way. Bury her campaign by sleeping with the enemy." She was smiling an evil, satisfied smile.

"I feel like I hit the daily double," Joey said.

She said there was more. She'd gotten to know Ron Rice on the campaign trail, and knew for a fact that he was not a happy man. Ham was closing the gap on him, Rice was nearly tapped out, and the Republican Party wasn't doing a thing for him. "He thinks it's because he's black," Maggie said. "He told me he wants to switch parties."

Joey tied his shoes and told Maggie he had to run, but he'd stay in touch. He'd definitely stay in touch.

Augie was in his chef's outfit—sleeveless undershirt, gray slacks. He answered Joey's ring and hurried back to the kitchen, where the gravy bubbled on the back burner and the sausage sizzled in a black cast-iron skillet. "Smells beautyful," Joey said.

"Let me dump the sozzich in the gravy here," Augie said, spearing brown links out of the pan and plopping them into the pool of marinara. His slippered feet were parked in the worn grooves in front of the oven. "You want some coffee?"

Joey poured a cup and took a seat. "Take a look at the paper there," Augie said. "We got a good ride on that PECO message board stunt. Fuckin' newspaper tryin' to figure out how it could be that we got Ham and Izzy up there in lights." The "City &

Region" section was face up on the table. The story was in the upper right-hand corner of the page with a box around it, Ham and Izzy's names in the headline. Joey only skimmed the article, which quoted Augie saying it must have been God's will, and voters should follow his cue.

"Senator, I got two things," Joey said when Augie pulled up a chair. Joey thumped the table with his fingers, a little drumroll.

"What?" Augie asked, elbows on the table. "What?"

"Number one, Debra Sharperson's got a little problem." He recounted his conversation with Maggie at the TV studio, and Augie's mouth opened wider as Joey went on. When Joey was done, Augie grabbed his face and kissed him on the lips.

"That's the best fuckin' news I heard since we struck oil," he shrieked. "How 'bout we call Bonguisto, lay it in his lap? This thing'll be everywhere inside of a day." Augie jumped up and danced around the kitchen. He rubbed the top of the Jesus statue on the stove and then went over to the light switch, which had a plastic Jesus around it. Augie touched the halo and closed his eyes to say a prayer of thanks. When he opened his eyes again he had the face of a little boy. "I got it, Joey! We go into one of these apartments Sharperson has, put a tenant family on the air. They're shivering in the corner of a room with no heat. On the wall behind them they got our new campaign poster—WEINER'S A WINNER." Joey said he'd call the ad agency in Harrisburg right away, tell them to jump on it.

Augie was like a cat, back and forth across the kitchen floor, scheming and plotting. "What else?" he asked, suddenly remembering there were two things.

"Have a seat there, Senator." This was the tricky part, and Joey wasn't sure how to couch it. As big an asshole as Ham had been, you still had to be careful with Augie on the subject of loyalty. Augie could tell by Joey's voice that something was up. He sat down like he didn't want to, his eyes level with Joey's. Joey leaned on the table and dropped his voice, talking like a priest in a confession box.

"Senator, what I'm hearing, Ron Rice don't like what they're doin' for him. The other side."

Augie said, "You can't blame the man, can you? You get a *melenzane* like that, the Republicans naturally figure he'll pick their pockets and poke their daughters."

"What I heard," Joey said, "maybe he wants to be with us."

Augie pushed himself off the table, leaning back on the chair. He closed back in, cocked his head, and then pushed away again. "Be with us?"

"Maybe if he wins, he wants to tell the Republicans to go fuck themselves."

Augie slumped when he realized what Joey was saying. He wanted Augie to cut Ham and pick up Ron Rice. Augie took in a breath that seemed to blow his body back up. He stood and went over to his gravy, staring into the pot as he stirred.

Joey knew exactly where he was. He was thinking twenty-five years. That was how long he'd been grooming Ham as his protégé. "Loyalty works two ways," Joey said. "Otherwise it don't work at all, Senator."

Augie came back to the table and leaned on the chair. His spindly arms, with knotty elbows, had never looked so old and frail. "Gives me the shakes, Joey."

"I'll tell you what gives me the shakes, Senator. Ham forgetting what he's got, where he came from. That gives me the shakes."

Augie ran his fingers over his mustache and stared at his reflection in the china cabinet. "My word is everything, Joey. That's my whole life."

"Senator, this ain't no issue of who's loyal. It's about who's disloyal."

Augie sat down, his body folding in flat pieces on the wooden chair. He rested there several minutes before saying, "I'll tell you what. I gotta think about this."

He'd already been thinking about it. Joey knew that, and he knew Augie had been within a hair of dropping Ham after that night at the South Broad Diner. This was how good a heart he had. That no matter how many times Ham slapped him in the face, Augie wanted to give him one more chance.

"Oh shit," Augie said, looking at the clock. The Sunday Macaroni Club would be coming through the door any minute.

Joey touched the muzzle of his gun through his sweater. Maybe he would make a call, hire a freelancer, get this thing over with. Of course, there were risks involved in contracting out. The local wiseguys weren't geniuses, and they weren't exactly marksmen, either. One time they had Harry the Hunchback in a phone booth and still managed to miss. That's the thing you wanted to avoid, Joey thought. Wing Ham and then the fucker ends up getting a sympathy vote.

CHAPTER 17

IT WAS THE FIRST TIME in the history of the Sunday Macaroni Club that someone didn't show. Izzy and Lou had just left and Joey was scrubbing dishes and pots, talking it over with Augie, who had the wrong reaction, as far as Joey was concerned. He wasn't angry; he was disappointed.

"Not even a phone call," he was moaning, further into the Chianti than he usually got. "The cocksucker used to come up with a lie when he missed this or that, some fish story. Now he don't even bother."

Joey decided he had to step up, that's all there was to it. Augie was going to agonize forever about whether to cut ties with Ham once and for all. "Senator, you just let me handle it." Augie was standing against the green tile counter. He crossed his arms and looked at Joey. Not mad, Joey didn't think. Just surprised. "If you don't mind my asking, what're you gonna do?"

Joey said, "I'll take care of it, Senator."

Augie was grinning as he came closer. His ears pushed out, elflike, when he smiled or grinned. He touched the gun through Joey's shirt and patted him on the back. "Don't get goofy on me, Joey. All right? Don't get fuckin' goofy." Joey said it wasn't that. He was cooking up something else for Ham. Augie had started to ask what it was when the phone rang in the living room.

Joey couldn't hear what was said, but he could tell by Augie's tone that something was wrong. He stopped scrubbing the pot and rinsed his hands. Augie stood in the arched doorway now, his face gray and his eyes heavy. "It's Angela," he said.

Joey's heart jumped. "She OK?"

"I don't know. She's got a fever and she hasn't eaten. They asked could I come by, see if I can get her to eat something."

Joey tried to reassure Augie on the way to the home, tell him she was going to be OK. But she wasn't. They both knew that. Lately, every time they visited, it seemed like there was less of her to see. Augie was mumbling to himself as they drove east on Washington Avenue, chuckling every now and then between yep-yeps. "I ever tell you how we met, Joey?"

A hundred times. A thousand. Joey sometimes wondered who it was had Alzheimer's. He said, "No, Senator."

They'd gone to Palumbo's to see Eddie Fisher. Augie with his date, Angela with hers. The moment Augie laid eyes on her, he pretended he was sick and called for a cab. He took his date home and raced back to Palumbo's, where he moved in on Angela the moment her guy went to the men's room.

"She was the prettiest girl in South Philadelphia," Augie said. "My Angela's beautyful, Joey." Augie asked Joey to turn right on Eighth Street and take him to Termini Brothers bakery so he could pick up a cannoli for Angela. "They come out with this vanilla and chocolate years ago," Augie said, in a zone now, going back to a time when everything seemed less complicated. "But the ricotta was always the best. That's the one she always asked for."

Halloween decorations were already up in row-house windows and kids in Eagles helmets and Notre Dame jerseys played football on Eighth, a one-way, one-lane street with a solid line of parked cars on the right side. Augie watched one kid run straight down, cut between cars, and take in a long touchdown pass on the sidewalk.

"Out of bounds!" the other team screamed. "That's no good. He's out of bounds!"

Augie stuck his head out the window. "Out of bounds? It's a touchdown, boys. You don't wanna penalize this boy for bending the rules a little bit. That's called ingenuity."

Joey double-parked while Augie went into Termini's, which had opened in 1921, the year Augie was born. His mother tried to keep him out of here as a boy, because it was cheaper to bake at home, but Augie would get a few coins in his pocket and sneak over. His mother couldn't bake pastries and cakes and cookies all at once, like Termini's did, and she couldn't set everything out in glass display cases, the same way the jewelry was laid out at Wanamaker's department store.

Augie turned back to Joey before opening the door and asked if he wanted anything. Joey shook his head no. He was trying to diet, make himself a little more presentable for Maggie Sharperson. An old man who looked like he just stepped off the boat was playing accordion in the corner of the bakery, and Augie danced a jig for him when he walked in. "Phyllis, how you doin' today?" he asked a clerk.

The staff wore white smocks, and one pulled string down from a spool mounted on the wall, lacing up a pastry box. That spool had been there since Augie was a boy, and he remembered wanting to have that job when he grew up. "Look at this," Augie said, doing an inventory of the display cases. *"Pignoli, amaretti, pasticiottini, filbert, imbutitti, musticolli. Madonna mia, sfogiatelle."* He turned it into a song, keeping time with the accordion.

"You want a little of each?" Phyllis asked.

"You know what? I'd like that, Phyl, but I came in here to get just one little cannoli for my Angela is all. You got the ricotta?"

"For you, Senator, anything."

Augie bent down and looked at the cookies through the glass

while the cannoli was wrapped. "You know what?" he said. "Throw a dozen or so of the filbert in a bag for me, I'll give them to these kids outside." Augie tipped the accordion player a five on the way out and called to the kids down the street. They came running when he waved the bag of cookies at them.

Bridgeview Garden, a plain three-story building of yellow concrete, was on Columbus near Snyder, across from the shipyards. The docks used to be one of Augie's campaign stops, back when the port was alive. Augie had the longshoremen, the shipbuilders, the pipe fitters. He'd work the river north to Fishtown, where they used to process the shad that came in every day, and while he was in the neighborhood, he'd chat it up with men who made ball bearings, hats, hosiery, and railroad cars, drinking beer with them in union halls and taprooms along the waterfront. Philadelphia had been the nation's manufacturing center and Augie could pull votes out of the river wards like no one else. But most of that was dead now. The jobs were in places where nobody got dirty, and where guys like Augie were too much a part of the past.

Bridgeview Garden, rehabbed twenty years ago, had been a health clinic for men who worked the waterfront. Augie and Joey walked through a lobby that smelled of urine and disinfectant, waving to staff who knew they were VIPs and didn't need to check in at the desk, they could get right on the elevator. Angela had her own room, 314, a privilege bestowed on her because Augie had killed a state investigation into insurance billing irregularities at Bridgeview. She sat in a chair against the window in a flannel nightgown—white, with pink flowers and red stitching—and looked into the dying light of day, the Delaware River turning gray and the Walt Whitman Bridge fading out.

She didn't turn when they walked in. Augie threw his coat on her bed and sat in the chair across from her, so they were knee to knee. She still hadn't looked at him. He leaned forward, took both her hands in his, and kissed her on the forehead.

When she turned to him, her expression, pleasantly lost, showed no recognition. Her face was nothing but cheekbones and sunken eyes, her skin yellow. Augie's beautiful Angela was a memory, and the Angela who sat here in this room looked old enough to be his mother. She had white hair cut short and her shoulders were turned in.

Joey leaned against the wall and watched. They were silhouettes, the river behind them in the twilight.

"Angela, how you feel? It's me, Augie." He gently unwrapped the cannoli and waved it in front of her, but she wasn't interested. Augie took a bite of it himself, as if teaching her how. She looked away, out the window again and into a place Augie couldn't get to.

"Angela, Joey and me went by Palumbo's on the way over and what should happen but it brought back a memory." He told her the same stories over and over. A dozen or more tales randomly recycled. Sometimes she smiled when he did this, but her smile never seemed to have anything to do with the story, as far as Joey could tell.

"It reminded me of the time I met you," Augie said. "Back when you had a little meat on your bones. Jesus, you gotta eat something there, Angela." The collar of her flannel nightgown was turned in and Augie fixed it, then kissed her on the neck and heard her wheezing, each breath a chore. He told her the story of how he proposed, serenading under her window on Federal Street with a hired violin and cello. The street was blocked off for the party and they danced till morning.

"You remember how your parents were about you marrying me?" he asked. And then he told her. Angela Carmella Goretti had an older sister and her parents lived by a family rule they brought with them from the old country. Augie and Angela couldn't be married before Angela's older sister was married. In what turned out to be the start of his career as a politician, Augie set up Angela's sister with one date after another, two dozen in all, but they didn't take. The older sister didn't have Angela's looks, and despite Augie's best efforts, which included the offer of a cash bribe to one prospective groom, he couldn't find anyone to marry Angela's sister.

Six months into it, he began lobbying the parents to reconsider their position, flattering them with gifts of wine, cheese, and numbers tickets. This went on for six more months until one day, the same day Augie lit a candle at St. Mary Magdalen, Angela's mother hit a two-thousand-dollar number, and that was it. The family sent wires to relatives in the old country, called a party, and gave Augie and Angela their blessing.

"Those were the days," Augie told Angela, still holding her hands. She didn't appear to have heard any of it. But Augie wagged and fawned, carrying on as if everything were OK, as if she were waiting on his next word. The leukemia was diagnosed before Augie went to prison. From jail, he prayed for her health and his redemption, believing that his fall had opened her body to the spread of the disease. It looked for a while as if she had beaten it and then, five years ago, it was worse than before. She'd been wasting away ever since; leukemia taking her body, Alzheimer's taking her mind.

Augie hadn't been able to stop thinking about it lately. His wife, all these kids. He'd tell Joey five times a day that there was no way of knowing for sure how Angela got sick. Same thing with the kids. He didn't know a lot about leukemia, but he knew that much. Augie looked up from his thoughts and realized Angela was staring at him. "What?" he asked.

She did this every once in a while. Suddenly lucid, with an expression that was like an unspoken question. Augie's mortal fear was that there was nothing wrong with her aside from the leukemia. That she didn't have Alzheimer's, she just wanted to forget she was married to an ex-con hustler. Maybe she knew he was in the middle of a campaign and taking money under the table. Money from an oil company that some people said was poisoning the air. Augie was the one who looked away and out the window this time.

"I go through that market and I can feel it," he said, the same story, the same defense, he'd always given her. "You know how I get, 'lection time. Well, guess what? It's still there. I still got something to give." He said it apologetically, as if there were absolution in admitting his vices.

His arrest and conviction hadn't surprised Angela, even though he had always shielded her from his work. She was a wise woman. She saw, she heard, she knew. It was like being a mob wife. If you loved the man, you either pretended you didn't know anything or you convinced yourself there was nothing to know. Augie went off to jail a hero to some, a bum to others. Angela was left alone, sick and ashamed, to face them all. When Augie came home from prison, he promised he was through with politics because politics had robbed them of those years together. Angela, knowing how much he loved her, knew he meant it. And knew it wasn't possible.

"Angela," Augie said. "I got a few tricks for these guys is what I got. I just wish you could watch me and enjoy this, the campaign we're putting on. They had me on TV there the other day. You should've seen me. Anybody thinks Augie Sangiamino's finished taking care of people, they got a surprise coming."

She looked out the window. Augie tapped her shoulder, but she didn't turn. Augie got up to leave. He kissed her again and set the cannoli in front of her on the windowsill. He got his coat off the bed and stood in the doorway with Joey, looking back at her. She was in the same pose as she was when they came in. "Joey, I ever tell you where Angela grew up?"

"Yeah, sure. Seventh and Federal."

Augie shook his head. "That was where the family moved when she was fifteen."

"Where'd she grow up, Senator?"

"Mercer, Joey. She grew up in Mercer, right downtown there. Her father worked in one of the factories. Come on, let's go and let my Angela rest. She'll feel better in the morning."

CHAPTER 18

WITH TWO WEEKS to go until election day, Ham Flaherty had closed to within a point of Ron Rice, a surge the newspapers attributed to a flurry of TV airtime. Izzy Weiner had pulled even with Debra Sharperson in the first poll since she was scandalized with a story about a slum tenement she owned. She had explained that her ex was responsible for the building, but Weiner's ad, with its shivering tenants huddled under blankets, was a shot to the gut, and it was all over the state.

So was the news that a third child had died of leukemia, and the entire southeastern corner of Pennsylvania was on edge, frightened residents wondering what was killing their children and who would be next. The latest victim was nine years old and her name was Toni Clark. She wore her hair in braids, wanted to be a nurse, and spent her entire life in the William Penn housing projects. Three years, her fight had lasted. She died at St. Bartholomew Hospital with her family at her side.

Lisa Savitch, just back from a morning run, laid the newspaper on her kitchen table and dripped sweat on the photo of Toni Clark. William Penn. William Penn. Why did it ring a bell? She went to the living room for her briefcase and brought it back. The Liberty Oil file was so thick she'd transferred it to an accordion folder, which she dug through now as if working against a clock. She pulled out a yellow legal pad and flipped through the pages, certain she'd written down William Penn at some point, for some reason. She found it in a September 10 entry. The old women who went to the hospital after inhaling silica alumina lived there. Savitch pulled a map of the city out of the briefcase and spread it flat on her table, drawing her finger down to the southwestern edge of the city. There. William Penn Homes abutted the city line. On the other side was Liberty Oil.

Savitch took a sip of coffee and lit a cigarette, checking the clock. Was it too early to call Jack Singer?

She'd been tangled in the sheets at night, groping for the loose end that would tie Izzy Weiner and Ham Flaherty's miraculous comebacks to Liberty Oil. Muldoon had come around on it—reluctantly. He hadn't actually conceded that she was right, but he liked the possibility. With all these thoughts climbing into bed with her at night, Savitch would fight for sleep and then shoot up with an idea that faded before it took shape. Then she'd be on her back again, reading the ceiling for answers until something pulled her out of bed and pushed her into the kitchen, where she'd sit in cold yellow light and go back over her notes. When she couldn't wait any longer, she'd call Jack Singer at home, hoping she didn't wake him and hoping he didn't mind having another half dozen ideas and two dozen questions thrown at him before his first cup of coffee. She wouldn't have done it if he seemed bothered, but he was playing detective right along with her, calling with information she hadn't even asked for.

She'd joined him twice in the neighborhood for coffee before work, and the last time, they'd talked about something other than pollution. Movies, running, tennis, New England, the Philadelphia accent. He liked to read legal thrillers and had a hundred questions about what it was like to stand in a courtroom and do battle with a fancy, high-priced defense attorney. Do you get nervous? he wanted to know. Of course, she said. No matter how many times you've done it, you get nervous. You just don't let it show. She asked about his family and he asked about hers, and she showed him the ring Noah had given her. She also told him more than she'd told anyone about her father's emotional distance, saying she felt a combination of empathy and disappointment. Maybe it was impossible to know what it meant to lose a child, she said. Her father had been against Noah's plan to be an actor, and maybe it was guilt that kept him locked away in his den. She didn't know because they'd long ago stopped talking about anything but the things that mattered least. Savitch apologized to Singer when she realized she'd been rambling on. He didn't say anything. He just reached across the table and put his hand on hers.

Savitch was practically in a trot on her way to work. She had to talk to Jack Singer about Toni Clark and she had to talk to Muldoon about something Singer had dug up on Liberty Oil. Distracted by all of this, she didn't see the commotion on Market Street until she was in the middle of it. She noticed the police first. Police on horses, police on foot, police coming out of the back of a paddy wagon. Then she saw the bodies. She was standing twenty feet from the nearest of a dozen bodies that lay in the middle of Market Street. Her first thought was hit-and-run, and then she looked up at the skyscrapers, thinking sniper. Her instinct was to duck for cover, but dozens of people were standing around calmly, and she finally realized what was going on. She was in front of One Liberty Place, corporate headquarters of Liberty Oil, and she had walked into the middle of a demonstration. The people lying in the street were wearing NOT IN OUR BACKYARD T-shirts.

Savitch lit a cigarette with trembling hands. Market Street traffic had been stopped at Seventeenth, and police were rerouting cars and buses while officers picked the limp bodies up off the street and hauled them to the wagon. The demonstrators, their eyes closed or rolled back in their heads, sagged in the middle like flour sacks. A voice crackled over a megaphone, leading a chant. "Liberty Oil, you can't hide. We charge you with genocide. Liberty Oil, you can't hide. We charge you with geno-cide."

Police moved a blue-and-yellow wooden barrier at Seven-teenth to let a limousine through. The limo had to weave around bodies as it made its way to the curb in front of Liberty Place. Demonstrators pounded on the car as it came to a stop and yelled through the tinted windows until police galloped in on horses. A new chant began. "Whitney Pritchard, you can't hide. We charge you with genocide."

When Pritchard emerged, the booing picked up and the sound of it bounced off the walls of skyscrapers and settled back down over the growing crowd. Savitch looked west down Market, all the way to Thirtieth Street Station, and then east, to City Hall. It looked like an identical demonstration was going on across the street from City Hall, outside the headquarters of PennDel Petroleum, which also had a refinery south of the city. Savitch, in jeans and sneakers and a black leather jacket, looked like she could be one of the demonstrators, except that none of them were smoking. She moved in close enough to see Whit Pritchard hold both hands up, trying to quiet the crowd. He was middle-aged and wore the basic conservative gray suit, and he was smiling. Savitch was sure she'd seen him somewhere and was trying to remember where, but then she realized she hadn't seen him at all. It was the smile that was familiar. A politician's smile. She'd seen it in the photos in Kevinne McGinns's office.

Pritchard decided to speak whether he was heard or not, so Savitch moved in closer. Close enough to see dark circles under his eyes, just like she'd just seen in the mirror when she got out of the shower. It was good to know that if he was keeping her awake, at least he wasn't getting any sleep, either.

"I'd like to say that while we appreciate your concern for public health and the unfortunate illness that has befallen some of our fine young citizens, your passion here on our doorstep is misguided," Pritchard said. He waited for the booing to level off before continuing. "We'd like to get to the bottom of this just as much as you would. But there is, at this time, no evidence of any correlation whatsoever between air and water quality in the industrial corridor and any single case of death or illness."

They booed even louder at that, and one of the demonstrators threw a plastic skeleton at Pritchard, who ducked and kept on talking. Savitch had pushed and squeezed her way to within ten feet of him and heard him say he had just returned from delivering a one-hundred-thousand-dollar check to the Leukemia Society of America.

"You son of a bitch," Savitch said through her teeth, begging herself not to jump up there and strangle him. He probably figured he could buy his way out of any jam he got into, the sleaze. This was so typical.

"You might consider doing something in the same vein," Pritchard told the unruly crowd, "instead of taking cheap shots at a business that has provided hundreds of jobs and essential products for three generations."

Maybe she was reading into it what she wanted to, but Savitch thought she saw something other than arrogance and contempt on Whitney Pritchard's face. She thought she saw fear. The same nervous fear she had seen in a thousand thugs who had looked her in the eye and said, over and over, that they didn't do it.

Kevinne McGinns had transferred Carla Delmonico to the complaint unit, telling her it was a well-deserved promotion, and ordered someone to keep an eye on her while they figured out what to do with her. A new secretary knocked on Savitch's door and brought in a cup of coffee.

"Any word from Muldoon yet?" Savitch asked.

"No."

"Let me know right away."

"I'll put him right through."

Savitch was taking no chances with this secretary. Rather than fish her out of one of the patronage cesspools, she'd insisted that McGinns hire from a private agency. Muldoon ran a check on her, too. No political ties.

Savitch had her own map now, borrowing the idea from Jack Singer. She had just put up a red pin for Toni Clark and was going over the names and ages of the dead kids in her head. Joey Napolitano, twelve. Jessie Piatkowski, seven. Toni Clark, nine. An eighth case of leukemia had been reported. A five-year-old boy in Mercer. She went to the window and looked down the Benjamin Franklin Parkway to the art museum, the sky a dark blue behind it. Some of the trees still had color back there, where the river came out of the woods, but the brown of winter was moving in on the city, reminding her how little time she had.

A pile of paper, the history of a case Jack Singer had told her about, sat on one corner of her desk and Savitch looked through it again. Liberty at one time had a Texas subsidiary that was accused of contaminating a municipal water supply with underground leakage from storage tanks. But six months after the Texas attorney general launched an investigation, he was voted out of office. The man who replaced him had been backed by the Liberty subsidiary, and the state investigation, like the contamination, was buried deep and eventually forgotten.

Savitch jumped when the phone rang. She hit the speaker button and Muldoon's bass voice filled her office.

"Listen, I couldn't get a wire inside the place last night because the son of a bitch sleeps in there."

"Joey Tartaglione sleeps in the Pennies from Heaven clubhouse?"

"What can I tell you? He sleeps in there at night and somebody's in there all day. We've got a problem."

"Muldoon, you see that this girl who died yesterday lived practically inside the Liberty Oil property line?"

"The little black girl. Right. Look, I'm more convinced every day that you're right about Liberty, but as far as the connection to our favorite meatballs, I still don't know."

"Muldoon, I went back over all the stories about the

campaign, and Ron Rice and Debra Sharperson have been beating up on Liberty Oil from the start. But guess who hasn't had word one to say about it."

"Weiner and Flaherty."

"You're starting to catch on, Muldoon. You'll like this, too. Ten years ago in Texas, Liberty bought the attorney general's office to kill an investigation into groundwater contamination out there, where they used to have a storage plant. I talked to the former AG and he said there was some sleazebag involved with Liberty, a lobbyist or backroom lawyer, who he thinks is working in the Philadelphia area now. You ever hear of a guy named Richard Abbington?"

"No, but I'll check it out."

"The other thing is, I called Common Cause, and Liberty Oil's political action committee made a contribution to every single congressman and senator who helped roll back the Clean Air and Clean Water acts."

"That's lovely, Savitch, but I don't see how that helps us here."

"Muldoon, I'm just trying to establish that these guys will do anything to cover their asses in Congress and anywhere else. They're whores, and if they're the ones behind Izzy Weiner and Ham Flaherty, there has to be some way we can find out how they're getting the money to them."

"Look, maybe this is something. Three days in a row, Joey Tartaglione picks up Augie Sangiamino, they go to an early mass, they go to Ninth Street where Augie does a little dog-and-pony show through the market, and then they go to Milly's Lunchbox. Maybe that's where the drop is."

"Good. Can you wire the diner?"

"I'll try tonight. And I'm sending one of the detectives to go get a sandwich there today, see if he picks up anything. Anyhow, while Sangiamino's in there at Milly's Lunchbox, Joey Tartaglione comes out, he goes back to the church, and then he goes to that bank I told you about."

"First Columbus Trust?"

"Right."

"Why would he go back to church again?"

"Good question."

"Let's have someone follow him in. And do you want a search warrant for the bank?"

"You can get the paperwork started, but I can't go in there yet. They've got their own people inside the bank. Before I'm out the door, somebody's on the phone to Augie, Ham, Izzy, that whole set of donkeys."

"You're probably right."

"Also, I finally broke through with someone at the Oil, Chemical and Atomic Workers local. He told me to look up a guy who left Liberty Oil about three years ago who might know something."

"Three years ago?"

"Yeah."

"He still live here?"

"No. Believe it or not, he lives in Barbados. I don't know if it's even worth pursuing."

Savitch checked the clock and told him she had to run, they'd talk later. She had a one o'clock appointment in Mercer with the family of Jessie Piatkowski, the seven-year-old leukemia victim. She'd noticed in one of the stories that the boy's father worked at Liberty Oil.

As for putting it all together in two weeks, Savitch didn't know if that was possible. But there were two things she did know: Liberty Oil was bankrolling these hacks, and it was sitting on one hell of a secret. Lisa Savitch would have a cigarette in her mouth and circles under her eyes until everyone knew. Forget the lack of sleep, the ticking clock, the thousand and one loose ends. She hadn't felt this good in months.

CHAPTER 19

THE LIMOUSINE looked like a carving of black glass, catching all the clear fall sun as it gleamed into Roosevelt Park and stopped at the cluster of old men in berets near the bocce pavilion. The driver walked around to open the door, and two men stepped out. Richard Abbington was one of them. Mister peach fuzz. The other guy was out of some WASP catalog—one of those guys who had their underpants monogrammed and made their wives iron the bedsheets. Look at these two jerkoffs coming here in a limo, Joey thought. Probably pulling each other's puds in there behind the tinted glass. They actually looked the type. Abbington with his pretty-boy face, and this other swisher, who looked like he should be in deck shoes, a turtleneck, and a little sailing cap.

"Good morning," Abbington said, extending his hand. He was wearing that camel hair coat again, but he didn't seem to have quite the swagger he had last time.

"Who's your partner here?" Joey asked, even though he knew.

Abbington said, "I'd like you to meet Whit Pritchard."

"All right," Joey said, shaking hands. "Pleasure to meet you." Abbington, the flunkie, had mentioned that his boss had some questions, and Joey figured Pritchard would show up to baby-sit Abbington. It wasn't part of Joey's plan, but that was OK. This could work just as well. He had set it up for Liberty to hand a check to the president of the bocce club for losses sustained in the yellow cloud incident that wiped out the tournament. It's a nice little PR dance, for one thing, and it's a windfall for the bocce club, which was planning a cruise to Sicily for an international tournament. But more importantly, it sends Muldoon sniffing up the wrong trail to chase after the money.

Joey squinted into the glare toward Broad Street and across to Veterans Stadium. He checked the golf course, too, wondering if Muldoon was out there now. That would be his style. Out there lining up a putt with a pair of binoculars. The son of a bitch had gotten to Augie years ago by falling onto a singing judge he was eyeballing through the ceiling, so you couldn't put anything past him. Joey thought he had spotted a tail yesterday when he and Augie left the nursing home, and then last night, in the middle of the night, someone was messing with the lock on the back door of Pennies from Heaven.

Joey had always held fast to a simple rule of self-preservation. Some prick tries to enter your domicile, you shoot first, ask questions later. He blew three holes in the door with his Colt, and when he looked outside, nobody was there. Augie was right. Muldoon and his posse came through the cracks, but Joey Tartaglione was somebody who slept with one eye open and one hand on his gun. He stuffed the bullet holes with filling from a cannoli, and son of a bitch if it wasn't the next best thing to wood putty once it hardened.

Joey looked to the north and west, but there was nothing suspicious out there, either. It was open parkland and then, to the west of the Naval Hospital, row houses that were too far away to worry about. Joey led his guests over to the bocce courts, where four games were under way, the old men sounding like a flock of geese as they crowed at each other in Italian. Joey called to a man who'd just rolled one over the crushed seashells, the ball moving like a pearl on a bed of silk until it had kissed the pallino. A perfect roll. "Zoey, come here, will you? Mr. Pritchard, I'd like to introduce you to Enzo Moricone. This here's the current president of the High Rollers Bocce Federation. The guy you'll hand the check to."

Pritchard barely made eye contact before looking away. This was the kind of bullshit Joey couldn't handle with these guys. They came off like they were visiting a leper colony or something. Enzo Moricone worked all his life as a longshoreman and ended up with a limp, a little row house, and maybe a day trip to a casino once a month, that was it. He deserved a little respect.

Abbington spoke up as Moricone went back to his game, saying he and Pritchard would like to chat privately with Joey for a minute before the check-passing. The three of them walked over toward the concession stand, which was used as a storage shed in the off-season. The wind was coming in from the east, which was unusual, bringing with it the noise of jet planes making their descent. The airport was south and west, same direction as Mercer. Joey watched a plane drop out of the sky, picturing Muldoon in there with a telescope.

"Will Mr. Sangiamino be joining us?" Pritchard asked.

Joey said, "I handle all the senator's business matters, is the way that works. Tell you the truth, he's been sick."

"This flu bug that's going around?" Pritchard asked.

"Not that kind of sick," Joey said. "His age. I don't think he's altogether lucid, if you know what I mean. Half the time he doesn't know what day it is. He's about ready for the home, if you ask me."

"He looked all right in that debate," Abbington said.

"That's the thing. He's in and out, but mostly out. I've been handling all the business."

Whit Pritchard didn't hide his annoyance. "Let me be frank," he said. "We're spending a lot of money here, approximately three hundred thousand dollars to date, and we've simply taken your word for it—you're our only contact, in fact—that Weiner and Flaherty are on board."

Joey rolled his tongue around in his mouth. These fuckwads decide to go swimming and now they complain about getting wet. Joey hated working with amateurs, and he didn't appreciate the insinuation that he was a liar and a thief. This was the risk you ran, doing business with bigshots who thought they knew something. Joey looked across the golf course and all the way down to the Liberty Oil smokestacks on the horizon. He could only imagine what was blowing out of those things, as nuts as these guys were to have Ham and Izzy in public office. Joey looked back at Pritchard and said, "Let me explain something to—"

Pritchard cut him off. "Maybe if you could arrange a meeting so Mr. Abbington or myself personally could get to know Mr. Weiner and Mr. Flaherty. As big an investment as we have here, you might also consider our input as to how it's spent. I know Mr. Abbington has talked to you about that dreadful ad for Isadore Weiner."

Joey nodded and looked away. What a surprise that A. Whitney Pritchard III comes down here in his limo and treats him like some fucking rube. He'd probably never in his life had anyone around him he didn't think of as one of his lackeys. "Let *me* be frank now, Mr. Pritchard. You run a big business, something that if you put me down there, I wouldn't know night from day. But this here's a little different neighborhood, and I gotta tell you, I don't know if that's smart business, you getting together with my boys. Somebody sees that, it could be interpreted the wrong way. You see what I'm saying?"

A crease started between Pritchard's eyes and branched off on his forehead, making a Y that expanded as he stood there. Joey could tell he couldn't believe the position he'd put himself in. He turned his glare on Abbington, laser shots at the head. A look that said, What the hell have you gotten me into? Joey enjoyed the moment, a millionaire Main Liner coming down here to take control of a situation, and then it hits him. Here's some fat little fuck in a threadbare pair of gray slacks and his father's overcoat, a regular row-house guy telling him the way it's going to be, and there isn't a thing he can do about it.

Pritchard was still burning a hole in Abbington, who started to say something and then held off until a jet passed. It gave him time to organize his small thoughts behind those magpie eyes. "Just a phone call could do the job," he said to Joey. "I'm sure we're on the same page. If you just let me go over some things with Flaherty and Weiner by phone."

Joey nodded, like Abbington's idea earned an A for effort, but was the dumbest fucking thing he'd ever heard. He said, "I gotta tell you, Mr. Abbington. I have to guess you know your own business, working for a man of Mr. Pritchard's stature. But any type of record, such as phone bills and such, with me personally, that's the first thing I try to avoid." Joey let them chew on that awhile and thought it looked like it was finally sinking in. Once they did business with you, you had them by the balls, because who were they going to run to? Pritchard and Abbington were speechless, both of them looking at Joey like they'd discovered a new species.

"I want to pick up the pace," Pritchard finally said, flat and mechanical, like somebody had pulled a string in his back.

Joey had suspected he was the scarier of the two. Abbington was just plain stupid, but Pritchard was desperate. "You wanna do what?" he asked him.

"I don't want to have come this far and see it all go to waste."

Jesus, he was fucked up. Joey had seen this a million times. Guys with the fever. The deeper you're in, the more you throw on the table. But Joey was having trouble handling the flow as it was. He never thought he'd see a day when he wanted some-one with money to back off. What a slush fund these guys must have that they were this liquid. They must be printing the fucking money. "Tell you what I'm gonna do," he said. "Since you got your checkbook with you, why don't you make out a check to Roe, Barry, and Murray and give them a call soon as you get back to the office. You tell them you need a little bit of legal consultation, send them the check. I'll call over there, set the whole thing up. You'll get a receipt, the whole deal. It's indictment-proof, one hundred percent, provided you never open your mouth about it to anybody."

Abbington put his hands up, as if he still had a role other than to shine his boss's shoes. "What's the point of that?" he asked.

"It makes it a little easier from my end," Joey said. "Say it was twenty-five grand, for the sake of discussion, for legal services rendered. That's what your receipt will say, anyway. You follow me? Then the law firm turns around and makes a twenty-five-thousand-dollar contribution to the candidates, which is legal because this particular firm operates as a partnership and not a corporation. A corporation can't make political contributions straight out, as you know."

They were two blanks again. Complete fuckin' zeroes, Joey thought. And he could tell this was the first time in Whit Pritchard's life, past the age of ten, probably, that anybody had told him what to do.

Richard Abbington pointed to the park entrance and Joey turned. Two TV news vans were pulling in.

"What's this?" Abbington asked.

"A little free publicity for Liberty Oil," Joey said.

"You called them?" Pritchard asked.

"Mr. Pritchard, let me tell you something. You're taking a beating in the press, and we both know it's undeserved. You've had this company for what, three generations? Good, strong company run by men who happen to be leaders in the business community, and the press is on your back like this?"

Pritchard said, "They don't know the first thing about business, science, or medicine."

Joey went over and said something to Louis Bonguisto of Channel Nine, then stepped out of the way as the news crews set up on the bocce courts. Pritchard called Enzo Moricone over and put his arm around him like they were weekend barbecue buddies. He'd stepped into a new skin, going from panicked oil baron to slick PR man. It was like the rolling cameras charged a different battery in his head.

"On behalf of Liberty Oil, a member of this community reaching back into the last century, I'd like to welcome you all today. At Liberty, which was founded by my grandfather, we like to think of Roosevelt Park as part of our own backyard."

Joey wondered what would feel better—putting a bullet in Ham's head or in Pritchard's. It was a toss-up.

"Few other companies routinely grade themselves in several categories of environmental safeguarding and share that report card with you as part of an ongoing public service."

Joey couldn't remember the last time he'd heard so much bullshit. Here they were, standing on top of an oil slick, with who knows what coming out of the smokestacks, and Pritchard is telling a team of bocce players he's on their side. He could be a politician if he realized he wasn't as smart as he thought he was.

"And it is that sense of community that brings us here today, with a check for fifty thousand dollars, for the expansion and beautification of the High Rollers Bocce Pavilion." He handed the check to Enzo Moricone, who thanked him and put it in his pocket to applause from the bocce players.

Pritchard and Abbington waved to Joey and were on their way to the limo when a stubby man in khakis and a plain zippered jacket approached them. Joey had seen him earlier and thought he was one of the bocce players. "Excuse me," he said. "I'm Wallace Roach of the *South Philadelphia Bugle,* and I wonder if I could just ask a question."

Pritchard kept moving, saying he'd be happy to answer any

questions, but he had to keep an appointment. Call at the office, he said.

"I left six messages at the office," Wallace Roach said, trotting to keep pace with him. "I was just wondering, given your sense of community, if you had anything to say about kids getting leukemia in the vicinity of your refinery."

Pritchard stopped suddenly and turned. He looked for an instant as if he might reach out and grab Wallace Roach by the neck and strangle him, get rid of the little bastard and get rid of this whole fucking mess he'd gotten himself into. Instead, that change came over him again, like when the cameras started rolling.

He said, "Mr. Roach, is it? Mr. Roach, we are all, no matter where we live, exposed to carcinogens and suspected carcinogens on a daily basis. You are, I am, everybody is. But you and I don't have cancer or leukemia now, do we? I've been in that plant two and three times a week for thirty years, and I'm perfectly healthy. The truth is that there is no scientific means to determine how anyone contracts a specific case of cancer or leukemia. That is common knowledge and it is irrefutable. Do me a favor and put it in your newspaper. Maybe it will begin to balance the sensational stories that have needlessly alarmed the general public."

Joey memorized it. It'd be something to tell Augie when the boss looked into Angela's eyes and wondered how she got so sick.

CHAPTER 20

Lisa Savitch swept past a flurry of signs for Atlantic City casinos and under the Walt Whitman Bridge. The navy yard was off to her left, PennDel Petroleum to her right, the airport and the sewage treatment plant up ahead under a flat sky, the blue washed out by aerial debris. Savitch, heading south on Interstate 95, rolled her window up tight, but the odors poured in anyway. She got a blast of sulfur and then a more putrid smell, like fertilizer. She opened the window to let it out, but more poured in.

This stretch, through the southern reaches of the city and beyond, was the logical place for an industrial corridor. The Schuylkill and Delaware Rivers met here before emptying into Delaware Bay and then the Atlantic Ocean, and the interstate stretched to Boston in one direction and Miami in the other, a sooty, gray, fifteen-hundred-mile strip of American industry. By ship, train, plane, and truck, Philadelphia was a major shipping and receiving point on that route, and that was one reason Pennsylvania was fourth in the nation in hazardous spills, explosions, and emissions.

From the top of the Girard Point Bridge, Savitch could see the flat plane of row-house rooftops in her rearview mirror. The same snapshot was up ahead and to the right. Tens of thousands of people lived close enough to the factories to see and smell them, and it seemed like a thoughtless piece of municipal planning. Savitch didn't know which had come first, the factories or the houses, but it didn't make sense to have them so close to each other.

She took the the last Philadelphia exit. It wasn't the fastest way to get to Mercer, but she wanted to drive by William Penn Homes first to see the place where Toni Clark had lived. This part of the city had none of the charm of South Philadelphia proper. The streets were wider and the houses were newer, but more sterile looking, and instead of walking to corner cafés and mom-and-pop stores, residents drove to low-slung strip malls with sprawling parking lots. Savitch could see Liberty Oil's stacks looming over rooftops to her left. It was probably psychosomatic, but she felt a tightening in her chest and a light-headedness. She turned left onto a wide avenue, and the refinery opened up ahead of her, dominating the skyline and growing before her as she drove south. Just before crossing into Mercer, Savitch pulled over and checked her map. She had to be close. She drove two more blocks and saw the sign.

William Penn Homes was a cluster of six three-story brick buildings scarred by graffiti, with laundry hanging from every balcony railing. Savitch got out and walked to the open spaces behind the buildings, where twenty kids played on a dirt field tramped down hard as concrete. Boys played football and girls were jumping rope. A chain-link fence ran along the edge of the property, and beyond that was a creek, then flat, plain brown marshland, and then Liberty Oil. Savitch walked past the kids, who paid no attention, and went to the fence.

In sheer size alone, the refinery was frightening. A dark, hissing, sprawling empire that looked like it was unfinished and still growing, the primitive and ingenious invention of a mad scientist. Thousands of miles of pipe did synchronized flips and twists, running into, over, and around tanks, corrugated roofs, and gunmetal gray walls. Towers with legs of crisscross steel climbed the sides of chimneys, and catwalks stretched between the towers. Smokestacks pierced blue sky, and white and gray clouds vented from a half dozen spouts at once, bending with the breeze and trailing away, for now, from the William Penn project where Toni Clark spent her entire life.

Savitch sniffed. It was hard to distinguish between sewage, sulfur, and petroleum. She turned and watched the girls jump rope for a few minutes, wondering if they even noticed the odors. She thought about asking them if they knew Toni Clark, but changed her mind. Behind them, in the windows of the projects, she saw reflections of Liberty Oil.

A short bridge took Savitch across the creek and onto a two-lane road that carried her past a chemical plant, a sewage treatment plant, a landfill and trash incinerator, a toy manufacturer, a plastics company, and the edge of Liberty Oil's property. As she drove into town, she saw a sign.

WELCOME TO MERCER
POPULATION 8,204
A GOOD PLACE TO LIVE, WORK AND PLAY

Savitch passed the school, the library, and the town hall, and then she was in the heart of the business district, which had been crippled by the opening of a discount superstore out near the interstate and consisted mainly of vacant storefronts with peeling paint and cracked windows. Mercer still had a tavern—The 4 O'Clock Whistle—a diner, and a drugstore. The movie theater was shuttered and the marquee announced a flea market that had been held two years ago to raise money for the drum-and-bugle corps. An old man sat on a bench in front of a gas station, killing the day. Savitch was five minutes outside the city, and it looked like she'd entered a small town in the South.

Turn right at the theater, Jessie Piatkowski's father had said. Go two blocks, then right again, on Elm. It's the last house on the right, with the For Sale sign. Unlike in the city, there were no row houses here. The houses, like the town, were old and

tired. They were mostly freestanding wooden clapboard structures, with sagging rooflines and scruffy, brown yards. Hedges
and bushes marked property lines. The last house on Elm was a
white two-story with a gabled roof and a porch that ran along
the entire front of the structure. A bicycle lay in the front yard
and a blond girl of about five was on a swing bench on the porch,
holding a plastic bottle for a doll cradled in her arms. Savitch
parked and as she walked up to the house, she wished for a
moment that she hadn't made this appointment.

"Hi, my name's Lisa. What's your name?"

"This is my daughter," the girl said.

"Oh. Well, what's her name?"

"Ruth."

"Ruth. That's a good name. Are Ruth's grandparents here?"

The girl called her mother, who came to the porch with a
boy, about a year old, in her arms.

"Hi, I'm Jodi Piatkowski," she said, inviting Savitch in.
"You can have a seat here in the living room and I'll get my
husband. He's out back."

The living room was filled with wilting flowers. A photo of
the seven-year-old boy was on the mantel over a wood-burning
stove that was built into the fireplace. He was smiling, teeth
uneven, hair in a crew cut. A cute boy with freckles, wearing
his soccer uniform.

"That's Jessie," the man said, pulling work gloves off as he
entered the room. He was tall and thin and walked slightly
stooped, like someone who'd been teased for his height as a kid.
Jerry Piatkowski said he was out chopping firewood, trying to
get ahead of the season. He wore a red checked flannel shirt and
sweat had beaded on his forehead and above his top lip. Savitch
gave condolences and thanked them for letting her come by. It
had been just over a week since they lost their son.

Jerry Piatkowski asked her to have a seat on the sofa and he
sat in an easy chair, laying his lanky body out flat to stretch his
lower back. Jodi Piatkowski excused herself and went out on

the porch with her daughter. "My wife's not doing very well," Piatkowski said, and Savitch noticed a slight drawl. He hadn't shaved that morning, and in the low light of the house, his face was in shadows. He wore jeans and boots. A working man.

"I'm interested in learning a little more about health risks in the area, and I just have a few questions, if you don't mind. It won't take long."

"It's no problem. But I thought your office only covered Philadelphia County," Piatkowski said. "This here's another county."

"That's true, but three of the cases so far, kids diagnosed with blood disease, are on the city side of the border. We're just looking at all the possibilities right now."

"Well what can I tell you?"

Savitch reached for a cigarette and stopped herself. In four years of doing this, she hadn't gotten any more comfortable with survivors. She'd done seven murders in Boston. In each one, the victim was an adult. That was hard enough, but here was a child. That had to be his bicycle she saw on the way in, and those were probably his video games on a shelf under the television.

"I see you're moving," she said. "The sign out front."

"Trying. It's been out there six months, but no bites yet. I'll take a loss if I have to. I just want out."

Savitch looked around at the simple room and imagined the boy on the braided oval rug by the television, playing with his video games, or sitting on the too-soft sofa, where she was now. A beige bedspread with tassled fringe was draped over it and tucked in at the creases of the seat cushions. She said, "I can imagine it must be difficult, his presence being here in the house."

"It's not that," Piatkowski said. "I need to get out before I lose my other two children." He got up from the chair and walked to a window, pulling the drapes open. It was like pulling a cover off a painting of Liberty Oil. Except for a leafless tree in the side yard, the refinery filled the window. On the other side of it, not visible from here, was Toni Clark's home, and Savitch thought about the tie. Two children who lived in different worlds two miles from each other and probably had never met, but were connected now.

"You said you work there," Savitch said. "That's actually one of the reasons I wanted to meet with you."

Jerry Piatkowski nodded, studying the refinery as if there were more to see than the structure itself. In the light, his face aged and his skin paled. "I've been a janitor on the night crew," he said. "The cafeteria, the administrative offices. We moved here ten years ago from West Virginia. Coal to oil. I started out on one of the cracking units, but they eliminated some jobs a while back. I was lucky enough to be able to bump down." He told her he was taking courses at the community college, studying computer programming and paying for it with money his wife made as a crossing guard at the local elementary school. "That's the future, everybody tells you. But with my track record, I'm thinking I may never catch up to it."

Savitch, her hands in her lap, wished she had worn something nicer than jeans. She was sitting here with a father who had just lost his son. "Mr. Piatkowski, what do you mean about getting out before you lose your other children?"

He wiped at the sweat with the back of his hand and asked her to follow him. He led her through the dining room and kitchen—a big pot of soup was simmering on the stove—and out the back door. A black lab came bounding over to them from across the yard. "Down, Jim. Be nice now," he said, patting the dog's head. "Jessie's birthday present when he turned five. He wanted him to have a *J* name. I guess it's kind of stupid, but everybody in the family's a *J*. Jerry, Jodi, Jessie, Janie, and Jack—he's the baby. And a dog named Jim." He picked a stick off the pile of wood he'd been chopping and tossed it the length of the long, narrow yard. The dog bolted after it.

"He goes to Jessie's room every morning to get him out of bed," Piatkowski said, leading Savitch to the back of the lot, which was marked by a low picket fence. They went through a gate to a dirt trail that cut along the backs of all the houses on the block. At the end of the property line they turned right, and fifty yards down, the trail opened up to a set of ball fields. A fence ran the length of the fields on the left, three rows of barbed wire at the top. On the other side, the nearest structures only a hundred yards away, was the refinery.

It was even more mammoth and improbable from this side, a crude geometry of pipes, tanks, and chimneys sprawling over the plain to the marshes on either side and throwing itself at the sky. Savitch was reminded of the Erector Set her brother Noah played with in the basement of their house, magnified thousands of times. The refinery exhaled clouds of white steam and black smoke, hissing, whistling, and screaming. Tongues of fire flared from the tops of two chimneys. The odors were sharper than at William Penn Homes. Sulfur and oil, mainly. Savitch put her hand over her mouth.

"It'll gag you at first," Jerry Piatkowski said. "But you get used to it. That's the worst part. That you don't even notice it after a while, except for the headaches and the sinus infections everybody gets around here. The kids growing up here think this is how air smells." There wasn't much wind, just a slight breeze, but the smokestacks told Savitch it was coming their way.

"Is this typical, that it blows right over you like this?"

He smiled. "The day we bought the house the wind was blowing the other way and the real estate agent was smiling," he said. "We should have known better. Generally, it's right at us or just to the east. That's what the prevailing wind does with it. But it's all over the place. Sometimes it'll even shoot north. There isn't a day goes by, though, except maybe when a southern storm shoots up, that we don't get a direct hit for at least an hour or two and a smaller dose the rest of the time."

The ball fields were empty except for two women walking the edge of the property for exercise and a man throwing a rubber ball that a dog kept bounding after. Jim, seeing that, froze like a pointer. "Don't get excited," Jerry Piatkowski said. "You stay here, Jim."

When they reached the infield of the first diamond, he pointed out a scoreboard behind one of the dugouts.

LIBERTY OIL SPORTS COMPLEX
PLAY WITH PRIDE

"Jessie'd walk or ride his bike over here, meet up with his pals, throw a ball for the dog. This is where he played Little League, soccer, all that. I coached his T-ball team."

Savitch thought about the boy she used to baby-sit, playing in the abandoned railroad yard. "How long was Jessie sick?" she asked.

"They diagnosed it when he was four. He was still pretty active for a while, even after the chemotherapy started. You see that spirit in them, see how tough they are and how badly they want to live, and you don't know what to do but tell yourself, Yeah, he died, but he lived, too. We have a lot of good memories that we'll always keep."

"That's a good way to look at it," Savitch said.

"I know," he said. "But I have to admit it's not always that way. There are times when I don't believe in a damn thing, least of all that there's any way to make sense of this."

Savitch, without thinking about it, took his hand and squeezed it. He seemed to not mind, but he took his hand back after a few moments and put it in his pocket. His eyes filled and he apologized for getting emotional as they walked behind the backstop and toward the next field.

"I'm sorry," she said. "I didn't mean to make this harder for you."

He shook his head. "It's not a problem. I appreciate your interest, in fact."

Savitch's thoughts drifted to her parents as they walked. Her mother had tried to carry on after Noah died, consciously

making an effort to remind Savitch and David—and herself—
that they still had lives to live. She began walking them to
school every day and she talked to them more than ever about
what they did in class or after school, compensating, maybe, for
their father. Savitch cried one day on one of those walks and
David got mad and smashed his lunch box down on the sidewalk. Noah wouldn't want them crying for him, he said. Savitch
called him a jerk. It was the first time she'd cursed in front of
her mother, who just smiled and said David wouldn't necessarily
want them to cry or not to cry. He would just want to be remembered as someone who loved both of them.

They were in the outfield of the next diamond now, walking
toward home plate. "There are people in town who say their
families have been here since before Liberty Oil, and nobody
ever had so much as a head cold," Piatkowski said. "Even with
a half dozen recent cases of leukemia, they're saying God takes
you when he wants, it doesn't matter where you live, and we're
fortunate to have Liberty Oil still up and running when so many
blue-collar jobs have disappeared. It's understandable, really.
These jobs put food on the table and shoes on the kids' feet, but
that kind of thinking plays right into their hands, if you ask me.
That's what all these industries want you to believe—that the
compromise is worth it. The town fathers are on that wagon,
too, because they can't afford to lose any more of the tax base.
What you end up with is a town of people burying their doubts
and feeling grateful for the privilege of having their children
killed off."

He looked away from her and through the fence. "But I don't
think I exaggerate in saying most people wonder about it. You
wonder what you're breathing all day and what it means down
the road, five years from now, ten years." They sat on the bleachers, the refinery angled off to their right. Jim sat in front of them,
still trained on that other dog. Piatkowski looked at the refinery
and then at Savitch. "Excuse me. Your last name again?"

"Lisa, just call me. It's Lisa Savitch."

"I'll tell you what, Miss Savitch. I believe that refinery right there killed my boy, and I won't let them take my other two children. You might think I'm psycho or something, lost my mind because of what happened. But it's something I got from my mother, that I just know things in my bones, and this is one of them."

"No," she said. "I don't think you're crazy at all. Just a good father who has a lot to be proud of and a lot to be angry about."

"My boy loved the outdoors so much, which he got from me, that he'd come over here no matter the weather. It could be five below, I'd have to drag him and Jim home, sit them by the stove to thaw them out. My boy wanting to play is what killed him. I'll never stop believing that, because he was out here breathing these fumes his whole life." He seemed to want to say something else, but had to wait to compose himself before he could get another whole sentence out. "I sure didn't put that old house up for sale soon enough."

"You can't do that," Savitch told him. "You can't hold yourself responsible."

He shook his head and said, "They say it's impossible to know the particular cause. And somebody did point out that all the kids who got sick go to the same school, which is next to the landfill and the incinerator. It could be that that's it. But you can't tell me that living right here in the draft of that refinery didn't have something to do with Jessie getting sick. I started doing some of my own research about a year after he took ill, and the one thing they know is that benzene will cause leukemia. You know about benzene?"

"A little bit. As I understand it, when you crack crude oil to break it down and make gasoline, some benzene may separate and go up the stacks as a gas. That's if the equipment isn't working just right."

"Exactly," he said appreciatively. "It's got a sweeter odor than gasoline. You've smelled it pumping gas into your car."

"I hate that odor," Savitch said.

"Sometimes I'll just stand in the yard or come to the field here and sniff. I might stand here for a couple of hours, me and Jim, and damned if I'm not smelling benzene."

Piatkowski leaned down and made lines in the dirt with a twig. "Ever since they broke the union, you hear the employees talking about how we're out of the loop now as far as safety procedures go. And they've got fewer people doing the same job that used to be done, which can make for some corners being cut. Things are just a little frayed at the edges as compared to when I first started. Now I'm just a janitor is all, and even when I was on the line, I was no chemist. But I keep my eyes and ears open. I read the papers, too, stay on top of what's happening with regulation, how it keeps getting pulled back. From what I see, that refinery could go years without a good inspection. That's just the way things are set up."

He waited a moment, not sure whether to take the next step. But she could see it was where he wanted to go, and she nodded, encouraging him. "So what I've been doing," he said, "I've sort of been nosing around there at night, looking to nail that down." He turned to her as if afraid to see her reaction.

"What do you mean nosing around?"

"I've looked on a few desktops, opened a few drawers. There's nobody in the executive offices at night. I know the headquarters is up in Center City, but if somebody's fixing numbers, maybe there's a memo down here at the plant. A copy of something I can get my hands on in one of the plant managers' offices." He picked at a callus on a fingertip and said, "It isn't their money I'm interested in. I just want what's right. It isn't like shooting somebody, I know. But it's murder just the same."

Savitch felt the cold of the metal bleachers in her tailbone and stood up. He did the same, and they started back toward the house, Jim running along ahead of them. They were halfway there when she said, "Mr. Piatkowski, you need to be careful." She didn't want to go so far as to tell him not to keep snooping around. The man was trying to avenge his son's death. She asked, "You didn't happen to find anything we should know about, did you?"

"I don't think so," he said. "Closest I came was one night one of the management people was still up in the office. I didn't know he was there and he didn't know I was there, I guess you'd say. And I overheard what sounded to me like a phone conversation, something about off-the-books costs and then something about a trip to an island, which doesn't mean anything, I know."

Savitch asked, "That was it?"

"He got off the phone after that. Maybe he heard me or saw me or something."

"You know his name?"

He looked at the refinery. "Not off the top," he said. "I've seen him just a time or two. One of the men in suits. But it slips my mind right now."

"You should be careful," she repeated. "You have your wife and two beautiful children to take care of, and they don't need you getting into any kind of trouble."

He didn't answer that until they were back in his yard.

"Miss Savitch," he said, "I appreciate your concern. But I can't have any trouble that tops losing my boy."

CHAPTER 21

JOEY'S LATEST PLAN for calming Augie's nerves was to let him take some of the phone calls Joey usually handled himself. It'd keep him busy. Augie had one going now, the fiftieth call they'd taken this morning at Milly's and it was only eleven o'clock. A ward leader from the Northeast wanted to know if he could legally cast a vote for his mother, who was in a coma. Augie asked if anybody else in the hospital was comatose, and promised to have a half dozen absentee ballots delivered within the hour.

Joey felt under the table again, his hands like metal detectors down there. He'd found a bug earlier in the morning inside the telephone. It must have been put there overnight because he checked every day. Joey had ripped it out and flushed it down the toilet, not saying a word to Augie. Let that prick Muldoon keep coming. Joey could handle him.

Joey scanned Milly's Lunchbox for unfamiliar faces. Even a bullshit thing like this, casting ballots for people in comas, would have them busting your chops with vote fraud charges while half the Puerto Ricans were up selling drugs twenty-four hours a day in the Badlands. Joey could never understand that. Why they came after people trying to do honest community service while millions of dollars in drugs were moved through the city every day. Joey saw nobody new in the Lunchbox. It was the regular crew of cartoon-faced old-timers telling the same bullshit stories they'd told a thousand times. One new guy had come in for a couple of days, but it was so obvious he was undercover, Joey and Augie had to work to not laugh. Augie had given the visitor a tip on his horse, telling him I Didn't See Nothin' was a good bet at six-to-one in the fifth at Garden State.

The senator handed Joey the phone and told him to give the caller further instructions on absentee ballots for unconscious voters. Then Augie went back to the newspaper, half wondering if he'd see the same story there again or if he'd only imagined it. Izzy had nudged Debra Sharperson out of the lead for the first time. Augie had crossed himself when he first saw it. Who fuckin' knew? Joey himself wouldn't even have offered odds. Izzy coming out of nowhere in the primary, and then in the general, when it looked even grimmer, clawing his way back. Here he was, the little brisket boy, a reasonably competent but thoroughly unremarkable judge, ten days away from being on the state supreme court. It was a modern miracle.

By rights, Augie should have been coming out of his shoes, because he was finally within reach of the thing he'd wanted more than anything else—to be a player again. But instead he sat slumped at the table like a birthday boy who just found out his guests hit a telephone pole on the way to his party. An empty box of antacid tablets was on the floor under his chair, and Augie accidentally kicked it as he read the story what had to be the tenth time. Not the one on Izzy, but the one next to it, with the headline that ran across the top of the page:

LEUKEMIA CASES UP TO 9; FEDS JOIN PROBE

You couldn't open the goddamn paper any day of the week now without seeing another one. This leukemia thing was all over TV and radio, too, the press handling it like it was a murder mystery, the killer on the loose somewhere in the neighborhood.

Now the Centers for Disease Control had sent a team to Phila-delphia, see what they could come up with.

Sleep was no escape. In Augie's dreams, black clouds hung over the city and thousands of hollow-eyed children roamed the streets like orphans, retching in gutters. The same fucking dream every night, he had told Joey, his eyes bloodshot and droopy. The newspaper shook in Augie's hands now. To Joey, it sounded like mice running over the pages. Boxed inside the story was a list, in boldface type, of all the pollution violations in the area over the last ten years. The leader, with forty-three, was Liberty Oil. Liberty fucking Oil.

Augie dropped the paper, got up, and paced the Lunchbox. He'd been doing it all morning. Up and back, up and back on the chessboard floor, a man who didn't know what move to make next. One corner of his shirt had come untucked and his suit, brown wool, was rumpled. Augie always had his suits pressed after one wearing. Always.

Augie told Emiliano Falcone to please turn down the radio, which Joey could barely hear, and now he fingered his mustache and slicked his hair back with his hand, the manicure job all chewed to hell. When he tired of pacing, he stood in the corner behind his table and picked under his nails with the point of his pocketknife, his face nearly disappearing in the shadow under his hat.

Joey wondered if Augie was OK physically. Thin was thin, nothing wrong with that. But if Augie had been this skinny in prison, he could have slipped through the bars and caught a bus home. And those eyes? Augie could always come get you with those Mediterranean blue eyes of his, charm the wallet out of your pocket or scare the pants off you. They were eyes that knew something nobody else knew, but not now. Now, they didn't even know who was behind them.

The phone was ringing like it used to, no problem there. Everybody wanted to jump on the bandwagon, the fucking hyp-ocrites. Politicians who hadn't spoken to Augie in ten years were calling up as if they'd never been away, taking turns genuflecting in the event they needed him for something down the road. And money was pouring in, too. Especially for Izzy. The exposure from Liberty Oil's money was shaking legal campaign contributions out of pockets all over the state. Attorneys, doctors, businessmen—if Izzy managed to pull this thing out, they wanted to be able to pick up a phone and get to him so they could get over on someone else. But every second or third call was about sick kids. Anyone living within sight of a smokestack was in a panic, and clinics and hospitals were flooded with kids by the hundreds coming in for blood tests. Parents and grandparents who couldn't afford the checkups were calling Augie to see if he could make a call, set them up somewhere. Others said they were counting on him to crack down on these cretins who were filling the air with poison, making millions, and living like kings in their Main Line castles, miles from any of this poisoned air.

Augie had burned up enough caffeine to sit down again. He grabbed the paper and it fluttered once more in his hands. He said, "I don't know, Joey."

It could be taken a lot of different ways. I don't know if we can pull this off without getting caught. I don't know if I can handle the pressure. I don't know if this is worth it. I don't know if I can look at myself in the mirror. It all added up to a single question that had been forming for weeks and now hung there as sure as the blades of the fan that churned above him. A question Augie was afraid to ask or answer. Was the price of his new life the death of his constituents?

And what about Angela? The bug that was eating her red blood cells could have been planted in her body years ago when she was growing up in Mercer. Was Augie taking money from his own wife's killers?

Joey, who'd told Augie a million times that he was exaggerating the whole thing, just like the media, was running out of reassurances. He'd repeated that answer Whit Pritchard gave out at the bocce courts enough times that he had it down word for word. He decided to come at it a different way this time.

"You know what your job is, Senator?"

Augie sipped more coffee and thought about it, then shook his head no. He'd never really thought of himself as having a job. He did what he did, but he didn't think of it as work.

"Your job is helping people."

Augie brightened. "That's right," he said.

Joey's hand swept the width of the photo gallery behind Augie, taking in all the people who had counted on Augie for one thing or another over the years. Four decades worth of satisfied customers. "That's what this is all about, Senator. You're a little over a week away from being as big as you were twenty years ago. Am I right?"

The cloud seemed to lift, if only for a moment. "I can't fuckin' believe it myself, Joey. You know, I'm layin' awake nights, thinking back over a few things. One day you're in the United States Senate, the next day you're in jail with a whole different set of crooks, and you figure you'll never dig your way out of that hole. Then something like this comes along. God is telling you something, Joey. He waves another chance in front of you like this, it's a calling. You see what I'm saying?"

"Absolutely," Joey said. "We wrap up this election, that's when we cut fish like we used to, Senator. Helping people with this or that. You see what's going on here already with these phone calls. They fuckin' love you."

Augie floated on that awhile before sinking back down and staring into the black depths of his coffee cup. Joey knew he was trying to figure out what was more unfathomable: taking money from a polluter while kids were dying of cancer, or passing up the chance. That was the problem with politics. The needle on the moral compass kept jumping, and truth was a moving target. In the past, Augie had turned to a steadier guide for inspiration and direction. Survival.

"One thing about it," Joey said. "These rich bastards have

got it to give. Whit Pritchard, I don't know if you're aware of this, lives in a castle out there on the Main Line, and he doesn't cross a street without a fucking limo. If we don't grab it, someone else does."

"You think I don't know that, Joey? I worked in Congress, for crying out loud. You go down there to see what you can bring home, and you find out in a hurry you better be up with the sun to grab your fair share. And there was no nickel-and-diming down there. They ought to paint that pig from the gym on the front of the Capitol. Bobby Magnifico's House of Pork."

Joey tapped his pencil on the pad, bringing Augie out of his thoughts. "Senator," he said, tapping the pencil point, "we can't blow this chance on account of a little problem here with people getting sick, which is something blown all out of proportion. That's how they sell papers, with this kind of sensational BS."

Augie lifted his eyes out of the cup and acknowledged the logic in that.

"Look at it this way, Senator. If seven, eight kids have leukemia, you know what the big story is?"

"Talk to me, Joey."

"That seven or eight million don't. But you don't see the press doing that story, the puds."

"Geez, I never thought of it like that." Augie, who hadn't eaten since yesterday's lunch, covered page one with the sports section.

"One way or another," Joey said, "a fat company like Liberty gets what it wants. You, at least, turn it into a benefit for the little guy."

The phone was quiet for the first time all morning, and Joey convinced Augie to eat something. "Milly, fix the senator a nice grinder or hoagie, whatever you got back there, will you?"

"Make it a prosciutto with tomato and oil," Augie called to him.

Joey opened the sports section for Augie and told him to check the racing page. One of the handicappers had picked I

Didn't Hear Nothin', which finished second yesterday at Garden State, as one of ten horses to watch in the next few months. It seemed to lift Augie's spirits, and he went up to the counter to talk up his horse, nibble on the sandwich, and flirt with Tina the waitress.

Joey used the break to work on a poem to Maggie, who had been putting him off after two more afternoon lie downs, neither one as sweaty or satisfying as the first. Maybe she needed a jug of wine in her. She claimed she was bisexual, not to mention that she was addicted to Percocet and cough syrup. But Joey said he could get her some help for the drug problem, and if she wanted, she could have a girlfriend in on it, they'd go trio. He didn't have a problem with that.

She hadn't answered his calls since then.

Augie came back to the table and asked, "What have you got there, Joey?"

Joey looked at his poem and said, "It's a list of who else we can hit up for limos and whatnot." This was an Augie tradition. He always got hold of every car dealer, limo runner, and cabbie who owed him a favor, and sent the armada through South Philadelphia with megaphones on election day, picking up voters and taking them to the polls. So far they had a dozen cabs, six limos, and three luxury coaches from Atlantic City Gamblers Express. Termini Brothers bakery was donating cookies for all riders.

Joey picked up the phone again. "Senator Sangiamino's office. Yeah, yeah. Just now? All right. Keep an eye on it." They'd put a tail on Muldoon for the stretch run of the campaign. A fundamental rule of Augie's. You gotta watch the guy watching you. Their spotter was checking in to say Muldoon had gone to the airport.

"Good," Augie said, running his hand under the table. It was like Pavlov's dog. Mention the name Muldoon, and Augie pawed the nearest piece of furniture for bugs. "If he gets on a plane, see if we got anybody on board. Maybe we can hijack that prick to China."

Joey wanted to change the subject. Before he could, Augie said, "They got nothing on us, Joey." But it wasn't a statement. It was a question, and Augie was looking for the answer in Joey's eyes. He knew Joey was moving a ton of money, and nobody knew better than Augie how difficult that could be. With Muldoon sniffing after them, they'd have to be able to show where the money for all the TV airtime came from.

"Trust me, Senator," Joey whispered, looking over his shoulder to see if there were any unfamiliar faces in the diner. "They could bring Sherlock Holmes down here, he'd end up so dizzy he couldn't find a mushroom on a pizza."

"What about Carla? You get ahold of her?"

"She says they transferred her to complaints and bumped her up because they were short over there, is what they told her."

"She can't wander back to the Hall to take a peek for us?"

"I don't think we can hang her out there like that, Senator, but I'm telling you, you can relax. Everything's taken care of." Joey looked at the walls and ceiling. He'd checked three times, but Augie was making him nervous. On a day that began with finding a bug in the telephone, they ought to be a little more discreet than to talk about lifting records out of the DA's office. "You got these next two ads running soon?" Joey asked, changing the subject.

"Tonight," Augie said, and the thought of it buoyed him. Augie was like a little boy that way. Not a single emotion hidden, and the swings from happy to sad, glad to mad, were quick and complete. "The first one starts tonight, and it's strong. You got the money to keep it out there a few days?"

"It's getting tight, tell you the truth, as much airtime as we've been buying all over the state. But I think so."

"Rob a bank if you have to, Joey. This ad puts us all in black robes. And you know what? Maybe this little problem down at the refinery blows over. Maybe it turns out it's something in the water that didn't even involve Liberty. Who knows? They fish it out, whatever the hell it is, and two years from now nobody remembers what happened. This ad, though, they'll remember."

Lou had rounded up a dozen of Sharperson's Temple University law students, who opened the ad on the steps of the law school, chatting about Sharperson cutting more classes than all of them combined. The spot ended with a dramatization of Izzy on the bench, pounding his gavel and sentencing a black man—photographed from behind and played by Lou wearing an Afro wig he picked up on Chestnut Street—to fifteen years in prison for missing child support payments.

Augie was saving the other ad for last. It was built around a photo of a spacy Debra Sharperson in her college days. She wore an earth-mother dress with puka shells and puffed on a joint while holding up a Tastykake butterscotch crimpet for the camera. Maggie Sharperson had given Joey the photo.

"Seriously, you have problems pushing enough money through bingo, or however you're doing this, let me know. I always got an idea or two up my sleeve," Augie said. "One year Lou and I had to raise a few dollars for a guy I was backing for judge, so we head down the shore and what should happen but we see one of those valet kids with a jacket on, that park cars. We buy the coat off the kid, and Lou stands in front of hotels up and down the strip, one fuckin' mo-mo after another pulling up and handing him the keys." Augie picked up his nameplate and ran his fingers over the letters, as if reading SENATOR by touch. "I had a guy down there with a chop shop, we head back home that night with money comin' out of our ears, Joey. Bing, bang, boom—my guy's a judge. Fargedaboutit."

The oak nameplate made a solid knock when Augie clunked it back down on the table, and there was a heaviness in his voice, too, as he brought up a subject he'd been avoiding. "Ron Rice, Joey. You're taking care of that?"

Ham had hired his own ad agency and was running his campaign out of his state office in Queen Village. Joey's thinking all along had been that the less Augie knew about what was going on, the safer he'd be in the long run. He had made sure Augie never spoke directly to Izzy or Ham about what Liberty Oil wanted in return for their money. And he hadn't told Augie the other piece of it. That for every dollar he gave to Ham, he was slipping two to Ron Rice, not telling him where it came from. It was a sweet deal, Joey thought. Rice picking up money from the people he was bashing.

Ham was such a whoring drunk, he had no clue he was getting clipped. And as far as Liberty Oil knew, everything was fine between Ham and Augie. Joey still had Ham convinced that if he didn't need Augie, he at least needed Joey to launder his money for him. He also had him convinced that if he broke publicly with Augie, Liberty Oil would cut him off. Joey was playing Ham and he was playing Liberty, slipping the knife in so cleanly, neither of them had felt the blade yet. It was all timing now—waiting for just the right moment to flick his wrist.

"Senator," Joey said, "all you gotta know, there's nothing to worry about." Nothing except that Augie was up and down and twisted around, torn up by the notion that he was buying back into the game with the bodies of dead kids. Joey hadn't figured that into the plan, and he didn't need Muldoon on his back at every turn, either. But it would still turn out fine. Izzy would breeze. They'd bury Ham. The Prince of Pennsylvania would be back in business. And they'd have a new face in the Sunday Macaroni Club. Joey would see to it, whatever the cost. It was the least he could do for the man who'd saved his family.

When the phone rang, Joey wedged it between his ear and shoulder, trying to finish the poem for Maggie. It was Lou.

"You sitting down?" he asked.

"What've you got?"

"Ham just hit the jackpot."

"What are you talking about?"

"He went to A.C., threatened a few of the hotel and casino people that if he loses this election, he goes to the police and tells them the casinos bought his vote to block riverboat gambling here."

"Fuck me," Joey said, breaking the pencil tip on the table. He rocked on the back legs of his chair and looked up at the fan spinning over him.

"He had them in a fuckin' panic is what I hear," Lou said. "Had them running all up and down the Boardwalk to put something together, a little testimonial dinner, and Ham carries away a hundred grand."

Joey slammed the phone back into its cradle. With that much money, Ham would own prime time the rest of the way. Radio, TV, newspaper. Like a cockroach, he was. You sweep him out the front door and he's crawling in the back.

Joey told himself to relax. There was more than one way to get this job done, and he'd known that all along. The cost was higher. A lot higher, in fact. But it was worth the sacrifice, because the result would be the same.

The phone rang again. Joey thought it was Lou and picked up where he left off, cursing the cowards running the casinos. But it wasn't Lou. Joey stood up and looked around the diner, calling Augie's name. No sign of him. "Milly, you seen Augie?"

Emiliano Falcone pointed to the bathroom. Joey dropped the phone and ran to the back of the diner, nearly plowing into Augie as he came out still zipping his fly. "Senator, it's somebody calling about Angela."

Augie paled and his voice trembled. "What is it, Joey? She all right?"

Joey led him back to the table and Augie sat down, staring at the phone a moment before picking it up. He listened calmly, putting his hand over the mouthpiece to tell Joey to go get the car.

"What hospital?" Augie asked. "I'm on my way." He stood

too fast and the blood drained from his head. He reached for the table to get his balance.

"Augie, you OK?" Emiliano Falcone asked.

Augie didn't hear him. He steadied himself, then lunged for the door as if there were no air in the room, thinking about the fastest way to get to St. Bartholomew Hospital.

CHAPTER 22

THE LAYOVER IN San Juan was one hour, then it was ninety minutes to Barbados. Mike Muldoon wore a Hawaiian shirt he'd bought for the trip and sat in an airport lounge with the sports page spread in front of him, thinking the baggage guys better not bend his shafts. He had a new set of graphite that should give him an extra ten, fifteen yards off the tee.

Carla Delmonico had gone to the ladies' room, giving him a rare moment of peace. She'd been talking his ear off since the airport in Philadelphia. Come to think of it, she hadn't shut up since they called her in and told her she could go to jail for sabotaging an investigation. When Savitch—who was too much of a bleeding heart, in Muldoon's estimation—realized that every man in Carla's life had treated her with roughly the same respect as Ham Flaherty had, she went soft, telling her they might be able to keep her out of prison if she helped them.

The way Carla reacted, they thought she might send out announcements and throw a party. Yes, she said. She'd wear a wire. She'd do anything. Eager little deputy that she was, she even asked about getting into the police academy and wondered if they'd write letters backing her up. Here she came now, wiggling across the corridor on pencil-thin heels, still smacking her lipstick into place. Her skirt was at midthigh, nearly as tight as her

Lycra top, and she wore a flower in her hair because she said that was what people did in the islands.

Muldoon watched guys watch her as she came smiling back to him with her frizzed-out red hair and smiling green eyes. She could get on your nerves with the little-girl voice and the constant chatter, no question about it, but damn it if this didn't beat anything he'd done in retirement. Here he was, on his way to a tropical island to hunt bad guys and maybe sneak in a round of golf, Carla Delmonico doting on him like an obedient trophy wife. He'd rather have Savitch along, frankly, and almost got up the courage to ask, but he didn't want to hear her say no, or have her go into another fawning account of Jack Singer and all the help he was giving her. Carla was back now, sliding onto the stool next to him and asking if she had time for another planter's punch.

"What the hell?" Muldoon said, checking his watch.

"That's really a beautyful shirt," she said. "But I don't think I've ever seen a Hawaiian shirt with a little pocket protector in it like that. Sort of defeats the purpose, doesn't it?"

Muldoon turned slowly, made eye contact, and went back to his newspaper.

"You mind if I ask the bartender to take our picture?" Carla asked. She'd brought a Polaroid.

Muldoon didn't look up from his paper. He said, "It's not going to happen."

Carla turned her attention to the two women next to her, who were on the same plane coming in. They were talking about seeing Julio Iglesias at the Valley Forge Music Fair. "Best show I seen since Paul Anka came down the shore this summer," one said.

Carla jumped in, saying, "Oh my God, I was at that show."

"Julio Iglesias or Paul Anka?"

"No, Paul Anka. After he had those Kodak commercials on TV is when I started liking him. Good morning yesterday?"

They were from King of Prussia, on their way to St. Thomas.

One of them asked Carla, "If you don't mind my asking, who does your hair?"

Carla said, "I go over Julius Scissors. On Locust Street? He does it himself."

"Because it looks beautiful."

"Thank you."

Muldoon looked at his watch again and told Carla maybe they better head over to the gate.

It was late afternoon when Muldoon drove the rental through Bridgetown and up Highway 3, working from a map. "We can check into the hotel later," he said. "I want to drive past this place first, see how these guys are living."

"I been to the Bahamas a couple times," Carla said. "Nassau. Cable Beach. You been to the Caribbean?"

"St. John's," Muldoon said. "One time. I'm not a beach person."

"Oh, I love the beach. I practically grew up down the shore in Wildwood. My God, it's gorgeous here. Do you feel this air?"

Muldoon's FBI pals had set him up with more information than he asked for. It seemed that there were two former Liberty Oil employees living on a sugar plantation that had been in Whit Pritchard's family since the 1600s, when English settlers imported slaves to harvest the cane. Richard Kelly had been Liberty's operations manager and Daiman Heidorn, a lab technician, was a shop steward. They'd both been in Barbados three years. According to Muldoon's contacts, they were still official residents of the United States, but hadn't filed income tax returns since jetting to the island with their wives. He could throw that at them. Use it to draw out their story.

Everything pointed to Kelly and Heidorn having had their hands on the smoking gun. If Liberty Oil had been belching poison out of its stacks over the years, something that went undetected by state and federal regulators, Whitney Pritchard couldn't be the only one who knew about it. Muldoon suspected even the regulators. It wouldn't be the first time a public servant took a dive in Pennsylvania. As for Kelly and Heidorn, Muldoon didn't know a lot of guys who retired to tropical islands in their forties. They had to have worked a sweet deal for themselves. Send us to paradise or we talk. But exactly how much they knew, and how much Muldoon could squeeze out of them, remained to be seen. He was hoping Carla Delmonico might be able to use one or two of her many charms to draw them out.

The terrain rose gradually as Muldoon headed northeast through fields of hibiscus and orchids. The plantation house was supposed to be in something called the Scotland District of St. Joseph's Parish.

"Flower Forest, that sounds beautyful," Carla said, reading a sign.

Muldoon said, "It's supposed to be just past this fork. Here we go."

Westminster House was three hundred years old, a grand wood frame structure with a wraparound porch sheltered by an overhang. The yellow building paled in the late afternoon light, light that was softened by the Atlantic mist climbing the limestone slopes from the water's edge. The cane fields, leased to a local grower and still farmed, stretched north behind the main building. Off to one side was a row of guesthouses.

"That's where they're supposed to live," Muldoon said.

Carla said, "Honey, I'd take it any day. These guys got it made."

Muldoon had checked them into adjoining rooms at the Tradewinds in St. James, the heart of the touristed west side. You never knew what you were getting into, working with local police on an island outpost like this, but he'd called from Philadelphia and was told that Richard Kelly and Daiman Heidorn were well-known at the Tradewinds Bamboo Bar. A police captain said they were known to troll the international crowd flashing money and year-round tans, especially when their wives were visiting another island or were back in the States.

Muldoon showered and put on a blue three-button sport shirt, short sleeves, with a pair of beltless, pleated beige golf slacks. He set up a morning tee-off time and called the police captain to let him know he was on the island and would drop by tomorrow to talk about Kelly and Heidorn. Then he went out to the pool bar, where Carla was sipping planter's punch under a thatched roof.

"Will you look at this place?" she asked, gazing past the palms and torchlights to the moonlit Caribbean. A light breeze was coming off the water, the temperature in the eighties. "It's even better than the Bahamas."

She sniffed the tropical air and threw her head back, like she was having sex with the island. Muldoon kept thinking, Here's a girl who knows I've seen her in the Ham slammer video giving a desktop fuck to that slimy degenerate, and there's no sign of awkwardness. Not the slightest. He had never known women like this, except the ones married to the mob guys.

"Do I get to use like an undercover name?" Carla asked. She was wearing a flowered sarong, tight but not trampy, with matching halter top and an orchid in her hair. Looking like she belonged nowhere else in the world.

"I don't think it's necessary."

"Because I always wanted to be a Trish."

"Fine, be a Trish. Just don't mention you work for the district attorney's office, if you don't mind."

"Maybe I'll just use my job before that."

"What was your job before that?"

"I worked down at Tiffany's. The gentleman's club? Oh. I figured you would've knew. That's where I met Ham and he got me in the DA's office. That was years ago."

A stripper. No, he hadn't known. Muldoon was half repulsed, half titillated, and completely embarrassed, though he didn't know why he should be. He looked away until she turned to the ocean, and then he took a good look, the sarong twisted tight against her legs and the halter clung to her chest. Maybe three-fourths titillated. She definitely wasn't his type, but it wasn't every day you could say you hung out with a stripper at a seaside resort. He felt a quick pang of guilt, wondering what his wife would say if she knew. She'd asked if Savitch was going with him because she probably suspected he had a crush on her, just from the way he avoided saying much about her except that she was young and kind of headstrong. Muldoon said no, Savitch wasn't going along. He hadn't added that Carla was. Muldoon ordered a beer and took a long drink, making it a private toast to Kevinne McGinns for rescuing him from his boredom. Retirement was a great idea until you actually did it, and then you're sitting there wondering, all right, what now? Even golf wasn't all that much fun to look forward to when it was something you did every day. Going back to work had made things better with his wife, too. They'd even resumed regular relations, although Muldoon usually imagined it was Savitch, at least at first. Just to get himself going.

A calypso band was setting up on the terrace, the flat Caribbean slapping at the shore behind them. It was a narrow beach of white sand, a few people strolling at the water's edge toward the lights of Holetown. Muldoon told Carla that Kelly and Heidorn usually showed up after the dinner hour, so maybe they should get something to eat and then Carla could come back to the bar alone, see what happened.

She couldn't hide her enthusiasm. "This is great," she said, "because I always wanted to be an actress."

Muldoon took a little umbrella out of her drink and snapped it. "Listen," he said, "this is not a James Bond movie we're in. You're not an actress and you're not a detective. If you try to be something you're not, it'll tip them off. All I want you to do, like I've been telling you all day, is just be yourself. Let them know you're from Philadelphia, you're Carla—excuse me—

Trish, and oh my God, what a coincidence. They're from Philadelphia, too." Carla was draining her planter's punch through a
straw, staring up at Muldoon like an eager student. "Let them
talk, see where it goes," he said. "If we get nothing out of it,
then tomorrow I just knock on their door and do it that way."

They moved to a table on the terrace for dinner and when
they were done Carla slinked back up to the bar alone. She sat
sidesaddle, legs crossed, sipping drinks through straws she held
with her little finger up like a wing. She fended off a dozen come-
ons before she heard the bartender greet Mr. Kelly and Mr.
Heidorn like they were VIPs. She looked back at Muldoon, who
was nodding.

What a couple of assholes, he was thinking. They looked like
they were dressed for a a bad TV show. Pastel sport coats over
T-shirts. Loafers, no socks. Take them out of Philadelphia for
ten minutes and they acted like they discovered the fucking islands. He studied them for a few minutes, watching them clink
glasses with Carla, the stripper-turned-dick. What a life they
had. Sleep in, sip a cold lemonade on the porch while the plantation workers sweat in the sun, maybe get in a round of golf or
a swim, then come down here and chase skirts while half of
Philadelphia gets gassed by Liberty Oil. Muldoon would have bet
the mortgage on extortion.

After two rounds of rum, Kelly, Heidorn, and Carla were out
on the dance floor. There had to be a hundred fifty people on
the terrace, Muldoon figured. People from all over the world, and
you could guess the three from Philadelphia in two seconds.
Carla was doing the limbo under an imaginary stick, and her
dates, their laughing faces shiny with sweat, were doing the
Mummers' strut to a Latin beat. Muldoon hadn't felt in months
what he was feeling right now—the high that comes when you
know you're getting close and you're about to wipe the stupid
smile off some idiot's face. Savitch was right. She'd been right
all along, damn her. Instincts, smarts, she had something. Of

course, it could have been luck, too. Muldoon said a Hail Mary, asking the Virgin Mother to make them slip up just once, say something to Carla, so he could knock on their door tomorrow and throw it back at them. These guys would be blubbering on the floor. Muldoon wondered how much Kelly and Heidorn knew about the kids getting sick and dying back home, their families shattered forever. He wondered if, in three years, they had lost one night of sleep.

Muldoon had taped a microphone inside a lampshade in Carla's room and ran wire along the baseboard and under the door that connected their rooms. On his end, he listened on headphones plugged into a cassette recorder. It probably wouldn't get into court, but he could use it to muscle the two of them. That and the IRS jam they were in. You could never predict how hard or easy it would be to break someone down. But some of them, when they saw where they sat, dimed people all the way back to high school.

Kelly and Heidorn had brought a bottle of rum back to the room and Carla was telling them she made the trip with her brother, a gift to celebrate his divorce being finalized. He met a woman on the beach this afternoon waiting to take a parasail ride, and she hadn't heard from him since. Muldoon smiled. Not bad.

"What do you think they're doing right now?" one of the men asked. Probably Kelly, who looked like more of an operator than Heidorn. Muldoon could tell, out at the Bamboo Bar, that he was someone who couldn't keep his pants zipped.

Carla giggled and said, "Wouldn't you like to know?"

The other one said that was a nice gift for her brother. Expensive. He asked what she did for a living.

"You won't guess it," she said.

"Then tell me."

"You tell first," Carla said. Shit, she wasn't bad at all. "What do you guys do, and do you have any openings? Because I could handle this life. This tropical air makes me feel romantic." Careful, Muldoon whispered to himself. Don't overdo it.

"That depends," Kelly said. "Would you do practically anything to get the job?"

"God it's hot in here," Carla said. "Let's see if they got some ice." Her voice moved across the room, and then she said, "Would I do anything? It depends on what the job is."

Heidorn said, "We're sort of consultants. To a company back home."

Carla slid the door to the terrace open to let the breeze in.

"That's even hotter," she said. "But I hate air conditioning. It's false air, you know what I mean?"

There wasn't another sound for about fifteen seconds, and then Kelly, his voice higher than it had been, was asking, "Trish, what are you doing?"

"You don't mind, do you? It's just so warm."

"Oh my God," Kelly groaned. "Those are amazing."

"Thank you."

Muldoon put his hands to his head. She was stripping?

Heidorn asked, "Are they real?"

"Who gives a shit?" Kelly said.

Muldoon hadn't discussed how far she should go with these guys. Maybe Carla thought she was supposed to sleep with them. Muldoon got down on the floor and put his eye to the crack of light coming in under the door. As he did, he imagined his wife walking in the door behind him, catching him in this pose. Then he imagined Savitch doing the same. Hell, she'd caught him watching Carla wiggle out of her office that day. But why should he feel so self-conscious about this? It was normal and healthy, and besides, it's not like he cared about Carla. She was a stripper, for Christ's sake. You were *supposed* to look at her breasts. All he wanted to do was steal a peek, anyway. But as hard as Muldoon pressed his face into the rug, he couldn't see anything but feet.

Carla was saying, "Why don't you road test them, see if you think they're real."

Kelly said, "Unbelievable."

And then it was Carla, saying, "So do I get the job?"

Heidorn said. "Yes. As my personal secretary. I'll tell Richard to put you on the payroll."

"Richard? You mean Richard here's your boss?"

"Not this Richard. Someone you wouldn't know. He's sort of the company treasurer."

"Well if you're not going to tell me who to call about getting a job, maybe the girls here wanna go back inside."

Heidorn said, "Abbington. His name's Richard Abbington. And believe me, he wouldn't want the girls to go back inside."

Abbington. Richard Abbington. Hadn't Savitch thrown that name at him the other day? Muldoon couldn't remember the context, but he was almost certain she'd mentioned that name.

Carla said, "I don't really get it why a Philadelphia company has consultants in Barbados."

"It's a long story," Heidorn said. "Let's just say we know so much, we got promoted to the Caribbean division."

Muldoon heard ice dropping into cups. Heidorn told Kelly not to kill the bottle, he'd like to pour some rum on those things and lick it off.

"Wait a minute," Carla said, excitement in her voice. "I almost forgot. I've got a camera!"

They took turns taking shots of each other licking rum off Carla's breasts. Muldoon got down on the floor again to see if he could press his head far enough into the carpet to see through the crack, but it was nothing but feet again. He remembered Carla referring to him as Clark Kent. If he were, he'd be able to see through the door.

Carla set the camera to take a picture of the three of them together, one man at each breast. They went on like this for a while, the men carrying on like high-school boys who'd never had a pair wagged in their faces, Carla giggling along, trying to draw more out of them, but it was running dry. All they wanted to talk about now was the weather, saying it was so hot, maybe they should take their clothes off, too. Carla said she actually was getting a chill, and she better put her shirt back on.

"You don't want to do that," Kelly said. "Look, I've got my pants off."

"Come on," Carla said. "Really. Would you guys just give me my shirt back?"

"You don't want to be a party pooper, do you?" Heidorn asked.

"I'm just not feeling that well. Maybe that's why I took a chill."

"You're fine," Kelly said. "Probably just need some fresh air is all."

"No, I mean I'm really sick. Like maybe it was something I ate. Excuse me."

Muldoon heard the bathroom door close, and then he picked up one of the men, he wasn't sure which. "Fuck this," he was saying. "Two hours, this prick tease has her tits in our faces, and now she pulls this? I'm not leaving."

"I'll go see if I can talk her back out," the other one said.

Muldoon was out his door one second and banging on Carla's the next.

"Who is it?" one of the men asked.

"It's Trish's brother, who's this?"

No one answered.

"Open up," Muldoon ordered.

Heidorn opened the door as Kelly was zipping up his pants and Carla was coming out of the bathroom in a robe. Muldoon glowered at Kelly and Heidorn.

"How was the parasailing?" Carla asked.

Muldoon was still staring at her guests.

"I met these boys at the bar," she said, "but they were just leaving."

Muldoon held the door as they walked past him and out. "If

you're going to be around, Trish, maybe we'll catch you at the bar tomorrow night," Kelly said.

"Good. I'll look for you," Carla said, and Muldoon slammed the door closed.

"You all right?" he asked.

"Yeah, I'm fine."

"It sounded like they were getting carried away," Muldoon said.

"Tell me about it," Carla said. "The one guy had his pants down and was starting to pull his thing out."

"Well maybe they got the wrong idea when you took your top off," Muldoon scolded.

"Are you mad at me?"

"Am I mad at you? No, why?"

"I was just trying to get them to open up is all. But I couldn't get them to say anything."

"You did fine," Muldoon said. "I was impressed, actually."

"I got these photos, at least. I figured maybe you could threaten to show their wives if they don't talk. You wanna see them?"

Muldoon hesitated. Yeah, he wouldn't mind perusing them. But he said, "Tomorrow. I'll have a look tomorrow, all right? I need to go turn the tape recorder off and get some sleep. I'm playing golf in the morning and I'll call you when I get back."

He went into his room and was getting into bed when he heard a knock on the door that joined their rooms. He waited, then heard it again, firmer this time. He went to the door and spoke through the wood. "What is it?"

"I won't be able to sleep if you're mad at me for not getting something better out of those guys."

"Carla, you did fine. Honestly."

She waited a few seconds, then knocked again.

"What now?"

"Can I come in?"

"Can you come in?"

"It's still pretty early and we're in Barbados, after all. You wanna go for a walk on the beach or just talk or something?"

Muldoon was holding the doorknob. He flashed on his wife again, then imagined that it was Savitch on the other side, asking if she could come in. When he pulled the door open, Carla stood there topless. The blush came over him in a wave, and Carla put a hand on his chest and pushed him back into the room until he fell on the bed and was looking up at her. She untied the sarong and had nothing on underneath.

"An FBI agent," she said. "This is a first for me."

Muldoon had put in for a six o'clock wake-up call. The phone rang at five-thirty and he woke up with Carla's head on his bare chest. It was the police captain.

Richard Kelly and Daiman Heidorn had been forced off the road on their way back to St. Joseph's Parish some time after midnight. Both men had been shot in the head and the police captain said it looked like robbery.

Muldoon hung up the phone and said, "Not a chance."

CHAPTER 23

JOEY BOUNCED THE OLDS over the curb and onto the grass, delivering Augie to the front steps of St. Bartholomew Hospital, a modern six-story brick building on Broad Street near the Schuylkill Expressway. Over the years, Augie had funneled tens of thousands of dollars worth of state grants, loans, and other giveaways to St. Bart's, driving a nearby nondenominational private hospital into bankruptcy. In return, he never paid a nickel in medical costs.

Augie galloped through the halls as fast as his long, seventy-five-year-old legs would allow, his fedora bobbing high on his forehead. Joey huffed along behind him, his jowls flapping and his gun digging into his ribs. An emergency room doctor told Augie they'd gotten Angela stabilized and moved her up to the fourth floor. When the elevator doors swooshed open on four, Augie nearly trampled a nurse who was waiting there for him.

"This way," she said. Father D'Anunzio was performing last rites when Augie walked into the room. You knew it was going to happen, Joey was thinking. Of course you did. Everybody had to die. But now that it was here, it felt as if it had sneaked up on them. Last rites for Angela.

Augie's heavy breathing sounded like the wind. He made the sign of the cross and took Angela's hand. Father D'Anunzio continued his prayers. He didn't so much as look up at Augie, whose eyes were on his wife. His small, fading wife, who was seventy-two and looked as old as time. Angela lay on her back, asleep or unconscious. She had a clear green oxygen mask over her mouth and her chest wheezed and rattled, the outline of her ribs visible through a thin cotton hospital gown. Augie couldn't remember her cheekbones being so defined, her face so tiny. She'd been chiseled into a small religious figurine. Angela, patron saint of political widows.

When Father D'Anunzio was done, Augie started his own prayer. "Our Father, who art in heaven, halo be thy name..." He closed his eyes as he prayed, and when he opened them, he looked as though he had been praying for a miracle. Praying for Angela to be her old self. He was upset all over again.

"That's not my Angela," he told Father D'Anunzio. The priest put a hand on Augie's shoulder. "You remember what she used to look like, Padre? She was a beauty, my Angela. Am I right, Joey?"

Augie turned, but Joey was outside the room, looking in with sad wet eyes that made it worse for Augie.

"She's going to be all right," Augie told the priest, turning toward Joey again and nodding. "My wife, she's a fighter. If I had half her fight..."

A doctor came in and asked Augie to join him outside.

"I've gotta stay with my Angela," Augie protested. Joey poked his head in to say he'd watch over her, don't worry, and Augie went down the hall with the doctor, a man he'd never seen. They went into a small chapel, three rows of pews, candles, a Jesus statue, and a portrait of the twelve apostles. Bartholomew with a halo. The heavy door closed behind the doctor and the sound echoed through the chapel.

"Mr. Sangiamino, I'm Dr. Bhutto."

"Doctor what?"

"Kumar Bhutto."

Augie looked him over, trying to guess his age. He could be

anywhere from thirty-five to fifty. It was hard to say with these people. Dr. Bhutto was nearly as thin as Augie, four or five inches shorter, with jet black hair and black-rimmed glasses. "We got a doctor already," Augie said.

"Yes, I'm aware of that. But Dr. DePaulo is attending a conference in Chicago."

Augie said he wasn't aware of that. He asked the doctor to excuse him for a moment, and he went into the hall and called down to Joey, leaving the doctor alone in the chapel. Joey's heels pounded like mallets on the linoleum floor. "Can you believe this, Joey? That's my Angela in there, sick as all get out, and they got Simba the elephant boy lookin' at her."

Joey nodded as if he appreciated the sentiment, but he had calming words for his boss. "They're supposed to be a real smart type of person, Senator. I wouldn't worry about it. They're studying algebra in second grade, these people."

Augie wasn't buying it. "This here's fuckin' St. Bartholomew Hospital, Joey. Get hold of Father D'Anunzio if he's still in the building, tell him take care of this for me. Let's get Dr. DePaulo on the phone, at least." Dr. Bhutto poked his head out to ask if anything was the matter.

"I gotta be honest, Doctor," Augie said, going back inside the chapel. "It's just I'm a little uncomfortable with this setup. A doctor I don't know—not that it's anything personal against you or your people. But that's my wife in there and I'd feel better with somebody had a little more seasoning is all. You see what I'm saying?"

"Mr. Sangiamino?"

"Yes?"

"I'm chief of oncology. I'm Dr. DePaulo's boss." Augie nodded as if he knew that. He wasn't sure how else to respond. The doctor asked, "Would you care to sit down?"

Augie sat heavily on the last pew and Dr. Bhutto moved in next to him. He's got dark skin, Augie told himself, and his name ends in a vowel. Go with that. "I'm sorry," Augie said. "I didn't mean nothin' by it. I love my wife's all. She's gotta have the best."

The doctor didn't seem offended. "Mr. Sangiamino, your wife is a very sick woman. She has pneumonia, and the white cell count is up. She's had chronic myelogenous for how long?"

"Nah, it's leukemia she's got. About ten, fifteen years altogether."

"Yes, that is a form of leukemia. It might have entered transformation now, or what we call the blast crisis. But even if it's still merely accelerated, which is a less acute stage, she has other problems. Your wife is gravely ill, Mr. Sangiamino. I just wanted to make sure you understood this."

The pew felt like stone. Augie repositioned himself and said, "I'll tell you what, though, Doctor. She's strong, my wife. Angela's one hell of a fighter."

"I'm sure that she is, Mr. Sangiamino. But after a while, the body can no longer fight what she has. She might make it through the day, or maybe a couple of days. But unfortunately that's the best outlook I can give you."

Augie shot up off the pew, angry and afraid. His heart felt like a balloon somebody was inflating, and the room started to spin. He reached for the back of the pew to steady himself, and Dr. Bhutto held his arm and asked him to sit down. "I'm fine," Augie said, refusing to sit. "I'm fine."

"Try to take it easy, Mr. Sangiamino."

Augie thought, Take it easy? What kind of a jackoff was this guy? He said, "Listen, money's not a problem here, Doc. Let's take her to Penn or wherever they got a treatment for this type of thing. Whatever it takes. And I'd like to get Dr. DePaulo in here, if you don't mind."

The doctor was sympathetic, but didn't give any ground. "The best anybody can do is try to keep her comfortable the next day or two. You can stay with her if you like. I'm sure she'd like that."

Augie took a few deep breaths and slowed himself down. He

sat back down and leaned on the pew in front of him, looking at the statue of Jesus. She's dying, he said to himself. This was it. He could keep fighting it, but it wouldn't change anything. A different doctor wouldn't change anything, either. Angela was a goner.

Dr. Bhutto stood up, saying he had to check on other patients. "Can I get you anything?" he asked. "Why don't you let me arrange for someone to have a look at you downstairs?"

Augie brought his eyes up with tears in them. "I need more time," he said. "We had a problem there, Doc, and I had to go away for a while. I've been wanting to make that up to her, you know? Get it back the way it was. But she's been sick the whole time I'm back. I need more time is all. If she can just hang on a while longer." Dr. Bhutto sat back down and began to explain the situation once more.

Augie interrupted him. "You been following this thing, Doc? All the leukemia they got going around?"

Dr. Bhutto nodded. "I'm on a committee working with the Centers for Disease Control."

"What do you think?" Augie asked.

"What do you mean, specifically?"

"Is it something coming out of the refineries, you think?"

Dr. Bhutto didn't follow politics, but he knew Augie was involved. And he could see that something else, something besides the exact time of Angela's death, waited to be decided for Augie. "It's hard to say for sure," he said. "There are several refineries, as I understand it. And many more sources of industrial pollution."

"That's exactly what I've been telling people," Augie said, finding some relief in the doctor's answer. "You guys are the experts. Eagle-beavers that went to college, and you can't tell the elbow from the asshole on this thing yourselves, am I right?"

A puzzled look crossed Dr. Bhutto's face. His English was pretty good, but there must still be certain colloquialisms he wasn't familiar with. He asked Augie where Angela grew up.

"Mercer," Augie said. "Right there, like most of these kids."

"Is she a smoker?"

"Never touched it. This is a woman lived a clean life from day one. No tobacco, no alcohol. A glass or two of red wine with dinner is all."

"Let me tell you a story, Mr. Sangiamino. I grew up in an industrial region of Pakistan. Chemical plants, textiles, petroleum products. My father smoked his whole life, my mother never smoked. They both died of lung cancer in their forties."

"That's too young to die," Augie said.

"But not uncommon at the time, Mr. Sangiamino. And here, the cancer rate is not so high as in my home, but among the highest in the United States. I came here to learn more about the causes."

Augie said, "Nobody knows, though, is my point. You can't tell how anybody gets this stuff."

"That is true to an extent and partially untrue as well. You cannot take a single patient with a case of leukemia and determine the precise cause. But there are things we call carcinogens, and that means very simply something that is known to cause cancer. Also there are what we call suspected carcinogens. In a region of such industrial production as this, there is a higher rate of these substances and there is a higher rate of many cancers as well. It is something that will require much more study, because a number of other factors come into consideration: lifestyle, diet, these types of things. One thing we must do, in my opinion, and I've recommended this to the other doctors, is go into every industrial work site and test thoroughly for substances that could cause the problems we're seeing."

Augie stood as if in a hurry to get somewhere, then sat back down. He started to say something, but the words got caught.

"You must remember," Dr. Bhutto said, "that your wife is more than seventy years old. The sick children we have, they are five and six, seven and eight. The leukemia is definitely a factor in your wife's condition, but she has a different type than the children. We're seeing mostly acute lymphocytic in them. Your wife also has age working against her. As you know, Mr. Sangiamino, we all have to die." Dr. Bhutto stood again and asked Augie to come with him. He wanted him to see something.

"I need to get back to Angela," Augie said.

"It'll take just a minute."

They took the elevator up two flights that seemed like twenty-two, and Augie felt like he was suffocating in that little box. What if they did what the doctor was suggesting? What if they sent a bunch of doctors to Liberty Oil, let them snoop around in there, and they came out saying this is it, we found the killer?

The door opened to a hall covered with finger paintings and other children's artwork. Dr. Bhutto led Augie to a window that looked into a room. A child lay asleep on the bed, a stuffed giraffe six inches from his outstretched right hand. A man and woman slept on chairs at the foot of the bed, blankets over them.

Augie had seen this boy somewhere. Late at night, when he heard the house creaking and thought it was Angela, he saw Joey Napolitano and he saw this kid, too. He was sure of it. The boy floated on white, just like this kid was doing now. Augie put his hands on the windowsill to keep them from shaking.

Dr. Bhutto said, "Two years ago, this child was perfectly healthy. All of a sudden, he had no appetite. He was tired. He was prone to fever and infection. This was a good little athlete, the parents say, and he was tripping over himself clumsily, and the bleeding from cuts didn't stop. Acute lymphocytic leukemia."

Augie asked where the boy lived. "Mercer," Dr. Bhutto said. "This is one of the kids you've been reading about."

Augie's heart felt like it was inflating again and his legs buckled slightly. He gripped the windowsill tighter.

"Mr. Sangiamino, are you all right?"

"It's fuckin' hot in here is all, excuse me."

"Nurse, could you please bring a cup of water?"

"Why you got me lookin' at this kid?" Augie asked. He took the water and gulped it down, then panted. "You trying to tell me something with this?"

"You expressed an interest. I thought you might like to see one of the children."

"I seen one already," Augie said. "I see them every night."

"Well this is one of the luckier ones. It's actually a very treatable disease these days. Many children go into remission, and more than half are cured. We have our fingers crossed, but this one started chemotherapy early, and I think he's going to be OK."

Augie looked at the frail boy, then at his parents. "He's going to make it?"

"It looks good."

"That's beautyful," Augie said. "I'll make a novena. And do me a favor. Could you tell the parents there, they need anything, they can let me know? Just tell them Senator Augie Sangiamino will take care of it. The hospital bills, everything." Dr. Bhutto said that was a generous offer. He took Augie back to Angela's room and left him at the window, peering in.

She hadn't moved. She was still on her back, facing the heavens, and Augie could see for the first time that she wanted to go. Was she waiting for him to come clean, so she could go in peace? He could live without politics. It wasn't everything, after all. There was a lot of other stuff Augie Sangiamino could do with himself, and he'd be square with Angela.

He looked at her for an answer. She'd always known his weaknesses, and even now, she was watching him. He knew she was watching.

CHAPTER 24

MULDOON PARKED by the art museum again, walked down the Ben Franklin Parkway with some spring in his step, and paused in front of the Basilica. He began to make the sign of the cross, part of his daily routine, but stopped himself. He probably should wait until he had his confession heard.

Savitch was already in McGinns's office and Muldoon could tell she was relieved to have someone join her in the menagerie. She was looking up at the birds as if she wanted to yank them down and let the cats have their way with them.

"Good morning, ladies."

"Welcome back," McGinns said. "So who would have thunk it? Now we have an international murder mystery on our hands."

"It wiped out my golf game," Muldoon said.

"Yes, I can't tell you how sorry I am. You've had a chance to fill Lisa in?"

"We talked for a couple of hours last night on the phone."

"Good. Have a seat then, Mike. We'll go over the whole thing in a minute. You'll have to tell us more about Carla, too. It sounds like she rose to the occasion."

"She can surprise you," Muldoon said, crossing his leg and

tapping a wing tip with his finger. He felt Savitch's eyes on him and turned to her. "What?"

"Did you get burned down there?"

"No, why?"

"I thought it was sunburn. Maybe you're just flush."

"Savitch, I worked the entire time. I wasn't out laying on the beach."

"I didn't mean anything by it. Why are you so defensive?"

"I'm beginning to understand why you two have gone two months getting dicked around by professional idiots," McGinns said. "I hate to interrupt such stimulating conversation, but I called you in here to tell you about something that's come up."

The gray cat was on Savitch's side of the sofa, the black one on Muldoon's, and even they looked at McGinns, waiting to hear what was so important. McGinns, wearing a macrame shawl, got up from the rocking chair and frumped over to the window carrying the weight of all the unsolved crimes in the city, and carrying something else, as well. Talking into the window, she said, "I thought you should know that over the years, I've bumped into Whit Pritchard once or twice at fund-raisers and various soirees, and he's asked in the past if I was interested in running for state supreme court or governor."

I thought you should know? They're out trying to nail this bastard and the boss is partying with him and all but lining him up as her campaign manager? Muldoon saw Savitch's fingers digging into the sofa, like she was sharpening her claws. He had to admit, this was a hell of a bombshell to drop at this point. He wondered, like Savitch must be wondering, if McGinns's contact with Pritchard had anything to do with her ordering Savitch not to go snooping after Liberty Oil.

"It was never anything more than that, and I don't recall a conversation that lasted beyond a few lines of cocktail chatter. But I got another call from him yesterday," McGinns said.

"What did he want?" Savitch asked. Muldoon looked over

and wished he had a leash or something. Savitch was marking off McGinns the way the cats marked off the birds.

"The same thing," McGinns said, coming back from the window and sitting in the rocker again. "He said he wasn't happy with the way the current election is shaping up, and he thought I should consider moving beyond the DA's office at some point. He said he'd be interested in supporting such a cause."

"I don't fucking believe it," Savitch said. Muldoon reached over and touched her arm. She was definitely the type to blow up, say whatever was on her mind, and then regret it later.

"This town will surprise you," McGinns answered.

"No shit."

Muldoon knew he better say something or Savitch was going to combust. "He basically offered you an outright bribe to lay off of him."

"Basically," McGinns repeated. "That's why I called the two of you in here. What do you think the chances are I can get him to commit on that?" She put her hands together in her lap and rocked, waiting for one of them to respond.

Savitch asked, "You mean actually get him to frame it that way? That if you'll drop this investigation, he'll back your next political campaign? He can't be that stupid, can he?"

McGinns said, "Why not? Nobody ever called Whit Pritchard a genius. It's his father and grandfather who were the brains of the operation. As I understand it, it's been sinking ever since A. Whitney III took over, and he doesn't have the constitution, I'm told, to handle defeat."

"It sounds like you know him beyond a couple of lines at cocktail parties," Savitch said, her arms wrapped across her chest.

"No. But I know someone who knows him fairly well."

"If he was crazy enough to order a hit on those two guys in Barbados," Muldoon said, "what would stop him from bribing the DA?"

"Exactly that," Savitch answered. "That he ordered the hit rather than doing it himself. I looked at some stories that were written about the family when he took over, and this is someone who grew up on an estate, hangs out at the Merion Cricket Club, rides horses on his farm in Devon, works out of a Center City high-rise instead of down at the refinery, and has his driver drive him three blocks to eat lunch at Republic every day. This is not a man who gets his own hands dirty. If you told me he sent Richard Abbington in here offering a deal, I could see that. But no, I don't think Whitney Pritchard is brave enough, or honest enough, to kill someone himself or to even offer a bribe."

"So he just wanted to plant the idea in my head?" McGinns asked.

"Or he wanted you to play your cards," Savitch said. "Give him some clue as to what you have."

"Well, this does prove that he knows we're looking at him," McGinns said. "Maybe the troglodytes told him, if not Carla herself. If she fucked Ham Flaherty, why not Whit Pritchard? I know you two insist we can trust her, but I don't think this is a particularly discriminating woman we're talking about."

Muldoon's leg kicked out involuntarily. McGinns looked at him and said, "Mr. Muldoon here speculated on the phone that the police in Barbados might be involved. Maybe they tipped Pritchard that our favorite detective was down there to knock some balls off the tee."

"I still like that," Muldoon said.

"You turn one stone," McGinns said, shaking her head, "and creepy crawly things slither around in every direction." She got out of the rocking chair and went over to her desk. She came back with a calendar that she laid in her lap, and she asked when they thought they'd be ready to bring the grand jury back in.

Savitch toed the fringe of the Persian rug with her shoe. Muldoon stroked his red mustache before leaning back and revealing the holstered gun he'd started carrying since Barbados.

He threw one of his big wing tips over his knee and said, "I think we're close."

McGinns said, "Close, as in maybe we'll call the grand jury back before they forget where City Hall is? Close, as in we're ready to charge?"

Savitch said, "We're not quite there yet."

"Well let me tell you where we are," McGinns said, back to her sarcastic, bitchy voice, her eyes narrowing as she held up the calendar. "Right here. Six days until the election. Six days away from Izzy Weiner being on the state supreme court and six days away from Ham Flaherty being in Congress." She dropped the calendar on the floor, frightening the birds. They rattled in their cage and the cats crouched on the arms of the sofa, ready to pounce. "We've got kids dying," McGinns went on, "an oil company buying protection, and two men with bullets through their brains in Barbados. Ever since you guys took this case, there's been a new crime every day. I feel like we just keep getting further behind."

The secretary buzzed McGinns, who excused herself and said she'd be right back. She had to go over something with a prosecutor who was on his way to closing arguments in a death-penalty case.

"I'm going to strangle her," Savitch said, bounding up as if she couldn't hold herself down any longer.

"Take it easy."

"Muldoon, if I'd listened to her, I'd still be trying to find out who sent Ham Flaherty a TV and a stereo. She came on like a hard-ass to keep me away from Whit Pritchard, and now we find out she hangs out with him at cocktail fund-raisers."

"That's not exactly what she said."

"And now she wants to know why we don't have more on him? I don't fucking believe this woman. I don't even know if I trust her at this point. She's a politician, not a prosecutor, and that's been the whole problem from the beginning. Why should

Muldoon was smiling. He said, "Tell her about the church."

"No, you go ahead."

"We put a tail on Abbington," he said. "The last two mornings, he goes to this church near the Italian Market."

McGinns interrupted. "Maybe he's praying that I keep you two morons on the case."

Muldoon ignored her. He'd worked with her long enough to know this was her way of paying a compliment, of saying you were good enough to come into her office and have her insult you. He looked at Savitch and thought he saw some recognition of that, finally. Her expression had softened and she'd removed her fingernails from the upholstery.

"So guess who's at the same mass as Richard Abbington every day," Muldoon went on.

McGinns threw her hands up. "Frank Sinatra? The pope? What am I on, *Jeopardy!?*"

"Joey Tartaglione."

"This is the moron who put three slugs through the door of his place the other night, nearly killing one of our detectives?"

"Yeah, Johnny Steele. He says he bent down to see if there was a space under the door, maybe he could slip a microphone down there, and the shots whistle over his head. One, two, three."

"Are all of your men armed, Muldoon?"

"I called them all this morning to double-check."

"Because I don't want to take chances with any of these characters. Lisa, are you licensed in this city?"

"No, but I'm fine."

"I've carried for years," McGinns said, touching the handle of her holstered gun under the shawl. "I could make a call."

"I appreciate it, but I really don't think it's necessary. I've got Muldoon here to protect me."

"So go on. Joey Tartaglione is at the same mass with Richard Abbington. What are you telling me by that?"

Savitch opened a folder she'd brought in. She handed

McGinns photos of Abbington entering and leaving the church alone. Then it was photos of Joey Tartaglione. Same thing. "We just need to get somebody inside the church and see what's going on in there," Savitch said.

McGinns said, "You don't think there's a chance they're all just good Christians? We should dress up Muldoon here like a priest. He looks the type, don't you think?"

"I like it," Savitch said. "Put the vestments on him, give him one of those little hats. He could be a visiting bishop."

"That's supposed to be funny? That was actually my backup plan. If I didn't get into the FBI, it was the seminary."

"Why am I not surprised, Muldoon?"

"What, now there's something wrong with being a priest?"

McGinns scolded them again and asked Savitch to go on with the story. Savitch said, "In other words, we think the drop is in the church."

"In the church. Do we love this city?" She rocked up and back, organizing her thoughts. One of the cats got off the sofa and jumped into her lap, but McGinns pushed it away. "Muldoon, get one of the detectives in the church. And as I mentioned on the phone, I'm sending two detectives to Barbados and I need you to brief them before they catch their plane. Maybe you can join them at some point and finally get in your round of golf, but I want you in town at least through the election."

Savitch asked McGinns if they were running into a jurisdictional turf war with the FBI or the U.S. attorney's office.

"Screw both of them," McGinns said. "This is my fripping case. If a murder is ordered by one of the central figures in an investigation run by this office, and the hit is ordered from Philadelphia, that's jurisdiction. I was on the phone half the day yesterday trying to keep those superior sons of bitches off my ass."

"And they're OK with that?" Muldoon asked. He knew the feds would be salivating over this thing. One of the reservations he'd had about taking this job was that it was rinky-dink. A man of his stature shouldn't have to give up a daily golf game to go after some nickel-and-dime payola to a dope like Ham Flaherty. But the original rap was scarcely a consideration now, and Muldoon, with his gun strapped back on, was lead investigator on what had become an international murder-corruption-conspiracy case. If Kelly and Heidorn were killed for what they knew about that refinery, it was a bigger case than he'd ever worked.

"They're crying to Washington," McGinns said. "My argument is since I've got their best agent working for me, what would I want with the FBI? I've got two friends on the Senate Judiciary Committee working on it for me."

"I went to the morgue before I left the island," Muldoon said. "Nice little job, right behind the ear on both guys. I went out to the highway, too. No skid marks. No sign of any scuffle. This was no fly-by-night crew pulling a random robbery. You want to rob somebody, you pick some dumb-fuck tourist who doesn't know east from west. Either the police in Barbados don't know what they're doing—"

"Or the police tipped Liberty Oil that you were down there and somebody ordered a hit," McGinns said.

"Exactly. Maybe somebody up here hires hoods down there, or they send someone in. Or, and this is another thought that crossed my mind while I was down there, the police do the job themselves."

"You have anything on that?"

"No. But they seemed to know a lot about Kelly and Heidorn. Who's to say Liberty doesn't own the police, like you suggested? All they'd need, actually, is one guy in the department. This captain I dealt with sounded like he might have skipped over the police academy."

McGinns rocked silently for a while, looking toward the light of the window. Muldoon knew she was enjoying the shit out of this. Not just because of the press she'd get if everything came together, but because she loved the chase as much as the capture. He wished Savitch could have seen her in her day. She'd have more respect if she could have seen how the courtroom filled up with attorneys when McGinns was working. They went to school on McGinns, hanging on the rails like babies watching the mother crow pick carcasses clean.

"You think maybe we're watching too much television, letting our imaginations run wild?" McGinns asked, looking at Muldoon first and then Savitch. "We've got a couple of small-time pols hooked up with one of the richest men in the country, and we've got him snuffing out children and offing anybody who knows about it. Maybe this is all a bit of a stretch."

"Not at all," Muldoon countered, knowing exactly what she wanted to hear. "You don't go into it a cold-blooded killer. Maybe you've just got a little emissions problem and you're buying time until you can get it straightened out. But things start to snowball, you get nervous and try to cover your ass, and now you've dug yourself in deeper. It's the classic story. One mistake on top of another."

"If you get low enough that you can gas off children," Savitch added, "how big a step is it to kill the people who are in on the conspiracy?"

"Killing kids. That's another big assumption on our part, isn't it, or have you two come up with something?"

"It is an assumption at this point," Savitch said. "But it fits the rest of the story too perfectly. I've done a lot of research, if you want me to explain the science of it."

"Not now," McGinns said. "I'm assuming that Richard Abbington, if he sings the way you two think he might, would do an aria for us on the science of pollution. So listen, if you think he's the weak one, let's put another brick on his shoulder. I want you two to pay a visit to Mr. Pritchard. He won't say anything, of course, but Richard Abbington won't know that. Then I want you to get Richard Abbington in here, strap him to a straight-back metal chair, shine a light so bright his corneas melt, and tell him he better sell out his boss before his boss sells him out. From this moment on, it's a full press. And we've got a man on every principal in the case, am I right? Good. I want both of you to sign out cell phones and check in with me every two hours the rest of the way."

Muldoon rose like a Boy Scout and Savitch thought he was going to salute McGinns. They were at the door when McGinns called out one last order. She was in the rocking chair, going fast enough to catapult herself out the window, talking straight ahead as if they were still on the sofa in front of her.

"I don't care if you have to work twenty-four hours from here on out. I want that grand jury back in here on Friday with something to look at. And like I said from the beginning, I want every one of these sociopaths dragged in by the balls."

CHAPTER 25

ANGELA CARMELLA GORETTI SANGIAMINO was buried under a dogwood tree at the top of a knoll in a corner of Holy Sepulchre Cemetery. One hundred forty vehicles, including six produce trucks from the Italian Market and a three-Lincoln caravan from the Philadelphia–Atlantic City mob, made the forty-minute trip from St. Mary Magdalen to the northwest edge of the city on a sparkling fall day. Joey had paid a neighborhood kid to paste IZZY CAN bumper stickers on all the cars during mass, so the cortege looked as much like a political rally as a funeral procession. Joey, Izzy, and Lou rode in the Oldsmobile, which was plastered with political paraphernalia and flags.

The majority of the people paying respects never really knew Angela, who once told a gossip columnist she had no interest in having her private life reduced to public trivia. They came for Augie, who followed Father D'Anunzio's homily with a few words about Angela having been his strength and salvation, and a far more honest person than anyone he'd ever met in politics.

Augie gazed out the window on the ride back to town, quiet like Joey had never seen him. When Angela was unconscious in the hospital and Augie was at her side, Joey had written a poem about a man in love with his wife and devoted to a whore. He wondered which one his boss would be true to now. Just after

Angela died, Augie was going on and on about how maybe he should get out, because that's what Angela would have wanted. The hell with this election and all the rest of them, too. He didn't need the headache. But if he'd come to any conclusion, he hadn't told Joey about it, and with the diggers still throwing dirt on Angela, this wasn't the most appropriate time for Joey to bring it up. They were on Lincoln Drive when Augie asked Joey if he thought the funeral went OK.

"Couldn't have been nicer, Senator." The blow of Angela's death was softened by the fact that she'd been away for years. Angela hadn't been Angela since before Augie went to jail. But in a way, Joey knew, that only made it all the more tragic for Augie.

"I'll tell you one thing, Joey, I didn't deserve that woman. We had some good years there in the beginning. But the way it turned out, she could've done better than Augie Sangiamino the ex-con. What was I in prison—two years? She turned it into twelve, fourteen years, Joey. Ever since I come out, she kept bars between us."

Lincoln Drive, which curled through the woods and under cliffs that plunged into Wissahickon Creek, connected the north-western neighborhoods of the city to the downtown area. Augie said he couldn't remember the last time he was up in this part of town. "It's kind of pretty, ain't it, Joey? I mean if you like lookin' at trees and rocks and all." When they passed the marker for a battle site in the Revolutionary War, Augie said, "I don't know if you're aware of it, Joey, but George Washington come through here with his boys. Marched all the way to Valley Forge in those little costumes they had. That was a stand-up guy, Washington."

Joey said, "Senator, you mind if I ask you something?"

"Help yourself, Joey."

"You believe there's a place you go after this?"

"You call yourself a Catholic? Of course I believe there's an afterlife, Joey. I just pray to God I'm wrong."

Augie clasped his hands like he was praying now. "The house makes noises at night, Joey. I'm lying in bed last night, I figure maybe it's the house settling, right? That thing's a hundred years old if it's a day. But then I think to myself, that ain't the house. That's Angela. It's Angela and these dead kids in there looking at me every night. Ghosts, Joey. They won't let me sleep."

He'd been talking like this since Angela died, and it gave Joey a shiver. Not that he believed in that sort of thing. He started to talk but Augie cut him off.

"There's only two things I ever had. I had Angela and I had this thing I do. I love her, you know that as well as the next guy. A couple of times, though, Joey, once in Harrisburg, one time down Washington . . . it's a thing with some of these women out there that maybe you're an important person in their eyes—a big shot. You understand what I'm saying?"

"Senator, it don't matter."

"I'm an honest man, Joey, in a manner of speaking. But I lied about that one. Not that it was more than a few times. A half dozen tops."

"Let it go. It's human nature that nobody stays with one person forever."

"They lower your wife in the ground, it matters. You think about that sort of thing. Lies you told her. Promises you didn't keep. Let's be honest, Joey. This comeback we got here, Augie Sangiamino's resuscitation, it comes from bad money. You wanna know the truth? I think it's why she went when she did. Probably couldn't bear the thought of me going away in handcuffs again."

"Senator, nobody's going away in handcuffs. That's crazy talk."

Augie looked into the woods through wet eyes and Joey wondered if this was it. He tried to read Augie, but he had to keep his eye on the road, too. It was narrow and looping and the Olds was a wide-body load. Joey kissed the shoulder and pulled back out. Was Augie trying to tell him he was done? Turning over a new leaf after fifty years? Joey hoped not. Augie had nothing else to live for now, and inside of six months, Joey would be back up at that cemetery watching them throw dirt on the senator. "I told you this a hundred times, boss. Somebody else gets that money, they don't use it to help other people."

Joey realized he had never told Augie why he wanted to work for him, and this was as good a time as any. He told him about the gloom and doom in his house when he was a boy and his father was laid off, and what it meant to the family the day he came home from his meeting with Augie. "As far as I'm concerned, Senator, there's no way I could ever repay you for what you done."

"It's nothing, Joey. You service your constituents. That's what it's all about. Especially good, hardworking people like Enrique Tartaglione. I'll tell you something. You take a city like this and ask yourself what happened to it the last fifty years. I'll tell you what happened. All the jobs where you did something with your hands, like your father, you made something or you carried something on your back, all of that dried up. They got frickin' Chinamen in straw hats making our pants and shoes for two cents an hour in Taiwan, and they got Japs building our own bridges for us. You're fuckin' A right I put a few people on the payroll and grabbed whatever wasn't nailed down in Harrisburg and Washington. It ain't like I got rich from it, Joey, although with a little better luck at the track we'd be on easy street today."

Joey was still wrestling the big wheel, watching Augie and the road at the same time. "This is what I'm trying to tell you, Senator, how you should think of yourself. A roof for the church. A job for this one, a favor for that one. It's God's work with you."

"Maybe so. But to be good at it, you gotta crack someone's head open every once in a while, and that was where Angela didn't have the stomach for it," Augie said. His eyes moistened again and he said that when he was younger, he had gorillas from the roofers union, or sometimes iron workers, go around tuning people up. "Angela would go in to have her hair done and how was she to know the girls were whispering because Augie Sangiamino, that bastard, ordered a beating for the hairdresser's husband? I took a few jobs away, too, from people who didn't back me. Cut them loose without regard for their family situation, and sooner or later, Angela heard about these things on the street."

"A few people might have gotten hurt, Senator, but it was for their own good. That's politics and business in the big city, and you know the game better than anybody. You either go in with your spikes up or you sit in the dugout pulling your pud."

"I come through for a lot of people, Joey, but the only thing Angela ever wanted, I couldn't pull it off. Can you believe that?" Joey wasn't sure what Augie was talking about, but he could tell it was something that had bothered him for a while. Augie's eyes teared up good and he began speaking in a confessional tone. "Strong It'lo-American fellow like myself with bad seed. That's one for the books." Joey had never suspected. But it was more than he wanted to know. "You talk about a ballbuster," Augie went on. "She still wanted to adopt, at our age, and that's when I got popped."

It explained a few things. The Saturday morning movies in the Pennies from Heaven clubhouse, for one. For a while there, Angela used to come by and hand out the popcorn to the kids. Joey wasn't sure what to say, but Augie saved him. "I been thinking about some things, Joey."

Joey's heart pounded, pushing up at his sweater. He was used to knowing what Augie had in his head, but he had no idea now. Augie slammed the heel of his hand on the dashboard. "We're through with Liberty Oil."

"What are you talking about? Senator, we can't afford..."

Augie's voice was strong and firm. "As long as I live, Augie Sangiamino doesn't take another dollar from Liberty Oil. Not a

Augie had a point. He won it at the track.

"What they ought to do in elections," Augie said, "is forget all this fund-raising bullshit, and they can even drop the voting. If it's about money, put the candidates on a bus, take them down to a casino, and see who comes out on top. How'll that be?"

It was no use. Augie wasn't going to be talked out of this. Joey might as well try to work up some kind of strategy for him. His stomach was turning flips as he thought it through. "The odds are against us all the way on this thing, Senator. There's not a game that works for us."

"No stones. You got no stones, Joey."

"You're thinking baccarat, blackjack, what?"

"I'm thinking roulette, Joey. I'm going to spin the fuckin' wheel."

"Roulette? That's no good, Senator."

"I just go red or black and I've got a fifty-fifty shot."

"That's not a skill game, Senator, it's luck. And it ain't fifty-fifty. There's one through thirty-six, red and black, then there's zero and double zero, both green, and the green is theirs. That's where the house gets you. It gives them a five-point-three percent advantage. It's only one percent and under for the house with baccarat and blackjack."

"How the hell do you remember all that, Joey? I gotta hand it to you, you got a head for numbers. But I wanna spin the wheel." They were up on the Wissahickon interchange, crossing the Schuylkill River, when Augie told Joey to stop the car.

"Right here, Senator? We're on top of the freakin' bridge."

"Stop the car, Joey. This is perfect." Augie was out of the car before the Oldsmobile came to a complete stop. Joey looked in the mirror, worried about traffic coming up on them. What the hell was he doing out there? Joey heard ripping sounds as he got out. Augie was tearing Ham's bumper stickers off the car.

"Senator, it's dangerous out here."

"Good, Joey. Maybe I'll get hit by a car and never have to

waste another thought on this prick again. I thought I told you to get this shit off the car, Joey?"

"I know. I'm sorry, Senator, but I been too busy. I'll take care of it when we get back."

"I can't go ten more feet in this car with his name all over the fucking thing."

"Here, let me help you."

"Leave it alone, Joey. I wanna do every one of them myself. Jesus, this one on the trunk's the size of a doormat. What has it got, like a magnet in it?"

Traffic had bunched up behind the Oldsmobile, motorists rubbernecking to see what was going on. Augie didn't even look up. He worked the car over until he'd picked it clean, stacking the magnets and stickers in a pile by the bridge railing. "That's a hell of a drop," he said, looking over the side. "What is that, about a hundred feet down to the river?"

"You throwing them in?"

"You're fuckin' A right. Give me some room here, will you?"

Joey stepped back and Augie tossed the wadded-up paper like softballs, getting some height and then watching them all the way down. He looked like a gentleman at a county fair, playing a carnival game in his Sunday best. He saved the rubberized magnets for last. Those, he flipped off the bridge with some spin, and they sailed out flat toward Center City, thinking they could fly, but finally plunging into the murky depths and disappearing with the current.

"He's lucky it was his posters," Augie said, dusting off his hands and peering over the railing. He climbed back into the Olds a new man, and Joey had never respected him more. He'd made his deal with Angela and he'd made his deal with himself, chasing away the ghosts that came after him at night. And he'd finally freed himself for good of Ham.

Joey made a prayer to St. Joseph and a vow to St. Augustine that he would make Augie's rebirth complete. It was a fall he'd take with pride, and at this point, it might be the only way to bury Ham. Muldoon was all over them anyway, drawing the net tighter. Joey hadn't told Augie about it, but one undercover guy was showing up at bingo games, one was at Milly's, one was in a vacant house across the street from Pennies from Heaven, and another dick was in front of the convenience store next to First Columbus Trust every time Joey went into the bank. They probably thought they had it all figured out, but they weren't as smart as they thought they were. Joey "Numbers" Tartaglione had one more trick to throw at them. He was smiling as he turned the wheel and aimed them onto the expressway.

Augie said, "Step on it, Joey. I got a feeling and I don't wanna let go of it. I can't lose, I'm telling you. I can't fucking lose."

Joey hit the gas and the Center City skyline flew by in a blur.

Atlantic City didn't wait for you to cross the Delaware River. It screamed out the minute you left Philadelphia and shot across the Walt Whitman Bridge.

TRIPLE SLOT PAYOFFS!
FOLLIES FANDANGO!
$4.99 PRIME RIB FEAST!
PAUL ANKA AND RICHARD SIMMONS!
BLACKJACK BONANZA!

Augie had a thing about being passed by gambling buses on the Atlantic City Expressway. He said it couldn't help your odds if they got there first.

"They all pull slots," Joey said. "That's a bunch of bag ladies that got a free roll of quarters and they got it worked out to the penny, how they can spend all day down there and go home even. That's not your competition, Senator." They passed a Wayne Newton billboard and Joey asked Augie if he'd ever caught his act.

"No, but I hear the son of a bitch puts on a hell of a show. I must've had a hundred people tell me that. That you get your money's worth."

"Senator, there's something I never told you," Joey said.

Augie looked across at him, waiting for Joey to go on.

"My real name's Wayne."

Augie cocked his head like a dog. "The fuck you telling me?"

"Nobody knows this, but my name's Wayne."

"Joey Wayne?"

"No. Wayne Tartaglione."

Augie waited for an explanation.

"My mother for some reason loved the name of Wayne. I don't know why. Anyhow, what should happen but I'm born and she's got a thing for that name, but there's no St. Wayne."

Augie thought about that. "I think she's right, Joey. I never heard of no St. Wayne."

"This is what I'm saying. So long story short, she names me Wayne Joseph Tartaglione, at least there's one saint in there. But she calls me Wayne growing up and I hate it. I'm living on a block, it's Louie, Tommy, Rocco, Vince, Tony. And one fuckin' Wayne. By the time I'm in third grade, I've smacked a dozen kids for calling me that. And by the time I'm in junior high, even my mother was calling me Joey."

Augie asked, "What's your driver's license say?"

Joey took one hand off the wheel and adjusted the rearview mirror to see if they were being followed. It looked like Muldoon and his dobermen had taken a day off, maybe out of respect for the funeral. He said, "I never got no driver's license, Senator."

They passed a billboard pitching one of those shows with the dancing girls in circus outfits, headdresses, the whole nine yards. Augie asked Joey if he was still seeing Maggie Sharperson.

Maggie. He'd meant to bring her up with Augie. If Joey ended up going away for a while, there were some things he had to take care of first. "You know, she helped us out quite a bit here, Senator. I was wondering if maybe we could set her up somewhere. The gas company or the port authority. Something not too involved." He felt uncomfortable asking because he'd never asked Augie for anything.

"I'll take care of it," Augie said, looking out the window as they went through the Pine Barrens. "Tell me something, Joey. You still trimming her bush?"

Atlantic City was a depressed seaside slum with a spectacular row of glitz and flash along the shore, and neither Augie nor Joey could ever roll in off the expressway without feeling a surge of adrenaline. The A.C. Expressway dumped cars into the heart of the downtown, and the '56 Olds shone with the neon glow of the hotel casinos, which sat literally across the street from pawnshops, by-the-hour motels, and some of the most ramshackle housing in America. On May 26, 1978, a line had stretched for a mile along the Boardwalk to the entrance of Resorts, gamblers itching to ice their fever in the first of a dozen hotel casinos that would open for business in Atlantic City. Augie used his connections to bypass the crowd and was among the first legal gamblers the city ever saw. He dropped four hundred dollars at the blackjack tables but went home a happy man. The risk—the thrill of it—was his payoff.

Joey turned left on Pacific. Augie usually went to the Sands, which was on Indiana between Bally's Grand and the Claridge, but he said he wanted to go to Evolution this time because he'd once seen Sinatra there. "It gives you an edge, that he was in the house," Augie said as they pulled up to the valet. "Not that I need it, Joey. Where'd you say the money is? You got it in your coat?"

"It's in the trunk."

A valet opened Augie's door and said, "Welcome to Evolution."

Joey pulled his St. John Neumann High School gym bag out of the trunk and Augie's eyes lit up. "Joey, I brought my bone chip off St. John Neumann as a charm. That's gotta be an omen."

Neumann, the former Philadelphia bishop, was the only American man who had been named a saint. His bone fragments were sold at a shrine in North Philadelphia, but Augie, as a VIP, got a freebie.

Augie unzipped Joey's bag and grabbed a hundred-dollar bill. "Young man," he said, handing the valet the note, "here's what I want you to do. You see this billboard we're driving here? You get behind the wheel of that thing, and I want you to drive it up and down the strip like it's a float, let everybody have a look. You do that for me, and when I come back out with four of these bags, maybe there's a little something in there for you."

Augie handed his overcoat to Joey, then turned toward the entrance in his best suit, a three-piece Italian the color of octopus ink, a white carnation in the lapel from Angela's funeral. He fixed his tie again, cocked his gray fedora at just the right angle, and pulled the tails of his coat down snug. "All right, Joey," he said. "Let's go rob the bastards."

A doorman held the door and Augie walked in like he owned the place, tall and elegant with that forward lean of his, arms swinging free. This was how you did it. You didn't walk into a casino like some fuckin' bum who didn't know if he'd get out with his shirt. You walked in there like a million dollars and that was how you came out. Augie was like something out of *Guys and Dolls* and Joey trailed five feet behind, giving him space. He had to skip along to stay up with Augie, who strode under glittering chandeliers and beveled mirrors like he was part of the show, headed for that glorious sound of coins dropping and bells ringing. He loved the spectacle of color and light, the smell of money and sex. Vulgarity without shame. The only place that had it beat, he had told Joey, was the floor of the United States Senate.

When he got to the edge of the gaming floor, he stopped in awe and said, "Listen to it, Joey."

"It don't matter how many times you walk in here," Joey said as a cocktail waitress walked by in high heels and a sequined cave-girl outfit that pushed her breasts up to her throat, "it's like you never seen it before." It was almost as intoxicating as the salt air that blew in off the sea in summer, and if Joey Tartaglione had a dream, this was it. Get a little shack down the shore and drink it in every day, maybe find a chubby little black-jack dealer to knock around with and live out his life in the place where, as a boy, his faith in the world was renewed and his love of Augie was cemented.

Even if you knew somebody, you couldn't just stroll into a casino with fifty thousand dollars in cash and trade for chips. There were laws against that kind of thing, because someone might come in here with proceeds from some illicit activity. Joey and Augie divided up the money and paid hundred-dollar notes to several gamblers who made the exchange for them, cleaning the fifty. They dumped the chips into a plastic slot machine cup and Augie walked up to a pit boss and asked where he could find the floor manager. The pit boss had a security guard make a call and a minute later, Augie felt a tap on his shoulder.

"Senator Sangiamino, welcome to Evolution."

Augie threw his arms around him. "Billy, how the hell are you?"

Augie had set him up fifteen years ago as a bellhop, and look what he'd done. He'd made something of himself. This was exactly what Joey had been talking about. "You see this guy, Joey? I knew him when he was hanging on the corner with his dick in his hand, and here he is running this joint. The family OK, Billy? Everything all right? Good. Listen, Billy, what I want, maybe we could raise the limit for a couple spins on the roulette wheel here. You think you can set that up for me, pal?"

A lot of the neighborhood had been taken out of Billy. He was a company man now. Dark blue suit. Hair parted and cut real neat. "What are we talking?" he asked uncomfortably.

"Billy, I got fifty thousand in the cup here. One spin is all I want." Joey grabbed Augie's arm, but Augie kept his eyes on Billy.

"Fifty," Billy said, like there was something wrong. "You know, it's a two-thousand-dollar table."

"Guess what, Billy. I'm not a two-thousand-dollar man. Once in a while, depending on who comes in, you boys take the lid off of that, am I right?"

"We do what we can for VIPs like yourself," Billy agreed. "But I never saw it go that high. Senator, I'm sorry, but this one goes over my head. Can you give me a minute?"

"Do what you can for me, Billy, and take your time. We'll be right here."

When he left, Joey grabbed Augie again. "Senator, one roll?"

"It's beautyful, Joey, ain't it? That a man could walk in here off the street, spin that wheel once, and need a suitcase to carry the money home?"

"This is not a skill game, Senator. It's all luck."

"Let me tell you something, Joey. I don't need no luck. The money in this cup is from Liberty Oil and it's no good. This place takes it from me, they did me a favor. But anything I win, that's mine. I got something better than luck, Joey. I got a deal where I can't lose. That's what I've been trying to tell you."

"I understand that, Senator, but maybe you should break it up. Go five shots, ten each. Build it up and work with it."

"If I have to," Augie said. "But if Billy comes back here and tells me it's OK, fuck the foreplay. It's a quick bang and we're in and out, like burglars."

Joey started talking odds, maybe that would persuade Augie, but Billy was back now. "All right," he said. "You're on. Someone's on the way over."

"Beautiful, Billy. That ball bounces my way, there's a little something in it for you, all right, pal?"

Augie went over by the roulette wheel and took St. John Neumann out of his pocket. The bone was the size of a fingernail clipping and sat on a piece of foam rubber in a small plastic case. "You gotta touch it, Joey. Go ahead, you touch it first."

"I thought you said you didn't need no luck, Senator."

"This ain't luck we're going for, Joey. It's divine intervention." The dealer was setting up and two guys in suits had shown up with a security guard. Billy was off to the side and these other guys were in charge now. Augie put St. John Neumann back in his pocket and asked, "What do you say, Joey? Red or black?"

Joey took out his handkerchief and mopped his brow. He was wearing one of his heavier sweaters, but that didn't matter. He could have been in his shorts and he'd be dripping. "Jesus, Senator. I don't know. You got a lucky color or anything?"

Augie thought about it and said, "Blue."

"I don't think that helps us right now."

"Come on, Joey. In your gut, tell me what it is."

This wasn't fair. If Augie wanted to piss their money away in one shot, why didn't he pick the color himself? Joey looked around the room for a clue. The carpet was red. He saw a woman in a black dress. Maggie had black hair. "Black," he said. "I'd go with black."

"Black. You feel good about it?"

Joey looked at the managers and the security guard, who were staring at them. "No. I don't feel too good, honestly."

"There's a reason, Joey. You don't feel good about it because it's the wrong color. Now give me those chips."

Augie piled the fifty chips in two stacks and set them both on red. Joey was hyperventilating, looking around to see if someone could get him a drink. A handful of gamblers had seen the commotion and came over to check it out. When they saw what was happening, they called to others, and now there were twenty people watching the skinny old man in the fedora take a fifty-thousand-dollar gamble on a single spin of the roulette wheel.

"Good luck," one of them said.

Augie didn't even hear it. "I'm ready," he said.

The dealer looked at his boss, who gave a nod. The dealer said, "I have fifty thousand dollars on red," and he spun the wheel. Joey was dizzy by the time the ball first jumped. There were twenty slots it could fall into that were the wrong one. He closed his eyes and said a prayer, wanting time to speed up and wanting it to slow down, too. What the hell had they done?

Augie didn't take his eyes off the action. The inside wheel spinning one way, the outside wheel going the other, the steel ball kicking hard. He was hypnotized. "Come on," Augie pleaded, coaching the ball, his hands in fists. "Come on red! Come on pink, you Commie whore!"

The ball finally died but the wheel was still a blur—the quietest moment in a casino. Augie's eyes spun around in his head, chasing the ball. Joey still couldn't open his. Not until the dealer said, "Fifteen. Red is a winner."

Joey threw his arms around Augie, knocking his hat off. Spectators cheered.

"Did I tell you, Joey? Did I fuckin' tell you? Easy money." Augie's smile wrapped around his head.

"It's beautiful, Senator. You had me scared to death, I gotta admit." Joey, out of breath, picked up Augie's hat and dusted it off. "All right," he said, panting, "Let's get the hell out of here."

Augie took his hat and put it back just where it was, cocked a little to one side. "Not yet," he said, turning back to the table. The dealer had stacked fifty thousand next to Augie's fifty. Augie said, "Let it ride."

Joey grabbed Augie's elbow and squeezed hard. If he had to drag him out of here, maybe that's what he'd do. "Senator, that's it. We won. We fuckin' won. Now let's go home with our hundred grand. We got what we came for."

Augie walked Joey over by a craps table and spoke in a whisper. "We only got fifty thousand, Joey. That first fifty is Liberty's, and I won't spend it." He waved toward the spectators and said, "I'll give it to them first. I'd even walk out on the Boardwalk and throw it in the fuckin' ocean before I keep a dime of it."

He strode confidently back to the wheel, where Billy and the other two guys in suits were huddled, trying to decide whether they were going to let Augie spin for a hundred thousand dollars. One of them walked over to a house phone and dialed.

"How about it?" Augie asked Joey. "Red or black?"

Joey took out his handkerchief again, but it was already soaked. "Senator, you gotta listen to me on this. You get two hundred thousand, or you get nothing. There's no in between. Why don't you take fifty of it off the board, put it in your pocket?"

Augie interrupted him to ask the date of the election.

"November fifth. Why?"

"That's eleven five, and guess what. Angela and I were married on May eleventh. That's eleven five and five eleven."

"What the hell does that mean?"

"Eleven and five is sixteen, which is black. Sixteen and sixteen is thirty-two, which is black. And Ron Rice is black. I don't need luck, Joey. I got the planets lined up."

Joey, in his line of work, had seen and heard every system and superstition. This wasn't one of the stronger ones. He was asking himself if he should just grab Augie and drag him out of here, but it was too late. They'd decided to let Augie have another go, and it couldn't have been a tough call, Joey didn't think. The more a guy played, the bigger the house advantage.

Augie pushed all the chips over to black, one hundred thousand dollars worth, and said he was ready. When the dealer spun the wheel, Joey closed his eyes again and Augie talked to the ball. "Go black, go black, go black. Come on you *shvartze melenzane* bastard!" The ball kicked around more than it had the first time and the wheel seemed to spin longer. Everything in slow motion and nothing real. The crowd, which was up to forty people, cheered along with Augie.

Black, black, black, black, black, black, black, black.

When the ball died, it sucked the air out of the room and the casino fell silent, a long and painful silence, and Joey had to admit he couldn't imagine Augie anywhere else at this moment than right here at this altar. Augie dropped to his knees to await the dealer's call.

"We have twenty-two. Black is a winner."

Augie flipped his hat and Joey lifted him off the floor in a bear hug. When he put him back down the Senator counted out fifty one-thousand-dollar chips and gave one to each of his forty fans, then split ten among Billy, the other employees, and the valet.

Neon filled their car on the way out of town and it looked as if they were lit themselves. Augie said, "I feel like I just got baptized, Joey. Angela'd be proud. Don't you think?"

CHAPTER 26

WESTBOUND TRAFFIC on the Schuylkill Expressway was light at six-thirty in the morning, and Mike Muldoon looked out at the scullers turning upriver from the boathouses and cutting wakes on the gray water.

"You used to be out there, didn't you?" Savitch asked.

"For four years at St. Joe's," Muldoon said, answering like a marine. "It's the best conditioning you can get. I'm thinking about going back out there a couple of times a week."

"Maybe we can race," Savitch said, puffing away on a cigarette. "I'll run and you row."

"Let me ask you something, Savage. Do you smoke when you run?"

"I chain-smoke, Muldoon. I carry spare butts in a fanny pack and light up every mile or so. Listen, can you turn up the heat a little bit? It's freezing in here."

"Of course it's freezing. You're a woman. You're either freezing or burning up, you're starving or stuffed, and you're wide awake or exhausted. Am I right?"

No answer. Muldoon turned on the heater and opened his window a crack, Savitch's lemon-scented smoke drifting under his nose. Maybe she rubbed lemons on herself. He caught her profile as she looked out at the river and chewed on a fingernail.

Her face was flat-looking from the side, and you didn't get the full effect of how deadly she was. He half wanted to tell her he'd slept with Carla, but he wasn't particularly proud of it. Maybe that was why he wanted to tell her.

"You all right?" he asked.

"Yeah, why?"

"You just seem so intense."

"Do I? It's this interview, I guess."

"It'll be a breeze, if he agrees to see us."

"It's not that. It's just that it's been a lot of sleepless nights, and now we finally confront the bastard. Hold me back if it looks like I'm going to wrestle him to the floor and rip his lungs out."

"I've got my gun. You want me to just shoot him?"

"That's too easy. I want the son of a bitch to suffer."

Muldoon looked back at the road and asked Savitch if she saw the car up there in the slow lane.

"Yeah, why?"

"What do you notice about it?"

"I don't know. That it's black, it's midsize, it's going in the same direction as us? What are you asking me?"

"It's going slower than we are, is my point. And do you see me speeding up to it and then slamming on the brakes, or do you see me changing lanes so I can maintain a steady speed?"

"My God," Savitch said. "Can you believe yourself sometimes? How long before we get to Pritchard's place?"

"It's in Upper Merion. Another fifteen or twenty minutes."

Savitch looked out at the joggers, cyclists, and rowers. The river carved a path through the woods, which climbed up from the banks on both sides, and the Girard Railroad Bridge, with lane numbers on it for the regattas, arched like a Venetian aqueduct across the water.

"It's not as horrible a city as you thought it was two months ago, is it?"

"Maybe I'll even unpack."

"Does it have anything to do with Jack Singer?"

"What do you mean?"

"Your deciding to stay awhile."

"No. He's a nice guy, though."

Muldoon was going to change the subject, but she did it for him. "You make fun of my driving, and look at you," she said.

"What?"

"Correct posture, textbook attentiveness. Have you got your hands at ten and two?"

"Excuse me for not dropping cigarette ash on myself and fishtailing around while I play with the radio."

She laughed, but not necessarily because she thought it was funny. It looked to Muldoon like she just needed to laugh, blow off some of the stress. "Muldoon, I'm your partner and you haven't been up front with me," she said. "I heard a rumor that you might be staying on at the DA's office."

"Who told you that?"

"Am I right?"

"McGinns asked me if I'd think about it, but that was it. I haven't made any decisions."

"I think you should, if you care to hear my opinion."

"Why's that?" he asked, anticipating a compliment.

"Because if you don't, all you'll do is play golf. I could understand it if you were going to travel the world or something. But if all you're going to do is chase a little ball around a golf course, what's the point?"

"Savitch, do you have any idea how much alike you and McGinns are? I know you hate her, but trust an impartial observer. You're two peas in a pod."

"I don't hate her."

"You don't hate her? All you've done for two months is bitch about the woman."

"I was thinking about her 'tough broad' act when we left her office the other day. Maybe it's what you have to do to survive three decades in a business dominated by men who think they know everything. Men who constantly question your fitness for the job."

"Spare me, please."

"You have no idea, Muldoon. I have to present at least the appearance that I'm as tough or tougher than any man in this business. Of course, it happens to be true in my case."

"I'm sorry I brought it up."

"You're right, I definitely have some problems with her. The politics, especially. But I can see why you've got such respect for her. So are you staying on, or what?"

"Why should I?"

"They need you. There's not a detective in the place who has anywhere near your experience. And if you were there full time, you'd get your pick of the cases."

"I'll think about it."

"We'd make a great team, Muldoon."

"You mean I'd have to work with you?"

Whit Pritchard lived in a township of rambling European-style hilltop estates and two-hundred-year-old stone colonials built into the curves of winding creeks. Woods gave way to meadows, and lush green hills rolled to the edge of the horizon, the fall colors fading to a soft rust. "You know you're in money when the houses have names," Muldoon said. "Look at this. Fawn Hill. Woodbrook Manor. Summerhill Glen."

"Frightening," Savitch said. "But it's gorgeous. Look at this covered bridge coming up." The wooden bridge, painted red, looked like it went all the way back to the time of a mill whose stone remnants were scattered along the creek. "I thought New England had the only covered bridges that were left."

"You forgot colleges, athletic stadiums, and fall foliage. Don't you guys have the only ones of those, too?"

"If Liberty Oil is in such bad shape," Savitch said, ignoring him, "what's he still doing living out here?"

"Old money runs deep. I think he's around this next bend. What's the name of the road again?"

"Bloomsbury. There. That must be it at the end of that lane. Oh my God."

A. Whitney Pritchard III lived on a two-hundred-acre estate at the top of a rise. The gated front wall opened to a tree-lined driveway that carried past a pond and a three-hole, par three golf course. Three service houses were in a cluster off to the right, and straight up ahead was the main house, a sprawling, dusty gray English Tudor, which had its own name on a sign planted in the perfectly attended garden. WESTMINSTER NORTH. "That's the name of the plantation house in Barbados," Muldoon said. "Westminster." An English Tudor–style portico was built off to the side of the house, with a half dozen rocking chairs and a swinging bench facing down the hill, offering a view of a creek and the woods beyond. Muldoon parked in front of a small horse stable in matching English Tudor design.

"I hope he's got the coffee on," Savitch said, shivering as she got out of the car. They hadn't called ahead. It wasn't hard to guess that Pritchard would have put them off, referred them to an attorney, or just hung up. This way, what could he do? Sending them away wouldn't look good.

A man in a suit answered the door. They identified themselves and said they had to see Mr. Pritchard. The man, who must have been a butler, asked them to wait there and started to close the door. Muldoon stuck his big foot in before he could shut them out. "Thanks," he said, stepping inside. "It's cold out there."

"You don't happen to have any coffee on, do you?" Savitch asked.

The butler didn't answer. He left them on the tile floor of the foyer, under a crystal chandelier. "Look at this bureau," Savitch said, running her hand over the finish on a cherrywood antique.

Muldoon had spotted a portrait on the opposite wall. "This

must be the triumvirate," he said. "A. Whitney the first, A. Whitney the second, and A. Whitney the third." The dour grandfather was seated in the middle with the next two generations standing behind. The bloodline was unmistakable, down to the triangular head shape and the sure, aristocratic bearing.

"Three faces you'll never see at happy hour," Savitch said.

"He must have a fire going. I love that smell."

"Yeah, it's nice and toasty in here."

"Maybe he'll offer to buy us off like he did McGinns," Muldoon said. Savitch whispered at him to keep his voice down. "If he throws in the golf course, I'm in." He heard what sounded like traffic from a police scanner and peeked into the kitchen, but pulled back and strained to hear the muffled conversation coming from upstairs. It sounded like a scolding. The butler came down and asked them to follow him to the library, Whit Pritchard would be joining them momentarily. "The library," Muldoon repeated.

The foyer opened to a dining room and beyond that a living room looked into a backyard with a terraced garden, a gazebo the size of a normal house, a swimming pool, and a putting green. The library was the next room down the hall. Hardcover bindings filled built-in, dark wood shelves. A low flame licked at a log in the fireplace, and a Matisse hung over the mantel. On the opposite wall, next to a window looking into the backyard, was a Cézanne.

"Muldoon, I think these are originals." Savitch was inspecting the signature on the Cézanne when she heard Whit Pritchard's voice.

"You have an excellent eye," he said. He was wearing a bathrobe and slippers and the same smile he had the day he pulled up to the demonstration in front of One Liberty Place.

Savitch held out her hand. She introduced herself and Muldoon, who was off in a corner, examining a gun collection in a glass display case. Muldoon came over and shook hands.

"The district attorney's office," Pritchard said. "Let me fetch you tea or coffee. William? And to what do I owe this visit from two emissaries of my good friend Kevinne McGinns?"

"Coffee for me," Savitch said to the man who had answered the door.

"Make it two."

"And I'll have tea, William."

"Will you be taking your breakfast now, sir?"

"Not today, William. Unless our guests would like something."

They shook their heads no. "Lovely place you have," Savitch said.

Muldoon wondered if Pritchard was picking up on the vitriol in her tone. "I like the golf course, myself," he said.

"Thank you, thank you. It's quite a bit of upkeep, but yes, quite comfortable."

Comfortable did not begin to describe it, Muldoon was thinking. It sort of put things in perspective. This guy was putting a few hundred thousand dollars into the campaign, and it was nothing. One room of furniture was worth more than that. Muldoon sat next to Savitch on a sofa with comfortable, soft brown leather that was like a broken-in jacket. Pritchard sat in a matching chair and closed the open flap of his robe. "That's a beautiful collection," Muldoon said, pointing to the gun case. "Nice matchlocks, especially."

"A hobby I picked up from my grandfather," Pritchard said. "He used to hunt in those woods you saw out front, and I have a shooting range toward the rear of the property. Several of those are Revolutionary and Civil War pieces that were found on this property and restored."

Judging by a tip Kevinne McGinns had picked up, Pritchard might not have heard that both wars had ended. Neighbors made routine complaints about shooting that wasn't confined to the range. Muldoon had an FBI pal whose son was a township sergeant, and he said they had made a call at Westminster North two months ago on a complaint from a neighbor a half mile away who had a bullet hole in his barn. Whit Pritchard and Richard Abbington, both of whom were taking target practice, denied firing any stray shots. The sergeant also told Muldoon that Pritchard seemed to have an odd fascination with police and had been deputized as an honorary officer. He had paid for new cruisers and the department's state-of-the-art communication system, and he occasionally threw lavish parties for the officers, township officials, and magistrates. Some of the officers took it as Pritchard's way of buying special treatment for his wife, who had a problem with the bottle and routinely cracked up cars around the township.

"Were you in the service?" Muldoon asked.

"My grandfather served in World War I as an infantry commander, my father in World War II as a fighter pilot. I have an unfortunate asthmatic condition that kept me out of Vietnam. And you, Mr. Muldoon?"

"Intelligence. I worked at the Pentagon for two years during Vietnam." Muldoon saw Savitch squirm and nodded at her to go ahead.

"Mr. Pritchard, we're sorry to intrude like this, unannounced. But we hoped you could help us by answering some questions about a couple of men who used to work for you."

"And who might they be?"

"Richard Kelly and Daiman Heidorn."

"Yes, of course. Good men. It's a tragedy I can't fathom, frankly."

"We understand that they were living on your property down there."

"Westminster," Pritchard said. "The plantation has been in the family for three hundred years, if you can believe that. Yes, they managed the property for me." The butler brought in the coffee and tea. Muldoon watched Pritchard pick up his cup with sure hands, no trembling. The scariest type. "Is that what you're doing?" Pritchard asked. "Looking into the robbery? I would have thought it was a different jurisdiction altogether."

Savitch saw an ashtray and asked if she could smoke. Whit Pritchard took a silver cigarette case out of the pocket of his robe and held it open for her, ready with a lighter. "Actually," she said, blowing smoke at the ceiling, "the murder is just part of what we're looking at."

Pritchard sat back down and lit one for himself. "What else might you be interested in?" he asked, still cool. Way too cool, Muldoon thought. He studied him through the clouds of Savitch's cigarette smoke, which blew toward the fireplace. The window next to the Cézanne was ajar, and the heat of the fire was sucking air across the room and up the chimney. "If we understand correctly," Muldoon said, "Kelly and Heidorn worked for you in Mercer for quite some time before moving down to Barbados. Was there some reason they decided to leave Liberty Oil?"

Pritchard drank in Savitch the whole time Muldoon spoke, as if he'd made a personal connection with her in the five minutes they'd known each other. Was the asshole flirting? Muldoon wondered. Or was he trying to intimidate her? "I liked to think of it as a reward for years of reliable service and loyalty," Pritchard said, finally looking Muldoon's way. "They were good men. I considered them friends, and I needed someone to look after things for me."

"What exactly did that entail, managing the property?" Savitch asked. "Because Mr. Muldoon here mentioned that he bumped into some people down there who saw them spending quite a bit of time playing golf, snorkeling, and fishing."

"Oh, so you were on the island recently?"

"Very recently," Muldoon said, as if the asshole didn't know. He was certain now that the police in Barbados were in on the murder of Kelly and Heidorn.

Pritchard looked at his watch. "Maybe they were on vacation," he said. "I can tell you that I trusted them to manage the books, which they did on their own schedule. When you have employees whose loyalty and work ethic you can trust, you don't need to baby-sit them, Mr. Muldoon. I'd say they were quite invaluable to me, which makes their demise all the more difficult. I'm sure you can understand that."

"Understand it? Yes, I'd say I understand. Especially since you also considered them friends."

"Yes, of course."

"That must have been difficult, attending the funerals."

Pritchard didn't respond. He took a puff on his cigarette and flicked ash.

Muldoon said, "You did go to the funerals, I assume."

"Unfortunately, things have been a bit hectic in the oil business these days. I wasn't able to make it." Pritchard called for William to bring more coffee.

Savitch said, "I guess we were thinking that with two men you think of as loyal employees—"

"And friends," Muldoon interjected. "It just seems odd that you wouldn't attend the funeral." They wouldn't get much further now, Muldoon didn't think. Pritchard had thought he was going to dance through this, but now he found himself backed into a corner.

"I frankly detest funerals," he said. "That may sound crude, but I avoid them at all costs."

"That's interesting," Savitch said, "because I read where you were a pallbearer at your grandfather's funeral."

Pritchard smiled coyly, still trying to maintain his cool. "Miss Savitch, I'm flattered that an attractive young woman such as yourself would take an interest in so boring a man as I. It is rather difficult to avoid attending the funeral of a close relative you so admire. Wouldn't you agree?"

"Actually, I think I can understand skipping the funeral for Kelly and Heidorn," Muldoon said. "With all the trouble Liberty Oil is going through, that's got to be keeping you busy."

"What trouble are you referring to, Mr. Muldoon?"

"All this news about the kids dying of leukemia, and people speculating as to the cause. You keep hearing about it in the campaign, too, from Debra Sharperson and Ron Rice. Have you been following the campaign?"

Pritchard kept a nonchalant bearing, but his cigarette had burned down to his fingers and he jumped. "Is that what this is about?" he asked, dropping the butt into the ashtray. "The other part of what you're looking at, as you say? I suppose it makes sense. Everyone else is playing detective and assuming there's a simple explanation for a very complicated disease, so why not the detectives themselves?"

"I don't know what other people you're referring to," Savitch said firmly, "but Mr. Muldoon and I happen to be the only ones who matter. We don't assume anything, and we definitely don't play detective." Pritchard didn't have an answer for that, but Muldoon knew what he was thinking. That no matter what they had on him, he could buy his way out. He'd bought everything he ever wanted or needed.

Pritchard looked at his watch again and said he didn't mean to rush them, but he had to get to the office soon. As they stood to leave, Muldoon said he hoped they hadn't disturbed Mrs. Pritchard.

"We have some stables a few miles away, and she's gone to take care of a few matters before going on holiday in Barbados. I hope to be joining her soon."

"I understand from Muldoon that it's lovely down there, if you can stay out of the line of fire," Savitch said. She handed Pritchard her card. "But before you leave town, could you let me know?"

"Is that necessary?"

"It might be, yes. We're close to wrapping things up, actually. Very close."

"Well it's good to know that you're on top of things. Whatever it is you're on top of. I'd expect nothing less from Kevinne

McGinns's staff. She's going to be governor one day. Do you realize that? Please give her my regards."

Jack Singer poured the rest of the wine while Savitch set the empty take-out cartons on the counter. "I can actually cook," she said, "in case you were wondering."

"I wasn't."

Savitch didn't mean it as in, I'm really good in the kitchen, a regular little housewife. She just wanted to let him know she'd eventually have time to do a normal thing like invite him over, cook a meal, and talk about something besides benzene or leukemia.

Jack Singer got more interesting every time she was with him. He'd traveled in South America and studied infectious disease there, and he'd worked as a doctor in Mexico one year. He spoke three languages, made his own wine, and put the toilet lid down. His story was that he'd been married once, for three years. No kids. He'd dated for a couple of years, nothing serious.

"I like your hat," she said, picking up the Red Sox cap he'd dropped on the counter.

"Red Sox fan?"

"No. It just reminds me of my brother David. He practically lived in Fenway Park. Let me see how you look in it." She put it on his head and laughed. "You look like every jock I went to high school with."

Singer got up and straddled her, playfully trapping her against the counter. "That didn't sound like a compliment. Are you saying you wouldn't have gone out with me in high school?"

She looked at his hands on the counter. They were strong and masculine, with long fingers and olive skin. The kind of hands an artist or photographer would love to work with. She pulled him in to her, her hands on the small of his back. "The first time I saw you in your little dungeon there at Temple," she said, "you know what I noticed first? Your hands and your eyes."

"Which one was it?"

"I don't remember." He had a little-boy look, a lack of pre-sumption is how she had described it to her mother, and she liked that about him. "Maybe it was the hands, because you came around the desk with a ruler. Professor Jack pointing to a map."

He brushed her blond bangs off her forehead and kissed her there. He pushed hair away from her ear and kissed her there, too, until he felt her skin rising, and then he kissed her sweetly on the lips. Savitch liked the feel of him and the smell, too. His skin had a clean smell. When he pulled away he took her hands and examined them. "This is why you like my hands so much," he said, touching the divots around her nails, where she'd torn skin away. "You're envious. What do you have, a pet coyote?"

Savitch buried her face in his chest and squeezed him. She couldn't get her mother's voice out of her head. Watch out. Go slow. Maybe it's too soon. "You didn't forget that we still have some work to do here tonight, did you?" she asked. "Why don't we move into the living room."

He'd brought a backpack with him and he set it on the sofa, sitting next to it. "So tell me. Are you just keeping me around to help with your investigation, and then I'm history?"

"You don't have a problem with that, do you?"

He didn't know her well enough yet to know if she was kidding.

She poured each of them a bourbon. Savitch wasn't much of a drinker. A beer now and then, a couple of glasses of wine with dinner. But she had developed a taste for bourbon in Boston, especially after long days trapped in a courtroom.

"This is a wonderful view," he said, lying back on the sofa and gazing out at the lights of high-rises across the square. The moon had slid into an opening between two of the buildings and looked like a giant softball.

Savitch had unpacked about half the boxes and pushed fur-niture into place right before he arrived. The coffee table, an end table, a cedar chest. The chest was behind the sofa and Savitch had put a red clay vase on it with a dried flower arrangement. She still hadn't set up her stereo, and all her books were still in boxes. "Here you go," she said, handing him a glass and kicking her shoes off. She sat down close and kissed him with cold bourbon lips. "I was just kidding," she said.

"About what?"

"About keeping you around just to help me. Although you and Muldoon are pretty good partners."

"What's his story?" Singer asked.

"I didn't think I'd like him at first. He's retired FBI and there's this superior attitude the feds have toward state and county agencies. But he turned out to be a good guy, very straight but very sweet and shy. And he's so earnest, you wouldn't believe it. He was actually giving me driving tips today."

"What does he look like?"

"Big tall Irish guy with a voice to match, good timbre to it. A nice-looking man, too. I think he might be a little jealous of you, but he turned up this whole new chapter in the case because of it."

"Because of me?"

"Well he knew you were helping me out, and maybe he was trying to keep up with you, I don't know. He went and leaned on one of his old contacts and ended up getting something on two guys who used to work at the refinery." She could tell that Singer was looking into her eyes for something beyond what she was saying. Some reassurance, maybe, that she wasn't interested in Muldoon romantically. But he wasn't pushy, which was a good sign. "By the way," she said, "do you understand why I can't tell you too much about the specifics of this case?"

"I'm OK with that. Just let me know how I can help."

She'd already told him more than she should have, but he didn't know much about the money end of it. Unfortunately, neither did she and Muldoon, and it had been eating at her. They had a detective waiting to follow Joey Tartaglione into church this morning, but he hadn't shown up, and neither had Richard Abbington. They'd have to try again tomorrow. Savitch took out a legal pad and sat hunched on the sofa, her thighs serving as a tabletop. "So were you able to go down to the refinery today?" she asked, lighting a cigarette. If he was the kind of guy who would try to change her, it'd be better to find out now.

"Yeah, and I think I saw the house you were talking about, too. A white clapboard at the end of Elm, kind of a scraggly tree in the side yard?"

"That's it."

"I went over to the ball fields, too."

"So here's the question. Could something have traveled across the fence there, or to the ballpark, in large enough doses to make someone sick?"

"I called a friend at the University of Texas, an authority on occupational safety."

He paused there, which worried her. "And?"

Singer took a swallow of bourbon and rattled the ice in his glass. "Personally, I think so. But it's one of those situations where experts can disagree. You bring someone in to say yes, they bring someone in to say no, both sides with good credentials, and it's hard to sort through the variables and uncertainties. Not a lot is known about how much benzene you have to inhale or ingest for it to be harmful, and people have different levels of sensitivity."

He took some papers out of his backpack and set them on the coffee table. "Let me read you this. It's from the Agency for Toxic Substances and Disease Registry."

Savitch scribbled down the name.

"All right. 'Benzene has been found in at least three hundred thirty-seven of eleven hundred seventy-seven National Priorities List hazardous waste sites. Other environmental sources of benzene include gasoline stations, vehicle exhaust fumes, to-bacco smoke...' " He stopped there and looked at her with one reddish brown eyebrow raised, rattling the ice again. Savitch took a drag, and the cloud she blew was his warning to lay off. He went on. " 'Underground storage tanks that leak, wastewater from industries that use benzene, chemical spills, groundwater next to landfills containing benzene, and possibly some food products that contain benzene naturally. In addition, certain industries may release benzene into the surrounding air. These include ethylbenzene- and styrene-production facilities, petroleum refineries, chemical manufacturing plants, and re-covery plants for coke oven by-products. People living near such industries may be exposed to benzene in the surround-ing air.' "

Savitch said it sounded like there were two or three ways benzene from Liberty Oil could have posed a threat. "But couldn't the source also be one of the other industrial sites nearby?"

Singer put his hand on her leg and stroked it. "Look, obvi-ously, I'm not an attorney. But I know some environmental law, and when an industrial facility knows it has had some kind of discharge that's beyond allowable limits, it has to report it to the government. It seems to me that if you can establish that Liberty knew something and didn't report it, or that they doc-tored the numbers they did report, which isn't impossible to do, then in my opinion, you've got a case."

Savitch scribbled this down. "I think I told you Muldoon found records of two state inspections in the last four years. They were clean both times."

"Yes, but if that's all they had, two visits, it means they went more than a year without an inspection. It's outrageous, but it happens, especially with all the regulatory cutbacks we've had. Liberty itself has led the industry in lobbying for those cuts, and with a refinery as old as theirs, it can be a serious problem. I don't have an engineering background, but I've done enough research so that I don't look like a complete idiot in court. If the equipment isn't kept up, the whole process is less efficient. There's thousands of valves, flanges, and gaskets, and there could be leaks there. The industry calls them fugitive emissions. But you also could lose product right up the chimney."

"Product?"

"Benzene, among other things."

"And the detection equipment the state and city have in the area wouldn't catch that?"

"No. It's for ordinary pollutants like sulfur oxides, or the silica alumina you choked on. Liberty's had a lot of those over the years, but it's easier to just pay the fine, which is peanuts for these companies. If it's ten thousand dollars or even a hundred, that's a lot cheaper than retrofitting the plant, which costs millions."

Savitch told him Muldoon had gotten ahold of someone at the Environmental Protection Agency and they were going out to Mercer with mobile emissions inspections equipment. The plan was to set up at the fence in the ballpark where Jerry Piatkowski's son used to play. A negative reading didn't mean there hadn't been a problem, but a positive one would get the grand jury's attention.

"You do understand they could very well come up clean," he said.

She nodded.

"That's one of the misnomers out there right now. People seem to think you can breathe something in today and get leukemia tomorrow, and that's not how it works. Anybody who presents today with acute lymphocytic was probably exposed three or more years ago, and it's going to be difficult to prove what the emissions were back then."

Not if someone talks, Savitch was thinking. That was still

the key. Muscling Richard Abbington or someone else, and getting them to spill their guts. That, or figuring out the trick of the money drop, a riddle that was torturing Savitch. "There's one thing I don't understand, though. Actually there's about a thousand things I don't understand. But if the air is poison around the refinery, why aren't the employees sick and dying?"

"It could be a couple of things. It's possible the benzene is going up the chimney and getting into the airstream instead of leaking inside the plant. It's also possible employees have gotten sick but didn't make a connection to an occupational hazard. You can test for benzene in urine and blood, but it's not good science yet, partly because benzene occurs naturally in the system and we don't know how much is safe. We also don't know the medical history of every employee and ex-employee. If somebody works there until he's fifty, and he gets cancer when he's fifty-five, he doesn't necessarily assume he was exposed on the job."

This was another thing she liked about Jack Singer. He explained things in understandable terms and never condescended. If she ever got back in there with her grand jury, she was going to put him on the stand. A lot of experts got up there and were so flaky or esoteric, the jury either tuned out or fell asleep.

"I don't know about criminal, but at least from a civil standpoint," he went on, "you wouldn't have the burden of proving scientifically that Liberty Oil killed anyone. You'd have a negligent company covering up a dangerous emission, if you can prove that, and you'd have major blood diseases in the immediate vicinity, where the community has been suspicious for years and has been up in arms lately. I'll tell you what. Maybe somebody will go to jail and maybe they won't. But if you can establish that kind of homicidal negligence, you might just put Liberty Oil out of business. They're kind of shaky as it is, and the defense costs, not to mention the fines, could cripple them."

Savitch took a deep breath. A weekend off would be nice. Even just a day. But the election was four days away and there was no time now. She went to the window and looked out on Rittenhouse Square and the skyline to the west. She opened the sliding door and nodded for Jack Singer to come out on the patio. They stood at the railing, seven flights above the city, and the wind shook the trees in the park. Savitch burrowed between him and the railing and breathed in the cool air. "Hold me," she said, and he wrapped his arms around her. She looked down to the street, closed her eyes, and imagined that he was saving her from falling.

They went back inside when she started shivering and Savitch went to the bathroom, took off her clothes, and put on a robe. When she came out, he was poring over the material he brought with him. She took a sip of bourbon and bent down and kissed him, pushing an ice chip over his lips with her tongue. He tried to tug her onto the sofa, but she resisted, taking his hand instead. "Come on," she said, leading him down the hall, undressing him along the way and then pulling him into the shower. The water ran hot and the room steamed, and Savitch closed her eyes as he massaged her neck and shoulders and soaped her entire body. They made love right there, water splashing on Savitch's face and into her open mouth, her lean body tighter and tighter and then every muscle collapsing in a wave.

She crawled into bed and lay on her side, curved against him like an oyster in its shell, and fell into a sleep that was deep and uninterrupted until two-thirty in the morning, when she shot straight up in bed. Before she knew why, she knew she had to call Muldoon.

"What's wrong?" Singer asked.

"Go back to sleep. I'll be right back."

She went into the kitchen to make the call. Muldoon's wife

picked up and Savitch apologized. When Muldoon got on he said, "This better be good."

"Muldoon, what was the temperature on Tuesday?"

A long pause, and then he asked if she was serious.

"Yes. What was the weather like?"

It was Muldoon's first day back from Barbados. He remembered getting off the plane and feeling like he'd stepped into a blizzard. "Cold," he said. "Sunny but cold."

"Right, and what was the weather like Wednesday?"

"Savitch, what the hell is this?"

"It was cold again," she said. "Very cold. And what do we notice about Richard Abbington going into the church and coming out of the church in those photographs?"

Muldoon was too tired to think straight. "I don't know."

"He's carrying a coat. Do you get it? It's freezing out there and this guy's carrying his coat instead of wearing it."

"What are you saying, Savitch?"

"Muldoon, the coat probably doesn't even fit him. He just uses it to carry the money. It's been bugging the shit out of me and it finally came to me in my sleep. Did you take those pictures with you tonight when you left the office?"

Muldoon said he thought they were in his briefcase, he'd go check. He picked up the phone again a minute later. "All right," he said. "I've got them."

"Look at Joey Tartaglione. Does anything look different about the coat when he comes out of church, compared to when he goes in?"

Muldoon put the photos next to each other. "I don't fuckin' believe it."

"What?"

"It's a different shade. I mean, they're black-and-white photos, but the coat is a little bit lighter going in. Like a lighter shade of gray. And when he comes out, it's longer. The hemline is past his knees."

"That's it, Muldoon. Abbington lines a coat with money every day and they exchange coats in church."

He paused a moment and she heard his breathing. Then he said, "Savitch, I think you've finally done it. You've nailed their pricks to the floor."

CHAPTER 27

JOEY TOOK AUGIE to morning mass but didn't go in with him. He had to call Richard Abbington and tell him not to show up at the church at noon. Since the trip to Atlantic City, he hadn't gotten around to telling him Liberty Oil's money was no good with them anymore. Augie still wouldn't budge on the subject. Ham still had a comfortable lead on Ron Rice, and one poll showed Debra Sharperson a point up on Izzy. But by evening, Joey would be closer to putting Ham away for good, and Sharperson would be known from Philadelphia to Pittsburgh as a dope-smoking flake. And they'd put out the word across the state that Augie's roulette jackpot would flood the streets by Monday, ward leaders in every county getting a piece of it to bring out the vote for Izzy.

Joey sped over to Robert Magnifico's House of Beef and Pork to use the pay phone outside the gym. Richard Abbington picked up on the first ring at his place out in Bryn Mawr, like he was sitting there waiting for someone to call. "Listen," Joey said. "Get out of your house, go to another phone, and call me here in five minutes." He gave Abbington the number and the phone rang three minutes later.

"All right," Joey said. "Now give me your number and I'll call you back." He didn't trust Abbington to have left his own house, the dumb fuck. If Muldoon had already gotten to him, Abbington was the type who would have flipped in ten seconds. Joey called back and said, "Listen, we got a situation here where we're looking to end this relationship."

"You got a situation?" Abbington asked, throwing it back at him.

"Yeah. That we don't associate with air-polluting, baby-killing fucks like you. So don't come by the church, is what I'm saying."

"Let me tell *you* about a situation," Abbington squealed. "I just got served with a grand jury subpoena."

Joey's heart jumped half through his Christmas sweater. Here we go. Here we fuckin' go. Don't panic, he told himself. They were OK. Augie was OK, anyway. It wasn't like this came as a big surprise.

"You hear me?" Abbington whined. He was hysterical, and Joey could tell that the pretty boy was already gone. Joey would have bet he wasn't wired, because he'd be pulling his Mister Cool right now instead of pissing his pants like this. "You guys fucked up," Abbington moaned. "And if your people don't have the sense to keep their mouths shut, I've got a couple of ways I could go on this."

A threat? Richard Abbington was making a threat? What a fuckin' jerkoff. If this guy was a big-time lobbyist, Joey Tartaglione could own Washington, D.C. "Listen to me," Joey said. "I don't know who the hell you dealt with before, but you didn't smack nobody south of Market Street. That's who you're dealing with now, tough guy, so don't give me with your 'couple of ways to go' fag talk. You just relax, do what I say, and don't fuck up, Einstein, because I don't wanna have to come out there and smack you. *Capeesh?*" Not a peep out of him. Joey could probably tell him to walk down to the Delaware and swim across to Camden, and Richard Abbington would ask backstroke or butterfly. As fucked up as he sounded, he had to be caught up in this deal down in Barbados, which Joey had read about in the newspaper. He wouldn't have thought this crew was up to murder, but an amateur job like this? It had to be them. They probably hired some fuckin' Gilligan down there. Joey had read about Barbados before. They must have a thousand caves where nobody would find a body for a million years, plus you had all that water. They're literally surrounded by water and these geniuses leave two bodies on the side of the road.

The one thing it proved, as far as Joey was concerned, was that Liberty Oil must be pushing horrible poison through its stacks, so he'd be happy to take them down. Let that whole fucking place sink into its own underground oil slick. "Listen," Joey said, "I don't have to do this for you, because as you know I've had a little bit of a temporary falling out with Ham. But I know for a fact that Ron Rice has come into some money. It's enough to buy out the weekend on every channel, and that could put Ham in some trouble."

Abbington said, "What are you talking about? Ham just came into a hundred thousand dollars from the casinos."

"Well guess what. He just dropped a few bucks at the track. I know you've got a sizable investment here, so I figure I'll give you a break. You get a few bucks to Ham, say ten thousand, and that should put him in the clear. If you want, I'll even set it up."

"It's too risky," Abbington said. "I've already been subpoenaed."

"Let me explain something to you. If they had anything on us, you think I'd be on the street? I didn't get a subpoena. This is bullshit, and it may not even have anything to do with the campaign. For all you know, it's about this bad gas you guys fart out of that refinery every day. But listen, you got a half million wrapped up in this by now. If you wanna flush that down the toilet and disappoint your boss there, don't let me stand in the way. It ain't my fuckin' money."

He could almost hear Abbington sweating out the decision. "Where?" he finally said.

"Be at the lake at two. I'll get Ham over there."

Joey called Ham's legislative office in Queen Village and they said he had a speech at J & A Catering on Broad Street, a Sons of Italy breakfast meeting. He blasted up Tenth Street and passed Pennies from Heaven, the curb feelers lighting up like sparklers as they clipped hubcaps on parked cars. There was no sign of anyone following him. Joey had moved nearly a half million dollars in two months, and could account for every last transaction in his head. He was going over them now one by one, thinking about all the people who'd have to back him up if Muldoon started knocking on doors and asking questions of contributors. Maybe he was being optimistic, but he didn't see a weak link anywhere in the chain. They were stand-up guys, all. The one group he couldn't trust 100 percent was Maggie Sharperson's set of friends, but even that looked solid. She was still on the warpath against her mother, and she'd recruited a half dozen people who gave their names as campaign contributors. It was against Joey's better judgment, but women had that over you. You stayed with one of them too long, you ended up dumber than a bucket of paint.

Ham was taking questions from the audience when Joey got there. One old vet in an American Legion hat asked about the trouble in the Balkans, wanting to know where Ham came down. Ham said that was a tough situation all around, but his first commitment was to the men, women, and children of the congressional district. "The Balkanese have to solve their own problems from within, just like us," he said.

Joey stood in the back of the room with his arms crossed, thinking he should have just shot Ham when he had the urge, and this whole thing would have been simpler. When his speech was over, Ham came through the crowd headed for the door with that swagger of his, like nobody else but him had a dick. Joey knew Ham had spotted him, but he tried to walk right past him anyway.

Joey grabbed him.

"The fuck you want?" Ham asked.

Joey pulled him away from the crowd. "Listen, we had our differences, but you and I go way back. I wanted to warn you there might be some heat out there. Richard Abbington got a subpoena."

Ham threw his hands up. "What's this all about?"

"Don't get carried away. That's what they're hoping somebody does, is go nuts. I think it's bullshit, myself. They don't have nothing. They call you in, just take the Fifth, keep your mouth shut. All right? I just wanted to let you know, for old time's sake, so you watch yourself the next few days."

Ham looked suspicious, but he said he appreciated the warning. "How's the old man?" he asked.

Joey knew it wasn't an honest inquiry as to Augie's emotional welfare. It was a shot. As in, look at me, I'm about to win this thing without his help. I told you I didn't need the cocksucker.

"Augie's all fucked up," Joey said. "He should be in a home, telling his stories to somebody who might listen because where can they go? I think he's got the memory problem like Angela had. If I wasn't there, he'd try to put his pants on over his head. But I owe him, Ham. You know what I mean? What're you gonna do?"

"It's too bad. In his day, Augie was the best."

"Forget about it. Fact of the matter is, I still love him," Joey said. "I mean, even to this day, anybody did anything to hurt him, I'd put an ice pick through his eyeballs."

Ham nodded like yeah, that would be the way to go. He took a half step back just to be safe, still not sure what Joey was up to. He put a finger to his head, like an idea might have just penetrated. "How about after the election, Joey? What then?"

"This is what I'm saying. I don't think I can carry Augie much longer. I'll stick with him through Tuesday, but after that, I don't know. Maybe I gotta look out for myself, you know what I'm saying?"

Ham said, "Let's talk. I may need somebody to run the office here while I'm in Washington."

"I don't know, Ham. I've been with Augie a long time. Maybe just out of loyalty, I should get out of the business when I call it quits with him. That's what I have to decide."

"Well think about it is all I'm asking. Listen, I gotta run right now. I got another one of these in ten minutes."

Ham was out on the sidewalk, pimping away, when Joey called to him. "I almost forgot," he said, running after him. "I had Richard Abbington on the phone—he's in a panic with this subpoena. He wants to know can he still get money to you to make sure you hold on. I said sure, but don't go near his office. He said he could meet you at the lake at two."

"Hell, I don't know. If he's under subpoena, maybe I better play it safe. I think I'm in the clear here, anyway. We've got one poll that puts me over him by six points."

"It's your call," Joey said, backing up and heading for his car. "But I know for a fact that Ron Rice has come into some money, and he's going to make a last-minute run at you. I think Abbington said he's got ten thousand, something like that. You do whatever you think's best."

Joey drove past First Columbus Trust and saw a yellow police strip tied across the entrance. Muldoon's car was in the parking lot. He was a bull, this guy, but Joey could handle him. The edge he had on all of them was that they weren't smart enough to realize he wasn't an idiot. Joey sped over to Pennies from Heaven and scribbled out a note for someone to deliver to Izzy.

Call Bonguisto, call every reporter you know, and bury Liberty Oil. Every speech you make today, tomorrow, the next day, rip a new asshole for those guys about the pollution. I'll explain later.

—Joey.

Augie had just come out of St. Mary Magdalen and was standing at the top of the steps when Joey pulled up. Look at him, Joey thought. Nice suit, beautiful fedora with a little feather in the band, a smile you could see from around the block. Augie was schmoozing the crowd, shaking hands, crouching in a boxing stance with old pals. Two months ago he was walking out of that church like he was leaving his own funeral, and nobody could have cared less. Joey would remember this scene. If there were days when he wondered if he'd done the right thing, he'd think back on this picture.

"Joey Tartaglione, son of Enrique, how you doing there?"

"Fine, Senator. Everything's fine." Joey wanted to get Augie away from the crowd before he broke the news to him. Augie was going on about all the parishioners who were congratulating him on Izzy. The election was still four days away, and they were already patting him on the back. Father D'Anunzio had made a blessing, too. A prayer for Senator Sangiamino's ticket.

When they got to Robert Magnifico's, Joey told Augie they needed to talk, and Augie could tell what was up by the tone. He'd seen it coming when he walked down the steps of the church and saw Joey standing back, watching him. He'd probably seen it before then, too, but he'd pushed it away. He tilted his hat back now and leaned against the warehouse wall, looking off in the distance at the movement in the Italian Market. "What have they got?" he asked. He was calm, his voice steady. He was a pro.

"They got nothing, Senator. You're protected on this."

Augie put his hand on Joey's shoulder and took him in with a look that cut everything else away. It was a look that said he understood everything Joey had done for him. "You hung yourself out there for me, Joey, didn't you?"

Joey took a breath and repeated what he'd said. Everything would work out. They'd probably all get called before the grand jury in the next day or two, but all Augie had to do was take the Fifth, and Joey would handle the rest.

"The Lord works in mysterious ways," Augie said. "I come clean for Angela, tell Liberty Oil to stuff it up their ass, and now we got trouble. Where's the justice in the world?" A weariness had crept into his voice. "When Angela died, I promised her I'd be the man she always wanted me to be."

"Senator, she loved you the way you were."

They began walking toward the Italian Market with slow, easy steps. Augie said, "Not anymore, she didn't. But I learned something about myself, Joey, and there's no way around it. I can't be no saint. I'm a politician." They waited for a delivery truck to pass and then Augie walked into the middle of Ninth Street, near the produce stall where he had grown up. He turned to the north. A square turn, like a soldier, and said, "I kind of like that line, Joey. Put it on my gravestone for me, will you?"

Augie leaned into the first step and was gone, walking the walk. It was a safe place to be right now because there was no good or bad here in the market. No right or wrong. This was where the line had been erased in the first place.

CHAPTER 28

MIKE MULDOON BREEZED IN over the Ben Franklin Bridge on a day so clear he could see all the way to Mercer, and Liberty Oil looked like a cotton-ball factory down there, shooting little puffs up into the blue sky. He took the Vine Street Expressway into Center City and picked up a bag of bagels at the Fairmount Bagel Institute. Then he went out to the art museum, parked the Bronco in his regular spot, and walked toward City Hall. On most Saturday mornings, he was on a golf course somewhere. But he could break eighty, and that wouldn't feel as good as what he was going to do this morning. It wouldn't come close.

He paused in front of the Rodin Museum and studied *The Thinker*, wondering why it was that so few people in Philadelphia ever did what that bronze creation was doing. They ought to take Billy Penn down from the top of the City Hall tower and put *The Thinker* up there. Let it be a reminder to everyone. The fountain was gurgling and hissing as Muldoon walked through the gardens of Logan Circle, and he paused again at the Basilica, made the sign of the cross, and said two short prayers. One was a prayer of forgiveness for boffing Carla Delmonico. The other was a prayer for the day. A prayer that everything would work out.

Richard Abbington said he'd like a cup of coffee, then changed his mind. Maybe water. Muldoon went to the door and asked a secretary to bring two coffees and a water. "You can help yourself to a bagel there," Muldoon told him. "Savitch, you sure you don't want one? I got you the strawberry." It was nine o'clock Saturday morning. The grand jury was coming in at eleven, but Lisa Savitch had called Abbington Friday night and told him it might be to his advantage to stop by her office a couple hours early if he wanted to. She left the map up intentionally, all those pins around Liberty Oil, and Abbington was pretending he hadn't noticed.

"So what's this about?" he asked, turning down the offer of a bagel. Savitch lit a cigarette and Muldoon made himself a bagel sandwich. He was the only one in the room with an appetite.

"What would you say it's about?" Muldoon asked her in a wise-guy tone. He took a bite and kept his eye on Abbington, who was staring at Lisa Savitch as she organized some paperwork on her desk and put it in her briefcase. She had on a black outfit, loose and flowing, like a judge's robe, and she looked great. What a show, Muldoon thought. The guy walks in off the street with a rope around his neck, and the person holding the other end isn't some battle-ax like Kevinne McGinns. It's a drop-dead blond who, under any other circumstances, Abbington would probably be hitting on. She looked even sexier without sleep. It gave her rough edges you wanted to smooth out.

Savitch brought her head up and looked at Abbington as if she were reading him, the left eye wandering and probably hypnotizing the poor bastard. Abbington had floppy brown hair and a clean, round face with hazel eyes. When she'd first seen pictures of him, Savitch told Muldoon he reminded her of a high-school classmate who was nice looking, but fragile and boyish, more pretty than handsome. She said she'd be able to use that. "I think Mr. Abbington knows what it's about," she said, drawing on that cigarette like it was the best one she'd ever had, and staring into him like she could see everything he was. He was spilled casually onto the chair, legs crossed, no worries. The guilty-man pose. Muldoon had seen it so many times he could sketch it with his eyes closed. Abbington put his arm on the chair back, revealing a ring of sweat that was coming through his sport coat.

"Have you two been formally introduced?" Savitch asked, pointing at Muldoon with her cigarette. "Mr. Abbington, Mr. Muldoon here is a former FBI agent working now with the district attorney's office as chief detective. One of his specialties is surveillance." Abbington's expression didn't change. He wasn't going to give anything away. Savitch asked Muldoon if the interview room was ready.

"I believe so," he said. "Let me just finish this first." He and Savitch were both playing it cool, like they dragged people in here every day and toyed with them. Letting Abbington think about how confident they looked. This room was perfect for an interview, as small and depressing as it was, almost like a cell. But Muldoon wanted to press the point by leading Abbington past a chain gang of prisoners in the gloomy, institutional corridors of City Hall. He had stopped by the holding cell and paid two inmates ten dollars each to put on a performance when he came back with Abbington. The sheriff's deputies were going to lead the gang into the hall as if they were shuttling them somewhere.

It came off perfectly. As Muldoon and Savitch came through with Abbington, one of the two bad guys said something about the other's wife and they went at it, spilling on the floor and trying to rip each other's faces off while the rest of the men in the chain gang, all of them in orange prison jumpsuits, cheered them on. Muldoon was wondering what they would have done for twenty each. "Watch your step," he told Abbington, moving around the scuffle as sheriff's deputies broke up the fight and got the gang moving again. Abbington's mouth had become a thin line and his walk stiffened, like he was wearing a metal brace that started at his shoes and went right up his ass.

Muldoon had arranged to do the interview in a courtroom holding cell. It was a small cave with nothing inside but hospital green walls, a rectangular table, and two high-backed metal chairs. The only window was a small Plexiglas square on the door, and it didn't open. Savitch took one chair; Muldoon motioned for Abbington to take the other. "You smoke?" Savitch asked. Richard Abbington shook his head no and asked again what this was about. The room was tight, and Savitch's smoke hung like fog. It was one time Muldoon didn't mind it. He could see a twitch under Abbington's eye now. Mr. Cool starting to melt. They let him squirm until he asked again, testier this time, "Would you mind telling me what this is about?" Savitch said she was obligated to tell him he didn't have to answer any questions here. At eleven o'clock, when he was called before the grand jury, he had no choice. But he could blow this off if he didn't feel comfortable. Nine times out of ten, a guy in that seat gave the response Richard Abbington gave now.

"I have nothing to hide."

"I didn't think so," Muldoon said. "Mr. Abbington, have you ever testified before a grand jury?"

He shook his head no.

"Maybe Ms. Savitch here can tell you what to expect."

She sizzled out the cigarette in her coffee. "Here's what it looks like," she said. "Twenty people, twenty-five, are gathering right now in a courtroom one floor below us. They're waiting to hear how you answer a series of questions I've prepared."

Abbington looked at Muldoon for no reason except that Savitch was making him uncomfortable. Something in the depths of those brown eyes was designing a new life for him, and he knew it. "Questions about what?" he asked.

"For instance, do you know a man named Joey Tartaglione?"

Abbington scratched his head behind his ear. He said, "I

meet a lot of people in my business. I'm a lobbyist and a consultant. A lawyer by training. I don't remember everybody's
name."

"In other words, to the best of your recollection, you never
met a man named Joey Tartaglione?"

Abbington stood up. He said, "Listen, you said I didn't have
to sit for this bullshit, and frankly, I think I've changed my
mind."

Muldoon, who was sitting on one end of the plain wooden
table, stood up and looked at his watch. "Thanks," he said.
"We'll see you downstairs in about ninety minutes." Abbington
made his way to the door, but stopped there. "So you're done?"
he asked.

"Not exactly," Muldoon said. "We've got time to get a
couple more people in here before the grand jury gets started,
see if they care to talk. But yes, we're done with you. Thanks
again for coming."

Savitch had pulled a folder from her briefcase and plopped it
on the table so a few photographs peeked out. Not far enough
for Abbington to see what they were, but far enough. "I think
it's only fair to warn you," she said, "that people aren't always
quite as cool under these circumstances as you are right now.
They've convinced themselves it would never get to this, and
all of a sudden, here it is."

Muldoon picked it up, saying, "You'd be amazed how
quickly people will turn on each other to save their own skin.
In my experience, the ones who decide to cooperate tend to
make out a little better than the ones who don't. There are certain deals that can be worked out."

Abbington went back to his chair and sagged into it. He
could see now that his name was on the folder in front of her.
He pulled out a handkerchief and patted his forehead.

Savitch asked Muldoon, "Do you like irony?"

"What do you mean?"

"Well you take a guy as good-looking as Mr. Abbington here,

and you figure that has to be an advantage in life. But now it takes a cruel turn. Can you imagine how popular Mr. Abbington would be in a joint like Graterford?"

Muldoon checked out Abbington and turned to Savitch. "Weren't those guys in the hall from Graterford?"

Abbington looked at the folder again. He couldn't tell who was in those pictures. All he could make out were the feet.

Savitch said, "Mr. Abbington, it turns out that Mr. Muldoon here is a photography nut. Would you care to look at some of his work?" She opened the folder and took the top photo off the pile, setting it down in front of him. Joey Tartaglione leaving church. "Does that refresh your memory as to who Mr. Tartaglione is?" The next photo was Richard Abbington leaving the same church. Abbington was still holding on, though more defensively now. "What does any of this prove?" he asked.

Savitch flipped more photos down, the daily comings and goings at St. Mary Magdalen, like she was the dealer in a poker game. "It proves that we've got a hell of a coincidence going, Mr. Abbington, in which day after day, a devout Catholic comes out of church with a different coat than the one he went in with. I mean, what are the odds on making that same mistake over and over?" She let him roll it around awhile, then she asked, "Where were you yesterday at two in the afternoon?"

"I don't keep a record of every move I make in a day."

"That's OK," she said, taking the next photo off the pile. "We do." It was Abbington and Ham Flaherty at Roosevelt Park, outside the concession stand at the High Rollers Bocce Pavilion. "You want to tell me you never heard of Ham Flaherty, either?"

Abbington looked angry now for the first time.

"Take a look at Mr. Muldoon," Savitch told him. "Does he look to you like the kind of character who'd hide in the bocce court snack bar, take pictures, and eavesdrop on conversations? My guess is the grand jury's going to love hearing him tell that story. I've already seen Mr. Muldoon testify in court, good St. Joe's alum that he is. Believe me, the jury loves this man."

Richard Abbington's eyes drooped and he leaned forward, elbows on the table. Savitch and Muldoon still didn't know where the tip had come from. Someone called anonymously Friday morning and left a message for Muldoon in the form of a poem.

Two o'clock performance
At Roosevelt Lake
In the Garden of Eden
Which one is the snake?

Maybe it was the same person who sent Judy Flaherty poems ratting out her husband. Who knew?

"These are some real geniuses you hooked up with," Muldoon said. "I've been doing this for twenty-five years, and damn it if people don't get a little more stupid every year. It just makes me feel so lucky, as hard as it is to hold a job today, that I picked the one growth industry in this state."

Richard Abbington was turning gray now and his eyes were sinking. Muldoon got more of a kick watching a well-heeled, educated man go down. Lowlifes tended to accept the fall as fate, and met it with a degree of recognition, if not honor. They didn't break. Richard Abbington looked like he might wet himself. It was a much better show, proving yet again a Muldoon credo: When it comes to crime, the smart guys are always dumber than the dumb guys.

"I want to see my attorney," Abbington said in a shrunken voice.

Savitch slapped the table and looked at Muldoon with a satisfied smile. "There it is," she said. "You owe me."

Muldoon took out his wallet and put a ten on the table. "We had a bet on which guy would be the one to cut himself a deal and rat out everybody else," he explained to Richard Abbington. "I picked you."

Savitch joined in, saying, "He thought you were a little smarter than the others. You go ahead and call your attorney and we'll see you in two hours in front of the grand jury. Muldoon, you want to go get the next one?"

The depth of Richard Abbington's trouble was becoming clearer to him by the moment. He was fucked if he walked out the door; he was fucked if he didn't. "You've got a couple of pictures," he said weakly. "That's nothing. Is it illegal to go to church? Is it illegal to make a campaign contribution?"

"Here's what we know and can prove," Savitch said, working with a pen and a legal pad now. "You're the bagman for Liberty Oil, which has been making illegal campaign contributions to Ham Flaherty and Izzy Weiner for nearly two months. You lined a coat with money every day and made the switch with Joey Tartaglione in church. You delivered another payment to Ham Flaherty yesterday. You sent checks to Barbados every month for two men who ended up with bullets in their heads because of what they knew about toxic emissions." She looked up from the pad and said, "Stop me when you get tired of listening, because I can go on all day."

Muldoon told Abbington he should have had a bagel, because it could be his last decent meal for a while. Abbington loosened his tie and pulled his collar open. "What do you want from me?"

Savitch slapped the legal pad on the table and leaped up. "I want you to wake up," she said, her voice sharper now. No more dancing around. "We know exactly what you've been up to. We've got photographs. We've got an eyewitness sitting right here in this room. You're in shit up to your eyeballs."

"The question isn't whether you do time," Muldoon said. "It's where and for how long. And this is where you can get us on your side and maybe help you out." Savitch looked at the clock. Nine-thirty. She picked the legal pad up again and read the charges he was looking at.

"Conspiracy. Bribery. Fraud. About four hundred tax crimes and twice as many election code violations. Not to mention murder, which is another distinct possibility." She smacked the legal pad down and waited for Abbington to look at her. "How old are you?" she asked.

Abbington dropped his head.

"He's thirty-nine," Muldoon said.

Savitch did some math, her lips moving as she went down the list of charges and probable sentences on each. "You just turned seventy-two. And that's without murder."

Muldoon, leaning against the wall, pulled away and said, "Jesus, he'd be in jail nearly as long as he's been alive." He sniffed under his arm and said that was a long time for a good-looking guy to go without a shower. At that, something gave inside of Abbington. It started with a quivering at his mouth and moved along a fault line all the way down his spine and to his feet. His hands shook and his legs trembled and the first tear ran down his smooth face. "What do you want?" he pleaded. "What the hell do you people want?"

Savitch reached into her briefcase and pulled out a newspaper. A fourth child had died of leukemia. He was nine years old and his picture was under the headline. She slid the newspaper toward Abbington and walked around behind him, bending down to speak directly into his ear, like the closeness would get the words to his brain faster. "I want the truth about this. I want you to give up Whit Pritchard and whoever else was involved in this, and tell us how long Liberty Oil's been covering up the benzene problem."

He turned palms up and shrugged. "What are you talking about?"

Savitch grabbed the back of his head and pushed down until his eyeballs were two inches from the dead nine-year-old. "This!" she screamed. "I'm talking about dead kids, you stupid piece of shit! You killed this little boy and he wasn't the first and he probably won't be the last. You, Richard Abbington. You killed this boy!"

She lit a cigarette, circled the table, and said, "We ran a test in Mercer yesterday with the EPA. There was three times as much benzene in the atmosphere as the law allows. I'm not a scientist but I'm not an idiot, either, Mr. Abbington. Liberty Oil has lied for years about emissions, and they didn't stop just because children started dying. Kids, Richard. Three boys and a girl. Do you fucking get it?"

"There's no way you're going to be able to draw a scientific connection," Abbington protested.

Savitch said, "There's no way you're going to like a dick up your ass every night for thirty years."

Abbington appealed to Muldoon now, figuring he didn't have a chance with Savitch. "How would I know anything about it?" he whimpered. "I don't even work full time at Liberty. I contract with them for some PR, some consulting. I do other lobbying that doesn't even involve the oil industry."

Savitch said, "Maybe you haven't made vice president yet, but this is not a company you're just getting to know, Richard. Ever been to Texas? Does that ring a bell? Don't sit here and tell me you have no idea why an oil company would throw a zillion dollars into an election and do everything in its power to keep the state off its property at a time when kids all around the plant are dropping dead." She had moved away, but went back and sat next to him on the edge of the table, her knees almost in his face. In a softer, smoky voice, she said, "Look at my legs here, Richard. Do you like what you see? Here, let me pull my dress up a little higher so you get a better look." Muldoon tried as inconspicuously as possible to get off the table and move to where he had a better look. Savitch said, "Nice, huh? Well guess what. You'll never get in there. You'll never get into another skirt the rest of your life, unless you can get it up when you're seventy-two."

Muldoon could have watched this all day. He'd been in on the same setup a hundred times and hadn't seen this move. McGinns, in her prime, didn't have the weapons Lisa Savitch had. "You're a cretin and an idiot," she was telling Abbington now, "and I could put you in a room half the size of this one until your hair falls out. But you're not the one I'm after."

Muldoon slid in closer, and now they were like McGinns's cats, one on each side of him. "There's one thing you're not taking into consideration," Muldoon said. "Here you are protecting the rest of the crew, assuming they'll do the same for you. But this isn't the honor society you're working with. Somebody even sold you out yesterday afternoon when you went to see Ham Flaherty. You think the next guy in here is going to protect your sorry ass if he can save his own? We had a little chat with Whit Pritchard yesterday. Did he tell you about it? He must have, but did he tell you everything, do you think? There's a man with a lot to protect. You think Whit Pritchard isn't thinking about grabbing the only chance he has to save his own ass? You've got something over all of them, Richard. You know what that is? You're the first one being offered a deal. But the train's leaving the station now. You can climb aboard, or walk out that door and deal with the consequences."

Tears flooded down Abbington's face now. "What are you offering?" he asked.

"It depends on how much you cooperate," Savitch said. "But we're talking about dropping some charges, lighter sentences on others. Best of all, the U.S. attorney's office may take a piece of this case, and it's possible we can arrange for someone to do time in the federal system instead of the state."

"Some people think of it as a little more cushy," Muldoon interjected. "Those state boys out in the hall, for instance, would probably kill for a chance to do federal time."

Abbington looked from Muldoon to Savitch and back again. "If you can give me certain guarantees," he said, "I'll tell you what I know. As long as you'll stipulate to the fact that I don't know anything about a lot of this."

Savitch leaned in to where her face was six inches from his.

"Mr. Abbington," she said, speaking through her teeth, "I won't stipulate to the time of day with you. All I'm doing is offering you the best chance you're going to get."

Muldoon went and got a stenographer and a tape recorder. He called Kevinne McGinns and asked if she wanted to sit in, and she said she'd be right over. Lisa Savitch stepped outside the room for some fresh air and slumped down on a chair. "If I've ever felt this tired, or this satisfied," she told Muldoon when he got back, "I can't remember it."

At eleven o'clock sharp in courtroom 598, Lisa Savitch called Mike Muldoon to the stand for a brief summary of developments since the last meeting of the grand jury, and then she called Richard Abbington. After introducing him, she read his statement into the record, and as she did, several jurors groaned or put their hands to their mouths. Liberty Oil had discovered five years ago that aging equipment was resulting in an unintentional release of benzene from several sources, primarily through the smokestacks. Tests performed by the company at the edge of the property showed three-tenths parts of benzene per million parts of air, three times the allowable limit for the cancer-causing substance. Liberty was struggling financially at the time because of legal fees relating to underground oil seepage from storage tanks. Whit Pritchard believed that a much-needed retrofitting would have put the company under, so he decided to delay the upgrades and try to reduce leakage as much as possible. And, in the meantime, to conceal the truth from employees, the community, and the government.

The ruse was facilitated by a state inspector who detected the benzene emissions and demanded a cash payment of twenty thousand dollars in hush money on each of two visits to the plant. In return, he doctored the numbers, giving Liberty a clean bill of health. A third time, he demanded ten thousand dollars for not showing up at all. A month ago, when stories about leukemia began dominating the news, the inspector died at his second home, a cabin in the Poconos, of what was believed to be a self-inflicted gunshot wound to the head. Two employees who knew about the benzene problem, Richard Kelly and Daiman Heidorn, had blackmailed the company for three years and lived on Whit Pritchard's sugar plantation in Barbados on money that had been sent, on occasion, by Richard Abbington himself. If Kelly and Heidorn were murdered by anyone associated with Liberty Oil, Abbington claimed, he knew nothing about it.

As for the election, Abbington said Liberty Oil used a slush fund—the same one set up to pay the state inspector—to make unreported cash payments to Joey Tartaglione with the understanding that the money would finance the campaigns of Isadore "Izzy" Weiner and William "Ham" Flaherty. In return, according to the understanding, Weiner and Flaherty would give special consideration to legislation and legal matters involving Liberty. Abbington said he didn't keep records, but guessed that the payments totaled in the neighborhood of a half million dollars.

After Abbington's statement was read into the record, Savitch went back over it with him, affirming each element of it for the jury's sake. The members of the grand jury were reduced to stunned silence.

When Richard Abbington was done, Lisa Savitch called a succession of witnesses to the stand, but got nothing out of any of them.

William "Ham" Flaherty took the Fifth.

Isadore "Izzy" Weiner took the Fifth.

Lou Canuso took the Fifth.

Joseph Augustine Sangiamino took the Fifth.

And then Savitch announced that there'd be a lunch recess of two hours before she called the next witness—Joey Tartaglione.

CHAPTER 29

AT THE AGE OF SEVEN, Wayne Joseph Tartaglione was beating his father at blackjack. The old man told friends and family about it and when they came by the house, they tried their hand at beating the boy. Joey always won.

When he was nine, his uncle Rocco bought him an abacus for Christmas. Joey did his math homework on it and by the time he was ten, he used it to help the neighborhood bookie do his daily accounting. They gave him the nickname China Joe.

At twelve, he threw the abacus away. Numbers slid through the circuits of his brain faster than the wooden discs slid along those metal runners, and with just a moment of concentration, Joey could see all the possibilities, see things through to their logical conclusion. It struck his friends on the street that his purpose in life had been predetermined, and he became known as Joey Numbers. To sharpen his skills, he read books on economics and accounting, and he occasionally dropped in on classes at Penn or Temple and sat in the back of the room, hoping the professor wouldn't realize he was a freeloader.

In one of those classes, he met Penn's female shot-put champion and they started going out. Joey went to a writing class with her one day and the teacher came around the room, asking everyone to tell a story about a poem that had touched them in one way or another. Joey, who couldn't think of one as sophisticated as the other students'—he preferred limericks and simple rhymes—left class so humiliated he never saw the shot-put champion again, even though he had been doing two-a-days with her. He had been reading and writing ever since. He would never be unprepared in his life again. He would never be humiliated.

In thirty years of bookmaking and independent study, Joey had combined his strength for the logic of numbers with an innate knowledge of man's weakness for risk, and the result was the gradual creation of a small fortune. He had kept it in the floor under the sofa at Pennies from Heaven, but recently transferred most of it to safe-deposit boxes and bank accounts in the names of seven people he had invented—Social Security numbers and all—at First Columbus Trust.

All told, Joey had amassed $720,000. He wasn't saving for anything in particular. A man could wear only so many Christmas sweaters. It was more about making numbers work for him, about proving himself—until this election. If his calculations were correct, and he couldn't remember the last time they weren't, Joey's fortune had bought him the only thing he wanted: Augie's resurrection and safe passage. The senator would have Izzy and he'd have Ron Rice, all of them free and clear. A new era in the life of the Sunday Macaroni Club.

The smell of Richard Abbington's nervous sweat still hung in the room. Joey Tartaglione sat in the chair where Abbington had been. Muldoon stood and Savitch sat, fidgeting with some papers, Joey calmly observing.

"Mr. Tartaglione," she said, "we asked you in here because we'd like to show you some things before we call the grand jury back."

Joey tapped his finger on the table in front of her. "What did you say your name was?"

"Lisa Savitch, I'm an assistant district attorney. And this is Mike Muldoon. He's—"

"Him I heard of," Joey said, his eyes still on her. She looked great, but the girl had no meat on her bones. Like a stick, she was. She reached for a cigarette and Joey grabbed the lighter in front of her and flicked it.

Savitch gave him a suspicious eye. He almost looked like he wanted to be here. She said, "You understand you don't have to do this, Mr. Tartaglione?"

He nodded.

"The grand jury returns from a lunch recess in one hour, and you're the first witness I'll call to the stand. At that point, you'll have to answer some questions under threat of contempt for refusing to do so. But you're not obligated to answer any questions before then."

Joey gave a safe sign with his hands. "I'll tell you what, though. Would you mind opening the door or maybe getting a fan in here? It's about a hundred forty degrees in this sweatbox."

Savitch was getting warm herself, and she nodded for Muldoon to go ahead and open the door. "Mr. Tartaglione, what is your occupation?"

Joey chuckled. "What am I, applying for a loan? I help out Senator Augie Sangiamino." He was wearing a sweater he hadn't pulled out of the pantry closet in a while—gray wool, with a black leather design on the shoulders and under the neck. Very sharp, Muldoon thought. He was tempted to ask where he got it.

"And what did you do before working for Mr. Sangiamino?"

"Prior to that I would have been a bookmaker."

It caught her by surprise. "Excuse me?"

"I was a bookie."

He'd already said more than the Fifth Amendment crowd combined. She glanced over at Muldoon and gave him a look that said they might as well dive right in. She reached into the folder and threw the photos on the table. Joey going in and out of the church. Richard Abbington going in and out of the church. "Nice coat," she said.

"You like it?"

"Do you know the man in this picture?"

"Why, did he say he knew me?"

"Mr. Tartaglione, let me give you a quick piece of advice. Don't fuck with me. I'm tired, I'm busy, and I can be extremely unpleasant when somebody irritates me. You're in a considerable amount of trouble here, and how it works out for you could depend on your ability to cut the bullshit and answer the damn questions."

Joey could almost hear Richard Abbington's echo in the room. The pretty boy sang opera in here, just as he expected. Joey looked at Savitch and then Muldoon, and he could tell by the way Muldoon carried himself and the way he looked at Savitch that he had wanted her but didn't get to first base. Joey didn't know a man who could hide either wanting it or having gotten it. You wore that like you wore a shirt and pants. Joey looked at Savitch. "What are you offering me here?"

"It depends on who you're willing to deliver," Muldoon said.

"Who would you like?"

"Whit Pritchard, for starters," Savitch said. "Richard Abbington, William Flaherty, Isadore Weiner, Augie Sangiamino."

Joey laughed at that. "Remind me not to go to A.C. with you guys," he said. "You're holding three of a kind and you're counting full house."

Savitch looked at Muldoon for help. He was leaning against the door, arms crossed, wondering how he had ever convinced himself to leave this life. That was the thing about these guys. They were crooks, but they were characters, all, and when you came face-to-face, it helped if you spoke their language. He sauntered over and sat on the edge of the table, two feet away from Joey Tartaglione. He said, "Listen to me, fuckface. Miss Savitch here has already pointed out that you're standing in a bucket of shit, and another one's about to come down on your head. Do you honestly think we don't know exactly what you morons have been up to? We've got photographs, we've got witnesses, we've got bank records, and we've got a statement from one of your yo-yo buddies."

Joey pushed himself away from the table, rocking on the back legs of his chair. "You got bad information is what you got. Because guess what, Inspector. Nobody knows dick but me. I had the purse."

Muldoon looked at his watch. He said, "You've got one hour to tell the story or forty years to think about it. Your choice, fat boy." If Joey was intimidated or insulted by that, he hid it well. "It's yours for a price," he said. Muldoon stood over Joey and stared down at him. Using that neat move of his, the same one he'd used on Savitch's ex, he kicked the chair out from under him and had Joey up against the wall in a heartbeat. "I got a 'guess what' for you. You don't roll in here off the street like some little meatball and tell us what the deal is. It works the other way around."

Muldoon let him go and Joey picked his chair up and sat down unfazed. "Tough guy," he said. "Well let me tell you something, Tracy and Hepburn. You got a hard-on for a couple of guys who don't even know what happened here. All I'm doing, I'm trying to save you the embarrassment of indicting people you can't convict."

Savitch had an inch of curled ash on her cigarette. "What do you want?" she asked.

"Five years maximum is what I want."

"Not a fucking chance."

"Let me ask you something," Joey said. "That grand jury you got sittin' out there, how many times today did they hear somebody take the Fifth? You think the boss will be happy with that, an aspiring lady like Kevinne McGinns? That's a hell of a press conference she's lookin' at. Ladies and gentlemen, I got a statement from one fuckin' moron named Richard Abbington, who happens to be nothing but the bagman, and I got about four hundred other clowns taking the Fifth."

Savitch asked, "Who would you give us?"

"I could give you Whit Pritchard."

"Not enough," Muldoon said.

Joey held his hands up. "I'm not done. I'll give you Ham, even though I'll take heat for that the rest of my life, ratting out a longtime friend and associate."

Savitch shook her head no. "Throw in Izzy Weiner and Augie Sangiamino," she said, "and maybe we can arrange ten years or less."

Joey sat back down and smiled at her. "This is what I'm trying to say. Izzy Weiner doesn't know what happened. Augie Sangiamino doesn't know what happened. They were like Reagan and Bush in Iran-Contra—out of the loop."

Muldoon knew Kevinne McGinns wanted Augie Sangiamino, just to say she'd bagged him twice, and she wanted Izzy Weiner just on general principle. But they had next to nothing on Augie, and outside of Richard Abbington saying the money was supposed to go to Ham and Izzy, they had nothing on Weiner.

"Correct me if I'm wrong," Joey said, "but in all the pictures you got, all the tails you put on everybody, which, by the way, you ought to send some of those junior deputies back to the police academy, you don't have Izzy Weiner or Augie Sangiamino one time coming into contact with anybody from Liberty Oil. Am I right?" He knew he was right. The one time Augie met with Richard Abbington at the lake, they didn't talk specifics. Everything was left purposely vague, and it was long before Muldoon and Savitch were on to them.

Muldoon turned to Savitch, who flicked ash on the floor, forgetting the ashtray on the table. She was studying Joey Tartaglione like she was in an anthropology lab and they'd brought in a rare specimen, possibly the missing link. But he was no idiot, and he clearly had seen this day coming for weeks. Muldoon wondered if he and Savitch were thinking the same thing. That Joey Tartaglione might even have predetermined this day.

"It didn't happen," Joey went on. "If Izzy Weiner was bought out by Liberty Oil, what the hell is he doing in the newspaper smacking them around for this pollution problem they got? You give that any thought?"

Savitch's eyes were red and puffy. She played with a matchbook absentmindedly and stared at the wall. Maybe she was just tired, Muldoon thought. It was clear that this wasn't going to fall into place as easily as they had hoped. Tartaglione was covering for Augie Sangiamino and Izzy Weiner, no question about it, but there was no way they could prove it—at least not yet. There'd probably be hell to pay with McGinns, but Muldoon wasn't going to let Savitch beat herself up over it. They were in this room today because of her, and she already had the piece she had wanted all along. From day one, she had gone after Whit Pritchard as if he were the one who had killed her own brother, and barring any unforeseen twist, he was already in the bag.

"Tell me something," she said. "Why are you so interested in cooperating against Liberty Oil?"

"Can I be perfectly honest?" Joey asked.

"Probably not, but give it a shot."

Joey took a deep breath and his eyes softened. "I can't sleep at night. Can't look in the mirror." Muldoon played air violin but Joey ignored it. "Liberty Oil comes to us with a deal. They want to help Ham and Izzy so they can catch a break with some legislation and whatever goes before the court, but there's not enough time to push enough money through legal channels. Besides, they don't want it public knowledge that they're supporting these guys, because the way they look at it, it's beneath them to be associated with us. Now am I going to take their money in a situation like that? Fuckin' A right I am.

"But I had no idea the cocksuckers might have something to do with these kids dying, which maybe they did and maybe they didn't. But if I would've knew there was even a possibility, I wouldn't have worked with them. I done some wrong things in my life, but I didn't kill nobody yet. Especially children.

"You know what I say? If these pricks had anything to do

with kids dying, give 'em the hot squat, every fuckin' one of them. A guy like me gets jammed up trying to help out the little guy, he goes to jail, am I right? One of these bigshot executives perpetrates a horrible crime against innocent people, a case of greed pure and simple, and he gets a slap on the wrist, maybe a fine. Fuck that. I'm happy to go to jail if it means these bastards fry. I gotta get some sleep."

Muldoon thought he better jump in before Savitch ended up buying in to Tartaglione's act. She looked like she was beginning to like him. Sure, it was a good performance, but that's what it was. It pained Muldoon to admit that he had underestimated Tartaglione, assuming he was nothing but a gofer and bagman. But his story had some holes in it, and Muldoon hitched up his pants and paced the room like he'd seen Savitch do with Abbington. "Very nice to hear your thoughts on social justice, Mr. Tartaglione, but why don't you cut the crap now and tell us exactly how much money Liberty Oil gave you?"

"I'd put it right around a half million altogether."

Muldoon raised his voice, and Savitch could feel a bass vibration in her chair. "They gave it to you, or they gave it to you and Augie Sangiamino?"

"Didn't we already go over this?"

"Listen to me, Fred Flintstone. We're going over it again, so shut up and answer the questions."

"Augie Sangiamino don't know a thing about this. Tell you the truth, he doesn't know much of anything. He's got that thing his wife had there."

"Alzheimer's?" Savitch asked.

"Sometimes he isn't sure where he is. It's a sad thing to look at."

Muldoon was still pacing. He said, "The last time I worked with Mr. Sangiamino, he had trouble remembering how three ghost employees ended up on his federal payroll."

"That's another deal entirely," Joey said. "That's past history."

"How stupid do we look?" Muldoon asked. "You want us to believe that you work with Augie Sangiamino every day— every fucking day of the week—and he knows nothing about this?"

"He wouldn't have allowed it. He's terrified of prison after the way you got him the last time. There's no way he'd take a risk of going back."

Muldoon's blood pressure was up, his face and neck beet red. He took off his navy suit coat and folded it neatly over the chair. Sweat was soaked through his white shirt on the small of his back. "So what exactly did you do with the half million from Liberty?"

"I pushed about two hundred thousand to Ham."

"And the rest to Izzy?"

Joey said, "You guys get something in your head, you don't let it go. Listen to me: Izzy isn't like Ham. Ham would steal from his mother and whore his wife if he could win an election from it. Izzy doesn't even know what's goin' on here."

Savitch asked, "Did you tell him Liberty Oil wanted to bankroll his campaign?"

"Bankroll his campaign? He didn't even know I had a deal going with Liberty Oil. This is not some common criminal, Izzy Weiner. This is a respectable judge." Savitch shook her head because by Pennsylvania standards, he probably was. He was no worse, in fact, than the boobs already on the state supreme court.

"You gave none of the money to Izzy," Muldoon said incredulously.

Joey slapped the table. "Not one thin bone. He was doing all right as it was, so I didn't think he needed any help."

"Abbington says the money was for both candidates."

"Abbington's not too smart a guy. Maybe you already noticed that. I told him Izzy was on board, but I played him. These are not the most intelligent crooks I ever worked with."

"But Izzy raised nearly three-quarters of a million dollars for his campaign," Muldoon said.

"Every cent legit," Joey said. Actually, most of it was. Once they put the ads on TV with the Liberty money, contributions started rolling in from the usual suspects trying to cover their asses in the event Izzy won. Joey had used Liberty's cash as seed money. "Look at the disclosure papers and see for yourself. He's got lawyers and law partnerships all over the state, he's got the state Democratic Party, he's got labor, he's got nickels and dimes from people everywhere who happen to think he's the best candidate, despite your opinion of him. It's called democracy, for your information. And he just got a nice little sum from Senator Sangiamino, by the way, who had a big night in Atlantic City. You may have read about it in the *South Philadelphia Bugle*."

Savitch said, "So Izzy wins the primary at a horse race, and he wins the general at the roulette wheel?"

Joey said, "It's a great country, ain't it?"

Muldoon had stopped the pacing and leaned over the table across from Joey. "You got a half million dollars from Liberty and gave two hundred thousand to Ham, am I right?"

"About that."

"How'd you get it to Ham?"

"Various ways. Mostly small cash contributions to his campaign fund, where I made up names."

"Then explain something to me. If you didn't give anything to Izzy, where the hell is the other three hundred thousand dollars?"

Joey looked at both of them and then bowed his head and made the sign of the cross. "This is where I ask God's forgiveness," he said. "Fuck me sideways if I didn't steal it for myself." They were both staring at him when he looked up. They knew he was lying, sure. But that wasn't the issue. The issue was whether they could prove it.

Joey had worked from the advantage of being able to move

money through several accounts at First Columbus Trust, where one of Augie's former legislative assistants was vice president. He'd even written campaign contribution checks drawn from the accounts of people who didn't exist. Of Liberty's half million dollars, Joey had actually given one hundred thousand to Ham early in the campaign, another hundred thousand to Ron Rice after they dumped Ham, and three hundred thousand to Izzy. But in a million years, they wouldn't be able to break it down. They couldn't prove a thing.

Joey used a lot of what he had learned from Augie to cover the cash trail, but he'd come up with a few of his own twists, too. In Izzy's case, Liberty cash passed through the hands of dozens of relatives and associates of Izzy's, Augie's, Lou's, and Joey's. Those people in turn wrote checks to Izzy's campaign fund. He had also broken the cash into dozens of contributions in the names of residents at three nursing homes where Pennies from Heaven hosted bingo games, including Angela's. A lot of those people were barely hanging on, and they'd be of no use to Muldoon and Savitch. They couldn't remember if they had their socks on, let alone if they gave someone three hundred dollars a week ago. Joey had also laundered money through Roe, Barry, and Murray, paying them for alleged legal consultation, and having them pass it right back to the campaigns. The one mistake he'd made was telling Pritchard and Abbington to write a check to the law firm. But the lawyers would know how to cover their asses. They'd been doing this sort of thing for decades.

"All right," Muldoon said. "So you stole it for yourself."

"What can I say? I'm thinking Augie won't be around much longer. And with Ham and Izzy, they don't owe me a thing, so maybe I better look out for myself. Maybe it's not too long before I'm out of a job here, and I don't particularly care to go back to bookmaking. I'm trying to get a clean start."

"This is your idea of a clean start?" Savitch asked.

"In a manner of speaking."

"Well in a manner of speaking," Muldoon said, "where's the stash? Because unless you've got three hundred thousand dollars socked away somewhere, your story is for shit. And don't tell me you dropped it at the track. You got a half million from Liberty and gave two hundred grand to Ham. Where's the rest?"

"Am I getting some help here?" Joey asked.

"Yeah, I'm offering some help. If you tell me where the money is in the next ten seconds, I might not break your fucking nose. And don't tell me it's in your safe-deposit box, because that's the first place I looked."

"You didn't look under the right name," Joey said. "Try Salvatore Costadura."

"How long's he been in the ground?"

"He died in the Battle of the Bulge," Joey said.

"Let me guess," Muldoon said. "He still votes, am I right?"

"Never misses an election. Sometimes votes twice."

"So there's three hundred thousand dollars of Liberty's money sitting in his box?"

"No, only about two hundred grand."

"And the rest?"

"If I have any say," Joey said, "I'd like it to go against the bills for the kids in the hospital."

"That's too happy an ending," Muldoon said. "Just tell me where it is. You got another dead vet with a safe-deposit box?"

"It's at Pennies from Heaven," Joey said. "I got a hundred thousand dollars in the floor." He'd even stacked it for them. Neat bundles, ten thousand in each. Handing it to them like this stung more than Joey had expected it to. He was giving up three hundred thousand dollars of hard-earned savings from years of honest bookmaking to make it look like Izzy hadn't taken a nickel of Liberty's cash. But it was worth it. Ham, that ingrate prick, would be in prison. And Augie, after all these years, would finally be out.

Besides, Joey still had four hundred thousand dollars stashed away. He'd pulled a lot of it out of the floor over the last two months and deposited it in the bogus accounts. He'd use it to hire Augie the best lawyer in town if they came after him, and in the end, he was sure, Augie would skate. Forty years ago, Augie Sangiamino had made the Tartaglione family whole. Joey's only regret was that it had taken so long to pay him back.

CHAPTER 30

FROM THE TIME he was a kid and got his first pair of toy hand-cuffs, Mike Muldoon was fascinated by them in a way that be-came a concern for his parents. He would round up his little friends, place them under arrest for various infractions, most of them imagined, and handcuff them to radiators, stop signs, and bike racks. As a federal agent it had always been his favorite part of the job because it was justice swift and sure. A man strays, violating the rules of society, and you put a leash on him. Muldoon sat tall in the driver's seat, hands at ten and two, the handcuffs on the seat next to him as he approached Delaware Avenue to make the first arrest of the day. Ham's wife had tipped them that they might find her husband hiding out at a couch-dancing salon named Jugs.

Muldoon was surprised the grand jury took only thirty minutes to sift through it all. At ten o'clock in the morning, on the eve of the election, they had found probable cause to bring charges against Whit Pritchard, Richard Abbington, Ham Flaherty, and Joey Tartaglione, but not Izzy Weiner or Augie San-giamino. McGinns had bitched briefly, but Muldoon suspected she was thrilled, and he knew Savitch was. Savitch had hugged him outside the courtroom, and then ran off to answer a call from the state attorney general's office. The state was going to

court for an injunction to shut Liberty Oil down pending an inspection, and the U.S. attorney's office was looking into the possibility of both criminal and civil charges. Regardless of what
happened on those fronts, Pritchard, Abbington, Flaherty, and
Tartaglione were already looking at multiple counts of bribery,
conspiracy, and obstruction of justice, along with tax- and elec-
tion-code violations. The case for the murder of Kelly and
Heidorn was still too sketchy, but that was subject to change,
and so was the status of Izzy Weiner and Augie Sangiamino. It's
not like the book was closed yet. Ham, for one, might be per-
suaded to talk.

Muldoon parked in the lot and flashed a badge at the front
desk, asking where the manager was. He blew through a shop
stocked with sex toys, magazines, and videos, and took the stairs
two at a time. When he got to the top, he flashed on a dreary
thought and stopped in the dark gloom of the hallway. He and
Ham had slept with the same woman. The thought simply
hadn't occurred until now. Muldoon suddenly itched all over and
scratched under his collar. What the hell was he thinking? He'd
betrayed his wife and he'd betrayed himself, and worst of all,
he'd been where Ham had been, that pervert. Carla was the Ham
slammer, for Christ's sake. The hallway led to the only door,
and Muldoon threw it open without knocking. "Where is he?"
he asked a fat bald man sitting behind a desk.

"Who are you and what are you talking about?"

"Give me a fucking break, will you? I've got a busy day ahead
of me." Muldoon began opening storage closets and found Ham
in the third one, surrounded by dildos. He twirled the handcuffs
as he read him his rights, then slapped them on and cinched
them tight. "Let's go, dickhead." Muldoon had tipped reporters
by phone and waited for the throng to arrive before tugging Ham
out past the flashing NUDE LIVE GIRLS sign. Ham's hands were
clasped behind him, a stoic Muldoon holding him by one arm
and trying not to squint even though the sun was blinding him.
In the local custom, Ham showed neither shock nor dismay. He

treated it as a temporary inconvenience. They were surrounded by microphones and Ham asked Muldoon if he could say something. "Sure, give it your best shot."

"I have only three comments to make. I am one hundred and ten percent innocent. I will sue the pockets off of any person involved in what is obviously a politically motivated attempt to destroy my good reputation. And most importantly, I will win election to the United States Congress tomorrow because voters are smart enough to see this for what it is. It's a low, trumped-up crock of BS."

Muldoon shoved him into the backseat and pulled another pair of handcuffs out of his pocket, handcuffing Ham to the door handle. He got into the driver's seat and said, "Nice speech, asshole. I put it right behind the Gettysburg Address."

"Fuck you," Ham said.

"Do me a favor," Muldoon said, turning the key. "Jump out while the car's going. I think you can make a run for it." He fixed a red light on top of the maroon sedan and roared up Sixth Street. Force of habit. The federal building was on Sixth, and Muldoon liked to do the liberty lap with his crooks, driving them past Independence Hall and the Liberty Bell. A little reminder of the patriotic trust they had betrayed.

"What am I?" Ham complained. "A fucking tourist?"

"Yeah," Muldoon said. "How about if I jump back there and mug you?" He turned right on Market at the Liberty Bell and delivered Ham to a City Hall holding tank crowded with crooks of every caliber. The moment the iron-barred door clanged shut, Ham was swarmed, pummeled, and relieved of three rings, four gold chains, a quartz watch, and a VIP card from Hooters.

Savitch was pacing the lobby outside Kevinne McGinns's office when Muldoon got off the elevator. "What's going on?" he asked.

"You're not going to believe it."

"What?"

"The state police are in with McGinns. They went to pick up Pritchard, and the place was surrounded by township police. He's holed up inside."

"What do you mean he's holed up inside?"

"His wife said she was getting ready to leave for Barbados at about nine this morning, and Richard Abbington barges into the house waving a gun."

"He pulled a gun on her?"

"No, on Whit Pritchard. She said Pritchard went and got a gun of his own and they were facing each other off, so she and the butler got the hell out of there."

"Why don't the police go in?"

"Pritchard's firing shots out the window to keep them back."

Muldoon looked at McGinns's closed door. "What the hell are they doing in there?"

"I think they're trying to get a helicopter to take some troopers out there."

Muldoon went in without knocking. "I'm going out there," he told McGinns.

"This is ours," the guy from the state police said.

"You guys should stick to moving violations," Muldoon snapped. "This could turn into a hostage situation or a murder-suicide, who knows? I've been in the house and I know both of those maniacs. I'm on that helicopter."

Savitch followed him down in the elevator. "Don't shoot them," she said. "Whatever you do, don't shoot them. And don't let them shoot each other."

"Wouldn't that be the best ending, Savitch, if they shot each other?"

"No. I don't want it to be that easy."

The helicopter landed in a meadow near the covered bridge, next to five TV news helicopters. Muldoon was met by the township sergeant who was the son of his FBI pal. Pritchard was still firing an occasional shot from the front porch or through one of the windows, the sergeant said. Muldoon asked if there was some way to approach from the rear of the house, and the sergeant said the nearest neighbor on the back side was a half mile or so from the estate.

"Perfect," Muldoon said, drawing his Sig-Sauer nine millimeter out of his shoulder strap. He pulled the slide back to make sure there was a bullet in the chamber. "Listen to me," he said. "There's a library at the back of the house, and the window was ajar the other day. If it's still ajar, I'm going in. Let's go tell your commander and then you can drive me around. And none of this can be put out on the radio, all right? That's important. Pritchard has a police scanner in the house and he's probably listening to everything."

Muldoon walked with his Sig-Sauer drawn, tiptoeing over horse droppings in the pasture behind Whit Pritchard's house, cursing each time he accidentally hit one. A police helicopter came up over the shooting range and Muldoon wondered briefly if he'd thought this through well enough. These guys both had guns, they both knew how to use them, and they were both desperate. But if they hadn't already shot themselves, doing it for them didn't seem like all that bad an option to Muldoon, despite Savitch's plea. If he took them in, they'd post bail, then hire the slickest attorneys in the country and drag this thing out for months, maybe years, and who knew if it would ever be proved that the pollution had anything to do with the kids dying. Savitch had been right about them all along. They were more dangerous than Augie Sangiamino and his gang because they operated under the cover of respectability, posing as business and civic leaders. Not that Augie ran a seminary, but at least his crew lived by a code. Look at Joey Tartaglione, taking the fall for his guys. As twisted as it was, it was probably more decent than anything these bastards had done in their lives.

He crouched down the last hundred yards or so, then made his way through the garden, careful not to rustle leaves. The library window was ajar, just as it had been. Muldoon peeked in and listened. Nothing. He swung the window out, pulled himself up, and stepped inside gently. It hit him when he landed: If he got out of here without taking a bullet, he was coming back full time. Working with Savitch would be fine, but with or without, this was what he needed to be doing. Leaving the FBI hadn't been the wrong decision; he'd done everything he wanted to do there. But he still needed to feel what he was feeling now, and down at this level, he'd have more authority and maybe even be able to train younger detectives. It had taken him until now to realize why he had resented Savitch so much in the beginning, aside from the fact that he was hopelessly attracted to her and knew he always would be. It was her sense of justice and moral outrage. She had the passion he had lost. Looking back on that night in Savitch's apartment, Muldoon couldn't believe he'd almost made a move on her, but he was glad he hadn't. This way, he could hold on to the dream that she might have wanted him to.

Muldoon tiptoed to the door of the library and heard voices now. Pritchard and Abbington were in the living room. He also heard the police scanner blaring from the kitchen and hoped they remembered not to blow his cover. He slid down the hallway, his back against the wall, inching up to where he could see into the living room. Pritchard and Abbington sat ten feet apart, facing each other, both with revolvers pointed at the ceiling. Muldoon drew back, trying to figure out his next move, and he could hear Pritchard saying something about his father getting out when he saw the end coming, saddling his son with this mess. Even now, the bastard couldn't take responsibility.

"All right," Pritchard said. Muldoon heard them cock, and he peered around the corner in time to see them put the muzzles to their own temples. "Now," Pritchard said, and they both clicked off empty chambers.

Muldoon couldn't believe what he was seeing. These two whackjobs didn't have the courage to shoot each other, so they were playing Russian roulette. He would have been perfectly happy to let them play it out, but he couldn't let Savitch down. She wanted her day in court with these guys, a chance to give the public a good look at them, and he was going to give it to her. But if they were determined to die, they had nothing to lose by killing him first, and Muldoon wasn't going to gamble on two more empty chambers. He got into a low crouch, both arms extended, and lined himself up so he'd be able to shoot either one without moving his aim more than a few inches. He started toward them, moving like a cat. An antique wooden cart with plants on it was between him and the living room, his last cover. Abbington sat in the nearest chair, his back to Muldoon. They were getting ready for another round, so now was the time. Muldoon took two of the fastest steps in his life.

"Freeze!"

Abbington leaped to his feet and threw his hands up, but still held the gun. Pritchard was Muldoon's first concern, though. He sat there with a crazy smile, slowly drawing the gun higher. "Drop it," Muldoon ordered, his Sig-Sauer trained and the trigger hot on his finger. Pritchard ignored him, bringing the revolver up higher and pointing it between his ear and his eye. The moment he cocked, Muldoon fired. He missed the gun, but got Pritchard's hand and the gun flew back against the wall and out of his reach.

Muldoon ordered Abbington to throw his gun over by Pritchard's and lie on the floor face first. What a fuckup. He'd come over here to kill Pritchard and couldn't pull it off. Abbington followed Muldoon's order, but Pritchard was still a zombie. He had a hole clear through his hand, blood all over the place, and he was fixing his hair like everything was OK. If this bastard got in there and pleaded temporary insanity or something, Muldoon would go find him and shoot him again, but in a vital organ next time. He grabbed him by the collar, threw him on the floor next to Abbington, and handcuffed both of them.

Abbington started to say something, but Muldoon tapped

him in the back of the head with the butt of his gun and told him to shut up. Two or three helicopters hovered and Muldoon went to the front door and waved. Everything under control.

Kevinne McGinns, surrounded by reporters in the lobby of the DA's office, started the press conference at two o'clock sharp. She was flanked by the U.S. attorney for the Philadelphia office, the Environmental Protection Agency's regional director, and the chief of the Pennsylvania Department of Environmental Resources. "Today," she began, "is a landmark day for the forces against corruption, greed, and the abuse of power and money in business and politics."

McGinns had shed the frumpy den-mother look for a sharp blue suit, and she'd had her hair done, too, taking off five or ten years with a color job.

"I barely recognize her," Savitch said. She had a cigarette going and drank from one of the six Styrofoam coffee cups on the desk in front of her.

Muldoon, who'd brought the TV into Savitch's office because she wanted some privacy, turned up the volume and sat back down. "That's exactly what she looked like the last time I worked with her."

"With all those dog-face stiffs flanking her, she looks great," Savitch said. "This must be the start of her run for governor, or whatever it is she's running for."

"I can't believe she didn't ask us to the news conference," Muldoon said.

"What, you haven't been on television enough already today?"

"People might have missed it."

"Missed it? They had live coverage, Muldoon. Not with Ham, but with Pritchard and Abbington. And then they replayed it about every ten minutes. If you want more airtime, why don't you run down there? I still get the shakes when I see a camera."

McGinns was working from a prepared statement, turning

the press conference into a speech. She went through the list of charges, then said, "The investigation, I want to remind you, is by no means closed. Joey 'Numbers' Tartaglione, a former bookie and one of the principal figures in the case, was an associate of Augie Sangiamino, a man I successfully prosecuted twelve years ago for political corruption. He also served as treasurer for Isadore Weiner, the candidate for state supreme court in tomorrow's election, and we will continue to examine the nature of these relationships."

"She won't give it up," Savitch said. "If she can't charge, she's at least going to slander him. I guess I can respect that. She told me that if he wins, it'll just make for a bigger fall anyway, dropping him when he's a sitting supreme court justice. You think he can still pull it out tomorrow?"

"Well, you've got your choice of a guy who took three hundred grand from killers, or a flake of a slumlord who's on TV every ten minutes smoking dope. Either one of them fits in nicely on this supreme court. But if I were a betting man, I'd say the state is more comfortable with a traditional crook than a hippie burnout."

Muldoon started clapping when McGinns got to the part about the state shutdown of Liberty Oil. Savitch smiled graciously and signaled for him to keep it down, she wanted to hear this part.

"The plant will remain closed pending further investigation by a joint team comprised of staff from my office, the U.S. attorney's office, the EPA and the state DER. In addition, physicians from the Centers for Disease Control and the American Cancer Society have been asked for help in studying air quality in the industrial corridor in connection with the recent deaths of four children with leukemia, as well as the diagnosis of five others with blood disease."

McGinns asked the gray suits if anyone wanted to add anything, and then she opened it to questions.

"Kevinne, we understand you're also looking into the

murder of two former Liberty Oil employees who were shot in the head in Barbados. Is it true that they were blackmailing the company, and are the people who've already been arrested also suspects in the murder?"

"We have people working that aspect of the case as we speak, and although it would be premature to comment on it, let me remind you what I said at the top. This investigation is continuing. The case is not closed. We anticipate additional charges, but I can't give you a timetable for that at this particular moment."

Muldoon flipped through the channels when the press conference ended, trying to catch clips of his arrests. "You're not going to make me watch those things again, are you?" Savitch asked. She stood up and began gathering her things.

"Come on, Savage, show a little appreciation. I risked my life out there for you today."

"I know you did. It was even on CNN at one point today, by the way. You're a national sensation."

"Where are you going?" He thought maybe she'd want to get a beer or something.

Savitch, who looked beat, stretched and yawned. "I'm going home to take a nap, and then, if I can get out of bed, Jack is taking me out to dinner."

"Oh," Muldoon said. "That sounds good."

"You doing something?"

"Yeah, dinner with my wife, I guess."

"Well take her someplace nice, Muldoon."

She came around the desk and patted him on the shoulder. "Thanks," she said, and as she moved toward the door, the phone rang. "I'm not here," she said.

"It might be McGinns. Maybe I better pick up."

"If she wants me, tell her I died or something."

Muldoon answered and put his hand over the mouthpiece. "Your mother."

"Damn, I told her I'd call to let her know what happened

and I never got around to it. I also need to call and thank Ham's wife."

"I'll go call Judy from my phone," Muldoon said.

He called his wife first and told her not to prepare dinner, he was taking her out. She said she'd watched the whole drama at Whit Pritchard's house and was worried sick, not sure where he was, and then she couldn't believe it when he came out of the house with the two of them.

Muldoon called Ham's wife to thank her and remind her that they'd need her again at trial. He wished her luck, then went back to Savitch's office. She was winding up her conversation when he walked in.

"So how are the proud parents?"

Savitch sat on the edge of her desk, the trace of a smile on her face. "They saw you on TV," she said.

"All the way up in Boston?"

She started for the door and Muldoon said he'd walk her out. He knew a rear exit where there wouldn't be any reporters.

"My mother and I had a quick chat and then she said my father wanted to say something."

"What did he want?"

"He congratulated me and all, said he was sorry he didn't know the specifics of the case but he'd like to hear about it. And he said they got a call from my brother David."

"Everything all right?"

"He sounded about the same, my father said. But he was calling to check in, which he doesn't always do. He's in Chicago and my father's going out to see him. He wanted to know if I wanted to go with him."

"You have to do it," Muldoon said as they stepped in the elevator.

"I don't know. He's going next week, and I don't think I'll be able to get out of here."

"Savitch, you're going. If you want me to talk to McGinns, I'll be happy to. But you're going to Chicago with your father."

"I'd like to," she said, stepping out of the elevator. They walked to the end of the hall and when they reached the door, Muldoon told her McGinns was sending him back to Barbados later in the week.

"You bringing Carla again?"

The way she asked, he wondered if she knew something. "No," he said. "Of course not." Savitch had arranged for Carla to get two years probation. She also got fired, but was working as a cosmetologist and taking criminal justice classes at night. She'd left Muldoon several messages, asking him to be a guest speaker in one of the classes. He hadn't answered.

"You look back on this thing," Muldoon said, "and we were after some small-time payola and a cocktail waitress we never got. But we end up with bribery, a white-collar scandal, a public health epidemic, two murders, thirty-seven felony counts. Where's our bonus?"

"You didn't get yours?"

"By the way," he said. "I told McGinns I'm coming back full time."

Savitch held his hand and kissed him on the cheek, making him blush.

"She wanted to know if I wanted to work with you in a new special investigations unit," he said.

"Did you tell her we don't get along?"

"I figured she must know."

"So what did you say?"

"I said I can't keep carrying you."

CHAPTER 31

THE KNOCK RATTLED the living room and the sound thundered into the kitchen, where Augie was going through drawers and cabinets, throwing photos of Angela into a shoe box. He hustled out, cursing Lou as he opened the door. "How many times I gotta say it, Lou? Ring the goddamn bell, will you?"

"Sorry, boss."

"Come on in," Augie said, looking at the clock. "You're early, too. I gotta buy you a wristwatch or what?" Augie finished a cup of coffee and grabbed his coat, and then they were on their way to the supermarket in the '56 Oldsmobile. This wouldn't have happened when Joey was around. Joey would have reminded Augie on Friday or Saturday that he needed to pick up some things for dinner. Now, with the Italian Market shut down because it was Sunday, they had to go to a supermarket, and Augie hated supermarkets. This was going to take some getting used to.

"Beautyful day we got here, Senator."

"A little frosty, but I'll take it," Augie said. He was waving to everyone, same as always, but something was off. He couldn't figure it out until he found himself wheeling around to look at people who were sweeping past him in a blur. He checked the speedometer. "For crying out loud, Lou. What're you driving here, a friggin' ambulance? I told you once, I told you a hundred times, you gotta go slow when we do this thing."

"Sorry, boss. I guess I got kind of a heavy foot."

Joey had been gone nearly a week, and Augie had been feeling his way in the dark ever since. They talked every day, Augie using up most of each conversation to make sure everything was all right, thank Joey for what he had done, and tell him his parents would be proud. Joey, who envied Lou and pitied Augie, tried to help organize Augie's days and schedule appointments for him, but it wasn't easy to do from behind bars. Joey was still in a city jail, waiting for word on whether they'd let him do federal time. Augie had arranged through the mayor to get Joey his own cell, a cordless telephone, his regular breakfast from Milly's Lunchbox every morning, and the nightly delivery of a pizza from Marra's. Augie was also trying to work out conjugal visits for Maggie Sharperson, but she hadn't returned his calls or Joey's.

At the ACME, Lou pushed the cart and Augie grabbed romaine lettuce, onions, tomatoes, garlic, olive oil, and sausage. He picked through the entire stack of tomatoes before finding what he liked, and bitched to Lou about the prices. "Not to mention that they give you the sozzich wrapped up in a starfame package here, no butcher around to toss in an extra link or two." On the way back, Augie asked Lou what they were looking at with tomorrow's schedule.

"It's backed up all day, Senator. One guy after another, you got coming in." Lou wasn't too happy about Joey going away just when the workload picked up after ten years of cruising. They'd been swamped since Tuesday night when the results came in. Izzy, despite the election-eve blowup, had held off Debra Sharperson by two points. Sharperson was screaming for a recount, complaining that even if you put aside questions about Izzy's connections to Liberty Oil and a campaign treasurer who was already doing time, there were enough fraudulent absentee ballots to have the outcome reversed. But for the moment, Izzy was a winner, and would join the state's highest court in less than two months. Ham had made a valiant run at becoming the sixth Pennsylvanian in the last ten years to win an election while facing criminal charges, pulling 36 percent of the vote. Ron Rice, the day after his victory, announced his intention to switch to the Democratic Party.

"Then you got Nat coming in at nine," Lou went on, still going through the Monday schedule. "He's bringing a couple of the other *melenzanes* with him that's been calling."

Augie waved to a group of kids playing ball in the street. He said, "It's a beautyful thing, Lou. You take in one of their people, all of a sudden they treat you like Martin Luther King."

"The ones that didn't deliver their wards, I told them fuck off."

"They'll learn, Lou. They'll learn. The bank's got nothing for you if you don't make a deposit now and then. This isn't some fuckin' welfare office I'm running here. How about Nat, what's he after?"

"His boy got jammed up on some kind of drug thing, lost his job. He wants to know can you make a call, set him up at traffic court or somewhere. Twenty, thirty thousand a year is all he's looking for."

"What else?"

"There's a half dozen no-bid jobs coming up through the port authority—paving, painting, 'lectrical work. We got a few contractors wanna buy you breakfast. Then we got those lawyers coming in."

"That's a tough one, Lou. Car insurance in this state runs three times the national average, the way everybody's got an angle on the thing. Now you got the governor trying to put a lid on malpractice settlements, and you can't blame him, but the lawyers want his hand out of their pockets. You see how that works, Lou? They're ready to take him all the way to the supreme court if they have to, but the road to Harrisburg just took a little detour, Mr. Canuso. It goes through Milly's Lunchbox now. You gotta love our spot, Lou. Everybody wants a piece of us. Can you imagine that people in this town said the Fifth Amendments were dead and gone?"

Lou helped Augie with the groceries and then went to pick up Ron Rice, who would never know that the hundred thousand dollars he got through Joey was from Liberty Oil. It was safer that way, and more poetic, as far as Joey was concerned. Liberty had unwittingly helped elect the man they were trying to bury, and Rice's first move in office would be to try to put them out of business for good.

Augie's kitchen, the whole downstairs, was filled with flowers people had sent after the funeral, and they'd been here long enough. Every bouquet reminded Augie of Angela. She was watching him from her grave, he was sure of it. He went to his front steps and called to a boy at the corner. "Albert!"

The boy came galloping. "Senator Sangiamino, how come you didn't have no movie yesterday?"

"I was busy yesterday, Albert. You like that movie? Come by Pennies from Heaven next week, we'll show it again." The boy, eight years old, had a crew cut and high-top sneakers. He wiped his nose with the back of his hand and cleaned it on his pants. "You're a healthy-lookin' kid," Augie said. Joey was right about that. A handful of kids is all that got sick. "How you feel?"

Albert said he was on a soccer team and they ran a lot. "My coach said I'm in good shape."

"That's right," Augie said. "Listen, you want five bucks?"

"Thank you."

"Thank you? It ain't for free, Albert. Come on in here, I got a job for you. You see all these bouquets and whatnot? I want you to pick up the ones that don't look too far gone and deliver them to all the ladies on the block."

"My mother?"

"You pick the best one, that's the one for your mother."

He wiped his nose again and stared at the flowers. He was working on something, Augie could tell. "What are you cooking up, Albert? What?"

"Can I sell them?"

Augie ran his hand over the boy's crew cut like he was doing his nails. "You remember my wife?"

"That lady used to live here?"

"Yeah."

"What happened, you got divorced? My parents got divorced."

"No. She got sick is all."

"How come you don't want the flowers no more?"

"What is it with all the questions? I don't like the way they smell, all right?"

The boy went over to a bouquet and sniffed. "They smell like flowers."

"That's why I say."

Albert, a skinny boy with big ears, looked back up at Augie. "So can I sell them?"

Augie shook his head. "You got a future in something," he said. "But no, you can't sell the flowers. They're my wife's and she wants to share them with people. That's the kind of person she was—honest and kind. Not the type person who'd cut a deal with the devil, if you know what that means."

"I'll do it," the boy said.

"You're makin' five bucks out of the deal as it is," Augie said, reaching for his wallet. When the flowers were gone, he gave Albert a two-dollar tip.

The shoe box was full, all the photos in there. Augie had been going through the house since the funeral, gathering them up. He put the box under his arm and went out the back door. Fifty years in a box. There had to be a couple hundred pictures in there, dating back to when he was courting her. Here was one of his favorites—Angela all dressed up for the honeymoon in Atlantic City. A pretty girl, Augie said to himself. Look at that outfit, too. Son of a bitch if she wasn't beautiful in her day. Augie set the box on the patio, a safe distance from the Virgin Mary in the voting booth. He reached into his pocket for the matches, bent down, and lit a corner. In thirty seconds, the whole thing was in flames.

Augie stepped back and leaned against the back of the house, watching the photos go up. He had never deserved her and she had never approved of him. She couldn't understand the essential truth of politics—that it was a game of survival, and nobody who was good at it stayed holy. Helping one guy sometimes meant hurting another, or bending the rules, or taking something off the top for yourself. If you were out of the game, who could you help? The box kept smoldering after the flame died, and Augie watched a flake of ash drift past the Virgin Mary and over the house. He kept his eye on it until it disappeared into the sky with the rest of the photos, floating free. Augie thought she'd like that. And if he needed her, he'd know where to find her.

Augie was dumping sausage into the gravy when Lou nearly put his knuckles through the door. Augie didn't even bother telling him again. The man just wasn't going to ring the fuckin' bell. "The hell you got there?" Augie asked.

Lou handed him a bouquet. "Some kid's up the corner sellin' all type of flowers," he said. "Two bucks for this whole thing."

Augie started toward the door, then figured what the hell. The kid was on the ball, anyway. "Where's Ron Rice?" he asked.

"He had to go down the Vet. They got a little deal planned for halftime, where they trot him out there, congratulate him on goin' to Congress and all. Afterwards he's coming by."

"Can you believe this thing that come out right before the

election, Lou, that Rice knocked up one of those cheerleaders there and loafed on the support? I think it's in the blood with these people, that you bend over backwards trying to help them and they shove it up your ass every time."

"It didn't hurt him, boss. He walked away with this thing."

"Of course it didn't hurt him, Lou. That's every guy's fantasy, to nail an Eaglette. I'm just making a point is all. Listen, you wanna come into the kitchen, taste the gravy for me?"

"This ought to be something today, huh, Senator? New face at the table after all these years." Lou dipped the bread and did his usual performance. Augie thanked him, then picked up with Ron Rice. "It's historic. Man of his type coming in here with us paesans. He asks me the other day what can he bring? I said let me tell you something—the only two rules, one, you don't bring nothing, the other, you don't take nothing away. Maybe a little *aciata* is all."

Lou said it didn't matter what color he was, Ron Rice showed proper respect. He'd even gone to Angela's funeral. "It's a step up from what we had."

"I'll tell you what, Lou. He brings in some of his people, we're a lot stronger in that neck of the woods than we were in the olden days. We're branching out now's what we're doing here." Someone was ringing the bell. "That's gotta be the Yid Kid," Augie said. "How about this handsome group of gorillas we got now, huh, Lou? We got a rabbi, a *shvartze*, us paesans. A regular international goodwill committee."

Izzy came in with a bouquet of flowers, same as Lou's. "Look at this deal," he said. "Three bucks up the street."

"Come here, you son of a bitch," Augie said, opening his arms for a bear hug and feeling Izzy for a wire. You never knew. Muldoon and McGinns were both crazy, and they didn't know when to quit. Now they had this young hotshot broad working for them, too. Some fuckin' eagle-beaver. "Look at this," Augie said. "I got a supreme court justice in my house. Be careful, Izzy.

I think out of the last three that come by, one's dead and two's in jail."

Izzy embraced Augie and felt him right back. He said, "We're in, cousin."

"Was there ever a doubt?" Augie asked. "They throw these *farshtunken* candidates at us, a *for-schimmel* investigation. I feel sorry for them, that they think they can keep up with this gang of hoods."

"You wanna know the turning point?" Izzy asked, dipping bread in the marinara. "When you toasted that carpet muncher there on the TV. That's what did it."

"Get the hell out of here," Augie said. "You won this thing on your own. I already got calls coming in, too. The mayor's talking my ear off on this contract beef with the union. That thing's headed for the supreme court, you know. I hang up the phone and who should call but the union boss. They all want a piece of us now. After all these years, we got them lined up at the door again." Augie went back to the stove and asked Izzy to do him a nice favor and set the salad out.

"Sure," Izzy said. "Where the hell is it?" Augie looked around and realized nobody had made a salad. Joey usually did that. "Where's Ron Rice?" Izzy asked. "Don't tell me this *shvartze* wants to jerk us off like Ham, the putz."

The doorbell was ringing as he finished the sentence. A short, clean ring, and Ron Rice, in a sharp black suit and crisp white shirt, moved into the kitchen like a deacon into a whorehouse, a little unsure of himself but happy to be there. He was carrying flowers. Lou told him it was a shame he wasn't still playing for the Iggles, and Izzy, nearly a foot shorter than Rice, asked him if he played basketball, because they could use some fresh blood on the Fifth Amendments. Rice had a gracious smile stuck on his face, as if he'd worked on it in the car mirror. He was still athletic looking at fifty-two, only a trace of gray at his temples. Just standing in place, he had a sleek, graceful look, like he did when he was playing ball, and he'd kept the sideburns from that era, too. Chopped at the earlobe.

"I don't think I'm old enough to play in that league," he said, waiting to see how that went over, a cautious friendliness in his voice.

"Fuck you," Augie said, and Rice's laugh took the edge off.

"Smells great in here," he said. "What're you cooking?"

"What're we cooking? Chop suey, what the hell do you think we're cooking here in the middle of South Philadelphia?" Augie offered him a piece of French bread. "Go ahead, dip that prick in there. Jesus, look at the size of this guy's hands. Will you look at those paws, Izzy? Hard to imagine that a man could drop so many passes with dogs like those."

Izzy didn't laugh too heartily. None of them knew Rice well enough to feel at ease yet, especially since he was black. But they preferred this to the tension that always walked into the room with Ham.

"That's a hell of a sauce," Rice said.

"Gesù Cristo. It's fuckin' gravy, all right? Don't say sauce or you can't come back." Rice didn't know what that was all about, but fine. He'd call it gravy. Augie called for Lou to crank up the phonograph and Izzy told Rice where his seat was—Ham's old seat. "You sit in the same place all the time. That's how we work it. That other one there's Joey's seat."

Rice nodded an OK, wondering what kind of crazy white man's club he'd gotten himself caught up in. The song was "Come Fly with Me" and Augie danced through the kitchen with Izzy. Lou came in from the living room and said the Eagles were down by only thirteen.

"They can still get back in this thing," Rice said.

Izzy set the macaroni and sausage on the table and then brought out the Chianti and poured a round. Augie went for the phone and dialed the jailhouse. "Joey, they set you up all right?" Augie had arranged for the sheriff's office to deliver penne and sausage to Joey's cell from Michael's Ristorante. A bottle of Chianti, too. Joey said he was all set. "All right," Augie said, laying the phone at Joey's setting, receiver up. "Let's go."

Rice closed his eyes and bowed his head when he saw the others do the same. Augie began, "We thank you, Lord, for this wonderful macaroni dinner, and as you know, this is a new day for us here. We welcome a new member to the Sunday Macaroni Club, somebody we're all proud to be associated with and intend to work our asses off for by the name of Ron 'Minute' Rice, the ex-football player, as you know." Rice, a church-going man, said Amen and praise the Lord.

Augie told him he wasn't done yet and yelled toward the phone, asking Joey if he could hear all right. Joey's answer was faint and static, but he said it was fine. "OK," Augie said. "Lord God, we thank you for the victory that Ron Rice so rightfully deserved on Tuesday, this being a man that from day one had the Liberty Oil boys pegged for the cocksuckers they were. We pray that with him in the group, we can use this as a bridge to all type of colored people out there. As for Izzy, we knew he had it in him to be a part of history, and we thank you for your help in that area."

Augie paused before the next part. Everyone at the table, except Ron Rice, knew what Joey had done for them. In their minds, it wasn't particularly valiant or courageous. You covered for your brother, took a bullet for him, whatever the situation dictated. There was no higher calling and no more obvious or natural one. "As for Joey, we pray that you watch over him. I don't know what went wrong with the mold up there, but we don't see too many stand-up guys anymore like Joey 'Numbers' Tartaglione, son of Enrique. Please send him back safe and sound, the sooner the better. And please take care of my Angela, who by now you already met. Amen."

The glasses met over the center of the table. Augie picked up the phone and said, "*Salud*, Joey. I wish you could be here to see this, because it's the start of something. *Salud* and *mangia*, and I hope to hell they didn't overcook your macaroni."